For
Anne + Alan,
with warmest
regards –
Lesley Stone

Fountain Hills, 1986

Riviera Story

Also by Lesley Stone

SIREN SONG

RIVIERA STORY

Lesley Stone

W.H. ALLEN · LONDON
1987

Copyright © Trevor Enterprises Inc., 1987

Phototypeset by Input Typesetting Ltd, London
Printed and bound in Great Britain by
Mackays of Chatham Ltd, Chatham, Kent
for the Publishers W. H. Allen & Co. Plc
44 Hill Street, London W1X 8LB

This book is sold subject to the condition that it shall not, by way of trade or otherwise, be lent, re-sold, hired out or otherwise circulated without the publisher's prior consent in any form of binding or cover other than that in which it is published and without a similar condition including this condition being imposed upon the subsequent purchaser.

British Library Cataloguing in Publication Data

Stone, Lesley
   Riviera story.
   Rn: Trevor Dudley-Smith   I. Title
   823'.914[F]   PR6039.R518

ISBN 0–491–03812–7

To

LIN and GARY

Contents

PROLOGUE

1. THE FUNERAL
2. A CARPET OF JEWELS
3. CRY OF A PEACOCK
4. THE FANCY-DRESS MASK
5. SHADOWS
6. RICH MAN'S TIGER
7. COUNTESS BIBI
8. DARK SECRET
9. RUNNING SCARED
10. THE INVITATION
11. *JE T'AIME*
12. THE ROSE GARDEN
13. CELESTE
14. ARABIAN NIGHT
15. A TABLE FOR TWO
16. THE TELEPHONE CALL
17. AT THE HOTEL D'ANTOINE
18. THE GIRL FROM MEMPHIS
19. NIGHT DRIVE
20. IN THE RIDING PARK
21. THE EAVESDROPPER
22. AN UNKNOWN HAND
23. PRINCE JACQUES
24. DREAD TIDINGS
25. CRISIS
26. THE NEW PATIENT
27. THE SNATCH
28. LA CONDAMINE
29. A TERRIBLE PARTY
30. THE VISITOR
31. GHOST FROM THE PAST
32. THE STAINED-GLASS WINDOW
33. A HUNDRED RED ROSES
34. MORNING
35. THE LETTER
36. HOME

Prologue

During the night the mistral had died away, and by morning, just before dawn, the sea was calm again. In the Port de Monaco the slender masts of the yachts were almost still. At this early hour the streets of the Principality were deserted, except for a van delivering the first edition of *Nice-Matin* along the Boulevard des Moulins.

In the Place du Casino the crimson geraniums in the little park glowed like embers under the lamps, and the heads of the palm trees were motionless. It was very quiet, yet the body of Prince Edouard de Montigny-Villiers made hardly a sound as it hit the pavement below the baroque facade of the Hotel de Paris, on the west side of the square. There was just a slight thud, as if someone had dropped a sack of potatoes, and then it was over.

Not far away, the doorman on the steps of the casino started forward as he saw the still figure on the paving stones; then, suddenly squeamish, he turned and hurried up the steps to find a telephone.

At the top of the square, near Cartier's, the woman at the wheel of the black Ferrari sat perfectly still, gazing through the windscreen with her green eyes expressionless. In this moment she had become sharply aware of all that her senses were bringing her: the raw smell of the stagskin upholstery; the lingering warmth of the orgasm between her thighs; and the salt sting of the tear that had crept onto her cheek, the first of so many. In a little while she moved her gloved hand to the ignition switch, and the street lamps sent their reflections rippling across the bright bodywork as the car moved away, a wax-white magnolia petal fluttering from its roof to the roadway of the now deserted square.

Below in the harbour, where the sunrise was casting a rose light across the water, a sailor on the deck of a white-and-gold yacht pulled at a lanyard to hoist the personal ensign of Prince Edouard, not knowing that soon he would be ordered to lower it to half-mast.

1

THE FUNERAL

TWO HUNDRED YEARS ago, the Chateau de Beausoleil had been built on a hillside of pines above a little fishing-village at the edge of the Mediterranean sea. It was ordered by the first Prince de Montigny-Villiers, whose title had been created by Louis XIV in recognition of the services of the former Duc de Montigny-Villiers to the throne. There were no estates granted; it was hardly necessary. At that time the family had already possessed half a million hectares of vineyards and agricultural land in the north, fifty thousand hectares of vines in the Vallée du Rhone, and nine villages clustered to the east of Bordeaux, where a thriving trade in livestock was then plied.

But Prince Michel de Montigny-Villiers' favourite corner of the world was the southern coast, with its gentle hills, its azure sea and its mild winters; and so it was there that he ordered the construction of the Chateau de Beausoleil, a pleasant building of four small towers and thirty-seven rooms, among them three major salons, a winter-garden and a ballroom – not a large residence, compared with the prince's two other chateaux north of Paris, but of a size, as he put it, that would allow the entertaining of a few selected friends. On two occasions, in 1772 and 1786, King Louis XVI was informally received at the chateau, each time with a mistress; and in 1789 it offered shelter to loyalist émigrés during the Revolution.

There had been twelve births here during the years, and seven deaths, three of them violent: a scullery maid, delivered of a child after seduction by the fifteen-year-old Baron de Tourquet and demented with guilt, swallowed a bottle of caustic fluid; an under-gardener, clipping a hedge in the ornamental garden, was accidentally shot dead by a visitor hunting pigeons; and in 1939 the young nephew of Prince Edouard de Montigny-Villiers was found floating in a lily pond at dawn one morning, unable – it was whispered below stairs – to face being called to the colours on the outbreak of the Second World War. During the German occupation the chateau was mercifully spared requisitioning by the enemy forces and, following the cessation of hostilities, those under its roof enjoyed gentler times for almost half a century, and the sound of croquet and tennis games was again heard across velvet lawns, and the music and laughter of masked balls and summer revelries.

Though closely touched by the death of Princess Grace of Monaco, the lives of those of the chateau continued without personal suffering until a year ago, when Princess Charlotte's physicians, concerned by her failing health, ordered tests carried out, and diagnosed leukaemia. The shadow of darker times was falling across the Chateau de Beausoleil, yet no one was prepared, only three days ago, for the news of Prince Edouard's deathplunge from the hotel balcony.

The family and those close to it were stunned. Even when the assumption of accidental death changed to the suspicion of suicide, it hardly seemed to make any difference. Edouard de Montigny-Villiers, a man beloved by so many, was gone from them.

Today the gates of the horse-paddock had been thrown open to provide extra parking space after the visitors had been put down at the chapel, and across the short, nibbled grass the cars stood in polished ranks – the Rolls-Royces, Lancias, Mercedes, Ferraris, Jaguars and Cadillac limousines, their chauffeurs beside them, some cupping a cigarette discreetly in one hand. Beyond the paddock and the west wing of the chateau the mourners were gathered by the family vault, the heads of the men bared and many of the women veiled in black. In the coffin, draped in purple silk and smothered in crimson carnations, lay the remains of the man who, fifty-nine years before, had stood here as a boy of three, seeing the sculpted stone vault as a doll's house where nobody played.

On this October morning the air was still, and scented by the pines and the drift of woodsmoke from the village. Pale sunshine sparked on the heavy gold handles of the catafalque, and lit the black polished shoes of the pall-bearers. The guests might have seemed to have nothing much in common, except for their kinship or friendship with the deceased; yet they were the same people one would find in the nightclubs of the European capitals, on the guest-list at society weddings, on the slopes at Gstaad, the polo grounds at Windsor, or here, of course, on the French Riviera at the start of the winter season.

Near the centre of the gathering stood a Greek king in exile; the third most bankable film actor in Hollywood; the Duke of Madeira; a Swiss watch manufacturer; and the former King Abdallah of Tunisia (who also bore the titles of the Sultan of Mascara, the Sultan of Titteri, the Shadow of God on Earth, the Sword and Glory of the Faith, Sultan of Sultans, the Lord of Lords.) On the far side of the coffin were Yuri Novikov, the defected ballet dancer; the Consul-general of Pakistan; a fast-food-chain heiress from Ohio; Lord Charles Kilroy-Fitzgerald of the Queen's Royal Lancers; and Madame Claire Rissaud, the Arabian horse breeder. Towards the fringe of the throng stood a motley group of diamond-merchants, bankers, dress-designers and people whose only claim to fame was their presence here today, by personal invitation.

Nearest the coffin stood the widow.

Before her illness, Princess Charlotte de Montigny-Villiers had been slender and fine-boned; now she was gaunt in her black silk dress, her hands like claws under their net gloves, her face concealed by a veil. 'Everyone will be looking at me,' she had told Madame Leclerc, her housekeeper, 'and I can't bear that.' There had been a time, and not very long ago, when the face beneath this veil had stopped the conversation when she'd entered a crowded salon or the Cathedrale de Monaco; it had the kind of beauty that is lit from within by the spirit. That time had gone.

As she listened to the final words of the priest, Charlotte de Montigny-Villiers was thinking of the man she could go on loving only in her memory, until – soon now – she could be with him again. Another year, perhaps, Dr Chirac had murmured yesterday, when she'd asked him to be frank. Too long, she thought, too long by far; she was ready to go tomorrow. Yet in another sense it wasn't long enough for her to do everything that must be done before she could die in peace. With the passing of Edouard the estates of the Montigny-Villiers would become hers, in their entirety, and she was determined that when her own time came she would leave them in proper hands. It wouldn't be easy. Edouard's unexpected death had brought a change to the fortunes of these people around her that would have the force of a whirl-wind in the days to come.

Her head moved slightly as she looked towards the woman who

stood alone at the edge of the crowd. She too was in full mourning, and her veil revealed only an ember of crimson lipstick behind the black lace, and the glint of her green eyes. Leaning on the arm of her companion, Charlotte knew that today, weakened by the ravages of her illness and stricken with grief, she must somehow find the strength to face the most daunting battle of her life, if she could live long enough to fight it.

2

A Carpet Of Jewels

IN TRENTON, NEW JERSEY, a chilling rain had been coming down since early morning, and by mid-afternoon the sky was winter-dark. Through the rain-haze, St Francis' Hospital looked like an ocean liner riding out a storm, its flag crackling at the mast-head above the visitors' entrance.

Coming into the nurses' lounge, Linda Terman found an aide mopping the floor. A wind-gust had broken a pane of glass and let the rain in.

'You know how many times I've told them about that window-pane?'

'How many times?' asked Linda. She watched the young black girl skidding around with the mop, glad she'd found her in here, glad of someone to talk to, not really caring what was said but just wanting to talk to someone who was young, and not dying.

'I don't know how many times, Linda, but it's an awful lot. Now look at this!' She squeezed the mop into the bucket.

'Maybe you should tell them again,' Linda said.

The girl looked up. 'You OK?'

'Sure I'm OK.'

'You look kinda beat.'

'No, I'm not beat.' She turned away, annoyed that it showed.

'Bad in there today?'

'I guess it's bad in there every day, Bessie.' It was always like this, they'd told her, the first few weeks in Terminal, until you got used to it. She didn't think she'd ever get used to it.

She went along to the nurses' station, and found that the Operating Room had called for Charlie West. He'd been premedicated and was ready, she knew that; but she didn't know how ready he was in his mind. She went along to his bed.

'So they're going to fix you up, Charlie.'

'Are you going to give me a bad time in there?' He was watching her almost without blinking, as many of them did at this kind of time when they didn't know if you were going to lie to them.

'Not nearly as bad a time as you've been giving me in here,' Linda said, and took his hand. It felt like the hand of a skeleton, and very soon it would be. You caught yourself thinking things like that, when you were off your guard. You had to let these people feel that everything was going to be OK, or if not OK, not bad, until you began believing in your own lies, and that was when the thoughts came flying into your head, the truths you never dared admit.

'Tell you this much, Lindy.' He was still watching her face, but the guardedness had left his eyes. 'If they open me up in there and find they can't do anything for me, OK, we all got to go some time. But if I go when I'm lookin' at you, it'll be a helluva lot easier.'

'I've told you before, Charlie, I don't fall for that kind of line.'

He didn't smile. 'There's somethin' a beautiful woman can never get to know, because she ain't a man. She don't know that on the darkest night just the sight of her can light up the whole goddamned world.'

'OK, Charlie, I believe that.' She wanted to keep him talking – flirting, actually, a seventy-eight-year-old man with his body riddled with cancer – until the transporter came to take him along to the Operating Room. 'But we were meant to be talking about me, remember?'

'You know what I mean, for Christ's sake. I could've had Mary-Louise as my nurse.'

'Mary-Louise is extremely competent and highly regarded. She – '

'Oh, sure. But she's got a face like a horse's ass.'

'Charlie,' she said, feeling the strangeness of laughter for the first time in weeks, 'I'm not going to listen to – '

'Mr Trowbridge, is it?' It was the escort in the doorway. 'Mr Charles Trowbridge?'

The skeleton hand tugged suddenly at Linda's, and she bent over him. 'Gimme a kiss, now, Lindy. One more, an' this the last . . . Ain't that what the guy said somewhere?'

Linda sat on the worn vinyl-covered bench with the other nurses on her shift, listening to their reports and giving her own. The rain was still trickling down the wall from the broken window, and a new puddle was forming.

'Two-forty-five, Bed B,' someone was saying. 'Alice Marino. Ovarian CA, and she's now deteriorating pretty fast. She's started strong pain medication now – Dilaudid 2 mg q3h p.o.'

'Two-forty-eight,' someone else took up, 'Bed A. George Jacklyn, sixty-four, CA, excision of rectal mass. The wound is draining pinkish serous fluid with no frank bleeding. Dr Betts has been notified.'

'Jimmy just died.' This was Linda's report now. 'One-twenty-one, Bed C. Jimmy Skaggs.' There was a brief silence. *I guess I totalled it*, he'd told Linda with a sheepish grin. He was seventeen, and it had been his first motor-bike. There was a hint of pride, too, in the way he'd said it – the young gladiator had burned up his first chariot of fire. *Maybe you should try riding the next one a little bit slower, Jimmy*, Linda had told him. *Oh, sure, I'm going to have to do that, right. It's really what I'm going to have to do.* But there hadn't been enough time left for him; he'd died just fifteen minutes ago. It hadn't been a good day today. 'One-twenty-nine,' Linda looked at her clipboard again. 'Bed B. Millie Jacobs. She's just hanging on, that's all we can say. We're putting zinc oxide on her buttocks to help the soreness.' She looked across at the young nurse who'd joined them yesterday. 'You took over Charlie Trowbridge, didn't you, Cheryl, when he came out of surgery?'

'Yes. He didn't make it to Recovery.'

There was another short silence. *Gimme a kiss, now, Lindy. One more an' this the last . . .*

Not a good day, today.

After report was over, Linda volunteered to stay until Marge Swensen got here for the next shift – Marge was late again; but Linda's Supervisor said no way was she letting her stay over; she was to go straight home and get her feet into a hot bath-tub and look at a TV show, or whatever she did for relaxation. They had a good supervisor, Mrs Weston, a woman who'd been a head nurse for thirty years and who knew when you still had some steam left in you or were ready to drop. She also knew it wasn't just the sheer physical labour of running to and fro for ten miles a day along the wards and humping mattresses and lifting patients that drained the energy out of the nurses in Terminal. *We wouldn't get nearly so beat,* one of them had said once, *if only they'd stay alive for us a bit longer*. It was true, yet it was strange too, because what they were really doing was helping people to die, to die with what little dignity was left to them, to die without too much pain. Yet when they succeeded in this, it seemed also as if they'd failed, because a death was a death, and you couldn't argue your way out of that.

'Why do you want to nurse terminals?' It was one of the standard questions they asked when you applied for the change of duty.

'I don't really know,' Linda had said. 'I guess it's a kind of challenge. I've tried helping people to live and now I'd like to try helping them to die. It's kind of a different dimension.'

But that wasn't the reason. For a long time she'd believed it was, until one day she realised the truth. Her mother had died of cancer, but it was only in the final few days that Linda had known she was even sick. They'd kept it from her because her mother was in Los Angeles and Linda was in Trenton, New Jersey, hacking her way through a whole series of special training courses and exams that meant a great deal to her in her career. She'd come through with flying colours and her state registered certificate, just three days before her mother asked if she could go out there and see her.

'I just didn't want to mess up your career, Linda. I'm so proud of you, and – '

'But gee, Mom, didn't you know I would have come and looked after you?'

That had been a pretty dumb question. Of course her mother had known, and that was why she hadn't even let anyone tell Linda she was sick. But it had left a gap, and Linda had been into terminal nursing for quite a while before she realised that every patient she helped, and gave her love to in their last days in this life, was her mother.

Yesterday, Susie Casciotti. Today, Charlie and Jimmy. And tomorrow? There wasn't time to think about tomorrow right now – tonight as she left St Francis' the rain was still coming down in torrents and the windshield of her beat-up Rabbit was leaking again just like in the nurses' lounge and the battery only just made it when she started the engine because she needed a new one – a *new* one, ninety dollars? – and there certainly wasn't going to be time to sit with her feet in the bath-tub and read the comics because she had to get to the supermarket before it closed and then she had to see Mr Kleinz about the rent before he carried out his threat and dumped all her furniture and belongings onto the sidewalk.

'It's nothing personal, Linda. We're putting everyone's rent up. We have to live too.'

Mr Kleinz lived rather well, with his Cadillac Seville outside whenever he paid a visit. She always called him Mr Kleinz – instead of Karl as he'd asked her to – not because he was her landlord but because she wanted to keep things strictly formal between them.

'You're a very lovely young lady, Linda, and you do a very fine job, I know that. Maybe if we could just have a little dinner together sometimes, or maybe take a drive out and look at the beach on a week-end, I could talk to my partners about the rent, you know?'

He didn't have any partners; he just used the royal 'we' to dodge the responsibility of his decisions.

'I'm not dating right now, Mr Kleinz.' (And if I were dating, Mr Kleinz, it wouldn't be with a beer-bellied, balding rent racketeer.)

'I wouldn't exactly call it dating, Linda. I just – '

'Thanks anyway, but no.'

Maybe she could have turned him down more diplomatically, but that was the time he'd told her that if she didn't come up with the extra rent today he'd put all her things onto the sidewalk.

The rain was so cold that she spent longer inside the supermarket than she meant to, and bought a half-dozen things like Daz and Windocleer and Drano that she could easily have left until next Saturday. The car started OK this time because the engine was warm, though the headlights were almost yellow as she turned into the street where she lived; but they were still bright enough to light up the pile of things on the sidewalk right outside her apartment with the rain soaking into them.

For a moment, as she stopped the car and jerked on the handbrake, she felt the overwhelming temptation to slump over the steering-wheel and cry her heart out; but instead she suddenly found herself getting out of the car and running up the steps and wrenching at the door of her apartment, because inside there was the telephone and she was going to call Mr Karl F. Kleinz and tell him that if he didn't come right on around here and put all her things back into her apartment she was going to slap him with the biggest law-suit he'd ever seen in his whole life.

But the door was locked against her and there was a notice on it with the word *Vacant* and Mr Kleinz's telephone number, and in any case she didn't have enough money to slap him even with the smallest law-suit he'd ever seen in his whole life. This did it for her, being locked out of the place she'd thought of as home, and she just slid down the door and sat in a heap sobbing her heart out, until Bob the janitor heard her from his office and came along to see what was happening.

'Hey, Linda! Are you OK?'

'Sure I'm OK. I just sprained my ankle, that's all.' She got up and limped away along the corridor, sniffling into her handkerchief – the janitor probably knew what had happened but she couldn't care less, she wasn't going to have anyone think that creep Kleinz could ever make her break down and cry, goddamn it.

Half an hour later the Rabbit was back in the hospital parking-lot with all her stuff crammed inside – her record-player and the classical music albums and all those volumes of medical books and the flute in the case that David had given her the day they'd got married and the household repair kit she'd bought herself the day after they'd got divorced, everything soaking, all her clothes and everything while the rain kept on coming down on the roof of the car and trickling through the crack in the windshield. She got out and slammed the door and ran through the puddles to the building.

'But I can't let you do that, Linda.' The supervisor on this shift was Miss Ogilvie, stiff, starched and a real stickler for rules and regulations. 'I'm sure you know it's strictly against the hospital regulations.'

Right. 'Look, it's just for tonight. No one will know.' Linda stood there with her dark hair dripping with rain-water. Anyone else, for God's sake, would have let her use one of the spare rooms just for tonight. 'I've been thrown out and I don't have anywhere else to sleep.'

'You don't have any relatives?'

Only Caroline, her ex-sister-in-law. She called her and had to apologise because it was getting late by now. Caroline said she was sorry, but she had a house-guest using the spare room tonight. Linda didn't believe her because of the way she said it, but she couldn't do anything about that. Caroline had always taken it for granted that Linda could have cured her brother David's drinking problem – she was a nurse, wasn't she? – instead of just divorcing him. Linda wouldn't have minded so much if it weren't for the fact that in a stupid moment she had promised David she'd pay off all his debts as soon as the divorce was through, to help him make a new start – which was why the only home she had tonight was a beat-up Rabbit in the parking-lot.

She came away from the telephone. 'My sister-in-law doesn't have any room,' she told Miss Ogilvie, 'so I guess I'll have to sleep in the car.'

The supervisor heard in her tone that she meant it. 'I can't let you do that, Linda. A night like this, you'll catch your death.'

'Too bad.' She was swinging through the door when Miss Ogilvie called her back and spent ten minutes persuading her that being allowed a spare room to sleep in was like being offered the guest-suite at the White House. By the time she'd thanked Miss Ogilvie as if she were the First Lady and gone down to the car and fetched her overnight things it was past eleven o'clock and she just dropped onto the bed and switched the light off, ready to sleep like a log until morning. But sleep wouldn't come; the sound of the rain beating at the window reminded her that tomorrow she'd have to deal with a car full of soaked possessions and somehow make the time to find a room to share before night came. That was if she could get the car to start, after using the headlights tonight. She'd need a new battery but she was overdrawn at the bank and would have to go see the manager – and how could she get there anyway if the car wouldn't start? Suddenly she was crying again, this time quietly, just letting the tears soak into the pillow as the fatigue and the misery drained out of her and she was left in that twilight zone that comes just before sleep. It was then that she found herself half-dreaming of the ad. in the hospital newsletter that her regular supervisor, Mrs Weston, had pointed out to her a week ago. It seemed kind of irrelevant, yet the idea persisted until she stirred herself awake and switched on the light and got the ad. from her pocketbook and read it over agin. Then she took a plain sheet of paper and wrote the brief letter of application that was required, and signed her name. It was a gesture of defiance, that was all, to end the day with, and sleep came easily now, undisturbed by the knowledge that in the last few minutes she had changed the whole course of her life.

'But I can't take that kind of a job,' Linda protested.
  'Whyever not?'
  'Well, I – guess I don't really know. It's just – '

'But you applied for it, didn't you?'

'Sure, but – '

'And you've been accepted. So take it. It's yours!'

It was two weeks later and Linda was in Mrs Weston's room on the fifth floor of the hospital. The rain still beat at the windows but she had a place to sleep now, sharing a room with a waitress at the coffee-shop around the corner; she also had a new battery for the Rabbit, together with a lecture from her bank manager on how to live within her means.

'I applied for the job on an impulse,' she tried to explain. 'It was a couple of weeks ago and I'd had a bad day, that was all.'

'But it's a good job anyway, isn't it?' Mrs Weston normally didn't try to give any of her staff her advice, but today she was being persistent.

'It's a good job,' Linda shrugged, 'sure.' In fact it was terrific, and she'd be surprised if half the nurses in St Francis' hadn't applied for it right away. *Competent private nurse wanted to attend leukaemia patient, female, French Riviera. Live in, all found, $2,500 per month.* That kind of money was unreal, but the name and address was the ringer. *Apply in writing to Princess Charlotte de Montigny-Villiers, Chateau de Beausoleil, Alpes Maritimes, France.* 'I guess,' she told Mrs Weston, 'it'd seem kind of self-indulgent, taking a job like that. You know, living among all those rich people.'

'Oh, for goodness *sake*.' Mrs Weston had three chins, an impressive bosom and her hair done up like a cottage loaf; some of her staff called her Queen Victoria among themselves, and it was generally accepted that doors had opened for Mrs Weston long before self-opening doors had been invented. Today Linda found her in her most Queen Victorian mood. 'You need a break, Linda. We've discussed that, and you've admitted it. This is a perfect opportunity for you and there's nothing in the world to stop you taking it. I simply don't understand.'

Linda looked at the rain slashing at the window. 'It's just the French Riviera bit, Mrs Weston. You know, Monte-Carlo and everything. I'd be kind of turning my back on the real world and leaving it behind.'

'It's the same kind of world all over, my dear, and people are the same kind of people, it doesn't matter how rich they are.'

'I find that hard to believe. I mean, this is a *princess*, in a *chateau*.' Last night she and her room-mate Cindy had taken it in turns to stuff their heads into the toilet cistern trying to jiggle the thing into flushing properly because the owner was out of town and this week they didn't have the money to call in a plumber.

'A princess is no different from anyone else,' Mrs Weston told her. 'They even get leukaemia.' She had a lot of work to do, so she used the only argument that would appeal to a nurse of this calibre. 'There's a patient over there, Linda, and she's dying. And she's asking for help.'

The telephone was ringing and she went across to the desk and answered it, while Linda looked again at the letter that had come for her this morning. It bore a discreet coat-of-arms in the top left-hand corner.

Dear Miss Terman:
I have your letter of application and will be pleased to receive you here. My secretary will send you your air ticket shortly and will make arrangements to have you met at Nice Airport. I shall look forward to your safe arrival.

Yours sincerely,

Charlotte de Montigny-Villiers

Mrs Weston put the telephone down and came around the desk.

'Well?'

Linda was still looking doubtful. 'Do you think I'd do a good enough job, in a place like that?'

'I can't think of anyone I know,' her supervisor said carefully, 'who'd do it better, in any kind of place, wherever.'

Studying Linda in the merciless light from the tubes overhead, she noted again the sign of strain she'd seen building up in this nurse over the past three or four months – the nervy eyes, the pale skin, the restless hands. There'd been other signs, too – her uncharacteristic readiness to pick on a doctor who was overworked and needed understanding, not criticism, and her lack of patience with some of the aides when they made mistakes. Mrs Weston knew, either from what Linda chose to tell her or from her own intuition, what this young woman had been up against for these past months – a disastrous marriage to a secret alcoholic who'd smashed up the car three times and spent a week behind bars on a drunk-driving charge and then run himself into debt. And this was aside from the normal strain of trying to help people to die in peace, day after day – the special kind of strain they even had a name for: the terminal blues.

What Mrs Weston was looking at, she thought, was something very close to a burn-out. 'Do you happen to know how many of my nurses – just *my* nurses – applied for that job in France?'

'No.'

'Fourteen. That's not surprising, in view of the pay offered. But that must have been a pretty good letter you wrote. It worked the oracle and you've got the job. And you're going to take it, Linda. You need a rest, like everyone does once in a while. You need a nice quiet private nursing job for a few weeks, maybe even for a few months. Then, if you want to, I hope like hell you'll remember us and come back here.' She took Linda's hands in her own for a moment, because what she was going to say next needed a little cushioning. 'If you don't take this chance, Linda, then I'm going to send you on forced sick leave. It's your choice.'

Linda stared at her. 'Have you had any complaints about me?'

'Nothing specific. You're just pushing yourself too hard, giving too much of yourself. So it's time you took a little of it back. Go and eat a few lotuses over there in that rich man's playground for a while. And don't worry – the real world isn't going to go away before you get back. I'll take good care of it for you.'

* * *

Ten days later, as Air France Flight 302 lowered into its approach path towards Nice-Côte-d'Azur, Linda checked her flight-bag under the seat in front of her and tightened her seat belt. On the long seven-hour flight direct from New York she'd been able to sleep on and off, in between snacks and the simply delicious *Poulet sauté aux olives de Provence* the flight attendants had served for lunch. She had also had time to do a little thinking and get a few things off her mind.

David had called her two days ago, telling her in his habitually slurred voice that he was going to be in Trenton for a 'day or two' next week and would love to see her. This meant that if she said no, he would still show up and go to sleep on her doorstep until she let him in; he would then cry on her shoulder until she lost patience and had to yell at him, which she hated doing. On this occasion she was able to tell him she wouldn't be in Trenton next week anyway. It had been easy to say and it was the truth; yet she had that familiar feeling that she was abandoning him again. But how much longer was she expected to be a thirty-two-year-old mother to a thirty-six-year-old man? It was just guilt, of course, the quick acceptance of blame that wasn't really hers. How many times had she told a visiting relative? *Yes, he's dying, but it's not your fault. It's sad and scary and heart-breaking – but it's not your fault.* Her brief life with David had been like that too. Although he was taking his time about it, he was dying, killing himself slowly, and it had been sad and scary and heart-breaking. But sooner or later she must make herself believe the truth: *it wasn't her fault.*

She had also told herself, between the snacks and the naps, that she was running out on little Cindy the waitress, who had so many troubles that the first night Linda had moved in as her room-mate she'd spent listening to them, through bouts of tears. What would that poor kid do without her now? The same thing as she'd done before. *And it wasn't her fault.* And there had been Mike Grubb, the old man who'd come into Terminal the day before Linda had signed off. He'd refused to see his wife, or his son, or even a priest. *They never took no notice of me when I was at home, an' they ain't goin' to start pretendin' to take notice of me now.* Blood on the pillows again and his blue-veined hand clutching at a shred of Kleenex, all he'd managed to claw out of his life on earth. *But it wasn't her fault.*

There was another thing she had found herself thinking about, soon after they'd left New York. There hadn't been time in the past ten days to give it her attention, because there'd been so many things to see to. It was something Mrs Weston had told her: that fourteen of her nurses had applied for this job she'd been accepted for. That was around half the number who came under Mrs Weston's supervision alone. In the whole of the hospital there were something like four hundred nurses, and their newsletter, the *San Franciscan*, was read by *all* of them – you'd miss your first call and you'd miss your coffee-break but you'd never miss reading the newsletter, because it was where everything happened. So, four hundred nurses had seen that ad. about the job in the South of France, and if half of *them* had answered it, the odds against Linda's being accepted were two hundred to one.

Was her letter of application that *good?*

Her flight attendant, still cool, trim and smiling after seven hours on her feet and running, came along the aisle checking their seat-belts. Linda could feel herself being pressed into the seat as the big jet levelled out for the landing.

There was another thing. However good her letter of application might have been, that newsletter had been lying around in her pocket-book for a whole week before she'd answered the ad. By that time, there must have been at least a hundred other applications arriving at the Chateau de Beausoleil, leaving out those nurses who couldn't leave their husbands or kids or various obligations for any length of time. *Call it a hundred, then.*

'*Mademoiselle.*'

Linda looked up at the attendant. 'Yes?'.

'Would you please straighten the seat-back? We'll be landing in a few moments now.'

'Oh. Sure.' She leaned forward a little and pressed the button.

'*Merci.*'

Call it a hundred, then, a hundred applications for this job. They'd reached the Chateau a whole week before hers, and they'd been good ones. For this kind of salary and in this kind of place, they'd been *very* good. *And they'd all been turned down, except hers?*

It was a mystery. But one of two things had to be true. Either her letter had struck some kind of personal chord when Princess de Montigny-Villiers had read it, or this dizzying change of direction in her life had happened for reasons she couldn't even imagine.

But her thoughts were suddenly submerged as the big jet lowered towards the runway and the windows on Linda's side became filled with the shimmering lights of the coastline, as if they were landing on a carpet of jewels.

3

Cry Of A Peacock

'Who is it?'

'Thérèse.'

She had knocked very softly; Charlotte had only just heard it; the peacocks were making such a noise on the lawns below, as they always did in the middle of the afternoon. She would have liked to get rid of them, but Edouard had loved them so.

When Thérèse came into the huge shadowed room she found Charlotte sitting upright against a cloud of satin pillows. She never allowed people to visit her lying down. *I shall lie down only when I sleep*, Thérèse had heard her tell her Swiss nurse last week, *or when I die.* The nurse was leaving today, Madame Leclerc had told Thérèse, and a new one coming, an American girl. Why American?

'Open one of the shutters,' Charlotte said softly, 'if you like.'

'There's no need.' Bright slits of October sunshine broke up the darkness of the Venetian shutters across the windows, and threw bands of light across the moulded ceiling. The room smelled of roses; a bowl of pink blooms stood on a night-table by the bed. Charlotte never wore perfume; there were always roses near her, in her hair or clasped in her hands or somewhere close. 'I came to see how you were,' Thérèse told her. Pulling a brocade chair a little closer, she composed herself on it with instinctive grace, her silk-clad legs together and to one side, her left elbow resting on the arm of the chair, her other hand lying on her lap. A band of light escaping from the shutters glowed on the emerald bracelet, her green eyes reflecting its colour. Thérèse de Valoise, as Charlotte knew, was the same age as herself, nearing fifty, but was taken to be much younger. The question of her age never came into mind when one was in her company; her grace and her smouldering vitality gave her the quality of a living flame. In the presence of Thérèse de Valoise one sensed the unquenchable fires of youth, and today Charlotte envied her, hungering for just a little of it.

'It was kind of you to come, Thérèse, so soon after your return. How was Rome?'

'Noisy.'

'And London?'

'Wet, of course.' Thérèse no longer enjoyed her trips abroad. As the head of *Maquillage de Valoise*, a cosmetics company whose worth was estimated to be one and a half billion US dollars, she found it necessary to spend a quarter of her life in one of the company jets and almost three quarters in the offices and boardrooms and salons and showrooms of the cosmetics industry in the major capitals of the world. The one small part of her life that offered her any happiness was spent here at the Chateau de Beausoleil; but even that was being taken away from her now. Edouard, whom she had known for thirty years, had been buried a month ago, and Charlotte, whom she had known for almost as long, was herself dying.

'I haven't see Jacques yet,' Thérèse said. 'How is he?'

In a moment Charlotte said, 'He still can't believe it happened, so he goes on rejecting it, as he always does with anything he can't deal with.'

'It's hard for him, Charlotte.'

'Oh, yes.' She had seen her son early this morning, riding one of the horses at full gallop across the park, ducking his head at the last moment under the boughs of the trees as if he were playing his own private game of Russian roulette. 'Help him, Thérèse, as much as you can.'

'Of course I will. As soon as he'll allow me near him.'

'He needs more time. Just as I do.'

Thérèse felt a rush of pity for the woman in the bed, and it surprised her. In these past weeks she'd been drained of emotion whenever she was here, as so many of them had been – wherever you went in the Chateau you'd hear someone crying. But for Charlotte the shock and the loss had been worse than for anyone, and if there were pity left, she must have it. At the funeral, Thérèse had thought that it would be easier for Charlotte, herself so close to death, than if she'd been in full health; but she realised now that it had been a double blow. With her strength already ebbing and her days numbered, a peaceful end had been snatched away from her. Worse, she must see that within the year –

according to Dr Chirac – she must be ready to hand over the sprawling family estates to someone loyal, capable, and of the blood. And there was no one, as Thérèse knew.

'Can I bring you anything?' she asked.

'Nothing. And I mustn't keep you here.'

There was a note of such loneliness in her voice that again Thérèse felt compassion. The subdued light in the room was kind to the woman in the bed, yet her face, once so beautiful, was now a mask of bones and hollows, with only those huge dark eyes giving her the look of life.

'You've a new nurse coming, they tell me.'

Charlotte turned her head so quickly that Thérèse wondered if she'd said something wrong; perhaps she wasn't meant to know. 'Yes. Today.' She reached her hand out suddenly, and Thérèse took it in her own, feeling the delicate bones. 'There's so much I have to do.' Again, Thérèse wondered if she were still talking of the new nurse, or had changed the subject.

'I know,' she told Charlotte. 'If there's any way I can help, I want you to tell me how.'

Sudden tension came into Charlotte's hand, and Thérèse released it. 'There's something on my mind, Thérèse, yes, that you could help me with. If you chose.' Her voice had become vibrant. 'I understand that you were with him, that night. With Edouard.'

Thérèse left the chair, moving towards the shuttered windows, her back to the bed for a moment. The cry of a peacock came again, an ugly screech. There was no point in asking how Charlotte had come to 'understand' that she'd been with Edouard on the night of his death. Some of the staff had seen her leaving the Hotel de Paris, and had reported it. Chief Inspector Risso of the Monegasque Gendarmerie had questioned her in private. 'It's my duty, Madame de Valoise, as I hope you'll understand, to set any doubts at rest concerning the circumstances of Prince Edouard's tragic death.' On the testimony of several witnesses, she had passed through the lobby of the hotel only six minutes before the doorman at the casino had seen the deceased fall from the balcony. Her black Ferrari had been seen driving away shortly afterwards.

Thérèse had wanted to avoid a long and painful interrogation, and so had been perfectly frank. 'M'sieur l'Inspecteur, I am without doubt the most valuable witness you could ever obtain for your enquiry into the death of my great friend Prince Edouard de

Montigny-Villiers. You also know me as someone with a profound sense of social responsibility. Let me tell you, then, that to my knowledge – which is deeply informed – Prince Edouard decided to take his own life. As you know, Princess Charlotte de Montigny-Villiers has not long to live. Her illness has been developing rapidly over the past year, and you can imagine her husband's misery during that time.'

'He was depressed?'

'But of course, m'sieur. They loved each other deeply.'

He seemed to accept most of what she told him, but kept coming back to what he called 'the deceased's last moments'. 'You must forgive me, Madame de Valoise, if I ask a rather intimate question. Your relationship with the late Prince Edouard is well understood. Monte-Carlo is not a place where one can hope to enjoy privacy, especially if one is a world celebrity like yourself. I am going to ask you, then, if there was any kind of sexual communion enjoyed during the time when you were there in Prince Edouard's suite on the night of his death.'

Thérèse glanced away. 'Would you take my word for it that whatever I answer, it won't help you in your investigation?'

'I'm sorry, Madame. Everything is important, everything is relevant, in a case where violent death occurs.'

'Then if I refuse to answer, M'sieur Risso, what will you take it to mean?'

'That there was such communion.'

'Then I refuse.'

It had been the best she could do to protect Edouard's privacy. Beyond that, she would never reveal the truth of what had passed between them in those last minutes of his life on earth. Not to the police, not to a living soul. Not even to Charlotte.

Not especially to Charlotte.

The strident cry of a peacock came again.

'Yes,' Thérèse said as she turned to face the bed, 'I was with Edouard that night.'

Charlotte watched her, but couldn't see her eyes; Thérèse was only a silhouette, the dark figure of a woman against the sunlight filtering through the shutters. 'And he meant to do that?' she asked in a moment.

'Yes.'

Charlotte watched her steadily, desperate to know the truth that only this one person in the world could tell her.

'Why?'

Thérèse took a step towards her. 'I can't tell you that.'

'Because he made you promise?'

'Yes.'

Charlotte felt the hope go out of her, and lay back into the pillows. It was a question she had waited so long to ask, knowing that Thérèse too had been grieving for Edouard during these past weeks. But the thought had haunted her in the quiet of this lonely room where the scent of roses barely managed to smother the smell of death. *If she, and not Thérèse, had been there with Edouard that night, could she have dissuaded him from that terrible act?*

'There was nothing,' Thérèse said quietly, 'that I could have done, that I didn't try to do. I wanted to telephone you, but it was impossible.' She moved again, taking another step towards the bed, wanting to touch Charlotte, to hold her and try to comfort her, but knowing she couldn't, that she'd be rejected, just as Charlotte believed that Edouard had rejected her in the last hour of his life, preferring to be with his mistress. That wasn't how it had been, but there was no way she could explain: she was sworn to eternal secrecy. 'And there was nothing *you* could have done,' she told Charlotte, 'if you'd been there. Nothing. All I can tell you is what you already know. Edouard loved you more than he loved anyone else on earth.'

'But in the end, he didn't want me. He wanted his mistress.' Her voice was infinitely bitter.

Thérèse turned away. 'Yes. That's true. But you know the classic role of the mistress in a man's life: since he doesn't respect her as he respects his wife, he can reveal himself to her without shame, exposing his weaknesses and his self-doubts and the private devils that haunt him. For Edouard, that was the difference between us, in the end. You were his great love, and I was just his concubine-confessor.'

4

THE FANCY-DRESS MASK

IN MID-ATLANTIC the *Queen Mary 2* was breasting rough seas, and the waves were tumbling white under a full moon. Nearly a thousand feet from stem to stern, she was cutting a swathe through the surface that left a wake a mile long. Her stabilisers were reducing a twenty per cent roll to less than five, and even in this sea she was so steady that at this hour the restaurants were filling up for first service.

On the forward deck starboard, underneath the steps to the bridge, Daphne Houghton-Downes lay on her back under the second officer, tearing her Thai silk dress to shreds as she pulled him harder against her, jerking her legs in a kind of desperation as for the third time she reached her climax.

She hadn't brought the man here because she had nowhere else to go. One of the terraced de luxe staterooms was permanently reserved in her name, whether she came on board or not. It was just that she couldn't do it quite like this anywhere else in the world; here under the moon and the wild sky with the salt wind stinging her skin she felt closer to the animal in this primitive act, closer to the truth. This was how it should be done, riding the night through the timeless sea. There was also the risk of their being seen from the bridge, and getting this poor man dismissed his ship. That was exciting too. But he'd be all right: if he were caught and given the sack she'd just ask Daddy to put him on board one of the smaller ships of the line as captain.

In the Queen's Grill the second service for dinner was just beginning, and the stewards were settling their guests, moving quickly along the lamplit balconies and through the well of the restaurant, helping with chairs and offering the menu, their eyes flickering over the tables to check for the slightest fault. Still only two days out from New York, they already knew which passengers would ask for caviar, which for smoked salmon. The champagne corks were popping, and occasional laughter was breaking out among the tables.

The American girl was sitting alone at a small table on the starboard side, her restless eyes taking in the scene. Her steward spoke to her in a lower voice than usual, which made it necessary for him to bring his face closer to hers. He was already arousing envy among his colleagues, for having the luck to get 'a little smasher like that' at one of his tables. Her eyes alone were fantastic – a deep kind of amber with flecks of gold in them; her raven-black hair hung to her shoulders like a cloud, and her long firm mouth could break into a smile that took your breath away. But the steward's manner was impeccable; she would never have known his thoughts.

On this crossing the chef was French, and the American girl at first ordered the *Fricassée de Lapereau au Vin Blanc*, but she seemed uncertain, and the steward made a point of mentioning that not many of the passengers seemed to like rabbit, so she changed her mind and let him steer her to the *Carré d'Agneau de Sisteron*, since she said she 'went for' lamb.

With her elbows on the table and her small dimpled chin resting on her clasped hands, Suzie Spinoza let her dark, liquid eyes go on roving around the restaurant, at the fine linen and silver wine buckets and cut glass goblets, at the sharp tuxedos and the evening gowns among the candles and the massed hydrangea blooms, and thought that what she was feeling was the exact opposite of *déjà vu*. Things didn't come like this in Memphis, Tennessee, or at least along the truck routes where she used to work. This whole scene was captivating, and the few sips of champagne she'd drunk had already filled her head with its golden bubbles. She moved her glass a few inches away, out of temptation.

So she was crazy. It could happen to anyone, and it had sure as hell happened to her. Is this what they meant when they said there are times in life when everything comes together? Could be.

'Look, kid,' the guy had said, 'maybe if you wanted to stay in one place for a while we could fix something up, you know what I mean? Something more permanent.'

That was all he'd said, and it wasn't very impressive in itself, but along with the other things it suddenly came together and made sense, a whole lot of sense. The other things were that she was still sore from that creep of a Greek at the Sizzling Chicken

Truckstop on Highway fifteen because he had a lollipop as big as a rolling pin and all it had got her was twenty bucks, and it was snowing fit to freeze your ass and if she couldn't raise the money to haul herself out to the sunbelt she'd never get through this next winter. The doc had said so. *You're delicate, Suzie. You got no circulation, see, and if you don't hop onto a Greyhound bus and head someplace where it's warm, you're going to be found under a snowdrift one day, stiff as a stone-dead cotton-pickin' coon.* That's exactly what he'd said.

The final thing that had come together in her mind was the coloured picture of Monte-Carlo in a magazine at her dentist's, with the caption *The Rich Man's Playground*. OK, she'd heard of Monte-Carlo and knew the kind of place it was, but now it made sense. Look, the first time her Uncle Fred had fumbled around with her when she was thirteen years old he'd given her fifty cents when she said she'd tell her mother, and the first time she ran right out of money at the Rolling Hills Truck Stop where she was a waitress and let that skinny guy with the one eye feel her up in the store-shed it had earned her two whole bucks and he never even made her fake it, and by the time she'd been working the truck route from Memphis to Nashville and back she was asking twenty-five bucks a shot and getting it. For a full lay, OK, but you had to give satisfaction. But it was when that guy made his little proposition that she figured it all out. His name was Mr Jones – hell, yes – and he wasn't a trucker, he was an attorney's clerk, and she'd called the number he'd given her and he said he'd pay her *a hundred bucks a week* if she'd find a little place on the south side and keep her mouth shut. *And he'd even help out with the rent.*

So there it was, all written out in big letters and staring her right in the face. *The more they had, the more they paid.* So what in hell was the point in sticking around Memphis, Tennessee, and getting along on a hundred bucks a week when there were places like Monte-Carlo – *The Rich Man's Playground?* It made sense, didn't it? Those guys wanted something to play with, and she had it.

It had taken her two more years to save a buck here, a buck there from her wages and the tips she got at the Golden Garter and Auntie Mame's and the Steamboat, plus what she made on the side when she was able to pick some guy who didn't actually make her hair ache for her to look at him. More than two years

– through two more winters – and here she was, right plumb in the middle of the goldfields with her little spade ready for digging. *There's no point*, Maisie had told her, *shipping out less than first class. They don't have the money at the back end of the boat.* She'd met Maisie at the Golden Garter, and she knew a whole lot about Europe and everything because she'd worked for a travel agency before they fired her for laying the customers. *Go first class, and you stand a chance of meeting some real nice guy and spending the rest of your life with him in the lap of luxury.*

Her *life?* That hadn't occurred to her, but the idea hit her right between the eyes. *That was the ultimate.* You didn't need to spend your time screwing around with a whole bunch of guys while you stacked it all up. *All you needed was one.* One rich man, out of all that playground. Then you got him into the church and just sat back – OK, lay back – for the rest of your life. In luxury.

The *Queen* didn't go there, they'd told her at the travel bureau, but this year she'd started going into Cannes. Was that very far from Monte-Carlo? A taxi ride. So she'd booked a first-class stateroom – they called the ones at the back end cabins – and here she was, toying with a glass of champagne while they brought her the *Carré* – er – *de* Whatever and the fat guy with the heavy gold rings on his fingers at the table over there kept catching her eye – *how much did he earn?* It was heady, the whole thing, and she just went on sitting here not believing it, and at the risk of sliding right under the table she reached for her glass and sipped a little more champagne.

'I say, you *do* look lonely!'

It wasn't the fat guy, it was the girl at the next table, flashing her a brilliant smile and waving her fingers. 'Won't you join us?'

'Well gee, I – I don't like to intrude.'

'But we'd love to talk to you – wouldn't we, Billy?'

'Of course.' The young man stood up immediately and drew back a chair for Suzie, smiling.

'The others aren't coming tonight,' the girl said. 'I'm Daphne, darling. Daphne Houghton-Downes. And this is Billy Davenport.'

'Hi, I'm Suzie Spinoza.' She sat down, taking in the two people as the girl moved a glass nearer and the man poured some champagne. Daphne looked like a china doll, with milky skin and smoky blue eyes and fair hair; her dress was just a sheath of gold sequins. Maybe she was a model. Billy was very tall, with a long

27

face and creases around his eyes, though he wasn't very old. He could be an actor, she thought.

'We were just talking about Charles, darling. Billy says that Diana nags him, but it simply isn't true. He told me himself, when we were dancing at Bishop's.'

'Absolute lie.' Billy gave a gusty chuckle.

Suzie was staring at the girl. 'You mean *Prince* Charles?'

'Of course, darling. The thing is that *he* says he *lets* her nag him, because otherwise he wouldn't be able to slip off to his polo matches – which of course she *hates*, and I suppose I don't blame her – it must be rather like playing croquet on roller-skates, mustn't it?'

'We've joined forces,' Billy told the steward as he came up, 'I hope that doesn't bother you.'

'Of course not, milord.'

'We'll need another ashtray,' Daphne said.

'Yes, milady, I'll see to it.'

'We're not married or anything,' Daphne flashed her brilliant smile to Suzie again, 'we just bumped into each other when we got on in New York. Billy lives just round the corner from me in London. Talking of *which*,' turning to Billy now, 'Alec's just bought a castle in Wales – did you know?'

'What on earth for?'

'He says his flat's getting terribly crowded with all those dogs, and they keep getting run over, so he's going to take them all with him – or what's left of them, I suppose – and let them loose on the moors, or whatever they have in Wales.' She waved her fingers to someone who was passing their table. 'But it's the real thing, apparently – a complete and utter ruin covered in moss and full of bats and birdshit, with rusty iron gates hanging off their hinges and cracked fountains and everything, absolutely marvellous, and Alec's invited me to go there for a weekend but I can't stand those bloody dogs.' She put her pale cool hand over Suzie's on the table, fleetingly. 'Don't you *adore* castles, darling?'

'I haven't ever seen one.' Suzie was trying to get her breath. These people couldn't be putting her on; they'd never seen her before. *Yes, milord*, and *Yes, milady* . . . They had to be the real thing, right here in front of her very eyes. *And that stuff about Prince Charles* . . . Jesus, it was like the cover page of the *National Enquirer*!

'You've never seen a castle? Is this your first trip to Europe, then?'

'Yes.'

'But how simply *marvellous*. Where are you going – all over the place?'

'Just Monte-Carlo.' (*Just* Monte-Carlo . . . Hey, that sounded like real class!)

'But that's just where *I'm* going, darling – or quite close, just a bit higher up the foothills, in Beausoleil.'

Suzie noticed a sudden change in Daphne's bubbling mood, and the smoke-blue eyes were lowered; then she was herself again, plying Suzie with questions – did she already know anyone in Monte-Carlo? Which hotel was she staying at? Did she like playing the tables? – while the food was served and the plates taken deftly away and Billy raised a finger for the wine-steward at regular intervals and Suzie listened to everything that was said because this was a new world for her, the one she'd glimpsed in that magazine at the dentist's in Memphis more than two years ago, and then dreamed about, and then thought about, and finally done something about. *You want something bad enough*, Maisie had told her once when they were sitting side by side under the hair-driers, *then all you have to do is go get it.*

They were sitting with coffee in tiny cups and a steward was pouring cognac in huge snifters when a man in a white uniform with gold braid on the shoulders came up and bent over Daphne.

'I'm sorry to disturb you, milady, but there's a telephone call for you in the radio room.'

'Oh bother, that'll be Daddy. Sorry – I'll be right back, darlings.' Billy stood up and the man in uniform pulled Daphne's chair back and the two stewards gave little bows. 'Which way is the radio room, please?'

'Allow me to show you, milady.'

'Thanks awfully.'

Billy sat down again and watched Daphne's slight sequined figure moving gracefully between the flowers to the exit doors; then he turned to Suzie with that charming hint of a smile that he seemed to wear all the time.

'*Such* a nice girl. She'll show you the ropes on the Riviera as no one else can.' Suzie noticed he seemed to be having trouble with his 'r's, closing his eyes over them and taking care. She leaned towards him.

'This is – this is kind of new to me, Billy. Does she *really* dance with Prince Charles?'

'Not *all* the time.' He gazed at her with his eyes floating a little. 'Just sometimes. It depends which night-club she finds herself in. Or which he does.' He gave another gusty chuckle, then swung his head suddenly and peered towards the doors. When he looked back at Suzie she saw he was having to take his time focussing. 'I say, would you do something *frightfully* sporting?'

Suzie leaned back a little. 'Uh – sporting?' She wasn't sure if this was how they put it in this kind of society. Was he asking her to go to bed with him?

'Yes. I hope it doesn't show, but I am now totally and utterly smashed.' This time the gusty chuckle had to be cut short, to make way for a hiccup. Suzie made a fast mental count of the bottles of wine and the number of trips the steward had made with the cognac. Right – Billy could easily be 'totally and utterly' smashed by this time. 'You see,' he said with his charming smile fixed on his face rather bravely now, 'I could *probably* get to the doors all right if no one got in my way. But I'm afraid it's not at all certain. So would you be *frightfully* decent and get me to my stateroom?'

'Uh – sure. Sure thing, Billy.' Did he mean *carry* him there? Jesus, he must be six foot two. She felt panic rising.

'Jolly good show. If you'll take my arm, it'll look as if I'm escorting you out, and then I can hold on to you if things become chancy.'

She took a deep breath. 'OK. I'm ready when you are, Billy.'

His stateroom was three decks down and Suzie got an elevator as soon as they'd cleared the restaurant because they'd sure as hell never make it down the stairs. Billy stayed upright until she'd opened the door of the stateroom for him, but as soon as he saw the bed he tilted straight over and hit it squarely, facing upwards.

'Oh, God, that's better. Now could you just get my clothes off, Suzie? I *hate* sleeping in them. *Frightfully* sporting of you.'

It took her ten minutes because he was like a log and his clothes were in a heap and he was lying naked on the bed except for his boxer shorts when the door opened and a plump woman in a tight dress and pearls came in without even knocking.

'What the *hell* is going on?'

Billy opened one eye warily. 'Oh, Christ. Er, Suzie, this is the Duchess of – oh, God, where was it, darling?'

'Chelmsford.' She was staring at Suzie with ice in her eyes.

'Ah, yes, Wellsford. And this young lady is – '

'It actually doesn't matter what the *fuck* I'm the duchess of, and frankly I do not *care* who this young lady is, providing she leaves as soon as possible.'

Suzie left even sooner than that.

She was in bed an hour later, adjusting her ideas on the British nobility, when the telephone rang. Her first thought was to let it go on ringing, because that woman with the pearls had looked real nasty and she could be calling her up now to ask what the hell she'd been doing in there with Billy on the bed without his clothes on. Then she thought it could be Billy himself calling her up to ask her if she'd like to join him for another cognac or something, and that could be very interesting – *was he married, for instance?* He seemed to have taken a liking to her – right? He seemed to depend on her – and you could say that again, all the way from the table in the restaurant to the bed in his stateroom. Maybe he was lonesome in his life. Maybe if she told him she understood him and would look after him better than anybody else in the world –

She picked up the phone.

'Hello?'

'*Dar*ling!'

It was Daphne.

'Oh. Hi!'

'I'm in *such* trouble. Have I woken you up, or could you come round and help me?'

'What happened?'

'I'm so unutterably *miserable.*'

'Oh.' Suzie didn't want to go along there because Daphne might suggest some more cognac and ask Billy along and then when they were all smashed out of their minds that duchess would come busting in and . . . oh, Jesus.

'I'd be so grateful,' the soft childlike voice came on the phone again, and Suzie detected a note of something genuine in it now, something serious.

'Which cabin – uh – stateroom are you in?'

'Suite No. 2, just above the Grill. Can you find your way?'

'Sure. I'll be there.'

She slipped her bathrobe over her nightdress and went four decks up, passing a stewardess and a cleaner working on something someone had spilled on the carpet at the top of a staircase. Daphne opened the door for her, clutching a bathrobe against her naked body.

'This is terribly sweet of you, Suzie.' She dropped the robe onto a chair and slipped into one of the twin beds and sat there on her haunches with the sheet up.

'What happened to your back?' Suzie asked her.

'My back?'

'Your shoulders.' In the soft lamplight it looked like bruises on Daphne's very fair skin.

'Oh.' She gave a strange little grimace. 'I fell over, on deck. Come and sit here, darling, and tell me what happened – I missed you when I went back to the table. Did you and Billy have a good time?'

Suzie sat on the end of the bed and told her about the woman with the pearls. 'Oh, that's Tabetha, darling. She's an absolutely awful person who's running after poor Billy. She hasn't got any money, you see, and Billy's got *oodles*.'

'But isn't she some kind of a duchess?'

'Yes, but there are quite a lot of duchesses who can't even pay their butlers.' She was watching Suzie pensively with her smoky blue eyes, as if she weren't really listening to what she was saying. 'I've probably spoiled your whole evening, haven't I? You see, I'm terribly fond of Billy but he can be such a bore, and when our friends didn't turn up for dinner it meant I'd be alone with him, and that's why I asked you if you wanted to join us. Do you mind terribly?'

Suzie found something strange happening to her. She'd never been slow at catching people's vibes, and right now it wasn't only that this little English girl was talking without even listening to herself; Suzie wasn't really listening either. But there was another kind of conversation going on, a very different one, and as Suzie went on gazing into these clouded eyes she knew that what Daphne was trying to tell her was something much more serious than all that bullshit about Billy, something very deep. There'd been a kind of act going on all evening; it was like Daphne had been wearing a fancy-dress mask, and now she was taking it off.

A tremor suddenly shook her whole body, and tears glistened in her eyes. 'For God's sake,' she whispered urgently, 'come into bed with me and hold me tight. Help me keep out the night.'

5

SHADOWS

CRIMSON ROSES LAY scattered among fragments of smashed glass in a pool of water on the floor, and Princess Charlotte lay beside them with one arm flung out. Madame Leclerc gave a sharp little cry.

'*Mon Dieu! Qu'est-ce qui se passe?*'

Linda dropped onto one knee and began feeling for pulse, respiration and broken bones, gently lifting the woman's head and passing her fingers under it; there was no bruising.

The light from the wall lamps wasn't too bright but when she lifted the eyelids she could see the pupils were contracting normally.

'*Elle est bien?*'

'What?'

'Is she all right?'

'Unless I'm missing anything. Nothing's broken. Help me get her onto the bed.'

There was no weight to the poor thing; it was like carrying a child. The bed had been made, and the Frenchwoman pulled the coverlet away before they laid Princess Charlotte gently down. She was wearing a long silk dress with a floral pattern; some of the water from the smashed vase had darkened it.

'We need her doctor here, ma'am. Would you call him for me?'

'*Le Docteur Chirac, vous voulez dire?*'

'Look, I don't speak French. I want her personal physician here right away, OK?'

'That is Dr Chirac, yes.' But Madame Leclerc remained hovering anxiously, a short-bodied woman in a black dress, her greying hair tied back in a bun. Her small olive-dark eyes were despairing as she stared down at her mistress.

'She'll be OK now,' Linda told her quietly, 'but I want the doctor to check her personally, you understand?'

The woman looked at her sharply. 'I will call an ambulance, perhaps?'

'No. No ambulance. She just needs rest.' Back home, a whole lot of people with nothing more than a mild heart attack died in the ambulance on their way to a hospital because of the siren and the jolting and the slamming doors; and if it were the same in Europe she could lose this patient to some clumsy klutz of a paramedic before she could even start caring for her. Madame Leclerc was no help either; she still didn't want to make a move.

Linda looked around the huge room but couldn't see a telephone anywhere.

'Ma'am, will you please call the doctor for me? She's OK, really, but I don't want to leave her right now.'

The woman looked at her sharply again, maybe not wanting to trust her mistress with a total stranger; then she turned away reluctantly and in a minute or two Linda heard her speaking in what sounded like the next room. While she waited, she explored a little and found a washbasin behind a screen of ruffled silk in the corner of the room, and brought back a moist towel for her patient's forehead. It was still clammy and the pulse was below normal.

Madame Leclerc was suddenly in the doorway again. '*Le Docteur* – Dr Chirac is not there.'

Linda asked her to get the number again and give her the phone. 'Go and stay by the bedside, please. If she wakes up she'll probably ask for a glass of water, and she can have one, OK?'

'*Qui est là?*' she heard over the phone.

'Do you speak English?'

'Certainly.'

'Then please listen. I'm a registered nurse just arrived at the Chateau de Beausoleil. Dr Chirac's patient here, the Princess de Montigny-Villiers – '

'Yes, yes, but Dr Chirac is not here, as I told the other lady. He – '

'Where is he?'

'I am not sure. We would need to page him.'

'Then please do that right away. It's a leukaemia patient and she's just taken a severe fall and it's urgent we have a doctor here, preferably her own physician.'

'I will do what I can, Mademoiselle, but – '

'Are you a doctor?'

'Certainly.'

'OK, Doctor, then you know we need an immediate examination made and I'm not qualified to do it. Nor am I prepared to take the responsibility if anything happens to this patient. Please find her physician and tell him that.'

There was a brief silence, then he said stiffly, 'As I told you before, mademoiselle, I will do what I can.' Then the line went dead.

Madame Leclerc was standing by the huge four-poster when Linda went back into the room.

'She does not wake, you see.'

'We'll just give her a little time. There's no need for you to stay, ma'am. I can look after her now.' She didn't want this woman's waves of anxiety around when the patient came to.

'But of course I shall stay, Mademoiselle. As I have told you, I am the housekeeper of Princess de Montigny-Villiers.' The bright black eyes regarded Linda steadily. 'There is much for you to learn, if you are to remain in her service for very long.'

'I'm sure of that. But please understand, ma'am, that my first concern is for my patient, and as long as Princess de Montigny-Villiers is my patient I shall do everything I can for her well-being. Right now she needs rest and quiet, with no one around her. I would like you to leave, and I thank you for your understanding.'

The silence drew out as they faced each other. Linda knew she'd just made an enemy, but that was OK; she'd made enemies before and would do it again, if anyone got in the way of her obligations to her patients.

'Then perhaps it is best that I will have a word with Dr Chirac, Mademoiselle, when he arrives.'

'Feel free.' Linda removed the face-towel from the Princess's forehead and took it behind the screen to re-moisten it. When she came back to the four-poster bed, Madame Leclerc had gone.

'*Qui êtes vous?*' The Princess was coming to, and Linda bent over her, touching her hand gently.

'How do you feel, ma'am?'

The patient's huge, feverish eyes regarded her. 'Is it Linda?'

'Linda Terman, ma'am, yes. Your nurse.'

'My nurse,' the soft voice came again. 'Yes.' Watching her carefully, Linda was aware that the patient wasn't so feverish, maybe, but just not fully conscious. After all, she'd taken quite a tumble. Or maybe it wasn't quite that, either; the woman watching her from the pillows seemed deep into thoughts of her own that were nothing to do with the present. Linda had seen this before; terminal patients had special worlds where you couldn't often go.

'I fell, didn't I?'

'Yes, ma'am. Are you in pain anywhere?'

'No.'

'Do you have any nausea? Do you feel sick?'

'No, I feel quite well.'

'Would you like to wiggle your toes for me, ma'am? OK, and now your fingers? That's great. Can you see me clearly?'

'Quite clearly, yes.'

'And you've no headache?'

'No. I'm a little thirsty, that's all.'

'Sure you are.' Linda fetched a glass of water for her, helping her to sit upright.

'Thank you, *ma chère*.' She looked at Linda intently. 'You see, I wanted to be up, to welcome you when you came into the room.'

Linda swallowed quickly, surprised to find herself so touched. So this patient, dying, had wanted to be on her feet when they met, and she'd finished up on the floor among smashed glass and roses. Linda pressed the slender, wasted hand.

'Then you sure get an "A" for trying.'

Half an hour later Linda was quietly clearing up the broken glass when the door opened and a small man in a dark suit came in with Madame Leclerc.

'This is Dr Chirac, Mademoiselle.' There was a strong smell of cologne.

He gave a brief nod. 'How is the patient?'

'I made neurochecks right away, Doctor, and there was nothing positive. She doesn't seem to be in any pain, but she has a low grade fever. I imagine you'll order a full neurological exam.'

He stiffened. 'Your imagination should be curbed, then, Mademoiselle; it's out of place in a clinical situation.'

Linda felt herself blushing with anger. Even in the give-and-take world of a big hospital back home she hadn't had a doctor talk down to her as if she were a schoolgirl. 'Then you're not concerned with the very strong possibility, Doctor, of an incipient subdural or epidural haematoma, after a fall like that?'

He tilted his narrow head on one side, raising an eyebrow.

'Since you're so ready to play the doctor, Mademoiselle, let me ask you what *you* would do with this patient.'

'OK, sure. I'd order a complete neurological exam and very close observation for forty-eight hours, with neurochecks every hour for alertness, orientation and pupil size and reaction.'

In a moment Dr Chirac asked with a certain interest in his tone, 'How much experience have you had, Mademoiselle?'

'Ten years as a state-registered nurse.'

He nodded and turned away, beckoning her out of the room. In the alcove at the top of the grand staircase he turned to speak to her again, his hands tucked behind his back, the light from a chandelier reflected on his balding head. 'You're quite good, Mademoiselle. Quite good. I agree entirely with your medical opinion. But each case is different, isn't it? In this case, since the patient has already refused chemotherapy and is quite prepared to take the consequences of ignoring my professional advice, it will make little difference if a haematoma develops – or indeed anything else. She has made up her mind to die, you see, and if that is her wish, I feel that it's not in the patient's interest to prolong her suffering.'

He nodded briefly and turned towards the stairs.

'Dr Chirac.'

'Well?'

'I've been told the previous nurse has left already.'

'I believe so.'

'Do you know why?'

'I can only assume that she felt she had not given satisfaction, since you were sent for by Princess de Montigny-Villiers in such great haste.' He gave a shrug. 'But she was extremely capable, in my opinion.'

'She should have at least stayed until I got here. I had the right to expect two things – an in-depth discussion with the nurse who was handing over, and a discussion with the patient's personal physician about his opinion of the case, plus his instructions for further care and treatment. I didn't get either.'

'You will probably find that Nurse Steiner left her report with Mademoiselle Pinalle, the private secretary to Madame la Princesse. To someone of your experience, a written report is all that is necessary.' He started down the stairs, then turned to look up at her. 'You will find Madame la Princesse a difficult patient. Very difficult.'

When Linda went back to check on the Princess she found her still sleeping peacefully; her pulse was a little lower than normal but that was typical with the ingestion of Oblivon at that dosage. She switched off some of the softly-shaded wall lights and went through the connecting doorway to the next room, a much smaller one, maybe a boudoir originally, but now with a single narrow bed in it with a pretty embroidered coverlet and a silk canopy above the bedhead. She fetched her two bags and unpacked; there wasn't another room next to the Princess's – on the other side there was only a big landing – so this was where she was supposed to sleep, obviously, within close call of her patient. When she'd put her few things away in the drawers and the wardrobe she looked around her at the beautiful furniture – the period chairs with their silk brocade and the heavy curtains gathered by huge gold tassels. Even the walls were panelled with shimmering blue silk.

So here she was, dopey from jet-lag at nearly ten o'clock at night in a princess's chateau on the French Riviera, bemused but a little uneasy. (How was poor little Cindy, her ex-room-mate in Trenton, New Jersey? Had she got the toilet fixed yet?) The problems here were different: she'd had a fight with the housekeeper and then with the doctor, who'd told her she was taking on a 'very difficult' patient. It wasn't a terrifically good start, and maybe she should do a little thinking. Had it been the jet-lag or the disorientation of finding herself someplace so different and so far away? Or the fact that the first time she saw her new patient she was unconscious on the floor? She didn't usually fight with people. Maybe she should go find Madame Leclerc and make it up with her. Dr Chirac would take a bit more working on, unless –

'*Pardon, Mademoiselle.*'

The voice from the shadows startled her. She turned to see a girl in a maid's uniform standing hesitantly in the doorway to the main bedroom, watching her.

'Er – hi. Can I help you?'

'*Vous voulez que j'arrange la chambre, Mademoiselle?*'

'I'm sorry – could you say that in English?' The girl looked vacant. 'In – er – *Anglais*, please?' The maid pointed to the bed. '*Je vais arranger le lit pour vous?*'

Linda searched her memory for any high-school French that might have lingered there, but didn't come up with much more than *oui*, *non*, *merci* and *bonsoir*. Everyone she'd talked to since she'd arrived at the chateau had been fluent in English, and it hadn't occurred to her that this was because they happened to be educated people.

'Er – this is my room, right?' She swept her hands around and then pointed to herself. '*Boudoir*, for me?' The maid shrugged, staring at Linda like she was something from outer space, and she realized now that if she were going to last another day in this place she'd have to grab herself a French-English phrase book, fast. She crossed the room and put her arm around the girl's shoulders, leading her through the bedroom. 'Would you take me to Madame Leclerc, please?' she asked softly. In the big four-poster the Princess was still sleeping. 'I need to talk to her.'

'*Madame qui?*'

Linda said it again, but didn't get any reaction; maybe she was pronouncing 'Leclerc' wrong. 'Never mind, it's OK. *Bonsoir.*'

'*Bonsoir, Mademoiselle.*' She gave a little curtsy and slipped away among the shadows of the long corridor. Linda stood at the top of the staircase, awed by its size. Goodness knew what it was made of, but the hand-rail looked like marble or maybe onyx, with gold decorated banisters and small sculpted angels set in niches where the wall swept down in a huge curve to the hallway below. It looked like something out of *Gone with the Wind*. She could hear no voices, either on this floor or below; the chateau was grave-quiet. Maybe ten o'clock was late in this country; or it was because of the Princess; the mistress of this domain was dying, and normal life would have been suspended.

But there was a chance that the housekeeper was still up, so she went down the stairs, listening for any signs of life. It looked as if most of the lamps had been turned low; all she could make out was the great circular hall with archways leading off it to left and right. Moving through one of them Linda found herself in a cavernous salon where the chairs and settees made ill-defined humps in the shadows. Along one wall were four massively-framed portraits, each with its own brass flood-lamp. At first she didn't recognize any of these faces; then it dawned on her that the beautiful, large-eyed woman on the left must be Princess Charlotte, either painted many years ago or certainly before the onset of her illness; it was painful to compare it with the gaunt, bloodless face that had looked up at her a little time ago. *You see, I wanted to be up, to welcome you when you came into the room.*

The figure beside her portrait would be her husband, probably, a silver-haired man with a patrician face, strong and high-cheek-boned. On his other side was a younger man, lean and brooding, his eyes watchful. The son of the house? But there was no resemblance to the older man, nor to Princess Charlotte either. The girl on the far side was unmistakably of her blood, though – fine-boned and with huge, luminous eyes, her mouth pensive. Linda had met only one of them; would she meet the others?

There was something about the silence of this place, *their* silence as they gazed down at her, that sent a sudden shiver through her.

New questions were always coming into her mind, adding to those that had puzzled her on the plane from New York. Did a princess normally make a strenuous effort to leave her sickbed to greet a new nurse when she arrived? And there was something Dr Chirac had said that she hadn't had time to think about before. *Since you were sent for by Princess de Montigny-Villiers in such great haste . . .* What did that mean? She hadn't been 'sent for.' She'd just answered an advertisement. And what 'great haste?'

A slight sound came and she turned her head, but couldn't see anything in the gloom. She shivered again. It was the first time she'd flown any great distance, and if this was what they meant by jet-lag she didn't want to feel it again. For the first time in her life she had the uneasy sensation that she wasn't in control of things; this place and these people were so different from those in the 'real' world back there where she'd been born. The atmosphere was sinister here, and she felt as if she were afloat on dark water, with strong undercurrents trying to tug her down.

A sound came again and she swung round, this time finding herself face to face with a creature watching her from the shadows, its head grossly deformed.

She screamed.

6

Rich Man's Tiger

The sea was mirror-smooth as the *Queen Mary* dropped her anchor two and a half nautical miles outside Cannes harbour. The sun, itself hidden behind the foothills of the Alpes Maritimes, was pouring gold light across the horizon and setting the sky on fire. Watching the scene from the bridge, Suzie Spinoza was astonished to feel tears creeping on her cheeks, and hastily brushed them away.

Beside her, Daphne Houghton-Downe smiled prettily. 'It has that effect on people, darling. It's the same in the Greek islands at sunset.' But she herself was clear-eyed; she'd done enough blubbing in the last few days, sometimes clinging to Suzie and sometimes alone. Now she felt better. It would happen again, of course, but for a little while it was over and she could enjoy herself.

'My God,' Suzie whispered, 'it's all so beautiful . . .' Along the coastline the lights were just beginning to glimmer among the palm trees, gradually taking over from the rose-coloured glow of the sunset. A great silence had come down as the transatlantic liner lay on the water without movement at last, leaving her wake still ruffling the sea from here to the horizon, like a huge brushstroke.

'We invented the Riviera,' Daphne said with a childlike pride. 'I mean the English. We wanted somewhere civilized to stay in the winter-time, out of that bloody fog. By the way, you know when I was helping you to pack this morning? Well I smuggled a couple of little dresses into your baggage. I *do* hope you won't make a fuss and give them back. One was made for me by Bellville Sassoon – the turquoise one – and the other by Caroline Charles. They both make things for Diana too, and they're really very good, but the trouble is just little *me*. I look simply ghastly in them.' She and this intriguing little American girl had shared a table since that evening when poor Billy had fallen foul of Tabetha, and Daphne had noticed that Suzie had only a couple of decent dresses to her name. Of course, it might be that she'd only *packed* those two and left lots and lots more at home; but Daphne doubted it. She doubted it very much.

'But gee,' Suzie said, 'I can't let you do that.'

'Look, darling, I'll only have to throw them away if you won't wear them. You'll look simply stunning in them, just as you do in *everything*, and then I'll have the pleasure of seeing them on you. After all, I never see them on myself, except in the mirror.' She saw that Suzie was still hesitating, so she threw in the kind of information she knew would impress her. 'They cost a couple of thousand pounds each, you see, so I'd *hate* to throw them away.'

'*Each?*'

'Yes.'

'Jesus.'

Daphne was satisfied she'd won, and turned away to speak to the captain. As a matter of fact she liked those dresses quite a lot, but she'd worn them twice, and this was Suzie's very first time in Monte-Carlo and she *had* to have something to wear.

A lot of small boats had put out from the harbour, and one of them was nosing in to the *Queen Mary*. Daphne shook hands with the captain and turned back to Suzie. 'That boat's for us.'

'We're not waiting for the tender?'

'No, darling, it gets terribly crowded. Come on.'

Suzie hurried after her. 'But how do you fix things this way?'

'I don't have to fix anything. Daddy owns the line, that's all.' Their shoes click-clacked down the steps of the companionway.

'The line?'

'The shipping-line. Transocean.'

Suzie tripped. 'You mean this ship too?'

'Lots of them.'

Suzie followed her breathlessly into an elevator. OK, so it was being a very nice evening. She and Daphne had been the only passengers invited onto the bridge to say goodbye to the captain and there'd been around five thousand dollars' worth of clothes 'smuggled' into her baggage and someone had sent a big shiny motorboat specially to take them off the ship, but it was all quite easy to understand because this whole ocean liner belonged to Daddy, among 'lots' of other ones. Sure, it was easy to understand everything when it was spelt out for you.

'This deck,' Daphne told her, and they got out of the elevator and hurried along a strip of red carpet to the big metal doorway in the side of the ship, escorted by two immaculate officers who guided them along the walkway and into the motorboat.

'Marvellous trip!' Daphne called back to them.

'Thank you, milady!'

A lot of salutes snapping up everywhere and then Suzie sat down suddenly on the thick blue-and-gold cushions as the boat throttled up and swung away from the liner's side with a rising throb of power that went straight into Suzie's stomach and vibrated there like an electric massager, because she recognised that sound immediately and instinctively: it was the roar of the rich man's tiger. And there was another thing she knew, right deep down in her gut. One day she was going to ride it, like this cute little English gal sitting beside her with her white silk scarf fluttering in the wind and her eyes smiling at the two uniformed crew and the other man in the blue serge suit. Lady Daphne Houghton-Downe had it all, and did it all, and this was what it looked like and felt like and sounded like, and if there was a single chance in hell of ever making it, little Suzie Spinoza from Memphis, Tennessee, was going to be there too, riding the rich man's tiger.

'Are you all right, darling?' The brilliant smile was turned on Suzie now.

'You bet!' She'd just avoided saying, *You bet your sweet ass I'm all right, kiddo!* In the last few days she'd decided that if she was going to hang out with this kind of crowd she'd better start straightening out her language, so she could tell people she wasn't out of Memphis, Tennessee, but maybe Boston, Mass.

'Boat's a bit bumpy,' Daphne was saying.

'That's a real shame.' She laughed suddenly and Daphne joined her, then turned away again to watch the incredible coastline coming up on them out of the twilight, looking just like a galaxy seen edge-on. The only thing Suzie couldn't quite understand was why her friend had broken down like that, the first night they'd met, crying her heart out in Suzie's arms like a naked and abandoned child until she fell into an exhausted sleep. It had happened again a couple of times and Suzie had just held her and let her get it over with, not wanting to ask what it was all about because Daphne would tell her if she wanted to. *I'm sorry, darling, but I just get a bit miserable sometimes*, she'd said once, but that didn't really explain anything.

Miserable? With all that money? With a 'Daddy' who kept a transatlantic shipping company in his pocket? It struck Suzie she was learning something: riding the tiger was OK for most of the time but maybe you had to take a few falls.

When they swung into the quayside the man in the blue suit took them through customs with an expertise that didn't keep them waiting more than a few minutes, while Daphne stood there patting a yawn and smiling to one of the officers. *Jesus*, Suzie thought, *these Frenchmen are real handsome!* When they left the hall the man in the blue suit led the way and suddenly threw his hands up to shield them as a flashlight went off, then another one and then a whole lot of them. There was a big crowd of people waiting for their friends to come off the ship, and among them were all these photographers, and Suzie wished the man hadn't spoiled the picture because she could have asked for a copy to send back home.

Then they were standing on the long jetty and the man was holding open the door of a gleaming automobile that even Suzie recognised as a Jaguar.

'Thank you, Johnson.'

'Not at all, milady.'

He looked a rather tough kind of guy under the sharp suit and the white cuffs and he didn't smile as Daphne got in behind the wheel, and she didn't smile back.

'Come on, Suzie!'

'I can get a taxi.'

A look of fright passed fleetingly across the pale and rather doll-like face of the English girl, and Suzie caught it.

'Don't you want to come with me?' Her voice was plaintive.

'Well, sure, OK.' She didn't want to take this girl's incredible generosity for granted, that was all. 'But we didn't get the baggage.'

'They'll see to it, don't worry.'

'Your chauffeur?'

'He's not my chauffeur, darling.' She was holding the door open, and Suzie got in beside her. 'He's only my bloody bodyguard.' She slipped her bag into the glove pocket and started the engine, backing up and swinging the Jaguar round in a quick U-turn.

'You need a bodyguard?' Suzie thought it was only rock stars and Frank Sinatra and people like that who needed protection against being mobbed.

'No,' Daphne said, 'I don't, but Daddy thinks I do, so I don't complain too much because he's such a darling.' She swung the sleek car along a boulevard of palm trees, her small gloved hands playing expertly on the wheel. Suzie sat breathing in the rich smell of leather and the other exotic scents that had been shut in with them on the jetty.

'You know something? This place *smells* so fantastic! I hadn't been expecting that.'

'This is the Riviera, darling. What you're smelling is a mixture of garlic and cognac and Gauloise and Chanel and sand and seaweed – you simply won't find it anywhere else in the world, except for Paris of course, but then there's no sand or seaweed and you've got to throw in the exhaust gas.' She waited impatiently at the traffic lights and put her foot down hard the instant they changed to green, flicking her eyes to the driving-mirror as Suzie felt the seat-back pressing against her shoulders.

'You always drive fast?' she asked Daphne.

'It's part of the game, really.' She took the next set of lights at the yellow. 'I told Daddy we'd have to compromise, you see. I've agreed to have these bloody guardian angels trailing me all over the place but I'm not going to have them in the car with me. It's too intimate. I mean I wouldn't mind stopping occasionally to have a fuck but I can't stand having to make small-talk.' Suzie shot her a quick glance of surprise but she didn't notice. 'That's why one of them's behind us now, in the Porsche, and the reason he doesn't like me is that he knows that as soon as we get clear of Nice along the coast I'm going to put my foot down and he's going to be bloody lucky if he can catch us up before Monty.'

Suzie adjusted her seat-belt, and this time Daphne noticed. 'Don't worry, darling, I'm a good driver.' She checked the mirror again. 'I got kidnapped once, you see, and it frightened the wits out of poor Daddy. Hence the bodyguards.'

'Did you come out OK?'

'It depends how you look at it, I suppose. I wasn't gangraped, if that's what you mean, but is that good or bad? I've always thought it might be rather fun, but I've never been able to find a big enough gang. There were only two men on that occasion, and I remember hoping to God they'd let me alone because one of them had dreadfully bad teeth and French kissing with *him* would have been absolutely beastly.' She went through the lights on the yellow again, speeding up. 'We could have turned left onto the

N7 a little way back, but I thought you might like to see the sights. That's Cartier's over there; it gets broken into regularly every month or so but they don't seem to be able to do anything about it; I think they do it for the publicity. This is the Croisette with all the lovely dress shops and that's the new casino on the right, where all the millionaires go to look for popsies.'

'Popsies?'

'Tarts, darling.' Suzie swung a fast look through the window so she could remember the place. 'Where will you be staying?' Daphne asked her. 'In Monty?'

'I guess I'm not sure. Some little place.'

'You didn't book?'

'No. I – '

'Oh, how marvellous! I mean to be so free. When I go anywhere they make reservations for me weeks ahead, and then if I'm two minutes late they start a helicopter search.' The traffic had built up and they had to stop for a moment. 'Let me help you find somewhere; there are lots of super little hotels.' She shifted her body around slightly on the driving-seat so that she could study the American girl while they were waiting for the traffic to move. 'Then I can go on seeing you, can't I, if I know where to find you?'

Suzie looked into those smoke-blue eyes and away again, finding herself becoming lost in a world that was far more strange than she'd thought it would be when she'd bought the ticket to get there. Everything was coming together tonight – the sight of the coast from the ship and the powerful throb of that motor-boat and all those handsome officers saluting them, and then the exotic scent of the Riviera and the lights and the palm trees and this slinky sports car with its rich leather feel under her body – and of course Daphne, above everything else, Lady Daphne Houghton-Downe, with her smoky eyes and her milky skin and her soft child's voice and her bodyguards and her zillionaire daddy. And her loneliness. It reminded Suzie of something someone had said about Marilyn Monroe: that she'd been the most attractive woman in the world – and the loneliest.

It's just that I get a bit miserable sometimes . . .

Suzie could still feel the quiet falling of the tears against her bare shoulder as she'd held this girl in her arms that time, until far into the night Daphne had gotten it over with and fallen asleep like a child exhausted from playing too much.

'Why don't you answer?'

Suzie snapped back into the present. 'I'm sorry, I guess I was . . . you know, dreaming. It's all been so much at once.'

'I said I hoped I could go on seeing you.' The soft, haunted eyes were on Suzie's, and in the voice there was a note of entreaty.

'Sure,' Suzie said. 'I'd like that.'

Her hand was lying on her lap, and Daphne put hers gently over it. 'I'm so glad, darling. If I thought I couldn't see you again I think I'd die.'

* * *

Outside the customs hall in Cannes harbour most of the crowd had drifted away, with chauffeurs and friends helping the passengers with their baggage, and cars swinging away into the town. The last tender was moving in from the *Queen Mary*, and Mario Romano, one of the freelance photographers, slung his gear over his shoulder and turned away, a lock of dark hair falling over his brow as he bent to light a cigarette.

There hadn't been many celebrities on this voyage – a couple of film actors, Madame Vouvray-Lebon, the choreographer from Paris, a handful of Swiss gnomes and the English girl, Daphne Houghton-Downes. Her bodyguard had stopped Mario getting a useful picture but it wasn't important. She was a boring little bitch, and if her father didn't own half the shipping world she wouldn't be of the slightest interest, in terms of a story. Just those fabulous little-girl looks. To Mario's surprise he felt a stirring beneath his hand-sewn Italian silk briefs as he remembered those few feverish minutes he'd spent with her at the Beach Club at the end of the summer. She had been sitting with a long cool drink at the bar and he had asked her for a candid shot for his collection and she'd slowly put down her drink and smiled to him and said *My God, aren't you handsome . . . No, you can't have a photograph of me, but you can have everything else.* And within seconds she'd pulled him into her private beach enclosure and ripped his white linen slacks down over his hips and was working at him with small frantic hands, snatching off her bikini and thrusting herself at him, crying and shuddering until he entered her, with the sand shifting under their feet and the noonday sun streaming against their faces and the sweat gathering and running off their skin as she moaned and went on moaning, clawing at him and leaving marks that later took weeks to heal. But only his body was satisfied. There'd been no gentleness, no tender approaches, not even love-play: she'd taken him like a tigress and drawn blood, and the moment it was over she'd simply turned away and pulled her bikini on and walked across the sand to the bar without once glancing back.

Mario Romano was an Italian, and that wasn't how Italians made love. He felt he'd been *raped*, and it was a long time before he could get over the rueful irony of that, considering his reputation as a Lothario along this coast. Yet now, three months after it had happened, he could still feel this stirring in his loins at the mere sight of Daphne Houghton-Downes this evening. As he walked to his scarlet Alfa-Romeo on the jetty with the heavy camera gear across his shoulder, he flicked his half-smoked cigarette away and found himself thinking for the first time that he would like to meet that neurotic little English bitch again. She was a nymphomaniac, and must have had dozens of men – hundreds, even – and that was just boring. But Mario sensed a challenge in her now. It made no difference how often she'd made love; when he was alone with her again he'd show her – for the first time in her life – how it should be done.

7

Countess Bibi

THERE WAS A soft explosion of sound, starting from behind Linda and then thundering past her, and she tripped and went sprawling across the pine needles. The images were still in her mind's eye – the huge horse with its rider bent low across its mane as they hurtled under a low bough, the creak of leather and the ringing of harness and the flying of giant hooves.

She picked herself up and stared after them; they were already small in the distance, swerving onto a bridge across the lake with the sound of muffled drums. Her heart was still bumping from the shock, and she let the anger come out, cursing the man in good old New Jersey idiom. Hadn't he even seen her, in her white shorts and tee-shirt, in broad daylight? Or was it his kind of joke to scare the hell out of innocent joggers? She didn't think it was terribly funny.

In a moment she started off again, keeping an eye on the horse and rider. The shocks you got here at the Chateau de Beausoleil were different from the ones you got in Trenton. In Trenton you'd have some idiot clip your fender running a red light or you'd find the supermarket just closing when you came off late duty and didn't have as much as a single French fry in the fridge or the IRS would inform you that they'd made a mistake about the substantial refund and actually *you* owed *them* the amount stated. In the two days she'd been here in Beausoleil she'd found a princess out cold on the floor and seen a monster watching her from the shadows and been sent sprawling by a galloping horse.

'*C'est le petit Baron.*'

It was all Mademoiselle Pinalle had said when Linda had asked her about the Mongol boy – because that was of course what he was, and not the monster she'd imagined in her fright. She would have spoken to him, but he'd shuffled away the moment she screamed. That night she'd hardly slept for shame – after the human wrecks and accident victims she'd seen in her career as a nurse she should have recognised a Mongol when she saw one, and she didn't have to scream at the poor boy. They were super-sensitive to people's reactions, and she could have wept at her stupidity. But it was just this place, its atmosphere, and the hostility she'd met with from Doctor Chirac and Madame Leclerc. And first nights in any strange place were always a bit unsettling.

Le petit Baron. OK, even she could work that much out. He was a baron, that poor kid? *It doesn't make any difference how rich they are*, Mrs Weston had told her, *they're still people*.

But they were still strange, here at the Chateau. Mademoiselle Pinalle was another one – very tall, very thin, and very quiet. She was the Princess's secretary, and had an office off the huge entrance hall. Linda had never met anyone so withdrawn. Mlle Pinalle was still young, not much more than Linda's age, and quite pretty, with clear eyes and blonde hair, the sort of fragile looks you saw in porcelain figurines. But she wouldn't let you talk to her – at least not Linda. A wistful smile, a *oui* or a *non*, and she was gone, closing the door of her office quietly. Didn't she speak English? Most people here did, though not the servants. Well that was OK: this morning Linda had taken her first French lesson, from Bibi.

Bibi . . . She'd been another shock, of a different kind. Yesterday, one of the maids – Marianne, with the waif-like air and the curtsy – had come to the door of Princess Charlotte's room with a whispered message. '*Henri part pour la ville, Mademoiselle. Vous désirez quelque-chose?*'

Linda only got one word that meant anything, and that was *Henri*, which was the name of the chauffeur. He was the young man with the seven o'clock shadow and the husky voice who had brought her to the Chateau from the airport two days before, his dark eyes lingering on her, his slight bow making her feel like a princess. His English was smooth and quietly delivered. 'Every day, Mademoiselle, I drive into the town. If there is anything you need at any time, it would be a pleasure to obtain it for you. Anthing at all.' His soft, ardent tone had conjured instant visions of black lace lingerie at the top of the shopping list.

Linda hesitated in front of the little maid. 'Yes, I'll – *oui, merci, Marianne.*' She got the list from her room and hurried down the stairs and through the marbled hall. Standing by the silver-grey Mercedes, Henri gave his captivating bow.

'You should be able to find all these things at the pharmacy, Henri; they're for the Princess. But if you could pick up a French-English phrase book for me somewhere, I'd appreciate it.'

'But of course. I will go to the – '

'You don't need a phrase book.' The face of a young girl was looking up at her from the window of the car. 'I'll give you lessons.'

The chauffeur half-turned, smiling. 'Allow me to present the Countess Bibi, Mademoiselle.'

The eyes of the pale-faced girl went on gazing up at Linda with an extraordinary concentration, and when Linda spoke it was like having to break a spell.

'I'm pleased to meet you, Countess.' That sounded kind of strange too, because Linda's idea of a countess was an elegant woman in a silk hoop skirt floating through a ballroom full of flunkeys.

'You may call me Bibi.' It was said rather formally.

'Thank you. I'm Linda Terman.' She held out her hand, and the girl reached hers through the window of the car and shook it solemnly, her blue-grey eyes still regarding her intently.

'*Enchantée*. And that's your first lesson – you can use *Enchantée* to practically *everybody* when you first meet them. Can I call you Linda?'

'Sure.'

'What time of the day would you like your lessons?'

'I guess I'll have to see how things work out. It's going to depend on how the Princess is feeling. I'm her new nurse.'

'I know. I know all about you, Linda.' She didn't smile, and Linda was suddenly reminded of the horror movies when children set fire to buildings or made people drop dead just by staring at them. She didn't think she was going to like this strange young kid very much; a French-English phrase book seemed relatively harmless. Then an extraordinary thing happened. 'Don't worry,' the girl said calmly, 'we'll get along perfectly – I know that too.'

Linda still remembered the shiver that had gone through her when Bibi had said that, taking the thoughts straight out of her mind. At odd moments throughout the rest of the day she'd found herself thinking up excuses not to take French lessons after all, and on one occasion when a hair-brush had slipped off her dressing-table she'd remembered the well-authenticated reports of psychic-research groups – that in every case of poltergeist activity there was always an adolescent child in the house. But this morning Bibi had come to the door of her room, and since Princess Charlotte was sleeping peacefully Linda had said she'd be glad of a lesson right away.

It was hair-raising. She followed Bibi along the wide carpeted corridor to an ante-room on the other side of the staircase, and the first thing Linda noticed was that Bibi had a slight limp. She wore a simple white blouse and blue tunic, with her fair hair done in a pigtail, and therefore looked like a schoolgirl; but there were glimpses in her of a fully-mature woman – even a *wise* woman, sophisticated and knowing.

'This room will do for now,' she told Linda, and pulled back the heavy velvet curtains, her hair catching the morning sunlight. 'I had an English nanny, and then an English governess, so that's all I speak – apart from French, of course. So you'll have to get used to my idiom.' She moved across to one of the ornate chairs and composed herself on it demurely, folding her hands. 'They tried sending me to the *Lycée* in Beausoleil – that's the school – but I used to get fits there, I don't know why.'

'You didn't like being with other kids?'

'Not particularly. Some of them smelled. Why don't you sit down, Linda?'

'OK. Don't I need a notebook or anything?'

'You won't want to put down anything *I'm* going to teach you in notebooks.' It was said without a smile; she sat gazing at Linda reflectively, swinging her thin black-stockinged legs. 'I've also been giving a few lessons to Mademoiselle Pinalle. Have you met her?'

'Yes, just for a minute.' Mademoiselle Pinalle was the withdrawn, uncommunicative secretary.

'I like her, I suppose. But she's too *tall*, you know. She can't get a man, and that's why she *masturbates*.'

Linda did a mental flip. 'Uh – OK, you gave me the word for greeting people for the first time – *enchantée* – is that right? Now will you refresh my memory with a few other words? I picked up one or two at school, and they'll come back to me with a bit of help. How about 'good-morning' and 'goodbye' and stuff like that?'

Countess Bibi put her head on one side. 'I'll give you a couple of words straight away that should mean something to you. You've heard of an *enfant terrible?*'

'That's a kid who – uh – says outrageous things to shock people, right?'

'Yes. And that's what you think I am. But I'm not. I'm a bit *odd* in my ways, I suppose, because when I was five my mother and father got very depressed for some reason and sealed themselves up in a big Chinese cabinet with a thousand rose-blooms and died from lack of oxygen. I was so furious with them for leaving me all alone that I jumped out of a window but didn't have any luck – that's just like me – and all I managed to do was break my leg. That's why I limp.' She let out a little sigh. 'Now, then – "good-morning" is *bonjour* and 'goodbye' is *au revoir* and 'good-night' is *bonsoir*.' She went through a dozen words and one or two phrases while Linda did her best to concentrate, and then Bibi said, 'Of course you realise that Henri, the chauffeur, is madly in love with you, don't you? He doesn't behave like that to *every* woman he meets, believe me – all that heavy Gallic charm. It's your looks, of course. What on earth are you doing working as a nurse? You could marry *anyone!* And I don't mean a chauffeur.' She leaned forward, lowering her voice to a stage-whisper. 'Actually, Henri told me in the car that he – '

Linda cut her short. 'Look, Bibi, we're going to have to make a deal. If you want to give me French lessons, OK, I can use some. But no bullshit.'

Bibi threw her head back and gave a squeal of laughter; then she jumped off the chair and limped over to Linda, her blonde pigtail swinging. 'I told you we'd get on perfectly, didn't I?' The laughter had quite died way and her eyes were grave now. *'I've been waiting for you, Linda. We all have.'*

There was a strange note in her voice, a kind of triumph, and Linda felt a moment of vertigo, while the room echoed with faint voices. Then it was over, and she found herself staring into the unwavering eyes of the child.

Jogging through the great park, Linda could still feel the chill that Bibi's words had brought, the sensation of vertigo. She was again reminded of her earlier thoughts of why she was here at the Chateau; it seemed as if she'd been drawn away from her normal life in New Jersey by some kind of psychic force. *But that was crazy.* Two days in this place and she was beginning to think like a zombie. It had to be the jet-lag and the disorientation, the total unfamiliarity of everything – after all, this was the Old World, where people were still almost medieval in their ways. It was just culture shock.

There was the drumming of hooves again, and she swung around quickly. The horse and rider were coming up on her at a gallop, and she moved deeper into the trees; but this time the rider saw her, and reined in his mount, slowing it to a walk. Foam smothered its mouth, and the whites of its eyes showed as it tossed its head.

'*Qui êtes vous?*'

Looking up at the man in the saddle, Linda was aware of tremendous, held-in power, though he sat perfectly still and his voice was not raised. It occurred to her at the back of her mind that she was looking at the most handsome man she'd ever seen in her life – and not for the first time, she realized: his was one of the portraits in the *grand salon*.

'*Je suis Linda Terman*,' she told him. ('A lot of people,' Bibi had told her earlier this morning, 'will be asking who you are in the next few days, because you're a stranger here, so just throw in the *je suis* before your name.')

'*Vous êtes une invitée?*'

'I don't speak very much French.'

'Are you a guest here?'

'No, I'm the new private nurse.'

'I see.' The big horse moved restlessly, and he calmed it, not taking his dark eyes from Linda. 'Did you see my horse spook when we passed you earlier?'

His voice had the resonance almost of a cello string, and she found herself listening to it rather than the words. 'Did you say "spook"?'

'You know nothing of horses?'

'Nothing at all.'

He looked away impatiently, his eyes narrowed against the sunshine. 'The horses are not used to strangers here, especially dressed in white; this one shied when he came upon you unexpectedly, right in his path. He is spirited and nervous, and could have thrown me. This is the riding park. Please do your running somewhere else.' He turned away, touching the horse's flanks.

'*He scared the hell out of me too, do you know that?*'

The man reined in again. 'What did you say?'

'I said he scared the hell out of me too. There aren't any notices around here telling people they can't use the park, so how are we to know?' She glared up at him against the bright sky, hands on her hips. She'd expected him to apologise, when he'd stopped to talk to her; but he was too damned arrogant for that.

The man looked puzzled, studying her for a moment longer; then he swung the horse's head away and touched its flanks again, and within a moment they were galloping into the distance towards the lake. Linda gazed after them, still angry. She had a pretty good idea who this guy was – he looked very like the portrait of the young, arrogant man she'd been looking at earlier: the son of the house. Too bad nobody had taught him any manners.

In a moment she ran on, taking a route through the pine trees where the horse wasn't likely to come; but the sense of elation that jogging always gave her had gone now, and she just went on trudging over the massed pine needles for the sake of the exercise. For the first time she felt homesick for Trenton, New Jersey, with its pouring rain and its flat batteries and its ordinary, understandable people.

'You're not in pain, are you, ma'am?'

'Oh, no.' The fragile, blue-veined hand moved slightly on the silk coverlet, brushing the idea away.

Linda knelt at the bedside, so that she could face her patient on the same level. Late afternoon sunshine was slanting into the room. 'I'd rather you didn't try to be brave, you see. It doesn't help you, or me. I can't always tell exactly how you're feeling, and you told me you wanted me to make things a little easier for you.' She put her hand over the dying woman's, lending it some of her warmth. 'I want to do that, very much.'

'I know.' The large, pensive eyes of the Princess remained on Linda's almost without blinking; she felt from this woman the same kind of intense concentration that Bibi possessed; it was as if they both had the ability of looking deep into Linda's mind, and it made her uneasy.

She had spent most of the day with the Princess, helping her to wash and bathe and dress for the meeting with her visitors this afternoon – four black-suited men with large briefcases who had piled out of a limousine, to be received personally by the Princess: bows, handshakes, and her brave flickering smile. Linda had wanted to be there at the meeting, in case her patient needed her, but the Princess had been very firm, telling her afterwards that it had been necessary for those gentlemen to be assured that her health was bearing up during these trying days.

'I have a great deal to do, Linda, before I die. The es   ies are very substantial, and I am determined they shall not pass ınto the wrong hands.' Climbing the great staircase together, the Princess's hand on her arm, she had refused to rest at every step, as Linda had suggested. 'Once I rest, you see, I shall never be able to move on again. The rest of my life is like this staircase, and I mustn't stop until I reach the end.' The smile had flickered again, like the light of a guttering candle, and it was today, in that moment on the staircase, that Linda had begun to feel something akin to love for her patient.

Why had Dr Chirac called her 'difficult'? This was answered soon after Linda had helped the Princess back into her bed. 'You don't fuss, *ma chère*, as the other nurses did. You give me the credit for still being a person in my own right – and in my own mind. Dr Chirac is a clever man, but he always talks of treatment for me – chemotherapy and new drugs and that kind of thing. He wants to keep me alive, *n'est-ce-pas?* That's what a good doctor should do, of course. But he doesn't understand me as you do. That is remarkable, for someone so young. You know that as soon as I've put this great house in order, I shall be ready to leave it, and join my beloved husband.'

Kneeling by the bed in the late afternoon sunshine, Linda told her, 'If there's ever any pain, ma'am, I'd like you to tell me, and then we can deal with it. It's OK to take a little, sure, but too much can be debilitating, and that's going to sap your reserves.' She'd already learned that she could talk to this patient frankly; Princess Charlotte was a very intelligent woman. But in the hospital wards there was always the problem of patients who 'didn't want to give any trouble'. They'd suffer in silence, simply because some nurses were short on patience and would veer past the people who made the most demands on their time.

'I'll let you know, *ma chère*, if I need relief.'

'Thank you.' As one of the peacocks screeched again from the lawns below, Linda saw a tightening of the Princess's face. It hadn't been a loud sound, but it always bothered her. Was it some kind of association? 'Ma'am, why don't we have someone move those birds to the other side of the building?'

'Birds?'

'The peacocks.'

'No. They were brought here by my beloved husband, and besides, Toinette likes to watch them.'

Toinette was Charlotte's sister, a much younger woman whom Linda had seen in the hall a couple of times: Mademoiselle Pinalle had introduced them. Bibi, of course, had come straight to the point this morning, during the French lesson. 'I like Toinette quite a lot, but I don't like her husband. He's a lawyer, *and he beats her.*'

'Would you like to sleep now, ma'am?'

'Yes. It was a busy day.'

She looked more comfortable now; while she'd been downstairs at the meeting, Linda had got Marianne, the shy little maid, to help her drag one of the mattresses off the huge four-poster, to make it easier for her patient to leave the bed and get back into it by herself. She'd also stopped the practice – which the Princess had become used to – of putting a pillow under her knees when she sat up in bed reading. Linda knew it was more comfortable, but the pressure tended to stop the venous return of blood from the lower legs and the feet, with the risk of thrombi forming.

'Would you like a Somnoril, ma'am?'

'No. I shall sleep well enough, *ma chère.*'

Linda went over to the shutters, pulling them to; there was enough air circulating between the slats. Then she checked the medication tray and the water jug, switched on the little shaded lamp that she used for a night-light, and settled down in the big brocade armchair, listening to her patient's breathing. In a few minutes it began slowing and deepening, and Linda heard it with relief: the Princess had forced herself to nearly a full day's activity, and Linda hadn't expected her to sleep so easily, without a trace of fever.

You had no business to let her leave her room, least of all to receive visitors. Dr Chirac. He'd called Linda half an hour ago to ask after *Madame la Princesse*, and Linda had told him what had happened. *She is your patient, Mademoiselle, and you are entirely responsible for her in my absence.*

Linda had told him the Princess was also her employer, and that she didn't have the authority to stop her getting out of bed and going downstairs, though she'd done everything she could to dissuade her.

We shall discuss this matter further, Mademoiselle. Meanwhile my instructions are that you give her 3.5 mg of Oblivon, unless she has a fever.

Oblivon 3.5 mg was Dr Chirac's answer to everything. The

Princess was in no major pain, and her temperature and pulse were almost normal for her condition. Linda had given her nothing. Sitting here in the lowering light of the early evening, she wasn't exactly sure how much more she was going to take from Dr Chirac – or Madame Leclerc, the housekeeper, for that matter.

But the shutters must always be closed, Mademoiselle, during the afternoon. There is enough fresh air coming between the slats.

Linda had explained that the Princess liked to see the rose garden below, and had asked for the shutters to be left open.

The previous nurse would not have allowed it, Mademoiselle. The bright light always induces migraine.

Linda had told Madame Leclerc that if the previous nurse came back here, then she would be in charge again. It was the first time that the idea had occurred to her of leaving the Chateau, despite her growing affection for her patient. In the States she'd worked in crises, when the Trenton Linen Works fire had destroyed three of the main buildings and sent a hundred first-degree burn cases streaming into St Francis' in a convoy of ambulances, and when the through train to Newark had jumped the frozen rails and rammed into a stationary freight-train on a branch-line, with a count of seventeen dead and a hundred and nine injured. But that kind of situation, when they'd worked thirty-six hours at a stretch because there weren't enough staff to go around, was part of the job, and nobody had ever thought of quitting. Here at the Chateau, the work was a thousand times easier, but there were hostile elements that didn't allow her to care for her patient in the way she wanted to, and that was a whole lot different.

Listening to the quiet breathing of her patient, she wondered whether the previous nurse had left because of Dr Chirac and Madame Leclerc and maybe other obstructive elements; it could be the reason she'd taken off in such a hurry.

Her thoughts were broken as a sound came from the corridor outside, and she left the chair and went across to the door, in case anyone tried to come in. There was heavy carpeting outside and she heard no footsteps before a knocking began on the door. She opened it at once, to see the man who had scared her in the park this morning with his horse.

'*You can't come in*,' she told him in a fierce whisper. '*Madame is sleeping.*' She half-closed the door behind her, making him step back.

'I have to talk to her,' he said briefly.

'That's impossible. But I'll give her a message when she wakes up, if you wish.'

He gazed at her for a moment with his dark, intense eyes, as if he didn't understand what she was saying; then he simply moved her firmly aside and pushed the door open and walked into the room. Linda followed him, thinking she could maybe get between him and the bed; but the Princess had already been wakened by the noise, and was trying to sit up. The man helped her with the pillows, and when Linda made to say something he swung his head impatiently.

'Please leave us.'

Linda hesitated a moment, and then went through into the adjoining room, closing the door quietly and crossing to the wardrobe, taking down her few clothes and opening a suitcase. Inside of fifteen minutes she was packed.

8

Dark Secret

As the graceful shape of the *QM2* swung broadside-on to the shore and three blasts from the funnel sounded farewell across the dawn waters, an executive jet was lowering to the runway at Nice-Côte-d'Azur, thirty kilometres to the east along the coast. Twenty minutes later, Julius Ariche, a frequent visitor to the French Riviera, was ushered into the specially-built Mercedes limousine waiting under the palm trees, and the rear passenger-door was closed and automatically locked.

Monsieur Ariche was a short, energetic man of middle age, his face shadowed, rather than tanned, by that strange and attractive bluish hue of the Levantine races. His eyes were of a blue so dark that in certain lights they appeared black, yet they were never without light or expression – he could, at will, show surprise, innocence, affection or compassion, according to the need at the time, and even those who believed they knew him were unaware that Julius Ariche was totally unsurprisable and lacked even the most rudimentary understanding of innocence, affection or compassion. But most people – especially women – thought him charming; his lack of height was an asset, in that it was non-threatening and therefore disarming; and his soft, deferential voice was not only pleasant to listen to but equally reassuring. One never doubted that one was obtaining the best deal possible in terms of bargaining – for Julius Ariche was a merchant.

He had no friends, by his own choice, and therefore nobody in the whole world knew of the one great tragedy in this man's life, for he never spoke of it nor gave any indication that it troubled him. However, he had found his own answer to it, and it was this that directed the whole course of his life.

When he had left the VIP lounge a few minutes ago, one of his bodyguards had walked ahead of him, his head turning rhythmically to left and right, while another had followed him, turning now and again to glance behind. At this moment, as the long black Mercedes limousine pulled away from the kerbside outside the terminal, a smaller model of the same make swung out in its wake, to keep station fifty yards behind throughout the journey from Nice Airport to the Principality of Monte-Carlo, another thirty kilometres along the coast by way of the Grande Corniche.

The escort vehicle was in constant touch with the limousine by radio, and concealed in both cars were six emergency alarms, bullet-proof vests, shotguns and trauma kits. The chauffeur sitting in front of Monsieur Ariche had been trained at the renowned Bondurant School of High-performance Driving, completing a seven-day anti-kidnap and anti-terrorist course. The bodyguard beside the chauffeur had received his specialised training in anti-terrorist operations from the Central Intelligence Agency in the United States, while the two men in the escort vehicle had both passed high-proficiency tests in explosives and sabotage devices at a special unit of the Federal Bureau of Investigation. The driver himself had spent two years in the US Secret Service on presidential protection duties. Julius Ariche was almost indifferent to these elaborate precautions against any threat to his welfare, since they were the best that money could buy, and there was nothing more that he could do. He was a fatalist.

Although the Basse and the Moyenne Corniches offered a slightly shorter route to Monte-Carlo than the Grande, Julius Ariche always preferred to take it. He liked the high, winding road that threaded its way between the pinewoods, and enjoyed the glimpses of Beaulieu and the Mediterranean far below. He was also attracted by the knowledge that he would pass very close to the place where the late Princess Grace of Monaco had met her untimely death, and this would have perhaps been taken as an expression of morbidity, had anyone known his feelings. No one did. And finally he enjoyed the zig-zag *virages* that led down the mountainside from the perched village of La Turbie, from where he could look down on the charming panorama of Monte-Carlo itself, a jewel set at the fringe of the ruffled satin waves of the Mediterranean. It was a popular route from Nice to the Principality, and it was in fact this way that Daphne Houghton-Downes had come the day before, driving her crimson Jaguar at her usual frenzied speed with Suzie Spinoza beside her.

Today, as the leading Mercedes took the curves of the Grande Corniche, Julius Ariche spoke occasionally on one of his telephones, listening carefully and responding in that soft, modulated voice.

'Of course, Your Majesty. I understand.' His quick, intelligent, midnight-blue eyes gazed from the smoked-glass window beside him as he listened, making mental notes of what was required of him. It wasn't often that a client would telephone him so soon after he had arrived on the Riviera; Sheik Ahmed of Abu Talha must have instructed his communications unit to inform him of Ariche's movements over the past few days. That was flattering: it meant that one of the wealthiest and most powerful men in the world valued his services. It also meant that he was at this moment in need of them.

Sheik Ahmed – a younger brother of Sheik Adnan's – was one of the most intelligent and astute business men among the new Arabian mega-tycoons, with an estimated personal worth of three billion US dollars and a network of investments whose labyrinthine complexity was known only to a few – Julius Ariche being among them, since it was his private business to inform himself as to the financial status of his clients. How else was he to know what to charge them for his services? But these days such information was becoming more and more difficult to acquire; the time was gone when the nouveau-riche from the desert had ostentatiously ordered champagne by the barrel to bathe in, and Cadillac limousines by the dozen at a time. They had learned it was embarrassing in polite Western society, and there had also been agitation in the British parliament for laws to be passed to prevent these billion-pound potentates from buying up half of London.

Today, as Julius Ariche was aware, many a British company was a satellite of an American firm controlled by a bank in the Bahamas which was in turn owned, through private trusts, by Sheik Ahmed of Abu Talha. His Majesty's interests encompassed commercial banks in Switzerland, hotels, meat packing companies and restaurant chains in the United States, together with movie theatres, hospitals and a silver mine in Colorado. In addition he owned a French fashion house and real estate property in London, New York, Florida and Texas, though not in his own name.

This priceless portfolio was the result not only of the Sheik's natural inheritance, but also of his shrewd capabilities as a businessman; and what amused Julius Ariche was that he should have at the same time, in his private life, the emotions almost of a child.

'Of course, Your Majesty.' Sheik Ahmed always appreciated the use of the courtesy title. 'I count the invitation as a great honour, and will look forward to the occasion with the keenest pleasure.'

After the usual exchange of formalities he cradled the telephone. He would look forward to the royal dinner party with less pleasure than he'd indicated, since the last time he had dined arabesque, so to speak, he'd finished up with violent indigestion, because as the guest of honour he was obliged to eat an underdone sheep's eye. It had also been his privilege to sit cross-legged on the floor opposite his illustrious host, and it had taken his masseur more than two hours to ease the ache from his calf-muscles. But perhaps it would be worthwhile to suffer the ordeal again, since Sheik Ahmed had just confirmed that he did indeed require his good services, for which Julius Ariche had already decided to ask half a million US dollars, provided he could locate top-quality merchandise.

One of the telephones sounded its electronic chime again, but he ignored it. He had no friends, so it could only be another client, who would have to wait until he had successfully fulfilled his assignment from Sheik Ahmed.

On the few occasions when Monsieur Ariche was formally asked his business, he described it as 'import-export', which was not at all inaccurate, though he devoted his energies mainly to export, and the merchandise he dealt with was not ornamental brassware from India, nor firstgrade leather from the Argentine, but women, from wherever he could find them.

* * *

In the evening of the same day, Toinette Cavaille, née Antoinette Madeleine de Montigny-Villiers, lay on the floor of a guest-suite in the west wing of the Chateau de Beausoleil, submitting to rape.

Only ten minutes ago she'd heard the distinctive sound of Raoul Cavaille's super-sports Lamborghini coming down the hairpin bends from La Turbie, where the road passed within half a mile of the estate, the tyres of the car squealing regularly as it was sent headlong into each *virage;* and as she listened to it, Toinette had stood in the middle of the gilded, high-ceilinged bedroom and shivered, torn between the idea of running downstairs and out of the building and through the pinewoods to escape, and the idea of what life would be like if she were never to see Raoul again –

for if once she left him, she knew she would never come back. In the end she did what she always did, going into her bathroom and taking the Heinlich diaphragm and rinsing off the antiseptic fluid and opening her legs to insert it. She always hated it: it was the least sensual object she could possibly imagine, more suitable to fit inside a coffee mill or a plumbing fixture; but the pill made her nauseous, and that was worse.

And now she was on the floor, still with her clothes on, while Raoul raped her, strongly and efficiently and with great energy, not letting her take any part in what he called their lovemaking, but forcing her to submit to whatever he wanted to do to her, straining under her thin mohair sweater to reach her breasts, tearing at her pleated skirt and clawing at the join in her silk panties in his initial foray, and then pulling the clothes from her body one by one and forcing her arms above her head and her legs wide open while she made small sounds, timing them so that he heard them just before the pain began but not always getting it right: it was a more subtle game than it seemed, because if she hissed through her small clenched teeth too soon he would know she was bluffing, and would use his hard spade-shaped hands more strongly, punishing her for cheating; and of course if she left the sounds of pain too late they'd become real.

But even now, after almost five years, she wasn't sure whether the tears that were now staining her face were of pain or passion, for there was something deep in her that responded to these primitive attacks; and this was why she sometimes wondered what would happen if she left Raoul, with his dark animal looks and his flared nostrils and his shimmering black eyes under the heavy brows – whether she would ever be able to find a man so fierce, so ravenous after only three days away from her.

'There's never anyone else,' he'd told her more than a few times when he'd come back from a trip, 'there's only ever you, Toinette. I could never find what I find in you in any other woman.'

But she knew that if he could, he'd have that woman too.

It was her own sister, Charlotte, who'd introduced them, on one of the yachts in the harbour, she'd forgotten which one: it was just another party. But from the instant Raoul Cavaille had looked into her eyes she'd had the immediate and overwhelming knowledge that she could never, from that fateful moment, escape him. In his dark, saturnine face and his shimmering gaze she had recognized someone she had in fact never seen before, someone perhaps from another life, or other lives, a known entity that had always been with her in the centre of things, and would always be with her, world without end.

Raoul had known what was happening too: he'd put it straight into the first words he'd ever spoken to her. After offering his formal homage, he had straightened up from kissing her hand and looked deeply into her eyes. *'It's time we met.'* The effect on her had been dizzying, and she'd had to excuse herself from his presence, going on deck and leaning at the rail and taking in deep breaths of the cool sea air. Then later, when she went below again, it was to him, and she spoke to no one else for the rest of the night.

She watched him now as he rolled away from her, his long, inflamed phallus still erect as he stood up, flexing it so that it moved up and down as he looked at it with the triumphant smile of a swordsman who had just killed. It was the only way she could think of it: he'd conquered again, and must gaze at his weapon with a warrior's pride before he sheathed it. Yet what had he conquered? Not her: she knew that. Perhaps something in himself; perhaps some deep fear of inadequacy.

Toinette got up slowly, as if a little drunk. There were new bruises, or at least the pain of them: they always took an hour or two to blemish her fair skin, but they would be there for days. It was always at this moment that she looked at him and thought of killing him, not of course immediately, because she had no weapon, as he had; but later, perhaps in the middle of the night when he was sleeping, or when she was sitting opposite him at the dinner table, watching him sip the wine that she had doctored. But even if she were successful, she knew she would meet him again in another life, just as she had met him again in this one. She would never be free of Raoul.

'How is your sister?' He asked her later. It was still warm enough, even in early November, to take their aperitif on the balcony of their suite, overlooking the lake in the twilight.

'She's a little better,' Toinette told him briefly.

She knew what was coming. Since Edouard's funeral, she had asked Charlotte if she could stay here at the Chateau. She'd never been close to her sister, who was almost twelve years older than she: they'd been to their separate schools and colleges at different times, and had never had much in common; but Toinette felt enough for Charlotte at least to want to comfort her a little if she could, especially now that she was ill. Raoul had agreed at once to stay on alone in their apartment in Geneva, near his office, and fly to the Riviera every week-end to be with her. But it was not for his love for Charlotte.

'What does Dr Chirac say about her this week?' he asked Toinette.

'I don't know. I haven't spoken to him recently.' What Raoul really meant was: *How long is she expected to live?*

'But he's still attending her?'

'Yes.' She sipped her dry Tio Pepe, still feeling the soreness of the ravishing she'd just suffered, and wondering if anything showed on her face or her arms; it was always her worry, at this time, that something would give her away – she even had a packet of disposable plastic bags in a cupboard in her bathroom, to hide her torn clothes in until she could take them down to the dustbin in secret; the maids were always inspecting anything she threw out, hoping to salvage something useful.

'Do you think Charlotte would like to see me for a few minutes?' Raoul was asking her.

In a moment his wife said, 'I don't know.'

The situation was hateful to her. Despite all she did to hide the secret of her married life with Raoul there were some who knew it, and Charlotte was one of them. Toinette and her husband had stayed here many times since their marriage five years before, and Charlotte was a discerning hostess. Although she never liked intruding into the affairs of others, she had nevertheless dropped a hint now and then that her sister might be happier if she left Raoul for a gentler mate. Toinette suspected that Charlotte saw Raoul Cavaille as nothing more than a monster in the sheep's clothing of a smooth, cultivated international financier.

'I'll risk knocking on her door,' Raoul told her. 'She can only tell me to go away.'

He said it lightly; his mood after their violent bouts of sex was always cheerful, as if he'd been liberated from some kind of demon.

'You could take her some roses,' his wife said reluctantly, 'from the garden.' She couldn't stop his going to see Charlotte if he wanted to.

Raoul shifted his chair a little so as to face her directly. 'Have you made any progress with her yourself, Toinette?'

'I can't really tell. She doesn't say much to me.' He'd brought the matter into the open now, as she'd known he would. 'In any case, what can I possibly do to influence her? Jacques is the only possible inheritor.'

'Surely you don't still believe that, Toinette!' He was impatient now. 'The last thing your sister will do is leave property worth five billion francs to an irresponsible playboy!'

In a moment Toinette said quietly, 'Is that what it's worth?'

Raoul looked away quickly. 'That would be an approximate estimate, yes.'

But it was not too approximate, as Toinette knew intuitively. Since Edouard's death Raoul had made his own energetic but discreet enquiries into the worth of the de Montigny-Villiers fortune. When Charlotte had become ill, nothing had changed; Edouard, always in good health, had been expected to live for another twenty or even thirty years, during which time his estates would have been safe in his own hands. After his totally unexpected death, nothing would have changed either, had Charlotte's health been strong; she would have managed the estates, together with her advisers, wisely and well. But now there remained only two people with a legitimate claim to these vast properties once Charlotte was gone; they were Jacques de Montigny-Villiers, the heir apparent, and Charlotte's sister Toinette, who was also of the blood.

But there were two problems. Charlotte would never leave the estates in the hands of a playboy, as Raoul rightly said. Charlotte's love for Edouard was stronger than ever, reaching beyond this life, and she was determined to see the property pass into good hands, or at least not fall into bad. The line went back more than four hundred years, and today there were countless employees of this family spread throughout France who had regarded Prince Edouard as their patriarch. Their employment must remain secure, and their trust in the family name must be returned. The estates must not be broken up and put on the market to be fought over by the dogs of commerce – and that was what would happen to them if poor Jacques were granted his inheritance. He neither wanted such an appalling burden nor was fit to shoulder it.

The second problem facing Charlotte was that she couldn't pass the estates to her sister – at least not while she was married to Raoul. Toinette herself was indifferent to the idea of inheriting such a vast fortune. She had no quarrel with her sister; she could feel only compassion for her at this moment. She had loved and admired Edouard, as most people did, and would be willing for the sake of his memory to take over the estates and see that they prospered. But if Charlotte were to put a condition on Toinette's inheriting – that she first divorced Raoul? She would need to think about that. There were times when she almost made up her mind to see a lawyer and get it over with: in France it was difficult for a woman to claim her rights; but a doctor's testimony to her husband's evident sadism would carry weight. But there were times when she wondered what life would be like without Raoul. Outside the bedchamber he was civilised, charming, attentive and generous, and she knew she was envied by many women in their circle; his smouldering carnality attracted them, and it could even be possible that they would enjoy his brand of sex, as perhaps she did herself, at some level of her own carnal needs.

But there was no point in thinking about it now. If Charlotte chose to offer her the inheritance, on that one condition, she would have time enough to consider.

'A little more sherry?' Raoul asked her.

'What? No. No thank you.' The twilight had deepened to dark in the last few minutes; the day died quickly in this latitude. She looked at Raoul in the faint light coming from the room behind them; his face was in shadow, the face of an enigmatic satyr, his eyes two points of light as he watched her in turn, half-smiling, conspiratorial, sharing with her the secret of their most intimate privacy as its force went on flowing between them, between his now flaccid weapon and her plundered loins. She knew it would always be like this, that she would never leave this man, this demon, this Raoul.

'We must go down to dinner,' she said, looking away at last. He drew her chair back for her. 'I think there's no question, Raoul, about what Charlotte will do. I can't ever inherit the estate. So she'll have to leave it to Jacques.'

He took her glass and put it onto the little ironwork table. 'Unless something happens to him,' he said.

She turned her head quickly to look at him. 'Why should it?'

Raoul gave a shrug. 'He rides the horses like a madman, he drives suicidally fast, and if he's not racing his sports plane he's racing his speedboat. I wouldn't care to guess how long that young man is going to live.'

9

RUNNING SCARED

'*C'est pour quelle destination, Mademoiselle?*'

The taxi-driver stowed Linda's two bags into the trunk and slammed the lid down.

'Do you speak any English?' she asked him.

'A little.'

'I want to go to the airport.'

'OK. We go.' He closed the door for her and got behind the wheel. As the taxi drew away from the Chateau de Beausoleil, Linda felt the urge to look back at the ancient stones and the huge arched entrance with its massive doors; but she managed not to. She didn't want to see the place again.

Halfway along the driveway that wound between the pine trees a low black sports car overtook them and slowed, blocking their way. As the taxi-driver pulled up, a man got out of the car and came back to talk to them, looking in at Linda through the open window.

'You are leaving?'

It was the lean, brooding son of the house, the last person Linda wanted to talk to.

'Yes.'

He gazed in at her, hesitating before he spoke again. 'Are you going to the airport?'

'Yes.'

'Allow me to take you there.' He was unsmiling.

'Thanks, but I – '

She broke off as he spoke some rapid French to the driver, who got out and went to the trunk of his taxi. The young man opened Linda's door for her and held out his hand. 'I am Jacques de Montigny-Villiers.' Linda didn't know whether to tell him to leave her alone or shake hands with him. She was impatient to leave, but her manners prevailed. She climbed out and shook hands.

69

'I know. We met. Linda Terman. Look, I – '

'It will be quicker for you,' he said, 'in my car.' She watched the taxi driver taking her two cases from the trunk and stowing them in the sports car. Jacques de Montigny-Villiers went over to him and gave him some bills.

'*Merci.*'

'*A votre service, M'sieur le Prince.*'

Jacques held open the door of his car for Linda, still unsmiling. She hesitated for the last time, furious with him, or more accurately with herself for letting him override her this way; but the taxi was driving past them now and there wasn't anything she could do about it. 'Thank you.' She dropped into the black leather seat.

Jacques said nothing until they were driving off. '*La Princesse –* ' then he corrected it – 'My mother will be desolated, you know.'

'Why?'

'Because of your leaving her.'

'I'm sorry about that.'

It sounded like a glib answer, but Linda meant it. Since she'd packed her things last night she'd done an awful lot of heart-searching, and had even changed her mind once or twice before she'd finally decided to leave. At first it had seemed impossible: she couldn't go without first explaining her reasons to her patient, and Princess Charlotte would probably try to make her change her mind – she'd been sent for all the way from New Jersey and up to now the Princess had seemed satisfied with her services. It would also be necessary to have a new nurse sent in, and to hand over to her formally – reporting on the condition of the patient and the medication history and everything.

Linda had finally decided that to talk to Princess Charlotte about it would only tire her and possibly bring on pain, so she had called Dr Chirac first thing and told him she was leaving and that a replacement nurse was needed immediately. He'd started asking questions but she'd cut him short, simply saying she had to get back to the States. (She'd wondered, as she'd talked to him, whether this situation hadn't happened before. *Had the previous nurse quit without warning like this – and for the same reasons?* She certainly hadn't stayed to hand over.)

Linda had left her report fully documented and updated in its folder, and written a short note to the Princess, apologising for leaving without notice but saying that it was necessary for personal reasons.

But now, as she sat beside Prince Jacques de Montigny-Villiers in the sumptuous sports car, she felt as if she'd just come out of a strange dream – or was going into one. *What she'd done, in quitting the job like this, was way outside of all professional practice.*

The previous nurse had left without handing over, sure, but that was nothing to do with it. For Linda Terman, out of St Francis' Hospital, New Jersey, it was inadmissible.

So what had got into her?

'What flight are you taking, Mademoiselle?'

Jacque's voice, with its low resonant timbre, almost startled her.

'I don't know.' They were climbing the hairpin bends to the high corniche, the way Henri the chauffeur had brought her from the airport only a few days before. 'I – er – I guess I'll have to go through Paris.' She was aware of his lean brown hands playing on the thin steering-wheel, aware of his quiet attentiveness.

'You haven't made a reservation?' He turned to glance at her, and she met his eyes. There was no smile in them, only a kind of brooding preoccupation.

'No. There wasn't – ' she left it unspoken.

He waited, watching her, then moved his gaze back to the road, using the short, stainless-steel gearshift with a rhythm that was hypnotic as the powerful car surged through the bends. On the dashboard she noticed the small gold plaque of a rearing horse, and the name Ferrari. Jacques said nothing until they were through the village of La Turbie, with the morning sunlight slanting through the parasol pines.

'I think it was my fault.' He said it casually, as if they were already in the middle of a conversation.

'Your fault?'

'Your impetuous decision to leave my mother.'

Linda thought about this for a moment. 'Yes. Partly. But you wouldn't be able to understand the whole picture.'

He gave a slight shrug. 'I can understand, perhaps, that on the two occasions when we crossed each other's path, I may have seemed discourteous.'

'Right.' She wouldn't have said that, in the ordinary way; she would have made some kind of polite excuse for him. But she needed to vent some of this strange tension in her – the self-anger that she'd quit the job on the spur of the moment, and the uneasiness of not really knowing why.

Though she was beginning to suspect.

'I can only apologise, Mademoiselle.'

She was surprised. This masterful, domineering son of the house, apologise?

'Oh. It's OK. Don't think another thing about it.' That sounded ungracious, a brush-off. Well, it would have to do. In another hour she'd be saying goodbye to this man and to everyone else in the Chateau de Beausoleil, and she'd never have to see them again.

And this was it. This was what she'd begun to suspect.

They scared her.

She felt surprise again as he slowed and pulled the sleek car off the road between the trees, switching off the motor and turning to look at her. 'Since you've no reservation, Mademoiselle, perhaps you'd let me have the pleasure of a few words with you.'

'I – I guess we don't have anything to say.' Looking into his sombre, fathomless eyes, she realised he was no different from the others. *He scared her too.*

People are the same kind of people, Mrs Weston had told her on that cold rainy day in the hospital, *it doesn't matter how rich they are.*

Wrong, Mrs Weston. Just like Scott Fitzgerald said, the rich *are* different.

'You're feeling a certain degree of culture-shock, Mademoiselle. That at least I can understand. I've been to America, and we have many American friends staying at the Chateau and along the Riviera, most of the time.' He looked away briefly, frowning. 'Not recently, of course. Not since the death of my father. The *ambience* – the atmosphere at the Chateau was very different, before then.' He was watching her again, his eyes intense and yet still private, still preoccupied. 'You came at a bad time, you see. First, my mother's illness, then the shock of my father's death. I can quite understand your . . . reluctance to stay with us. We're not very cheerful to be with just now.'

'Do you think I – ' and she broke off right there. She'd been stung by what he'd said. When she felt calmer she tried again. 'I've been nursing for ten years, mainly in hospitals, some of the time with terminal patients. Do you think I demand a cheerful atmosphere to work in? A nurse makes her own atmosphere, and gives it to her patients as best she can.'

'I'm sorry. I don't seem able to say the right thing, Mademoiselle.'

There was a new note in his voice; it was something like entreaty, a plea for understanding. Linda caught it, and slowed up in her mind. What he'd said was true – she'd come at a bad time, and it was more than enough to excuse Madame Leclerc's hostility and this man's boorishness. But it wasn't the overtone of grief that had worried her: God knew she'd experienced that from day to day, talking with the bereaved and trying to comfort them. And it wasn't, really, the shock of seeing the poor little "Monsieur le Baron" that night, or the strangeness in the child-countess, Bibi, with her sly, watchful interest in everyone else's privacy. It was the feeling of those dark undercurrents that were trying to pull her down into deep and unknown waters – the kind of feeling Linda had never in her life experienced before in her open, extrovert, all-American existence.

Culture-shock. OK. But there were still those unanswered questions in her mind. She'd got the job out of hundreds of applicants, sure, but maybe life was like that sometimes. But why had the position been advertised in an *American* hospital anyway? Wasn't there just *one* competent private nurse on the whole of the French Riviera? Or in Paris, Rome or London?

Put it this way, then. For some reason – *but for a definite reason just the same* – she'd been brought to the Chateau de Beausoleil to nurse Princess Charlotte. Personally. Linda Terman, personally. And nobody was going to tell her why, and maybe she'd rather not know. She didn't want any part of these rich, titled denizens of an ancient land, or of the shadowed, brooding mysteries that haunted them.

She wanted out, before it was too late.

But she owed this man at least an explanation. Not the real one, but not a fairy-tale either.

'When I said you wouldn't understand, *M'sieur le Prince*, I just meant you've no experience, obviously, of nursing.' ("When you meet him," the little Countess Bibi had told her during their lesson, "you should call him *M'sieur le Prince*.") 'It's just that in a big hospital, a nurse has a certain amount of authority. Her first concern is the patient, and she has the right to take *any* reasonable measure to protect that patient's welfare. Even the closest relative isn't allowed beyond the nurses' station – that's the kind of frontier-post outside the wards. And even if they get past that, they won't be allowed inside a ward or a private room without permission.'

Aware of his dark and attentive eyes on her, she felt she was giving him a dumb lecture that he didn't want to listen to, but now she'd started she might as well finish. 'Your mother had been through a tough time yesterday, and last evening when you came to see her she'd just fallen into a good, sound sleep, without any help from drugs. So I wasn't going to let anyone past that door if I could help it, and when you showed up and just pushed me aside, that was it. I quit.'

He looked down and said in a moment, 'I didn't realise the situation, of course.'

'I know you didn't – and it wasn't only what you did. I don't get on too well with Dr Chirac: I'm used to a lot more cooperation from my doctors, a lot more respect as a registered nurse. And the housekeeper was constantly giving me grief. You were the last straw, that was all. Do you think we could move on now? I'd like to catch a plane.'

He hesitated, tapping his long fingers on the wheel-rim, gazing through the windshield into the distance. Then he started the motor.

'Of course.'

Linda sank back into her seat with her arms folded across her new Saks suedette jacket and her head against the headrest. The jacket had cost her a fortune in Trenton and she'd bought it as a gesture to celebrate her new ritzy job and show it off on the Riviera; but now she was just sitting huddled in it wishing she'd stayed right where she was in the cold grey New Jersey rain where everything was normal and the supermarkets closed right on time, a minute before you got there.

The Prince hadn't said anything more. OK, she'd bawled him out for trying to see his own mother, so what did she expect from him now, a flow of friendly conversation?

'I really appreciate your going out of your way for me like this.'

He turned his head. '*Pardon?*' He'd been deep in thought.

'I appreciate the ride.'

'Oh. It's my pleasure. I was hoping, perhaps, that I could – ' He left it as an opening.

She closed it. 'Gosh, this is such a beautiful place, isn't it?' They were dropping from the high corniche towards the sea, with a sign saying *Ville de Nice*.

'You haven't been to the Côte d'Azur before?'

'No.' And I'm not coming again, she thought bitterly. 'Do you think there'll be a plane to Paris some time this morning?'

'Yes. We have a private executive jet at the airport. You can take that.'

She stared at him. 'A private – look, I'll just get a regular flight. But thanks.'

'As you please, Mademoiselle.'

There she went again, being ungracious. But there was no way she deserved a private plane trip to Paris considering she was running out on them like this. She sat with her arms folded again as they drove along the palm-shaded Promenade des Anglais, with the morning sunshine flooding now across the façades of the big hotels and glittering on the sea. It didn't look like any November day she'd seen before, except maybe for Florida when she'd been there as a kid. But there was still a big difference, though she wasn't sure quite what it was – maybe just because she knew this was the French Riviera, or that she was sitting right next to a prince who'd just offered her a flight to Paris in his executive jet. Or maybe it was the rich scent of coffee coming through the open window on the driver's side from the blue-canopied cafés along the sidewalks here, and the elegant clothes of the women. She realised she'd only been here a few days, but already knew she'd miss it.

Prince Jacques slowed the Ferrari into the airport, taking a side road past the terminal and pulling up. 'Will there be anyone to meet you at Orly?'

'At where?'

'In Paris, when you land.'

'Oh. No.'

'Then I hope you'll let one of our public-relations people meet you there and arrange your transfer flight to the United States.'

'I'm quite capable of – ' she stopped right there. It was a question of personal realities. She was jumping on him because he didn't think she was capable of changing planes in a foreign city, but it probably wasn't like that at all: he was simply trying to make up for having given her a bad time at the Chateau. 'It's very kind of you, *M'sieur le Prince*. But I'll be OK.'

His deep-set eyes remained on hers for a moment, but she still couldn't read his thoughts. They weren't hostile, though, and she didn't feel scared anymore. She was aware without exactly thinking about it that it would be pleasant just to sit here for a minute and let this brooding, handsome Frenchman go on watching her, without speaking. It was as if they'd somehow made contact at last.

'Then I'll wish you a safe journey,' he said briefly, and switched off the motor and got out of the car, going around to open her door. A policeman in a white peaked cap was coming across the sidewalk, checking the licence-plate; then he gave a smart salute.

'*Bonjour, M'sieur le Prince!*'

'*Bonjour, M'sieur l'agent.*' He opened the trunk of the car.

'*Vous voulez un porteur, M'sieur?*'

'*Non, merci.*' He swung Linda's two cases out and shut the lid of the trunk.

'I'll go find a porter,' she said.

'It's not necessary. I'll see you to the check-in.' He picked up the bags again, waiting for her. The policeman had gone back to the side door of the terminal, swinging his truncheon idly, so that there were just Linda and the Prince standing there on the sidewalk, with the breeze bringing the sea-smell from the Mediterranean and the shadows of the tall palm trees moving gently against the wall of the building. It was the kind of moment when time seemed to have stopped, as if the world were changing pace. Then it moved on again, as Linda took a hesitant step towards the Prince.

'I was running scared,' she said quietly.

He stood there looking puzzled, the two heavy bags in his hands. '*Pardon?*'

'I – ' and she stopped. With his eyes on her, watching her so attentively, she found it difficult to think of the words she wanted. She looked down for a moment. 'It's – it's just the title of a book. *Running Scared.*' He didn't say anything. She met his eyes again. 'I guess you had a better way of putting it. You said it was culture shock.'

He put his dark head on one side. 'I'm not sure I understand, Mademoiselle.'

'I think you do.' Their gaze held steady.

'You wish to stay?'

She took a breath. 'Yes. I guess your apology has changed things a little. Maybe we understand each other now.'

He lowered the bags to the pavement, and took the final step towards her that would bring them close. His presence was almost tangible; she felt she was standing in an aura that was emanating from his body.

'It's not a decision you can make lightly,' he said.

She shivered suddenly. 'No. But I'm making it.'

He lifted her hand and touched his lips to it. 'I shall make sure that when you are back there, you'll no longer be alone. Or running scared.'

10

THE INVITATION

IN THE YEAR nineteen hundred and seventy-nine, the *Société des Bains de Mer* decided to honour the increasing influx of American tourists to Monte-Carlo Casino by completely redecorating its second oldest gaming room. Originally designed by Dutrou in eighteen hundred and seventy-two, it was handed over to André Levasseur to redecorate, and there was only one possible theme he could use: the opulent, elegant extravagance of *le style Gone With The Wind*, straight out of the Deep South. With its vast and lofty domed glass ceiling, its crimson carpeting and curtains, its gold leaf and velvet and chandeliers, it lacked only a staircase with Clark Gable coming down it. (A member of the *Société* actually suggested taking a leaf out of Disneyland and creating a mock staircase with, in fact, a waxwork figure of Rhett Butler gracing it. He was put summarily in his place by the coordinator, who said that it would be going too far, even for the Americans.)

On this evening in early November the *chef des croupiers* at No.1 roulette table was amusing himself by watching the spectators as well as the players, his eyes under their deceptively sleepy-looking lids moving from the chips and the croupiers' rakes to the throng of visitors who were here to watch, dabbling their feet in the shallows, so to speak, before taking the plunge at the wheel. Some of them, as always, were not here to watch the table or the wheel at all, but the players. The chief croupier, whose name was Michel, had noticed the young and exceedingly attractive American girl who had come into the *Salon des Amériques* perhaps a half hour ago. She'd spent only a few minutes looking around the tables and watching the play, and since then had been taking a keen interest in the players, especially the men. By now Michel had placed her with absolute certitude as a *belle de nuit* – yet he was puzzled. What was a *belle de nuit*, even one as arrestingly good-looking as this girl, doing in a dress he estimated to be worth thirty thousand French francs?

'*Mesdames, Messieurs, faites vos jeux!*'

The chief croupier moved his sleepy-looking eyes to the table again, watching the chips as they were thrown onto the soft green baize but still thinking about the American girl. What worried him, as an experienced observer of his fellow human beings, was that he was *certain* she was a prostitute, yet *equally* certain that such a person would never be wearing such an expensive dress. There was something very odd – and to a man like Michel – very intriguing about this.

'*Faites vos jeux, s'il vous plaît!*'

As the little ivory ball was thrown into the wheel, Suzie Spinoza watched it spinning and bouncing for a moment and then glanced up at the chief croupier. He was watching her again, and she moved away from the table, feeling her colour rising. It wasn't embarrassment: Suzie had left her ability to feel embarrassed somewhere along the road behind her, like an abandoned bra. The fact was that she was getting desperate. Her dream of moving in to this rich man's playground and setting up house with a millionaire had been fading, and fast. She'd been confident of finding some well-heeled guy the very day she arrived, and staying with him a week or two while she got her bearings; but they were street-wise in this place – they either cottoned on to her right away or they thought she was good for a one night stand with nothing but a friendly pat on the ass in the morning. After three days here she'd been asked to dinner a couple of times and gone to an apartment for the main course, but that had been it. Nice knowing you, girlie. And if she was going to do that again tonight, and tomorrow night, she'd be turning into a goddamned hooker, unpaid. And there'd only be one thing worse than that – a goddamned hooker, paid. She wasn't here to wear out her little pussy till the cops wheeled her into the hoosegow and booked her for deportation.

She was now down to her last fifty bucks and even the smallest hotels she'd checked out were way over any kind of budget she could try and balance on that kind of money and she had nowhere to cook any food even if she economised by buying it at the open-air market. She'd come here to turn herself into a real rich lady and she was already on the skids, and if the only thing for it was to jump on a ship back home she'd have to get deported anyway because she didn't have the fare.

All this didn't add up to anything she could throw a party about but the worst thing of all was that she was being made to take a good look at herself for the first time in her life, and what she saw wasn't pretty. Little Suzie Spinoza, out of Memphis, Tennessee, had thought she was too good for those truckers and travelling salesmen who'd helped to build up her savings account till she could buy herself a ticket to the promised land; but here she was in the promised land and she knew already she was way out of her class, and there was only one place where this little ten-cent hustler belonged and that was back in Memphis, Tennessee, and when she thought of the freezing rain and the sleazy truck-stops stinking of stale frying-fat and the unwashed truckers with their beer-bellies and their hairy chests and their bad breath and their lousy greasy greenbacks on the bed when they walked out hitching their pants up and leaving her like a bit of garbage they'd thrown out, she could have cried. She could have broken down and cried.

But not right now. Not right here in this ritzy place where even in this dress she felt out of her class by a zillion miles. She'd have to go cry her heart out in some back alley where she belonged. OK, lay it on thick, Suzie, but that's really what the score is. You thought a kid from the sticks could hit the big-time just by getting laid by the right people, but the right people know just who you are, so you'd better get out of here or they'll go on watching you like that goddamned croupier over there.

This was where the night would have to end. Yesterday Daphne Houghton-Downe had told her they'd meet up again in the American Room at the Casino and take it from there; but in her present mood Suzie felt that the last person on earth she wanted to be with was Daphne – who'd been so good to her that it had started to hurt her pride. Daphne had said eight o'clock, which it was now, or almost, and there was just time to get out of here and disappear and find someplace to go hide in and think what to do next.

A guy in a tuxedo made a pass at her with his eyes as she hurried through the doors but she didn't stop, even though it could have meant she'd at least eat tonight and maybe have somewhere to sleep. It was beginning to leave a taste in her mouth, the taste of something rotten, and if it meant that she'd at last dredged up a sense of self-respect it'd be the only thing worth while that had happened to her in the last twenty-three years, and as this thought struck her she walked even faster because if Daphne came in now she'd have to find some excuse to –

'*Dar*ling . . .'

The smoke-blue eyes were suddenly staring into hers as Suzie stopped dead and tried to fix up a quick smile. It didn't work.

'What's happened?' Daphne asked, with her eyes anxious. 'You look as if – ' she left it.

'What do I look as if?' Suzie wanted to know what was showing; she wanted to know if everyone else could see it in her eyes that she thought she was a cheap, washed-up hustler.

Daphne didn't answer the question. She just took Suzie's ice-cold hand and said, 'We'll go and find a drink, darling.' She hooked a bare, slender arm through Suzie's and led her across to the bar. 'You've had a rotten day, I can see, trying to find a decent hotel or something, but if it makes you feel any better, Suzie, you look absolutely stunning in that dress. I'm *so* glad I didn't throw it away!'

Perched on the bar stool next to her Suzie said: 'But you weren't going to. Were you?'

The misty eyes were on hers for an instant, then looked away. 'Of course I was. Now let's have a simply marvellous evening and then we'll go and pick at some caviar across at the Bec Rouge.' She said it lightly, still clinging to Suzie's arm, but Suzie heard a note of pleading in Daphne's voice, as she'd heard before as they'd sat together in the crimson Jaguar with Daphne's small fragile hand on hers. *If I thought I couldn't see you again, I think I'd die.* Suzie was beginning to know this strange little English girl: behind all the affected talk and the bright smile there was some kind of desperation going on. But she didn't have any idea if she – Suzie – was involved, or if so, how. After just one Tio Pepe – she had a light head for alcohol – she put the question, as soon as there was a chance. Daphne was talking about the hotels in "Monty".

'Lots of them are quite comfy, but terribly expensive, and those that aren't are too absolutely dreadful. Cockroaches and things that go squelch in the night.' She gave a theatrical shudder. 'I think you should come up to Beausoleil and stay with me at the Chateau.'

'That's a kind of castle, right?'

'Yes. Turrets and bats and everything, quite lovely.'

'I don't think places like that are for me.'

'But of course they are. Nothing but the best for my Suzie.' And here was the chance Suzie had been waiting for.

'OK, there's something I need to ask you, Daphne. What exactly do you see in me?'

The smoky eyes rested on hers for an instant and then dipped away. 'Oh dear, we *are* serious tonight, aren't we? Let's just enjoy – '

'I need to know. Really.'

In a moment the small fragile hand came to rest lightly on hers, and Daphne was watching her now without glancing away. 'It's not sex, darling, if that's what you think. You're lovely and cuddly in bed, but not in that kind of way, although of course you must be enough to drive men crazy.' She paused for a moment. 'It's something to do with my childhood, you see. You've brought one or two things back to me. Please don't take them away again.'

As Daphne's eyes remained on hers, Suzie was aware that at this moment the English girl was being more serious and more truthful than at any time since they'd met. What she'd just said didn't explain everything – it didn't explain why Daphne was so desperate for her company, when she must have hundreds of friends already, or why she was so generous all the time; but Suzie sensed that if she probed any deeper she'd lose out and be left with nothing but that bright smile for the rest of the night. And the thought came to her suddenly: maybe she was wrong about Daphne's having hundreds of friends already. Suzie hadn't ever seen her with anyone else, except Lord Billy on the *QM2*, and Daphne had called him a bore.

Did she have any friends at all?

Life could be surprising, as Suzie knew. Daphne was so rich that it hurt and she was pretty as a Barbie doll, but how many people wanted to be near someone with this kind of desperation smouldering inside of her, underneath the bright show-biz façade? Suzie herself was uneasy sometimes in her presence; it felt like being close to a ticking bomb. But it occurred to her that if she stayed around, it might help this strange, haunted creature from blowing herself to bits.

'OK,' she told Daphne, 'I won't take anything away from you. God knows you've given me so much. The only thing you could do to make me run like hell would be to look at me as an object of charity. So tonight, and for your sake, you're getting your two dresses back.'

There were tears suddenly in Daphne's eyes, and her voice was a tense whisper. 'For Christ's sake try to understand, Suzie. I could never give you a millionth of what you're giving me, just by – ' she shrugged her soft bare shoulders and for the second time touched Suzie's heart – 'just by suffering my company. So let's not talk about a couple of bloody dresses.'

In a moment Suzie squeezed her hand. 'OK, it's a deal.'

'And we can stop being serious?'

'Sure. If you want to kick the shit out of the rest of the evening then let's just go do that.'

'Oh, what a *splendid* way of putting it!'

Ten minutes later as they crossed the *Salon des Amériques* to the door at the end, the chief croupier at Table No.1 glanced across with his sleepy eyes and thought *merde, alors!* Not only was the little American prostitute wearing a dress she couldn't possibly afford, but she was now going into one of the *salon privés* arm in arm with the English heiress, Lady Daphne Houghton-Downe. It was beyond any puzzling out, and as a student of human nature Michel gave himself a well-rounded zero.

'No, darling, this is a private salon, mainly for Arabs, as you can see. They like high stakes.'

'You can say that again.' On the polished mahogany board above the roulette table the sign read in gold letters: *10,000 F Minimum*. 'You know that's around fifteen hundred dollars a shot?'

'If that's what it works out at, yes. Give me a number, Suzie.'

'A number?'

'Any number.'

'Uh – fifteen.'

Daphne dropped five gold-embossed counters onto Number 15. 'They're yours, darling.'

'Mine?'

'I bought some for you.'

Suzie opened her eyes wide. 'Oh Jesus, you shouldn't have – ' But the croupier was spinning the wheel already and dropping the little ball along the rim and Suzie could only stand there with her eyes half-crossing in concentration and her mind lurching under the rapid-fire impact of desperate ideas because those were

100,000-franc chips and there were five of them stacked up there on the green baize and that was around $7,500 and the chances of that ball hitting the right spot were exactly thirty-six to one against . . . So what if she just grabbed the croupier's arm *right now* and told him the whole thing was a silly mistake and could he throw the ball in again while she got those chips off the table? Or what if she went for the chips *first* and shoved them into red or black or odd or even to give them at least a fifty-fifty chance? Or maybe just faint or make like she was throwing up to create confusion so they'd declare a replay of the action and Daphne could get her chips back? *Daphne* get her chips back? But they weren't Daphne's anyway – *they were hers.*

'Isn't it fun, darling?'

'*Oh-my-God.*'

Suzie watched the little ball and started willing it to go right into that No.15 slot and stay right there till the wheel stopped, but it was bouncing around so much as it hit the bumps and she couldn't even see where No.15 was because the numbers weren't in any kind of sequence and it could be anywhere and by the time she found it she wished she hadn't because the ball wasn't even close as it bounced its way across the slots. The wheel was going real slow now and suddenly Suzie felt sick to her stomach and she might not even have to *make* like she was throwing up – she could do it for real because she just didn't give a damn how much this little English nut-case could afford to lose: seven thousand five hundred bucks was seven thousand five hundred bucks in anybody's language and there it was lying on the table ready to go right up in smoke. Another thought of a very different kind was flashing into her mind – *what if their number came up?* Seven thousand five hundred times thirty-six was . . . seven thirties were two hundred and ten and seven sixes – make it an even figure and forget the five hundred, OK – that was . . . oh, Jesus, that was *two hundred and fifty-two thousand dollars!* A quarter of a million! *More than that*, because of the odd five hundred. So if the ball went into the right slot she'd give Daphne back her chips and keep the rest, close to a quarter of a –

The ball hit No.15.

And bounced out again.

The wheel didn't seem to want to stop, and the ball hit –

Twenty-one.

And bounced out again.

But No.15 was coming around again and the ball –
Hit it and bounced on *and dropped into No.3 right alongside.*
And stayed there.
Right alongside 15.
'*Numéro trois, Mesdames, Messieurs.*'
Suzie felt herself swaying on her feet and the next thing she knew was hearing Daphne asking if she was all right.
'Uh?'
'Are you going to be sick, darling?'
'Yes. No. Could be.'
'Let's go over – '
'What? No. I'm OK now.' She got a hold of Daphne's arm and said in a fierce whisper, '*Don't ever do that to me again.*'
Daphne gave a quick trilling laugh. 'It's only money, darling. I've got lots more.'
'OK, I believe you. But you're lucky, that's all. There are people who – '
'Now you're being serious again. You see, money's got to circulate. That's what it's for. I've probably just paid that croupier's wages for about six months, and he's going to spend them on all kinds of things. It's people *hoarding* who cause all the trouble.' She studied Suzie anxiously for a moment, but the colour had come back to her face now. 'We'll just watch for a bit, and then go on to the *Bec Rouge.*'
Suzie spent the next ten minutes looking around her at the players, because if she watched that goddamned little white ball again she'd finish up wrung out. Most of them here were men, and about half of them dusky ones, with a few even wearing the kind of Lawrence of Arabia headgear she'd seen on the soaps back home. Some of them were standing back from the tables with their hands tucked behind them and their heads turning slowly from side to side, watching everyone in the room, and suddenly Suzie realized who they were, because the guy named Johnson – who'd met them when they'd got off the ship at Cannes – was among them. They were bodyguards – a dozen of them. Well, she guessed that kind of figured, with people playing around with two hundred and fifty grand a shot.
'Have you had enough, darling?'
Suzie turned. 'I don't want to spoil your fun.'
'Don't worry, I'm not playing. I never do, actually; I just thought it might amuse you.'

Suzie watched her for a moment as a thought tripped her mind. *Was this girl playing games with her?* She guessed that by this time Daphne knew the score: that Suzie was flat broke and if she picked up a ten-dollar bill on the sidewalk it would feed her for two days. That's why Daphne had given her those dresses, so she could take her around the night spots without being ashamed of her, and that was why she'd just invited her to stay at the Chateau up on the hill, so she wouldn't have to hustle herself into some stranger's bed every night just to get herself some sleep. So Daphne knew what it had meant to her to see seven and a half grand melt away on that table like a pat of butter on a red hot stove – and what it would have meant to her if their number had come up and she'd walked away with a quarter of a million bucks. So did she really think that might "amuse" her? Or was she just enjoying herself, watching this cute American kid from the wrong side of the tracks and the wrong side of the ocean spend her time squirming?

'What's wrong, darling?' The flecked and shadowed eyes in the blue haze of their makeup watched her steadily, the bright smile dying.

'Nothing, I guess. Sure – it amused the hell out of me.'

The English girl went on watching her, uncertain. 'Did you think I was – ?' but she left it.

Suzie waited, then asked: 'Did I think – ?'

Daphne moved right up close to her, and everything else faded out a little: the glitter of the chandeliers and the dark silk walls with their gilded panels and the white cuffs of the men in their elegant tuxedos, the sound of the ball in the wheel and the counters going down, the rich smell of cigar smoke above the hint of perfume, and all Suzie could see were the English girl's eyes and the torment in them.

'No,' she whispered on scented breath, 'it wasn't amusing for you, was it? I – I just wasn't thinking. Terribly poor taste, I'm afraid. Suzie, don't ever think I'd do anything to hurt you, because if I did, you wouldn't love me any more, and that would – ' she shrugged her pale bare shoulders. 'You're my lifeline, you see, and I don't want to break it.'

Somewhere in the background a man's voice sounded calling a number, first in French and then in English. A woman's low laugh came, and there was the clinking of the ivory chips.

'OK,' Suzie said at last. 'I guess you're just hard to understand.'

'I know. It's hard for me too.' The bright smile flashed, and Suzie was suddenly dazzled. 'Are you hungry, darling?'

'I guess.'

'Come along, then.'

Some of the men in their dark suits moved aside for them, their eyes appreciative, their smiles tentative. One of them, standing alone near the doors, didn't move, but offered a slight bow, presenting a card to Daphne.

'Excuse me, please.' His voice was soft, modulated. He was a small man, and his skin had a strangely attractive bluish tinge; his midnight-blue eyes were so dark that in this subdued light they were almost black. 'Allow me to present the compliments of Sheik Ahmed of Abu Talha. His Majesty would be delighted if you would grace a small dinner-party at his residence in Monte-Carlo.' His hooded eyes passed a glance across Suzie. 'With your companion, of course.'

Daphne had noticed the sheik at the next roulette table: his eyes had been on her when she'd happened to glance up a minute ago. She'd met him a few times in London, but only around the clubs. She didn't much care for cous-cous and things like that – they were rather greasy; but it might be good for Suzie's education.

Suzie was standing dead still. "His Majesty" yet . . . She was getting an awful long way from Memphis, Tennessee. There was someone standing almost next to her, and from the corner of her eye she saw he was Johnson, the bodyguard. He'd come up very fast when the little guy had stopped them on their way to the doors.

'How nice,' Daphne was saying. 'When?'

'That would be for you to choose, Madame. The occasion would be in your honour, of course.'

Daphne turned to Suzie. 'Darling, are you doing anything on Tuesday?'

'I guess not.'

'There we are, then,' Daphne told the little man. 'If that's convenient, please tell His Majesty we'd be delighted to come. I'm at the Chateau de Beausoleil, if you'd like to phone me there about the time and so on.'

'It will be my pleasure, Madame.' He gave another slight bow and stepped back for them.

'Isn't it fun?' Daphne said to Suzie as they went through the hall outside. 'We've just been picked up!'

11

JE T'AIME

THE COUNTESS BIBI was playing some Bach at the piano, one of his English Suites, *Sarabande*, though she didn't take any notice of the bit about *Avec les agréments* because they were too tricky for her. Winter sunshine poured through the high window above her, bathing her fair hair in light and making a golden rope of her pigtail. Had she seen herself she'd have called it a photographer's cliché, but Linda thought she made a rather pretty scene as she came into the music room and closed the door quietly.

There was the smell of polish in here, because of all the wood – the parquet floor and the oak-pannelled walls and the piano itself. Linda just stood by the door with her hands clasped in front of her, listening and not wanting to interrupt Bibi's studies. In a minute the child suddenly stopped playing, looking down at the keyboard in perfect silence; then her head swung up and sideways and she was gazing directly at Linda with those clear blue-grey eyes. The silence went on, and Linda had the impression that this strange little French girl was communicating with her in her own almost telepathic way, checking her out, asking her questions, maybe the sort of questions she couldn't ask aloud.

Wrong.

'Well, what's it like?'

'What is what like?' Linda asked her.

'Falling in love.'

Linda felt the blood leaving her face as she stared at the girl on the piano-stool. In a moment she said quietly, 'What exactly are you talking about?'

'Falling in love.' Bibi got off the stool and limped across the parquet towards Linda, but stopped halfway. 'Phew! You look really upset.'

In a whisper that could have only just carried, Linda asked: 'Were you there?'

The beams of sunlight poured from the tall windows, making a halo around Bibi's fair head. She said, 'I wasn't anywhere.'

'I don't believe you.' Linda swung around and turned the heavy brass handle of the door.

'*Don't go!*'

The child was stumbling towards her with her face white and her hands flung out. '*Don't leave me!*' The next instant she was clinging on to Linda's white linen jacket, her eyes imploring. '*I haven't done anything . . .*'

Linda hesitated, then took the girl's hands, just as she always took people's hands in hers when they needed help, even now. 'OK. OK, Bibi. Calm down. I won't leave you.' She'd never recognized the need this child felt for her. 'We'll go and sit together over there.' She led her across to the brocade settee that backed on to one of the windows. 'Everything's OK now, Bibi.'

But she still didn't know if she believed her.

The whole episode – was that what you'd call it? – had burst into her life like an electric storm over the past three days, beginning when she and Jacques de Montigny-Villiers had driven back to the Chateau from Nice Airport, hardly speaking to each other but not feeling that their silences were awkward – she'd known it was the same for him. It was as if she'd suddenly switched lives from the one she was living to this one – this one that she was still experiencing, with its strange haunting quality, like a note of music lingering on, the music, maybe, of his voice when he'd said, *I'll make sure that when you are back there, you'll no longer be alone. Or running scared.*

He meant back at the Chateau, where for the past three days she hadn't been scared any more, of anyone or anything. Jacques had quietly taken her two bags from the trunk of his car and brought them into the hall, where two of the maids hurried up and took them to Linda's room.

'I'm so very glad,' he'd said simply, 'that you've decided to stay here with us, if only for my mother's sake.'

And that was all. Linda hadn't even seen him the next day, but the feeling had been there, the feeling of a new life, a new dimension to things. Crazy, of course. In New Jersey she would have shrugged the whole thing off, and gone home through the rain in the VW and picked up some more washing-powder at the supermarket and ended the day helping Cindy with the plumbing problem. But this wasn't New Jersey and it wasn't raining and the palm trees reached right along the coast by the side of the bluebell-coloured Mediterranean until the lights came on and the whole place started shimmering like a sequin dress and the moon came out of the dark velvet sea and hung there like a Chinese lantern, something out of a fantasy. OK, it was just the scenery, right? Wrong. There was the rest of it – the sound and the smell and the feel of this place, the cry of the peacocks and the scent of the pines and the rich textures of the brocades and the gilt carvings and the velours and the rosewoods wherever she went.

It made a difference. It was just the furnishing, but it made a difference; it had got inside her soul somewhere. Or he had. Jacques.

The second day, two days after they'd driven back from the airport (she'd begun counting the days, now, the hours,) she'd only seen him once, as they'd passed through the great hall by chance, going in opposite directions; and all he'd done was smile briefly as he'd passed on his way; and that night she felt a desperation she hadn't known since the time when her mother had died and she'd realized she could have been there with her all the time, helping her to go peacefully. It was the same feeling – of a loss, of desolation.

And that was crazy, too; it was a kind of fantasy that had grabbed hold of her for some reason, and she'd spent half the night trying to work out what was happening to her, ending up with the idea that this too was part of the culture shock – Jacques had terrific looks in the nicest kind of way, not macho but sensitive, brooding, almost mysterious; and he had the kind of voice that reminded you of all the sounds you'd ever loved, as if they were still trembling on the air; and he'd been kind, and even tender, and had kissed her hand; so he'd sort of turned into a symbol for something she could feel safe with, and warm about, someone she could go to, if she got scared again. So she'd gone to sleep at last, slumped in the big cane chair near Princess Charlotte's bed, because her patient had been in pain that night. Everything was explained, then – Prince Jacques de Montigny-Villiers was just part of the culture-shock. Right?

Wrong. Because in the morning she'd realised it was craziness again, this idea of seeing Jacques as someone she could go to if she got scared. *She was a state registered nurse, damn it*. Nothing had ever scared her before – not suicides, not amputations, not death itself. She could run a whole hospital floor on her own in an emergency and keep on running it till the emergency was over, OK? In fact she'd done that once, when those two trains had crashed head-on because of the frozen rails. She was a nurse, and she wasn't scared of *anything*. And then the whole thing had come up and hit her right between the eyes. She was a nurse, sure.

And also a woman.

In love.

That was on the third day. Yesterday. Coming down the grand staircase, she'd had to hold on to the marble banisters for a minute while the realisation swept through her and left her trembling. The problem was, she'd been so busy doing her Florence Nightingale thing all over the place and being reliable and capable and indispensable and God's gift to suffering humanity that she'd put everything else behind her. Like being a woman.

'*Vous êtes bien, Mademoiselle?*'

There was someone else on the staircase, looking up at her. Little Marianne, the upstairs maid. Linda didn't need to think out the English for what she was saying: the girl's eyes were anxious as she stared up at her.

'What? Yes. I'm fine. *Je suis bien*, yes. *Oui.*'

Although she wasn't at all *bien*, as a matter of fact. She went down past the little maid and out through the salon doors into the great glass conservatory and stood there among the massed ferns and hydrangeas and arum lilies while somewhere a tap dripped in the warm steamy silence. OK, she had a lot to digest and she'd better start right now and get it over with. This wasn't an adolescent crush: she was twenty-eight years old and had been into a marriage and out again. It was just that she'd never fallen for anyone before. David had been a friend at med. school and they'd started dating and gone on dating until one day she'd said look, we're practically living together so why don't we get married and set up house and share expenses? And he said they should do that, but when she'd suggested a date he'd said there was a major league game on that day, so they'd waited another week and hadn't even told anyone because it didn't seem too big a deal and they could maybe hold a surprise party some time when they weren't grinding away at their studies.

That had been the major passionate romance that had swept her off her feet and into the arms of a man who'd actually turned up at the registrar's but had been smashed out of his mind before midnight and given Linda the first clue to what their future was going to be as man and wife.

This was different, this thing about Jacques, different by a million miles. Maybe if you didn't fall in love by the time you were twenty-eight you either never finally got around to it or you fell so hard that it was like the whole of the northern hemisphere coming apart before your very eyes. That's what was happening to her now and the thing was to make light of it, take a bromide to calm the nervous system down and then just laugh it off. But it wasn't quite so easy as that because there were tears on her face as she stood here with her senses bewitched by the heady scent of flowers and the gold light of the sunshine burnishing their blooms; it just seemed such a shame that the first time she'd fallen in love it had to be with a man who'd done nothing more than smile to her as their paths had crossed yesterday, a man who was so removed from her in his upbringing and lifestyle that there could never be any common ground where they could meet.

OK, that was tough. The thing was to stop snivelling and get back to normal. She'd come here to do a job and she was doing it pretty well because Madame Leclerc had decided to get off her back and even Dr Chirac had offered her a thin smile yesterday and hadn't questioned her medication report.

By the time she'd left the lush romantic atmosphere of the conservatory and helped her patient take a bath and changed the bed-linen and made out her report for the doctor, she'd managed to get back most of her functions. There was still an unsettling warmth floating around in her chest like she'd swallowed a sunset, but it was dying gradually, and when she put the tray out for Marianne after the Princess had eaten her dinner, she felt she'd be able to sleep tonight, and wake feeling normal again. And maybe that would have happened, but the sun was going down beyond the foothills of the Alpes Maritimes, flooding the sky with colours, and she went up the two narrow flights of stairs that led to the stretch of flat roof between the turrets that made a kind of verandah with a balustrade all around. It was time for her to take a break and from up here she could see the coastline as the lights came on. But it was the dying of the day, the flood of saffron light that shimmered across the vast reaches of the sky that brought tears to her eyes again, so that Jacques, standing perfectly still against the balustrade, seemed hardly real when she saw him.

He turned, hearing her.

She stepped back into the doorway. 'Excuse me.'

For a moment he didn't move; she'd never seen such stillness in anyone, and she wondered if she were breaking another of their rules, like jogging in the horse park; maybe this verandah was only for the people who lived here, and their guests.

'Is it Linda?'

The light was in his eyes.

'Yes.'

She turned to leave again but he said quickly:

'Don't go.'

And there was the music again, that soft resonance in his voice. He came across to her, and took her hands so naturally that it didn't surprise her: it was where they had always belonged – in his.

'I was waiting for you,' he said quietly.

She made one final attempt at leaving her world as it was. 'I – I just came to watch the sundown.'

'No. It only seemed like that. We knew where to find each other.'

Against the blinding gold of the light she couldn't see his eyes, but as he leaned down and kissed her mouth the whole new world began and now she could do nothing about it; the very presence of this man was overwhelming, and she faltered, her foot missing the threshold of the doorway, and at once his arms went around her, and she just closed her eyes and laid her head against him and was lost in a kind of timelessness. Her body was trembling and her tears came hot and she let them spring, giving herself to what she'd never suspected was her most desperate need – an end to loneliness.

'Why do you cry like this?'

'Because I can't stop it.'

'You are not sad?'

'No. Oh, no.'

And now she was doing things she'd never done before in her life, not with David nor the other men she'd known since the misery of the divorce. Lifting her face, she waited for this man's lips again with the knowledge that her life depended on their touch, and that when she felt them she would surrender everything that was in her to give him – her love, her body and her soul. Somewhere in her mind was the echo of a young girl's voice, a patient of hers who'd poured her heart out to her in the middle of the night when she'd lain dying, and had wanted Linda to know how it had felt to her when she'd first fallen in love – *I felt like I wasn't me any more . . . I'd kind of given myself away to him, and would have given more if there'd been more of me to give . . . I wanted him to have everything . . .*

And then his mouth was on hers again, this time hungrily, and she shivered, her blood quickening as his hands moved over her and she pressed herself against him to let him know that there'd be no stopping now, whatever he chose to do, wherever he chose to lead her. At the edge of consciousness she was aware of warnings and protests, like waves rising against her to beat her back, but she dived through them and under them, her hair streaming like seaweed and the hot salt tears drowning her in the unknowing as she offered no resistance, letting him take her into one of the little rooms below the roof, where they lay on a bed and he made love to her, in a way she'd never known before, so slowly and so gently and then so hotly that she cried again, saying his name over and over as if it were a note of music she'd learned and wanted to sing, while his dark lean body thrust into hers, playing on her with a rhythm that quickened and deepened until she was carried headlong into an orgasm that sent her threshing and crying out with her fingers hooking into him and her mouth searching for his again as she moaned with the weight of so much sweetness, moaned as if she were in pain and voicing the unbearable, pulling his strong hard body against hers and rocking with him on the little narrow bed as the dust of disuse rose from its coverlet and the springs gave off brief musical notes, while all the time the heavy gold light of the day's dying poured through the doorway and bathed them as they clung together, drowning in the hot sweet abandonment of all reserve and all strangeness with each other, and all fear of ever parting now that it was begun.

'Jacques . . . Jacques . . . '

'Mon amour, petite Linda, mon amour . . . '

And now they whispered together, not thinking of any words but bringing this new element into their love play, the voicing of secret intimacies while their blood ran hot and she rolled away from him and then across, on top of him, her legs spreadeagled and her hair covering his face as she set the rhythm now, drawing herself upwards and then downwards along the silk-smooth shaft of his phallus, slowly, slowly, never quite reaching the point where she would feel that fierce luxurious explosion again deep inside herself, but quickening her strokes as the urgency ebbed away and then slowing again before she went too far, tantalising herself and giving no mercy, wanting to go too far and get it over before she died of ecstasy, wanting to hold back and find out how long she could go on riding this trembling stallion before he threw her and she was plunged again into that hot wild sea of horizonless abandon, wanting to see how long she could make this last because once it was over she wouldn't ever know how to find herself again without him.

'*Plus vite* . . . ' he whispered urgently, 'faster, my darling . . .'

'No . . . oh, please no . . . not yet . . .' And she held on to him as hard as she could, trying to stop him thrusting faster inside her but only half-succeeding, her nipples brushing rhythmically against him, their tips hard and their nerves sending spider-webs of lightning into her breasts and down her body to her loins as he fought to quicken the rhythm while she fought him back, arching her body against his thrusting to slow it down but knowing at last that there was nothing she could do because he needed release and she gave it to him, letting herself go limp across him and feeling the huge eruption of his orgasm swelling inside her and exploding, bringing her to the point where she couldn't go back but was forced to the brink and then over it, falling and falling through the rose-red dark, the throbbing, flesh-red waves of letting-go as she moaned again, moaning now with him as they writhed together, slower and slower while the tides ran back and slowly back and left them stranded, clinging to each other for comfort as the heat and the tumult receded and gave place to the afterglow as they lay supine now, until she rolled off him and they enfolded each other in their arms, to kiss again, and murmur, and look into each other's eyes as the last of the daylight deepened and left a rose-red luminosity in the doorway and on the wall of the passage outside; and it was then that Linda, sated and half-dreaming, saw, or thought she saw, a shadow moving across the wall, and heard, or thought she heard, quiet footsteps fading away.

Little Bibi was trembling, and her hand was cold in Linda's as they sat side by side on the brocade settee in the window of the music room.

'I wasn't anywhere,' the child said again, her blue-grey eyes wide with innocence as she stared into Linda's.

Maybe it was true, Linda thought. Maybe she'd imagined the

shadow flitting across the wall last night; but when she recalled it, there was no question in her mind that it was the shadow of someone with a pigtail, someone whose quiet footsteps had betrayed a limp.

'What made you ask me, Bibi?'

'What it felt like, to fall in love?'

'Yes.'

The little countess shrugged. 'It looked so *obvious*, the moment you came in.'

'Oh, really? What kind of obvious?'

'Oh, your eyes were shining and your face – I can't explain it. You just looked so *different*. As if you'd got a terrific kind of secret.' Bibi looked down, hurt at an accusation that she didn't understand.

'Most of us have secrets, Bibi.'

The child looked up quickly. 'Of course. The thing is, we've got to trust each other.' She paused for an instant. 'Where did you think I was?'

'It's not important now.' Linda pressed her small cold hand and got up. 'I came here for my French lesson, if you feel like giving me one.'

'All right.' Bibi spread her pleated navy-blue skirt on each side of her legs, as if it were a ball gown. 'There's a little phrase you'll find rather useful, now.' Her face was not mischievous, but solemn as she gazed up at Linda. 'It's in the familiar, of course. It's "*Je t'aime*", and it means "I love you." '

12

THE ROSE GARDEN

'You look so happy today, *ma chère*.'

'I'm happy to see you down here in the garden, Madame.' Linda straightened a cushion for her patient on the chaise-longue.

'But there's something else,' Charlotte said lightly. 'You look like a girl in love.' She noted how quickly Linda turned away, to settle the blanket over her feet. 'But of course that's none of my business.'

Perhaps it was just that Linda, like everyone else, was glad that Charlotte had officially ended the period of mourning for Edouard, sooner than usual. 'He would have wished it so,' she'd confided to her nurse. 'He'd want us to remember him with glad hearts, not long faces.' The Chateau was coming back to life again, and Charlotte herself was feeling the burden of grief lifting from her a little; her periodic spasms of pain had regressed already, and Dr Chirac had told her that she could receive visitors in the rose-garden if she felt strong enough. Yet, lying here on the chaise with cushions behind her and the quilted silk blanket over her feet, she felt old before her time. At the same age as herself, Thérèse de Valoise still led a full life, flying between Rome and Paris and London and New York and back, keeping in touch with her cosmetics empire. And would she be seeing other men, now that Edouard was no longer here? Charlotte's thoughts clouded, then she cleared them again by an effort of will. The past was done with, and now there was only her short future to think about, and to deal with.

Linda had fallen silent, sitting on the smooth sweet-smelling grass, and for a while they remained like that, each absorbed in her own thoughts, while the heavy perfume of the roses steeped the air; and then, punctually at one o'clock – he would of course be punctual, that went without saying – Michel de Beauvais appeared from a doorway in the winter-garden and came across the lawn, a short, energetic figure in a dark suit, his head bare and his hands tucked behind him.

'*Bonjour, ma Princesse!*' A quick, elegant bow and he was kissing her hand, touching his lips punctiliously to his own thumbnail. '*Vous avez de très bonne mine aujourd'hui!*'

Linda was moving away, as she always did when the Princess entertained business visitors, but now Charlotte stopped her with a gesture. 'Thank you, Michel, I'm feeling a little better, yes. I don't think you've met my nurse yet, have you? Miss Linda Terman, from America. Linda, let me present M'sieur le Compte de Beauvais, one of my most valued advisers.'

'Miss Terman . . .' Another slight bow, but the Count didn't take Linda's hand. Charlotte noticed his interest in the American girl's looks.

'I'm pleased to meet you, M'sieur.' He reminded Linda of the smooth, dark-suited businessmen who'd come to the Chateau a few days ago, except that this one was younger, with searching, inquisitive eyes.

'I hope you find the Riviera pleasant, Miss Terman, in the winter time.'

'This is winter?' she smiled.

'The nights are chilly now – we try to make a gesture.'

'Michel,' Charlotte said in a moment, 'you may come and sit here by me. He's going to bore me with business, Linda, so I suggest you make your escape.'

'I'll go and see if I can find *le petit Baron*. I haven't talked to him today.'

'He's very touched, you know. People don't have time for him, but then of course they're not as patient as you, *ma chère*.'

Charlotte watched her crossing the smooth expanse of the lawn, for a moment lost in her thoughts. Then she turned to the young man beside her. Young? Forty was young, yes, for a man of Michel's experience and acumen. He had also shown his loyalty, coming to her as soon as good taste allowed it after the tragedy, to tell her that he was at her entire disposal if there were anything he could do to make her future easier. He knew also that there was no one else she could trust, completely.

The de Beauvais family was one of the most distinguished in France, and shared honours with the de Montigny-Villiers in wars dating back to the Middle Ages. Michel's father had been one of Edouard's closest friends, and had fought in the same regiment in the second world war. Above all, Michel de Beauvais was an ambitious man, and that was going to make it easier for Charlotte in what she had to do.

'It's good of you to come to see me,' she told him, 'considering how busy you are in all your enterprises.'

'I am yours to command, Madame.' His eyes became serious and attentive. She hadn't called him here from Paris this morning for nothing.

'Thank you,' she said. 'There's no one, as I believe you know, whom I can put my trust in more safely. On the other hand, you will need to trust me in return – not of course my regard for you, but my judgement in general affairs. Affairs that would concern you and involve you very closely.'

'I have no qualms, *ma Princesse*.' If he felt she were about to make mistakes, then he would tell her so; she would expect that.

'There is a certain enterprise,' she told him slowly, 'that has your interest, I know. And it's in my power to arrange matters so that you would achieve the greater part of your ambitions within a short time.' She narrowed her eyes against the sunlight; it seemed brighter than usual these days, just as sounds seemed louder, and the texture of the bed linen harsher to her skin. 'I'm sorry to have to put these things so mysteriously, Michel, but I need to protect certain people, and to keep certain others at bay. This can't be done openly, I'm afraid; there's too much at stake.'

'Then let me read between the lines,' he said.

'Very well. What you'll need to do is simple enough, though it might take a little time. That is all I have to give you, Michel . . . a little time.'

He looked down, and made no attempt at blandishments. She was dying, and not slowly now; and no hopes of medical miracles were worth entertaining at this stage – he'd talked to Dr Chirac over the phone yesterday. 'I'll work as quickly as needs be, *ma très chere Princesse*.' He put his hand gently over hers.

'I know. And you need to be sure of one thing, Michel. If my plans seem strange to you, it has nothing to do with the fact that my life is nearly over now – though of course it tends to give me a different point of view. And it has nothing to do with the drugs I'm taking. My mind is as clear as crystal, and I want you to remember that. So here is what you will need to do, and I know that you'll listen to me carefully . . .'

She kept him only ten minutes; to have said more to him would have tired her, and in any case there was no need; he'd agreed to stay here at the Chateau for at least a week, leaving his business in Paris in the hands of his partners. Watching him cross the lawn again towards the winter-garden, Charlotte wondered if she were involving too many lives in these plans of hers for the future of the de Montigny-Villiers fortune and estates – if she were presuming to play God. Earlier today, two very different people had urged her in two different directions: Marc Dorlhac, who had been the family lawyer since her marriage to Edouard thirty years ago, and Thérèse de Valoise, whose devotion to Edouard's memory and respect for his wishes were almost as fierce as her own.

'It's very natural for you,' Dorlhac had told her in his thin, precise tones, 'to wish to pass on the estates to your son and rightful heir, Prince Jacques. But we should consider his . . . personal predilections. He seems hardly fitted for the task of controlling so much property.'

Perched like a thin, cadaverous elf beside her, pulling with pale fingers at his overlong eyebrows, he had gone on talking, and Charlotte had let him, even when he'd launched himself into his main theme. 'I see your sister Toinette as far more practical a choice, *ma Princesse*, since she has Raoul by her side. After all, he's the head of a firm whose major occupation is the running of large estates for their owners. This would give us a personage of the blood – your sister Toinette – as the titular head of the estates, together with her husband, a man with great experience in management.'

'I detest the man.'

'Pardon?' He glanced up quickly.

'Raoul treats my sister brutally.' Charlotte hadn't meant to put it so bluntly, but it was out before she could stop herself. She suspected in any case that it was no surprise to the lawyer: he handled the legal aspects of Raoul's business interests on the Riviera, and Marc Dorlhac wasn't a man to miss anything in people's relationships. He was at this moment studying his finger-nails.

'Whatever your personal feelings in the matter, *ma Princesse* – which of course I respect profoundly – there is no one closer to the bloodline who can take over the estates when you – when it becomes necessary.' He went on to say more about Raoul Cavaille, picking his way cautiously but extolling his virtues as a businessman and quoting the names of some of his present clients, whose properties totalled several billion Swiss francs. 'On the other hand, if you feel committed by maternal loyalty to entrusting the estates to Prince Jacques . . .' He left it with a shrug of this thin shoulders.

'No, Marc, I don't. It's out of the question to burden my son with such a responsibility.'

Charlotte told Thérèse the same thing, an hour later; but Thérèse tried valiantly to support Jacques as the rightful heir.

'He's young, Charlotte, and strong. He's devoted to you and to Edouard's memory. He's also first in line to the inheritance, and would carry far greater authority than Raoul and Toinette together.'

In the close presence of the beautiful, vital woman by her side on the sunlit lawn, Charlotte thought it strange that their relationship could have developed so strongly over the years; most wives wouldn't have tolerated the presence of their husband's mistress under their own roof. Yet there were good reasons. Charlotte was quite certain that neither Edouard nor Thérèse had slept together at the Chateau at any time; it hadn't been in their nature to humiliate someone they both loved. There'd been a need in Edouard that Charlotte couldn't provide for: not sex in itself, but in some of its manifestations – the piquancy of stolen fruit, the spice of variety, and perhaps the kind of *outré* sex that Edouard hadn't wanted to demand from her, the carnal, frenetic passion of the flesh that Thérèse was able to respond to. And there'd been that aspect of Edouard's and Thérèse's relationship that she'd put so succinctly to Charlotte a few days ago. *For Edouard, that was the difference between us, in the end. You were his great love, and I was just his concubine-confessor.*

What had Edouard confessed to, before he'd sought such a cruel end to his life? She'd asked Thérèse, but in vain:

I can't tell you that.

Because he made you promise?

Yes. All I can tell you is what you already know. Edouard loved you more than he loved anyone else on earth.

Stretched in the chaise-longue beside her, Thérèse's lithe body, elegant in a camelhair sweater and slacks, had the tension of a tigress's, totally relaxed but expressing the potential ability to spring swiftly into life. She was here, as Charlotte knew, to keep her company for a time, to share her grief; but already life was moving on again, Charlotte's to its close, and others' lives to whatever their stars decreed. Jacques' was one of them.

'I know you think he's still just a playboy,' Thérèse went on, 'but that's partly because he's never been given any responsibility. I think the office would make the man.'

'The "office" doesn't appeal to him, Thérèse. If he managed to accept such a responsibility he'd feel so obliged to make a success of it that he'd burn himself out.'

'I'd help him, if you wanted me to.' The green eyes were turned on Charlotte as Thérèse waited for an answer.

'You're already busy running your own empire, Thérèse. And if Jacques took over my estates he'd need someone permanent at his side, as his wife. Even then, I'd be committing him to carrying a burden for the rest of his life. I could never do that – I want to die in whatever peace I can find.'

Thérèse considered for a moment. 'To do that, you'll want to respect Edouard's wishes.'

'Yes.'

'What would they have been, regarding the succession?'

'He wouldn't have wanted Jacques to succeed.' Charlotte turned her head to look at Thérèse. 'He didn't give you that impression? He didn't mention Jacques?'

'No. He . . . wasn't thinking about the estates when he – when I last talked to him.'

'What was he – ?' but she left it. What Edouard had been thinking about before he died would never be known to her. Carefully she asked, 'Thérèse, did he at any time suggest that you should take over the estates yourself?'

'No. I haven't the slightest claim, and it wouldn't interest me – unless you wanted me to help Jacques.'

Charlotte shook her head. 'There's no question of Jacques.'

Thérèse left her soon afterwards, feeling she'd only tire Charlotte if she stayed. The only other visitor to approach the rose-garden before Charlotte went indoors was Guillaume, *le petit Baron*, creeping up from the massed rhododendrons behind the two chaise-longues, not wanting to be seen crossing the open expanse of the lawn. That was his way. Charlotte didn't suspect he was there until she felt with a shock the soft warm hand nuzzling inside her own.

'I thought you were somewhere near, *mon petit*.' Throughout the Chateau, people were asked never to show surprise, if they could help it, when *le petit Baron* crept up on them, because he didn't do it purposely, and if he felt it was a shock for them he'd never go near anyone again. The only way he allowed himself to approach people was from the shadows or some kind of cover. He came and went like a little ghost.

'She is the most wonderful person in the world,' he said now, his Mongoloid head hanging down as he peered at Charlotte from under his swollen lids. Few others would have understood what he was saying; his speech was slurred and halting.

'Who is, *mon chéri?*'

'Mademoiselle Linda.'

'She's been talking to you?'

'Yes. We talked a lot. She can tell what I'm saying.'

'But of course she can, Guillaume. We all can.'

He considered this, watching her with that sidelong stare that had so much intelligence in it. 'No. Most people can't. But you can. You and Mademoiselle Linda.'

What had surprised him, as Charlotte knew, was that a stranger should have the courage to approach him and talk to him at all. 'Linda is like that, *mon petit*. She loves people.'

'Even me.' His head swung gently, like a scarecrow's in the wind.

'Anyone who didn't love you, Guillaume, wouldn't even be worth talking about.'

Pauvre petit . . . He'd been told, when he was old enough to ask, that his mother had been a pretty ballerina who had been lost in a shipwreck, and that his father had died soon afterwards of a broken heart; in fact it had been a scullery maid here at the Chateau who had borne him, seduced by the fifteen-year-old Baron de Tourquet. Seeing in her malformed infant the mark of her shame, she had poisoned herself. Charlotte had at once brought the child under her care, for it was the duty of a noble house to protect even the lowliest and most afflicted.

He went away as secretively as he'd come, shambling into the bushes and taking with him their brief conversation, to go over and over it again in his mind, like a dog with a new bone.

Alone again in the rose garden, Charlotte gazed through half-closed lids at the scene in front of her: the emerald sweep of the lawn and beyond it the groups of dark green firs that gave shade in the long summers, and then the Chateau, with its ancient stones piled one on another from the winter-garden to the mansard roofs.

On this side, the east wing, there were balconies with stone balustrades ranged along the upper storeys, and the pale winter sunshine threw soft shadows from the fir trees across the walls. Her mind dwelling on her talks with Thérèse, Dorlhac the lawyer, and Michel de Beauvais, Charlotte felt uneasy again that in struggling to protect the estates from passing into the wrong hands she might be putting people she loved in danger. But she was tiring now, and drifting into the twilight zone that comes before sleep. Watching the Chateau through half-closed eyes she believed she saw – as she'd seen so many times in her dreams since Edouard had died – the figure of a man falling, slowly and in silence as her heart ached for him in his last desperate act of despair.

But this time a *frisson* passed through her, and for a moment she was gripped by the frightening thought that she was not seeing Edouard falling from the balcony of the hotel in Monte-Carlo, but someone else, falling from one of the balconies of the Chateau, and not in the past, but the future.

13

CELESTE

'WE MUST TALK,' Dorlhac said over the telephone.

'Is it something urgent?'

'Very.'

Raoul Cavaille glanced across the room at Toinette, and was momentarily caught by the sight of her body as she slipped into a black silk cocktail-dress, skin-tight and perfect for her slim figure. Then he brought his mind back to the lawyer – Dorlhac's tone had been urgent.

'I have a business lunch at the Yacht Club in half an hour,' Raoul told him.

'You can't break it?'

'Impossible. It's with the American consul.'

'What time can you come to my office, Raoul?'

'Not before three this afternoon.'

'Try to be here at three, then. I'll hold off all other appointments.'

It was gone three-thirty when Raoul parked his Ferrari outside the offices of Dorlhac, Gavalais and Weissman, attorneys-at-law, along the Boulevard Princesse Charlotte. He was shown straight in to the sombre, oak-pannelled room where the lawyer greeted him.

'I trust your lunch was successful?'

'I believe so.' Raoul sat down in the big leather chair. 'The Americans are renewing their interest in the *Société des Bains de Mer*.' He watched the lawyer with his dark, shimmering eyes; sunlight filtering through the slats of the Venetian blinds sparked on a gold cuff-link as he folded his strong hands, his elbows on the arms of the chair.

'Oh, really?' Dorlhac raised his massive eyebrows. 'I appreciate your telling me.' He made a note on a pad beside him.

'We don't keep much from each other, Marc; it's only good business.'

Dorlhac inclined his narrow, greying head in agreement. Sitting half in shadow behind the huge Directoire desk, he looked rather like a ghost, Raoul thought, with his grey, shrunken skin and his hollowed eyes; his nose was large but so thin that it seemed to have been whittled away by a knife. Twenty years ago, when he was middle-aged, Dorlhac was told he had a year to live before he succumbed to adrenal failure, but here he was still, with his brain as sharp and brilliantly effective as ever. Raoul had once said of him that he'd decided to go on living if only to haunt his doctors from this side of the grave.

Raoul, younger and in vibrant health, was going to miss the lawyer's talents, when his ghost was finally laid. 'I'm sorry I'm late,' he said. 'The consul is a talkative man.'

Dorlhac inclined his head again. 'No matter. Now I have to go back quite a way into the family history of the de Montigny-Villiers, though it won't strain your patience, I think. That history is in some respects quite remarkable. I was at the Chateau earlier today, and I learned something quite by chance that you should be made aware of.' He pressed a button on his intercom and said, 'Absolutely no calls please, Mademoiselle.' Then he looked across at Raoul Cavaille with his domed head tilted forward and his yellowed eyes regarding him steadily. 'What I have to tell you is in the most sacrosanct confidence. As you know, I have the interests of the late Prince Edouard and his estates close to my heart; as far as I'm able, I shall remain loyal to Princess Charlotte, who has my utmost compassion as a newly-made widow, herself nearing her own demise. But in my opinion her plans for the future of the estates may have taken a quite extraordinary turn; she's not spoken of them – at least not concerning this new and bizarre possibility. She is ill, Raoul, and under drugs; we can't expect her to think rationally about weighty matters. Finally, there is almost no one else to whom I would offer this confidence, but you are Charlotte's son-in-law and your wife stands in the line of succession.' He glanced up at the tall satinwood clock in the corner, then back at Cavaille. 'I would ask you to let me tell you this story without interruption. We can talk afterwards, and the consequences of our discussion may be far-reaching indeed.'

She was not pretty, but her eyes were her feature: soft, contemplative and with a habit of dipping away in modesty when faced too steadily. She was thin, quiet, neat, and capable of hiding under this colourless exterior the fires of secret passion. That was why Mario Romano, with his lock of black hair and his Italian charm, had been able to seduce her within the space of one single evening at Chez Bacco, by the harbour, and subsequently of course at his apartment.

Her name was Celeste. She was twenty-nine years old, and for the past three years had been personal assistant to Maître Marc Christian Dorlhac, attorney-at-law.

On this mild November evening she was standing in the doorway of the little parfumerie halfway along the Boulevard Princesse Charlotte, not far from Maître Dorlhac's office. She recognized the bright scarlet Alfa-Romeo at a distance, and was at the kerbside the moment it pulled up and the passenger-door swung open for her.

Mario Romano threw down his half-smoked Gauloise and gave her a smile that shone right through into her heart and there burned. 'Every time I see you,' he said with his dark eyes narrowed as if he were judging a painting, 'you look more beautiful.' Her own eyes dipped away, and he slid the short knobbed gear-lever into mesh, not kissing Celeste because it was an open sports model and the top was down. The need for discretion irked a man of Mario's mercurial temperament, but he couldn't afford to be blatant about his affairs; discretion was an indispensable tool of his trade, which was mainly concerned with the indiscretions of others.

He drove Celeste to a tiny restaurant in the Rue Terrazzani, nestling not far from the sheer rock face whose plateau was graced by the Royal Palace. He'd only entertained – as Mario would have called it – this young lady four or five times, but each time it became more necessary to use discretion, and he no longer dined her at places like Chez Bacco or La Salière.

'I would like to give you the most delightful evening of your life, my lovely Celeste.' He poured some wine for her.

'You always do,' she said simply.

He made a mock grimace of despair. 'Then I'm becoming a bore . . .'

'No,' she said. Even his pretence of despair wounded her heart.

And he knew this, of course. Mario Romano would never have struck up an acquaintance with a girl so shy, so colourless, if she hadn't been the key to opening a door that even a battering-ram couldn't have pushed down otherwise; but now that he needed to entertain her from time to time he rather enjoyed his ability to throw fuel on those fires he sensed burning inside her. Besides, she was astonishingly good in bed, as sometimes happened with quiet, withdrawn young women. The first time he'd laid her so gently, so romantically across the divan in the arabesque room in his apartment, stroking her softly as the incense in the brass burner sent a tendril of perfume rising to the arched, stuccoed ceiling and the concealed cassette-recorder sent the lilting notes of meditative flute music through the scented air, little Celeste had waited until he was naked before she even stirred, but when he laid his tanned, rippling body across hers she began wriggling like a fish under him, writhing and squirming and clinging and arching herself and tossing her head from side to side in the kind of frenzy that would have put that neurotic little English milady to shame.

So it wasn't really too much of a chore after all, entertaining Celeste. Mario was not a cold-hearted brute. He used women, yes, but also he loved them, if he could find anything to love in them at all; with his dark curly hair and his smouldering Neapolitan eyes and his honeyed tongue he bought them, but he paid his way. And when he left them he did it honestly, telling them that it wasn't in his capacity to create a permanent relationship and that if he tried, they could never trust him. Some had taken this philosophically, others less so; there were occasional complaints from his neighbours of screaming and wailing sounds, and more than once he'd had to remain isolated in his apartment for days on end while the scratches on his angelic face healed presentably and the supply of *Ricca di Donna* and *panzerotti* and *cannaruozzoli* in his refrigerator slowly ran out. And once a powder-blue Renault had come swerving past him when he was crossing the Avenue de Monte-Carlo, so close that it left a tear in his elegant Italian-tailored trousers. But Mario was a nimble man.

'People say bad things about me,' he confided to little Celeste, and poured more Chianti Classico for her, 'but that's just gossip.' He always affected a slight Italian accent, knowing its power to melt otherwise quite rational women. 'I am not a bad man.' He looked around the tiny restaurant to make sure he was not overheard. Reassured, he leaned over the red-checkered cloth and brought his voice low. '*People say I have no shame as a photographer, and that I will sell any picture provided it's worth money.*'

He shook his dark curly head. 'This is not so. *I once took a picture of Diana's panties*. You know? Princess Diana?' He waited a moment for the sake of drama. 'She is very careful in public, and wears her skirts lower than usual, knowing that if one day she were bending over a child to receive a bouquet or something like that, and a puff of wind came, the nearest photographer would click his camera and be able to retire for the rest of his life. Can you imagine? Even if only one little inch of those royal panties were showing!' He leaned even closer, his voice now a whisper. '*And it happened. And I was there . . . La Princessa Diana* was coming down the gangway from a yacht, and there was a puff of wind. I am a good photographer, you know – very fast. So nobody else got the picture, only I, Mario Romano. A picture that would have gone around the world within an hour. A picture that would have brought me millions of lira. *Millions*. Can you imagine my excitement when that photograph appeared in the developing-dish? I held the negative to the light. *Mama mia!*' He tossed back his lock of dark hair. '*It was the picture of the year!* But I tore it up.' He spread his hands open in a gesture of helplessness. 'What else could I do? She is a lady, *la Princessa*. She is respectable, and does no harm to anyone. And *I* am respectable, my little Celeste, and I do no harm either.' He leaned back and lifted his glass of wine. 'I will give you a toast. To Princess Diana of England! And to the little princess of my heart who sits here so quietly while this helpless *inamorato* babbles on, trying to impress her.'

'You don't have to try,' she said, so softly that he didn't hear; then she spilled some wine as she took her glass to touch his, because she could look nowhere else but into his dark poetic eyes.

'*Focàccia di Fiori di Sambucco!*' announced their waiter, and presented the entrée with a flourish.

Despite Mario Romano's predilection for romance, his acquaintanceship with little Celeste had been designed in a mood of total practicality.

'Monsieur Romano,' Dorlhac the lawyer had told him sternly three weeks before, 'I have brought you here to my office in order to tell you categorically that if you don't cease trying to compromise certain of my clients you'll become the subject of serious litigation.'

'But Maître, I haven't the slightest idea what you're talking about!'

It wasn't the first time that Mario had been called into a lawyer's office or sent a warning letter, and he knew the ropes. On this occasion the meeting lasted some fifteen minutes and Mario left the office maintaining his complete innocence of any such conduct and the tacit understanding that he would cease it forthwith. But today he was in luck; there was a rather plain but very responsive young assistant in the outer office, and as he gave her his melting, heart-stilling Neapolitan smile she knocked a bottle of Waterman's Royal-Blue ink onto the floor in her haste to snatch her tortoise-shell glasses off and show him her limpid, dove-grey eyes in their natural state.

The next evening a scarlet sports-car drew out in front of her as she was leaving the car park, and she had to brake hard to avoid it. The fault, surely, hadn't been hers, though she knew at once that it must have been, when the other driver, a young man with dark curly hair, shot her a look of quick anger and then changed it to that breath-taking smile she'd seen only yesterday in her office. She immediately botched the gears of her little grey 2–CV, which leapt forward and struck the rear bumper of the Alfa-Romeo. It took until long after midnight to smooth matters out, first at Chez Bacco by the harbour and then in Mario's arabesque studio in the Place de la Crémaillère, on the border of Monte-Carlo and Beausoleil, where the cost of repairing the Alfa-Romeo's rear bumper became no more than a subject to be henceforth forgotten.

On their second meeting, Mario reluctantly confessed the reason for the worried silences that punctuated their conversation, the poignant wrinkles on his pensive brow and the heartbreaking melancholy in his clouded eyes. Celeste must treat this as *their* secret – she crossed her heart – but the truth was that a client of Maître Dorlhac was attempting to smear Mario's reputation as a well-known and respected celebrity photographer. There was much of this kind of thing on the French Riviera – professional enmities, jealousies and so on among the international-class reporters and photo-journalists. Now, Mario and the good Maître knew that the troublemaker was one of the lawyer's own clients. The only way to discover *which* of those clients was for Mario to listen-in to the meetings taking place daily in the lawyer's office. But that was impossible!

At this stage Mario became very halting in his story to little Celeste, and admitted regrets that he'd ever begun it. He had no right to burden her like this, and place on her young shoulders the onus of secrecy. It took her a long time – some of it spent on her slender haunches in front of him with her arms on his knees and her imploring eyes lifted to his in the light of the beaded lamp – to persuade him to go on.

Well, then, Mario knew that Maître Dorlhac would have liked to secrete a recording-device in his office, so that Mario could later listen-in to his meetings with clients. But again – impossible! Those meetings were highly confidential, and the good Maître was a man of impeccable honour, as Celeste herself knew. It would be feasible, of course, for such a device to be secreted in the lawyer's office *without his knowledge*, so that he would not be party to the ploy; then Mario could play the tapes and with luck discover the malefactor. He could then destory the tapes and give Maître Dorlhac the name of the person they were looking for. But that too was impossible! There was no one who would do it for him.

At this point Mario broke off and refused to ask his little Celeste to endure more of his wretched problems. He would deal with the situation himself, and if he failed, well then, he wouldn't be the first innocent victim of professional jealousy to face ruin; he could leave the Riviera, the beloved Riviera that had been his only home since he was brought here as a child by his father, who came in search of work as a young musician, playing his guitar in the seafront cafés. He, Mario, could go to Italy and find a living there, and perhaps a new life. Broken dreams were not the end of the world, and –

'*I'll* do it for you, Mario!'

He turned to Celeste, confused, surprised to see the shimmer of tears in her soft eyes.

'What will you do?'

'I'll find a hiding-place for your recording-device, in Maître Dorlhac's office!'

At first he'd have none of it, and she finally had to beg to be allowed to help him, to express the love she felt for him by exposing his malicious enemy. In the end, helpless against her entreaties, he agreed.

That had been three weeks ago. Since then he'd listened to many hours of tape from the Sasaki 2000–FJ miniature long-playing recorder that had found its niche inside the pearly conch-shell that had been displayed on Maître Dorlhac's windowsill ever since he'd brought it back from the South Seas ten years ago after attending an international legal convention. So far, Mario had erased tape after tape for re-use. Now party to the private affairs of many of Maître Dorlhac's clients, he nevertheless put the information out of his mind as soon as the tapes were erased. All he was looking for was some instance of malpractice on the part of Dorlhac, something that would give Mario power over him so that the next time the man summoned him peremptorily to his office he could tell him to go and fry *bouillabaisse*. So far nothing had come up, but he knew it wouldn't be long; an attorney-at-law possessed all the honesty and integrity of a second-hand car salesman.

This evening, sitting with Mario in the tiny Italian café below the walls of the Palais Princier, Celeste sipped from her glass of Asti Spumante and let him enfold her hand in his. At times, during the past three weeks, she had wondered at herself, at her readiness to deceive her employer by hiding the tape-recorder in his office; but it was in his own interests, a means of helping him to find Mario's enemy – and Mario was also a client. These self-doubts had assailed her only when Mario was not with her, for she had only to look into his eyes to know he was telling the truth.

'Have you found what you're looking for yet?' she asked him in the candlelight.

'Not yet, *mi amore*. But we will.' He pressed her hand gently.

She wondered if he realized how deeply exciting it was for her to have this added intimacy to share with him: a secret known only to themselves that lay buried within the pearly conch-shell.

'Before I forget . . .' she told him, and reached for her little handbag. Looking around her with the caution of a master-spy's mistress, she slid today's tape across the table for him, and within an instant it was in his pocket.

'You have not only the fire and the passion of a lover,' he told her softly, 'but also a sublime generosity of spirit in helping a man who has no other true friend, and nowhere else to turn.' He poured more wine for her.

Since she lived with her widowed mother she could never spend a whole night away, in case she was needed; so Mario drove her as usual back to the shabby apartment-house in the rue Princesse Florestine, after she'd gone with him from the restaurant to tremble and quiver like a little fish on the divan in his studio. The night was cool, but they had the canvas top down, and as the scarlet Alfa-Romeo thrummed its way through the lamplit streets Celeste leaned back and closed her eyes and let the slipstream flutter through her hair while the aftermath of all those orgasms burned in her body like embers.

With the goodnight touch of her lips on his, Mario turned the sports-car quietly and threaded his way home through the midnight streets, taking the cassette she'd given him and slotting it into the player on the dashboard, turning the volume up.

The recording seemed to have started soon after the beginning of a meeting, and he recognized the voice of Maître Dorlhac immediately.

What I have to tell you is in the most sacrosanct confidence, Raoul. As you know, I have the interests of the late Prince Edouard and his estates close to my heart . . .

Mario began listening intently, and turned the volume up a little more.

I would ask you to let me tell you this story without interruption. We can talk afterwards, and the consequences of our discussion may be far-reaching indeed . . .

Mario lowered the speed of his little car so that he could hear better, and ten minutes later he pulled up along the Avenue de la Costa and switched off the engine. Stunned, he sat listening to the voice on the cassette as he gazed upwards across the hillside to where the Chateau de Beausoleil stood among the dark pine trees, with some of its windows still lighted softly from within.

14

ARABIAN NIGHT

BEHIND THE LIGHTED window near the east turret, on the top floor of the Chateau, Linda lay naked, curled in the arms of Jacques de Montigny-Villiers. It was late, but neither wanted to leave the other. This was the same little room with the single bed and the two soft satin-shaded lamps that Jacques had brought her to on the evening of the sundown, when Linda had been whirled from her past life into this one.

His tongue found her nipples again, arousing her when she'd believed she was exhausted: they'd come here three hours ago. Jacques liked it with the light on – not too bright but enough for them to see each other's bodies. They'd shut and locked the door this time, on her insistence – though she hadn't told him about Bibi and her suspicions – but the window was still uncurtained, and she could make out a constellation of blue-white stars in the night sky. She'd never made love in the light before, and found it liberating, a kind of extension of the ecstasy; in the dark, the most vital sense was missing, but now she wanted to look at this beautiful man and watch the sheen of sweat on his skin and the play of his muscles as he moved, the curling mass of the hair between his legs and the flushed silk-smooth phallus as her fingers stroked it, their tips tracing its contours and encircling it, to squeeze and slide and squeeze again until it became so hard that she rolled sideways and guided its inflamed head against the moist, parted lips between her legs and rubbed it there, backwards and forward, feeling its heat caressing her clitoris until it responded, itself hardening and sending a sweet shock of sensation spreading and flooding through her pelvis, so that she closed her eyes at last, not wanting to look any more but just wanting to lie cradled in this man's arms and go on moving his hardened body against her, slowly, slowly, aching to go faster as he began catching his breath and making low sounds in the quiet of the little room, whispering her name and saying things in French that she didn't understand or need to understand, while all the time she moved him against her, back and forth as her fluid came springing again, seeping across her fingers until his phallus was slippery with it and the contact became so exquisitely sensitive that she could hardly bear it any longer.

She'd never made love like this with any man; there'd just been David, who had never been able to reach any kind of hardness because he was full of alcohol and half-asleep, and then the few other men, the mere acquaintances who were so eager to get at her once her clothes were off that the whole thing was over before she could enjoy anything more than the quick rush of the climax and the immediate clenching of her eyes and the biting of her lip because here it was again, the confirmation that sex was only sex and if you didn't have it you'd build up the tension in your nerves and take it out on other people, and if you had it then this was all there was, something not much more than a good sneeze.

But now there was this revelation, a body-to-body communion with the first man in her life who'd ever reached this far into her senses and found this much response. She felt free at last, free to let go, to trust in self-exposure, in true nakedness, in headlong and unrestrained abandon.

Jacques was writhing now as she kept up the unbearable teasing, refusing to move him faster against her and even slowing a little, sliding and pressing deeper, deeper, her face nuzzling into his shoulder and her legs moving against his own, her bare feet thrusting down the length of his calves in time with the slow, slow rhythm of her hand, as she found out that wherever a woman's body touched a man's, love could be made there.

'*Mon Dieu . . . mon Dieu . . . ça suffit, Linda, je vais mourir . . . je vais mourir . . .* '

'I love you, Jacques . . . *Je t'aime, je t'aime . . .* '

'*Maintenant,*' he was moaning, '*maintenant, je te pris, ah mon Dieu, maintenant . . .* '

She tried to ignore him, and ignore her own desperate need of the orgasm that was building inside her like a rising wave, and kept her hand clenched around his phallus, moving it slowly, slowly, pressing it harder and harder into her body until suddenly he seized her wrist and began moving it faster and faster until they were moaning together with their bodies locked and rolling from side to side on the narrow bed and his hand took over the rhythm and brought them both to the point of unbearable sensation that left them helpless in that limbo where the wave, leaping, hangs poised in timelessness before it falls, releasing its liquid fire and tiding through flesh and spirit and leaving behind it the echoes of the storm. They both cried out, and for an instant Linda thought of Bibi – or anyone else who might be on the highest floor of the building at this hour, maybe unable to sleep – but the flash of warning was lost in the tumult of the senses and she gave herself to it, biting into his neck as the sweet raging of the climax overwhelmed her and she twisted her body in time with his, entwined with him until their movement became slower and the heat burned low, and there was nothing more in the silence of the room but the whispering of each other's names.

Later, as she lay beside him under the coverlet, Jacques leaned over her, saying softly, 'And now you are no longer running . . . scary, did you say?'

'Scared.' She smiled in the starlight. A minute ago he'd turned out the lamps, and the cool glow of the night-sky filled the room. 'No. Not now I know you'll always be somewhere near.'

But he seemed concerned. 'There is nobody here at the Chateau who wishes you harm, Linda. Why should they?'

'I don't know. It was just a feeling.' She watched the little constellation of blue-white stars in the window, the Pleiades. 'Sometimes I get a sense of déjà vu. I could believe I'm not a stranger here – it's like I was here before.'

'That happens to all of us.'

'I guess it does.' She turned her head so she could look at him. 'Why did you try so hard to stop me leaving, the other day?'

'Because I knew my mother didn't want to lose you.'

'I don't think I'm that important to her, Jacques.'

Then why had his mother gone through all that hassle to find her and bring her here from three thousand miles away, singling her out from hundreds of others?

'She's very fond of you,' he told her. 'She has an enormous amount of respect for you, and she's in less pain now than she used to be. She's talked to me about it; with you here, Dr Chirac has stopped trying to persuade her to undergo treatment.' In a moment he asked, 'Do you think she should?'

'I'm not a doctor, Jacques.'

'But you're very experienced.'

'Even so, it isn't for me to give an opinion. I – '

'In absolute confidence, if I asked you?'

She held him closer, bringing his head down on her shoulder. 'I think she'd like to go. I think all she wants to do is get the estates settled, and then she'd like to . . . you know, join your father. And the thing is, if someone wants to go, there's no treatment in the world that can stop them.'

He was quiet for a time, and she wished she hadn't given him her thoughts. Then he said softly, '*Bien.* So be it.'

'Look, I could be wrong – '

'I don't think so. It's what I believe, too.'

She locked her arms around his shoulders. 'It's been a tough year for you, Jacques.' He and his father had been very close, Bibi had told her; and there'd been no warning. God, how many times had she listened to relatives, their faces stained with tears and their eyes bewildered – *But he never said anything . . . Couldn't he just have told us what the trouble was? We would have done something . . . anything . . .* But that wasn't the way it worked. Most of the time, a suicide was someone who knew that nobody else would listen, or understand. It was the only way out for the lonely. But had it been like that in this case? She didn't know anything about Prince Edouard, except that everybody seemed to have loved him. That didn't sound like he'd been lonely. And Bibi had said there'd been someone with him just before he'd died. A woman. But Linda was learning every day, and very fast, never to listen to Bibi's stories; the kid spent most of her life fantasizing.

For Jacques the first traumatic shock of his father's death was over now, but it would be a long time before he could start forgetting, and he was going to have to do it while his mother too was on her way out of his life.

'Jacques,' she said softly, 'the thing I want most in the world right now is to help you get through the next few months. Whenever you need me, I'll be here.'

*   *   *

The whole of the fifteenth floor of the Vista del Mar *grand-luxe* apartment block in La Condamine, overlooking Monte-Carlo harbour, had been redecorated to look like a tent.

But not a common-or-garden Boy Scout tent. It had taken five thousand square feet of raw, hand-woven, gold-threaded Persian silk to cover the walls and form the rising canopy and create the impression that one was no longer in Monte-Carlo at all, but in the Sahara Desert. With its opulent braided hangings and its huge gold tassels and its swathes of looped silk awnings it offered a spectacle that would have gladdened the heart of any film producer frantic to find a location for his forthcoming epic *A Thousand and One Nights*. It was camera-ready.

'Isn't it cosy, darling?'

Sitting cross-legged next to Daphne Houghton-Downe, Suzie Spinoza looked went on staring around her, and when she answered she found she'd been holding her breath since the minute she'd arrived here.

'It's out of this world,' she said with awe in her tone. 'It's strictly out of this world.'

Sitting a few places to her left, Mario Romano was amusing himself by counting the cost of the objects d'art that were ranged around the tent and on the table-cloth itself. Sheik Ahmed of Abu Talha was sitting in the middle of one side, among some fifty aides, retainers, bodyguards and guests, and in front of him stood the centrepiece: a cloisonné peacock and coach encrusted with precious stones, three feet high on a gilded base, presumably a gift from the late Shah of Iran. On each side of it stood the pieces of a solid silver George III candelabra suite in the rococo style, complemented by three silver soup toureens of the same reign with bold chasing, reeded handles and gadroon border design. In front of the guest of honour, the Lady Daphne Houghton-Downe, stood a Viennese rock crystal cornucopia with hand etching and a vermeil top and base, as tall as the Réné Lalique opalescent vase with lovebird motif that stood in front of Mario himself. The whole ensemble was a hotch-potch, because most of these things must have been gifts, and according to what Julius Ariche had told Mario, Sheik Ahmed was a bit of a magpie and treasured anything provided it was priceless – which Mario supposed didn't show a bad sense of value.

Mario was here as a guest because Julius had asked the Sheik to invite him. There'd been one or two occasions when the Levantine had requested the celebrity photographer to take some long-distance zoom-lens pictures of certain women, on the understanding that Mario named his own fee and didn't ask any questions. And it was here that Mario's own sense of values came into play. He knew why Ariche wanted the photographs: to show various clients as samples of his merchandise. But Mario also knew that these women stood the risk of being seized and shipped out of their native land, never to be seen again. He had therefore warned them, discreetly, to get as far away as possible from Monsieur Julius Ariche and his import-export operation. Three of them, so far, had taken the hint and got out so fast that the next time Monsieur Ariche had tried to ring them up the number had been indicated as no longer in service. There might come a time, of course, when Ariche would notice that the women Mario had photographed for him had seemed to vanish from the face of the earth. If that happened, Mario was going to buy himself a pearl-handled Walther 7–shot PPK .22 with a light alloy frame and sleep with it under his pillow.

Life on the French Riviera had its raw aspects, as Mario knew. Most of the guests here tonight were respectable – a handful of Swiss gnomes, a couple of world-class jewellers and two or three oil men from Texas. But the man sitting opposite Mario was of a different stamp. A millionaire arms-runner, his idea of a little fun was the taking of human life. He was one of the "big game" hunters who took a trip into Africa now and then and went on strictly private safari, organised by a group of entrepreneurs who undertook to act as beaters, driving a dozen or so jungle tribesmen out of the bush for the hunters to pick off with long-distance rifles. The fee was ten thousand US dollars a kill, including a quick getaway for the client from the scene by private plane.

This particular individual had developed his sense of fun in a different direction, by offering hard-up stunt-men a fee for public performances. Two months ago "Daredevil Dan" Mulligan of Oklahoma had pocketed a quarter of a million dollars for jumping off the roof of a Chicago hotel and falling three hundred feet into a twenty-foot high airbag, ostensibly promoting a campaign for anti-drug abuse ('because that's really one helluva trip,' as Dan told the press) and giving the crowd of spectators a cheap thrill by defying death. But only a few people knew that what his promoter was really paying for was the chance that Dan would miss, and hit the ground. Mario had been there to take pictures, and he'd seen the expression on the promoter's face when the stunt-man had safely hit the bag. Even multi-millionaires didn't like wasting money.

Compared to this funster, Mario might have been expected to consider Julius Ariche almost benevolent. He didn't. To Mario there was only one crime more heinous than killing a man, and that was abusing a woman. The idea of the gentle little Celeste's being kidnapped and transported to an 'eros centre' in West Germany or a harem in Marakesh would have aroused his own killer instincts. As he sipped his Dom Perignon champagne – which of course was being served only to the non-Arab guests – he looked around him at the company, deeply intrigued. He had a rough idea of what was going on here, because he'd been in the private salon at the Casino the evening when Ariche had gone trotting up to Daphne Houghton-Downe and presented a card. Tonight she was the guest of honour, seated directly opposite Sheik Ahmed – instead of at his right hand, where even his chief wife would never be placed. And the presence of Julius Ariche meant that the Sheik was looking for a new woman. But Daphne Houghton-Downe? Impossible. Unless she *agreed* to marry Ahmed, he'd never acquire her. Daphne's father was as rich as the Sheik, so there was no question of buying her through the services of Ariche, and if anyone tried kidnapping her they'd get shot down by her bodyguard, and if her bodyguard didn't draw in time and milady was seized and bundled into a Mercedes limousine with tinted windows there'd be a fuss big enough to bring down the price of crude Arabian oil to five US dollars a barrel and send the price of gold down the mines.

So what was the reason for this little dinner-party? Mario went on looking quietly around him, his interest mounting.

Exactly five places to his left, Suzie Spinoza was sitting cross-legged between Daphne Houghton-Downe and Lieutenant-Colonel Hassan El Sherif, chief aide-de-camp to Sheik Ahmed. He was courteously engaging the American girl in conversation while letting his dark eyes drift by chance to the soft shadows between her breasts, under the shining fabric of her dress.

'I had the pleasure of meeting her in London,' he was saying, 'in court.' He was speaking of the Lady Daphne.

'In court?' Suzie wondered whether to spoon the blob of rice off the cloth and back into the bowl or leave it there; eating in this position was tricky. 'What were you being charged with?'

'Charged with?'

'No, darling,' Daphne told her, 'he means he met me *at* court.'

'*At* court?'

'At Buck House.'

'Buck House?'

'Yes. Buckingham Palace. At a garden party.'

'Oh.' Suzie turned to Hassan. 'You did?'

'Did what?' He brought his glance up to her face just in time.

'Uh – you met her at Buck Palace? I mean House?'

'That's right,' he nodded, 'in court. *At* court.'

Suzie plied her gold spoon again, pulling her damascene bowl a bit nearer and not giving a damn what anyone thought because she'd had two glasses of champagne which for her was a whole night out and she was too dizzy to go on trying to keep up with a conversation in two different kinds of English while this guy risked losing his eyeballs down there between her boobs. This whole thing had gone to her head and she just wanted to try and *absorb* it while she toyed with her bowl of food (*were these things escargots or sheeps' eyes, and which would she much rather not have, for Christ's sake?*) This whole set-up had hit her for a home run and she wasn't sure how to handle it – the Kennedy Centre-sized marquee and the strange exotic smell of incense burning and these dusky masculine faces with their dark eyes smouldering just below flash-point, the eerie sound of piping from the three musicians squatting on the rug over there and the way these guys in their white silk robes moved around like tigers on heat, salaaming the Sheik and beckoning the servants and moving away again, two or three of them keeping their hands on their curved jewelled daggers like there was going to be a palace revolution any next minute. What was coming through to Suzie was the heavily-charged atmosphere of wealth, power and sex. She still wasn't long out of Memphis, Tennessee, and there was so much culture-shock spinning around in her mind that if Daphne hadn't been sitting right by her side she believed she might have suddenly decided to get her ass out of here before anyone had time to throw a dagger and pin her to the wall by her earlobe. And she wasn't quite sure even about Daphne, who'd once told her that the only reason she'd never been gang-raped was because she couldn't find a big enough gang.

Was this one big enough?

'A remarkable man.'

Suzie jumped half out of the gold lamé Jasper Conran dress that Daphne had given her to wear tonight.

'Pardon me?'

'I was just mentioning that he's a remarkable man.' It was the little guy in the sharp European-style suit sitting next to her, the one who'd come up to Daphne in the Casino that night. His name was Julius Ariche.

'Sure,' Suzie nodded quickly. 'Absolutely.' Which man was he talking about?

'It would be a mistake,' the soft modulated voice went on, 'for us to believe that just because these people are so immensely rich, they have nothing more than their wealth.'

So he was talking about the Sheik.

'How rich is he?' It had kind of popped right out of her mind, and she felt a flush of embarrassment. 'I mean it couldn't be less important, but – '

Julius Ariche allowed his large midnight-blue eyes to dwell on her for a moment. 'You don't think three billion dollars is important?'

Suzie tensed.

'No. *Billion*. With a "b." '

'With a "b"?' She could feel her eyes glazing over, and hoped he wouldn't notice. Three *thousand* million, sure – what a difference one little letter made. So putting up this whole Kennedy Centre-sized marquee had just been kind of like ordering a beach umbrella from Bloomingdale's. She suddenly realised she'd begun sweating, and hoped Mr Julius Ariche wouldn't notice that either.

'Some of these people,' he went on in his soft, confidential tone, 'are of course uncultured, as yet. Immensely rich, but uncultured. Sheik Ahmed of Abu Talha is not one of those. He is one of the world's most influential men – and here I'm not speaking of his wealth but of his well-known endowments of art museums, universities and medical centres. I'm sure you'll enjoy his conversation after the meal is finished – he knows America intimately.' He picked delicately at a fine bone from the dish in front of him.

'He looks – uh – a real interesting man.' Suzie felt an instant of triumph; in the last couple of days she'd finally got around to not saying 'guy' any more. Watching the Sheik across the banquet cloth she wondered what he'd look like in a tee-shirt and sneakers instead of this white silk robe with the gold trim and the tooled Moroccan sandals. Just as impressive, she thought. He had the kind of sculpted, eagle-like face that would make a Tennessee state trooper hesitate before giving him a speeding-ticket, whatever he was dressed in. She found his eyes on her again, and felt her stomach flip gently over as she looked right into their black, fathomless depths for a moment before she turned back to Mr

Ariche. She hadn't ever had that feeling before; from the time her boobs had gotten to be bigger than ping-pong balls she'd used her sex as a commodity, and the men who'd laid her had simply been customers, not people, and they'd been too busy staring at her boobs to look into her eyes. Just now, Sheik Ahmed of Abu Talha had been gazing right into her soul, from clean across the Sahara.

Suzie didn't really know now whether she might suddenly make up her mind to run for the door. She had the feeling it was already too late.

Mr Ariche was talking to her again, so softly that she had to lower her head to his. 'I should explain that my position *vis-à-vis* our host is rather special. I have the privilege of calling myself his friend and confidant, you see.' He lifted his large innocent eyes to Suzie's. 'So what I'm going to tell you is in the strictest confidence, you understand?'

'Sure.' Suzie began to feel nervous. The kind of confidence anyone offered you in this setup would probably rock the balance of power in the Middle East if you broke it.

'Tonight,' Mr Ariche said softly, 'your charming companion Lady Houghton-Downe is officially the guest of honour, as you know. This was made possible by the fact that she had met Sheik Ahmed socially before. It couldn't have been arranged had she been a stranger to him.' A slight frown wrinkled his brow. 'It would have been an unpardonable breach of etiquette. That is why I couldn't approach *you* the other night in the Casino. The invitation was therefore extended to Lady Daphne, but it was in fact *you*, Miss Spinoza, whom Sheik Ahmed wished me to bring here tonight as his guest of honour. You see – ' and Suzie had to bring her head so close to his that they almost touched – 'it is His Majesty's most earnest wish that you become his wife.'

15

A Table For Two

It was a few minutes after one in the morning when the specially-built Mercedes limousine left the Vista del Mar apartment building in La Condamine and moved at a moderate speed along the Boulevard Albert Premier. It was no longer followed at a prescribed distance by an escort car. The Principality of Monaco, despite the immense wealth of its residents and certain visitors, is a low-crime area, thanks in part to an alert and efficient police force, and even Julius Ariche, despite his obsession for security, felt safe there. It would in any case have required a fully-equipped commando unit to overcome the armoured strength of the limousine and its specially-trained crew.

The night was mild, and as the Mercedes took the left fork into the Avenue d'Ostende, Ariche pressed a button to lower one of the tinted windows so that he could see the moonlight spread in a sheet of molten silver across the sea, beyond the harbour lights. The evening had gone well for him, and he felt able to enjoy the simple pleasures that so often escape the very rich. Compared, of course, with the wealth of his host of this evening, Sheik Ahmed of Abu Talha, the assets of Julius Ariche were those almost of a pauper, able to call upon no more than ten or twelve million US dollars, including real estate. But he lacked no physical comfort.

Except for the love of a woman.

This was the hidden tragedy of Julius Ariche's life. Even the love of a man or an affectionate houseboy would have allowed Julius at least a semblance of sexual communion with his fellow creatures; but he knew nothing of carnal passion. He had been born, by ill fate, asexual. This would not have been so bad if, like a man born blind, he had no understanding of what sight meant. But in late twentieth-century society, whose naive and immature preoccupation with sex had spilled over into toothpaste advertisements, tee-shirts and bumper-stickers, Ariche was reminded almost every minute of his waking day that he lacked an aspect of life whose passion had inspired symphonies, cathedrals and lunar landings, and could also drive men mad, even to murder. Let a young and seductive woman with laughing eyes and a perfect smile, with breasts so tender that to touch them would inflame a man's hand, with loins so inviting that to bury himself there could cost him a marriage whose loss would leave him destroyed – let this young and seductive woman strip herself before the eyes of Julius Ariche, and he would see nothing more than a flower. A beautiful, scented, vibrant bloom that could appeal to the soul, but not to that heated and fiery nucleus of male creaturehood whose undeniable force had sired the human race on earth.

He would see only a flower. Something that could only be picked, and left to die. So Julius Ariche had grown to hate women, and since he could not have them, that was what he did with them. He picked them, and left them to die. Yet even then, even in his obsessive need for vengeance, there lay an irony that only his sadistic fates could have devised for him. He could pick these flowers only for other men.

Men like Sheik Ahmed of Abu Talha.

He'd been impetuous, as usual, and Ariche had had to exercise great patience. Despite his sophistication as an international tycoon, Sheik Ahmed had the emotions of a schoolboy when it came to women. It happened almost every year: he would see a pretty face in a crowd and become instantly smitten by calf-love, all over again. Though not *just* a pretty face – it had to have that exceptional, vital allure that Miss Spinoza possessed, with her heavy, curling locks of raven-black hair and those extraordinary eyes, a deep amber with flecks of gold in them, and that long firm mouth that could break suddenly into a smile so white and quick and generous that it caught you by surprise. Julius Ariche, who could see women only as flowers, would have compared this one to a tiger-lily. He supposed, as he gazed through the window of the limousine at the shimmering sea, that if he'd been born with the normal reactions of a man, Miss Spinoza would have started to drive him crazy, as crazy as she was driving Sheik Ahmed.

'But didn't you ask her?'

'No, Your Majesty. I simply *told* her that you wished to make her your wife. We mustn't rush her, you see. You are offering her an unimaginable honour, and for the moment she's confused.'

'If I ordered her seized, would there be . . . problems?'

'Devastating problems, Your Majesty, I can assure you.'

It took Ariche all of his tact and acumen to calm the man down. It hadn't helped, of course, when an hour before the first guests had begun leaving, that that little English nymphomaniac had almost dragged one of the Sheik's aides into an ante-room and come back five minutes later with her face flushed and her dress disarranged. Sheik Ahmed had noticed it, and Ariche had gone over quickly and urgently cautioned him. If the Sheik tried to drag Miss Spinoza behind those gold silk curtains he, Julius Ariche, could not guarantee the consequences.

But this was only to protect the deal. From Ariche's probing questions it seemed that the American girl was completely on her own in the world – 'I guess they're somewhere around,' she'd said when he'd asked discreetly about her parents. 'They got to be such a pain in the – uh – neck that I quit home pretty early, you know?' Her only friend appeared to be Lady Houghton-Downe, and here, certainly, there might have been problems if Sheik Ahmed had done anything against Miss Spinoza's will. Lady Daphne could go straight to the Palace here and obtain immediate and powerful aid; men of great wealth, like Sheik Ahmed, were respected in the Principality but they had to behave in a civilised manner.

What Ariche had needed to ensure was that the Sheik didn't seduce Miss Spinoza straight into marriage. That would have cost Ariche a cool five hundred thousand US dollars – the price he had decided to ask for this particular item of merchandise. She had to be bought, not seized or seduced before Ariche had time to impress on Sheik Ahmed how extraordinarily difficult it was to bring the American girl to the altar. One couldn't ask half a million dollars for a piece of trash that had been plundered by the Sheik's infamous horn behind the curtains.

He was to be here for two weeks, Ariche had been told. Ariche would therefore wait for three or four days and then contact Miss Spinoza again, this time for a private little talk in the palm-court of the Hotel de Paris, where he would detail the advantages of becoming the wife of his friend Sheik Ahmed of Abu Talha. He wouldn't say which wife. He would simply describe the assets the American girl would command – unlimited wealth, international recognition as the wife of a leading figure in the financial world, an entourage of her own personal servants and of course the undying love of a man beneath whose trappings of power there lay a capacity for tender devotion unmatched in the annals of romantic literature. There would be no mention of this same man's proclivity for outrageously deviant sexual practices among his wives, who aged so quickly that their sojourn in the harem was normally counted in months rather than years. She would not be warned, as she and Julius Ariche sipped their Earl Grey tea beneath the leaves of the palm-court in the Hotel de Paris, that if she attempted to flee the harem or the palace in Abu Talha she would be caught and thrashed; or that if she in fact succeeded in escaping the palace she would never reach the frontier, but would be abandoned by the Sheik and thrown to whatever secret police chief had caught and arrested her, to use as he pleased.

This had happened many times, as Julius Ariche had discovered during his difficult and exhaustive research into the background of his client. Of the seven women – three of them French, two English and two West German – who had tried to make contact with the outside world through their embassies, five had ended up as the victims of 'traffic accidents' after having been forced to supply the needs of an entire secret police barracks, and two of them had taken their own lives, one by saturating her robes with gasoline and setting herself ablaze.

To earn his fee, Julius Ariche must tempt, entice and inveigle the pretty little American girl into a willing agreement to go through a legal form of marriage with Sheik Ahmed of Abu Talha. Despite the Sheik's impetuous wish to press matters, he would better enjoy the slower process of infatuating his intended bride – through the good offices of Julius Ariche – with his wealth, his power and his manly charms. She must at first be confused, then dazzled, then perhaps allowed a period of modest hesitation, then finally overwhelmed by the honour, the position and the riches that would be spread at her feet, given her slightest word.

As the limousine turned off the Avenue de Monte-Carlo into the Place du Casino – where only a short time ago Prince Edouard de Montigny-Villiers had met his death – Ariche pressed the button again to close the window, his thoughts brooding on the days ahead. He expected all to go smoothly, but if for any reason Miss Spinoza decided to deny herself the title of Sheika, she would be seized clandestinely and shipped to the palace in Abu Talha in any case, and would never be heard of again. That much was certain.

* * *

'Now tell me if anything here appeals to you, Linda.' He glanced up quickly from the leather-bound menu. 'I may call you Linda?'

'Of course.' She held the gaze of his bright, curious eyes for an instant, wondering what she was doing here in the Belle Epoque Restaurant at the Hotel Hermitage, and what she was doing here with the Compte de Beauvais. She'd been aware that when he'd come across the lawn of the Chateau two days ago Princess Charlotte had made a point of introducing them. But she hadn't expected him to follow up with an invitation to dinner.

'They do the duck rather well here, and of course the filet. Take your time.'

She couldn't see anything but French on the menu. She didn't care for duck; did he mean steak when he said filet? She was aware that as she tried to seize on a familiar French word here and there, the Count was watching her in the lamplight. OK, that happened. But he hadn't asked her out to dinner just because he found her attractive, had he? He was still fairly young, maybe forty or so, but with his grooming and the cut of his suit and the wafer-thin gold watch and the diamond cuff-links he just radiated class – and money. Maybe success would be a better word for it; maybe he hadn't been born rich but had used this energy – which he also radiated – to get right to the top in his field before he was even middle-aged. He wasn't the type that Linda had met very often, and she could be wrong, but she didn't think he spent many of his evenings dating almost complete strangers.

'I'd like some chicken, I think, M'sieur le Compte.' She was beginning to enjoy some of what Bibi called 'forms of address.' There was an old-fashioned courtesy about them she found kind of appealing.

'The chicken's excellent, yes. But please call me Michel, won't you?'

'OK.' She smiled for the first time, and saw his eyes soften.

'Mademoiselle would like the *Sauté de Poulet de Bresse*,' he told the waiter, 'and I would like the *Filet de Saint Pierre – saignant, s'il vous plâit*. And shall we start with some caviar? Or smoked salmon? Oysters?'

'I'd like some soup, if – '

'Of course.' He glanced up at the waiter. 'Perhaps the *Fermière*, Bernard.'

'*Bien sûr, M'sieur le Compte. C'est parfait.*'

Michel de Beauvais handed him the menu and looked back at

the young woman sitting opposite him at the table. 'She's deceptively attractive,' he thought. She didn't have those *outré*, flamboyant looks of the starlets and the front-page models and the high-class mistresses who absorbed flashlight with their dazzling smiles. You had to look twice at this young lady before your attention was caught; and then it became difficult to look away. Maybe it was just her eyes, their unusual colouring – a blue so intense that it was a kind of luminosity – her eyes and what shone out of them, what was it exactly? Perhaps nothing *exactly*, but a mixture of sympathy, compassion, human warmth – and behind it all a hint of vulnerability, of confusion, that touched him strangely. She was a nurse, of course, and very experienced; she'd therefore be capable, cool-headed and courageous in the presence of traumas, accident victims and the routine unpleasantness of tending the sick; but there was nothing of this in her face, in her eyes. She'd somehow managed to remain gentle, to retain her special grace. She intrigued him, and he was even amused by the idea that someone who knew him well might happen to see them sitting here together in the lamplight, *tête-à-tête*. The word would fly around the office in Paris: de Beauvais had been seen dining out in Monte-Carlo *with a young lady!* Yet it wasn't that young ladies didn't have any appeal for him – he was just too busy.

'You should get yourself married,' one of his partners had told him a while ago. 'Life isn't all work, you know.'

'And when would I find the time to see anything of my wife?'

'You'd have to *make* time.'

'My God, if anyone could find out how to *make* time, he'd make a fortune!'

And even now he wouldn't have been sitting here with Mademoiselle Terman if it hadn't been for Princess Charlotte and her extraordinary suggestion. *There is a certain enterprise that has your interest, I know*, she had told him. *And it's in my power to arrange matters so that you would achieve the greater part of your ambitions within a short time. I'm sorry to have to put these things so mysteriously, Michel, but I need to protect certain people, and to keep others at bay. This can't be done openly, I'm afraid; there's too much at stake.*

She'd only been able to tell him, then, what he would have to do. She couldn't tell him *why*.

'Let me explain, Linda,' he said when the entrée arrived, 'why I have asked you to share this evening with me. I must say at once that I'm most grateful – we're virtually strangers, and you could easily have refused.' He broke another piece of his roll, let a crumb fall onto the cloth and put it with great care onto the plate. His face was serious now. 'I simply wished to know your opinion on Princess Charlotte's state of health. That's to say . . . what you believe her chances are of . . . remaining with us into the New Year. I find Dr Chirac difficult to talk to – he's so frustrated she won't submit to all his rather desperate measures to keep her alive.'

It wasn't of course why he'd asked her here at all, but it was the most plausible reason he could think of.

'It's not easy for me either,' Linda said in a moment. 'Life and death aren't that predictable. It's like I told Jacques – Prince Jacques,' she corrected herself quickly. 'I think that once the Princess has gotten her affairs in order, she'll just let go.'

'You mean she'd will herself to die, once she was ready?'

'No, that's putting it too strong. They will themselves to live, sure, till they settle their affairs, and then it's just an easy kind of letting go. I've seen it so many times.' She put her hand quickly over her glass as the waiter made to pour her some more wine. 'And in this patient's case there's even a positive reason for letting go. She wants to join her husband.'

'So I believe.' He let his eyes remain on hers for a moment. 'For someone so young, Linda, you've seen a great deal of life. Of its dark side.'

'It isn't really so dark – it depends on how much light we can shed. Sometimes it's the patient who does it for us – you know – very often they'll seem to reach right out there where the rest of us can't go, and grab a whole philosophy and then show it to us. It can sometimes blow our minds.'

'They reach "right out there." Where?'

'Oh, some kind of beyond, I guess.'

'There's a lot more,' he said slowly, 'to nursing, then, than – ' he gave a little shrug.

'Than those famous bedpans,' Linda smiled ruefully. 'Yes. Yes, there is.' She realised he'd changed the subject in the last few minutes, from Princess Charlotte's life expectancy to her own career.

'And you've told Jacques – Prince Jacques,' he said, not looking at her now, 'what you've just told me, is that right? That his mother will go when she feels ready?'

Linda suddenly began paying attention. He'd changed the subject again – and he'd noticed the way she'd corrected herself a minute ago.

'Yes,' she said, and waited.

'He's a most attractive young man.' Michel de Beauvais was watching her now.

'He's . . . he's having a rough time. I think I'm able to help him a little.' She looked down, making a pretence of enjoying the chicken. *So what was going on?* Michel had suddenly brought Jacques back into the conversation. Why was he interested? Did he know anything about – the way they were?

Had Bibi said anything?

She reached for her wine glass, but it was empty.

'Let me – ' Michel said quickly, and poured her some more.

'Thanks, I – it's so good, isn't it?' But when she glanced up at him she saw he wasn't taken in. Was her face flushing? It happened sometimes, and there was every reason for it to be happening now. She'd already got herself into the classic trap that always gave lovers away – she just hadn't been able to keep Jacques out of the conversation, and now he was in it she wanted to go on talking about him all evening.

She sensed danger suddenly.

'I'm sure you're helping Prince Jacques,' Michel said easily, 'just as you're helping Princess Charlotte. She's grown quite fond of you in the short time you've been here, did you know?'

'She compliments me on my nursing skills.'

He watched her steadily, his right hand fretting at the stem of his wine glass. 'That's not quite what I said.'

Linda thought quickly before she spoke. What did he mean? Was this some kind of trap? She'd started feeling she was under interrogation. 'A lot of times there's a growing bond of sympathy between the patient and the nurse. I – I have a great admiration for *Madame la Princesse*. She never complains, even when I know she's in pain.'

Michel de Beauvais inclined his head, and Linda sensed again that her words were being carefully analysed. All she knew about this man was that he was one of Princess Charlotte's financial advisers, but that could mean quite a lot – he'd be one of the few people who knew the life of the Chateau intimately, and possibly most of its secrets.

'And what would please you for dessert, Linda?' He was smiling again, the charming host, beckoning their waiter for the menu. 'Some crêpes? Patisseries? A sorbet?'

'I guess I'll just have some coffee.'

The waiter leaned over her. 'Expresso, Mademoiselle? Cappuccino? Turkish?'

'Just – uh – regular.'

'Some excellent café Français, Mademoiselle, but of course.'

Linda said no to a liqueur. She was technically on call for her patient at any time; private nursing was different from the routine of a hospital. She never left the Chateau without telling someone exactly where she was going, and giving them a telephone number as a backup to the beeper she always carried. She'd had a glass and a half of wine this evening but her head was perfectly clear, and Michel de Beauvais' probing questions were keeping her on the alert.

'It must have been quite a decision for you, Linda. I mean to leave your home country and make such a long journey.' He swirled the cognac in the big balloon glass, inhaling the fumes. 'This is your first trip to Europe, I think you said?'

'Yes, I – yes, it was quite a big decision.'

'And there must have been quite a lot of – shall I say – competition for the post.'

'Absolutely. At first I thought I'd just been lucky.'

She studied him while his eyes were lowered for a moment, trying to make up her mind to go for some kind of break-through; she had the gut-feeling that this evening she'd come closer suddenly to the truth of things. Michel sipped his cognac, the light reflected from its surface playing on his small intelligent eyes. He looked somehow out of place here; Linda could see him better behind one of those huge polished tables in a boardroom, doodling with a gold pencil as he listened to the chairman. But then of course he'd *be* the chairman, of his own company: according to Bibi he was a big wheel in international estate management. So what was he doing here tonight, playing host to a registered nurse of all people? She was certain now that he hadn't decided to spend the evening with her just to ask about her patient's condition – he could have drawn her aside for a few minutes at the Chateau for that.

'At first you thought – ?' His eyes were on hers suddenly, and for a moment she couldn't remember what she'd said.

'I – uh – just thought I'd been lucky. To get the job.'

'And then – ?'

Linda hesitated, then plunged. 'And then I began wondering, and asking myself a whole lot of questions.' Without stopping now she told him everything that was on her mind – that somehow she'd got this job even though there must have been a hundred highly-competent nurses available along the French Riviera, and even though there'd certainly been at least a hundred others who'd applied from New Jersey.

'The position was only advertised in New Jersey?' Michel was watching her intently now.

'Only at my own hospital there, as far as I know.'

'As far as you know.' He leaned forward with his arms on the table, the diamond in his gold ring sparking in the light. 'The advertisement wasn't in some widely-circulated newspaper or newsletter?'

'It could have been, yes, but then it would have made the odds even greater, wouldn't it?' She too was leaning forward, believing he could help her – unless he'd brought her here tonight to find out how much *she* knew. Or how little.

Michel inclined his head. 'Certainly. But after all, *one* applicant had to be finally accepted, and I can well believe your qualifications are of a very high order.'

'Thank you, but that just isn't so. I mean, sure, I'm qualified and experienced and my record's pretty good, but I wouldn't stand out in a crowd that big. And here's the clincher – I didn't send in my application right away, because I thought I'd be kind of running out on my hospital. It was a whole week before my supervisor persuaded me to apply, and there must have been a great many applications sent in before then.'

'And rejected.'

'Right. And rejected.'

He glanced down for a moment at his polished nails, and Linda watched him. There must be a whole lot of thoughts flashing through the head of a man like this; it was like watching a computer. Then he looked up again.

'Your own application must have been exceptional, then, in some way. Better written, better phrased . . .'

'No, Michel.' She found it easier to use his first name now; she felt he was on her side. 'I'm not a writer. I just put down the facts.'

'I see.' His brow was wrinkled for a moment, then it cleared, and he looked into Linda's eyes with an expression of something close to revelation. Maybe he was going to say something, but she couldn't wait.

'There's another strange thing, Michel. Quite apart from anything else, I've been getting a distinct and rather . . . rather creepy feeling that I've been here before. Here on this coast.'

For a moment he went on gazing at her face; then he spoke very softly.

'I think perhaps you have.'

16

THE TELEPHONE CALL

THERE WAS FIRELIGHT in the room, sending shadows fluttering across the ceiling and reflections from the silver champagne-cooler and Daphne's diamond earrings. She was sitting on a velvet-covered stool near the hearth, giving herself a manicure; her diaphanous nightgown had fallen around her waist, and her slight breasts were rose-tinted by the light of the flames.

'This is much cosier than some ghastly hotel down in the town, isn't it darling?'

Suzie Spinoza was in her pyjamas, standing by the big gold-framed mirror between the fireplace and the four-poster bed, her hands stroking the moulded frame. She'd been prowling round the room like a cat in a new house.

'*Cosier?*' she said with a little laugh, 'Jesus, it's absolutely incredible. Is this real gold?'

Daphne glanced up, thinking how boyish Suzie looked in her pyjamas. 'Gold leaf. Come by the fire, darling, you'll freeze to death over there.' Mademoiselle Pinalle had told her the central heating was giving trouble; it was always the same with these bloody chateaux.

Suzie came slowly over and sat on her haunches on the rug, clasping her knees and leaning back, her dark head tilted. She was quiet for so long that Daphne looked up from her nails, to catch Suzie glancing away. The quietness went on, with only the soft popping of sparks from among the logs and the call of an owl somewhere; and this time when Suzie looked up again she found Daphne watching her. Neither smiled; the moment seemed too intense for that.

'You know something?' Suzie said at last, but didn't finish, just shaking her head a little and closing her eyes. 'I guess I'm not used to champagne.'

'Was that what you were going to say?' Daphne sat very still, the emery-board between her finger and thumb.

Suzie's eyes came open a little; she looked drowsy, lulled.

'Going to say?' She shook her head again. 'No. I was just going to say you turn me on.'

'Oh.' Daphne laughed softly. 'How nice.' The quietness drew out again until she asked, 'Do you want to do anything about it?'

Suzie let out a breath and buried her head against her knees. 'Christ, I don't know. I don't think so.'

After what seemed a long time she heard Daphne taking the bottle of champagne and pouring some into their glasses.

'Have a little more bubbly, darling.'

An ember tumbled, sending light flaring against their bodies.

'I've had too much already.' Suzie was looking up at her friend. It was the first time she'd thought of this rich, neurotic English girl as her friend, despite all the things Daphne had done for her, all the things she'd given her. It had been too one-sided for friendship, and maybe it still was, but now the friendship was kind of breaking through. She took her glass and gazed into the yellow bubbles.

'Cheers,' Daphne said.

'Yeah. I guess it's just that – ' Suzie broke off, then drank a little, sinking herself into her shoulders and pressing her knees tighter together, feeling the cold of the room at last on the side away from the fire, or feeling something else that she couldn't identify. 'I've never made it, you see, with anyone I've liked. Not with a friend. They've all been just – you know – clients.' She shuddered suddenly. 'I was a hooker. OK?'

'You mean a tart?'

'I guess.' With sudden anger she said – 'I fucked for money.'

Daphne was leaning closer, her small breasts filling. 'We've all got to do it for *some* reason.'

Suzie stared up at her. 'You never did it for money.'

'Well, no.'

'Then you must have done it for love.' She drew back as Daphne gave a sudden trilling laugh that set her nerves on edge. She remembered how, at the sheik's party, Daphne had gone off somewhere with one of the men, and come back looking so strange, sitting down next to Suzie smelling of sex and with her dress down across one shoulder, her face drawn and haunted-looking until Suzie had asked her if she was OK, and then she'd thrown her blonde head back and flashed that dazzling Marilyn Monroe smile.

'No, darling, I've never done it for *love* . . .' She finished her champagne and flung the glass into the fireplace, where it smashed and sent bright splinters glittering among the flames, one of them glancing back and pricking her bare shoulder, breaking the skin. 'I've only ever done it because I had to get there – ' she was staring at Suzie with her smoke-blue eyes far away in some other place – 'to get there before *she* did.'

A drop of blood was seeping from the cut on her shoulder, and Suzie licked the tip of her finger and wiped it away. It was kind of typical, with Daphne, the drop of blood; she had such a cool, milk-clear body with perfect skin, but she was always damaging it. The first night Suzie had ever seen this girl naked she'd noticed the red raw bruises on her back; she hadn't realized then that Daphne must have been under some guy up there on deck, humping. That was the night she'd broken down and cried in Suzie's arms. *Hold me tight . . . help me keep out the night . . .* Was it some kind of problem she had? Fuck and freak out?

'Before *she* did?' Suzie asked hesitantly.

She saw Daphne's eyes come all the way back to the present. 'What? I had a sister. Sandra. I hated her. She was so like you.'

The silence came in like a cold wave, washing from wall to wall and leaving Suzie shivering, drawing back, her breath held for so long that she felt close to drowning, to being drowned. It didn't sound like her own voice when she said, 'She was like me?' She felt tears starting, and couldn't believe it. She hadn't cried since she was just a little kid.

'What?' Daphne had been away again on another trip and now she was back, and remembering what she'd been saying. She slipped off the velvet stool and knelt on the rug, throwing her pale arms around Suzie and holding her so hard that it hurt – 'Oh my God, oh my God, I didn't mean it that way, Suzie, not that way, no – ' and there were tears again on Suzie's face, and not her own – 'I love you, my darling, I love you with all my heart, you've got to understand that, *please* . . . you've got to understand . . .'

They stayed together like that for a long time, while Suzie's thoughts crept slowly back to before the time when Daphne had said what she had, about hating. So it was OK now, but it had been a real shaker, and had left her kind of numbed. Something had happened to her that had never happened before, even when she was a kid and Dad had screamed at her all the time, *you wear them white shorts to school again an' I'll tan your goddamned little ass 'til there ain't nuthin' left of it*, because he'd wanted to screw her, she'd realized later, and didn't dare, and couldn't bear to think of the boys at her school looking at her little white shorts and wanting to put their hands up them . . . even when Mom had told her every time she came home so hungry she could have chewed on a chair-leg, *I just ain't got the time to fix you anythin', Suzie, I got these two jobs goin'*, her white drained face not even able to look at her, *why don't you see if you can hustle your Dad for a buck an' then go find a MacDonald's or someplace?*

There'd been nobody who loved her, so it hadn't made any difference when they'd bawled her out all the time, her Mom and Dad and the teacher and everyone, she'd finally learned not to give a shit. But just now when she'd realised she'd found a friend who really meant something for the first time in her life, and then Daphne had said about hating her, or it had sounded that way . . . it had been like a bucket of freezing water right in her face, and then there was the other feeling, just after, of losing someone she'd only just started to be friendly with . . . Jesus, it had been a real double whammy . . .

She held onto Daphne, just as hard as Daphne was holding onto her, and after a while they drew away from each other and Daphne went over and got some tissues and they both had a good blow and Suzie picked up her glass and poured out some champagne and gave it to Daphne first and then drank the rest of it herself.

'You know something? I'm going to get smashed clean out of my mind.'

'Then we'll need another bottle, darling.' She gave a shaky laugh.

'Are you kidding? Just one more glass is going to do it for me.'

Later, holding each other again under the lavender-smelling sheets and blankets of the huge cold bed, Daphne filled the rest of it in for her, or some of it. Claudia was actually a step-sister, as dark in her colouring as she was fair, and she'd looked so like Suzie, with the same flecked honey-coloured eyes and the same mop of thick black hair – 'She was terribly pretty, darling, just like you.' But Claudia had been five years older, and had got everything first and done everything first, riding her own horse for the first time, driving her own car, discovering sex with a boy on the stairs at a Christmas party – 'They did it all the time after that

– I heard them from behind doors and in one of the stables and the back of the Rolls – it drove me absolutely mad, and one day I managed to watch them through a keyhole, and that was when I started to play with myself, just so that I could make that fantastic fuss that *she* was making, crying out and everything. I got quite furious when I didn't get the feeling, even though I rubbed and rubbed at myself till it bled. It was *beastly*, and I just hated her guts for years and years.' In a moment, and more quietly, she said, 'And then she died, still quite young.'

She began shivering, and Suzie held her tight until it was over, watching the last of the firelight across the high frescoed ceiling as the embers died. When Daphne spoke again her voice was very soft, though it sounded to Suzie that there wasn't any feeling in it now; it was like she was reciting something she'd learned by heart.

'And then of course I was old enough to realise it had just been a case of sibling rivalry, and perfectly normal, and I began feeling absolutely rotten, and wished I hadn't hated her so much – or hated her at all.' She stirred against Suzie, and warmth came back into her voice. 'When I first saw you, sitting at that table on the ship, it was like seeing Claudia again. That's why I asked you to join us. And although you're really quite different from Claudia, I started thinking about her again, and it all came together, and I began feeling the love for you that I should have felt for her, do you see? That's why I need you so.'

It was almost three in the morning before Suzie could get to sleep. The champagne had left her stimulated, and she lay awake thinking about what Daphne had told her, and trying to figure it out. It explained a lot of things – why she didn't want Suzie to leave her, for instance; it would be like Claudia dying all over again, with nobody left to love. She almost wished Daphne hadn't explained, or tried to explain – it was kind of like being a stand-in for a ghost. And she felt there was something more to it, something she hadn't been told, something that maybe she could never be told. It was just an impression, but Suzie trusted it. Maybe she couldn't ever expect to hear the whole truth from someone as mixed up as Daphne, with her terrific amount of money and her feverish obsession for laying any man who was around, and that lost, haunted look that came to her face that she had to cover up with her sudden show-girl smile.

Suzie was beginning to think it hadn't been all bad, being treated like shit by her Mom and Dad and then humping for bucks at the truck-stops to earn some kind of a living; at least it hadn't screwed her up like the poor little rich kid lying beside her in the big four-poster bed. A couple of times when Suzie had turned over, Daphne had reached out for her, half-asleep, like a frightened child; so Suzie had put her arms around her again and kind of rocked her back to sleep. This was what she was beginning to love about her friend the English girl – her need of Suzie. It gave her a little confidence, a little dignity, so she didn't feel so bad about being just a shit-kicking little trucker's whore from Tennessee.

She hadn't told Daphne about what had happened at the dinner party with the sheik. It had sounded so crazy, and she didn't want her friend to laugh. But in the morning, when the sunshine was coming through the shutters and they'd had breakfast – croissants and caviar sent up on a silver tray, OK? OK! – she took the risk, and told Daphne what the little guy – the little man had said: that Sheik Ahmed of Abu Someplace wanted to marry her. It didn't make the kind of waves she'd expected.

'Oh, they're *always* doing *that*, darling!'

'You mean he wasn't serious?' She felt let down; suddenly.

Daphne was brushing her long fair hair with a silver brush, and some loose hairs drifted down across a sunbeam. 'Of course he was being serious! That little party was thrown for *you* – it was obvious. Ahmed couldn't keep his eyes off you. I thought you realised.'

'It wasn't my usual kind of scene.' Suzie hesitated, then asked in a small voice, 'So do you think I should?'

'Should what, darling?'

'Marry him.' And now that they were actually talking about it and Daphne had said the sheik had meant it seriously the whole idea suddenly burst upon Suzie like a Fourth of July firework show.

Marry a billionaire sheik?

'Well,' Daphne said thoughtfully, 'one does hear so much about those people – I mean kinky sex and masterful ways and so on; but perhaps they're more civilised these days. After all, they buy places like Harrods and play polo and everything.' The silver-backed hairbrush flashed in the sunlight. 'But I'm not really sure an *American* would find that kind of life acceptable.'

'An American?'

'Yes, your ideas about freedom and independence and women's

rights. The clever thing to do is to marry him and then apply for divorce – you'd probably find plenty of good reasons – but make sure you do it in a Western country, where a sheik can't throw his weight about. That's what Dena did.'

'Who?' Suzie found herself getting short of breath. They'd finished talking about whether she ought to marry one of the richest men in the world, and now they were discussing the divorce.

'Dena al-Fassi. She sued for divorce in California and asked for half her husband's estate, which was estimated at six billion dollars. She only got about half a billion, but that wasn't a *complete* disaster, was it?'

'Jesus.' Suzie stared at her. 'How do you know things like that?'

'I was at school with Dena, and I'm always bumping into her at the dress shows.' She looked into the huge gilt-framed mirror. 'You know I really ought to get my hair shortened, but I don't know anyone on the Côte d'Azur who can do it.' She put down the brush and turned quickly in a little pirouette. 'Why don't you just wait a few days, darling, and see if Ahmed gets in touch again? That's what I'd do.'

The same evening, Toinette Cavaille was sitting on the balcony of the guest suite in the same wing of the Chateau, the tears drying on her face as the last of the daylight faded from the sky. The scent of the roses in the garden below was still on the air, and crickets sang in the gloom. She would never smell roses again without thinking of Charlotte. Toinette had come here to be near her sister while the last agonising days drew out, and she hadn't expected it to be easy; but sometimes she thought that if the choice were ever hers she'd like to go out with a plane crash, quickly and with no time to think, with no time for others to grieve so interminably.

Since the new nurse had come, taking over from that little Swiss martinet, Charlotte had even rallied, and gone downstairs to meet people. Toinette had felt a leap of hope, and had started thinking of miracles; but Dr Chirac had made it quite clear. Nothing had changed. It was a question of waiting.

As she came in from the balcony the fluted brass telephone was ringing.

'Hello?'

'Toinette.'

She was surprised, alerted. Raoul didn't normally telephone until Friday, to let her know which plane he was catching from Geneva; this week he'd already phoned from London and Paris, and had sounded tense. Now it was Thursday, and again she heard the tension in his voice.

'Raoul – are you all right?'

In a moment he said, 'Yes. But I'm tired. I'll be on the Swissair flight tonight arriving at Nice at 7:40.'

'All right.' Raoul, *tired?* She'd never heard him say that before. 'I'll be here.'

She rang for a maid and asked for some thin toast, just a hint of butter, no *confiture*. She was starving, and wouldn't be able to last out until dinner time now that she had Raoul to worry about. She already weighed too little but was trying to lose more, never riding less than a full hour in the park every day and most of the time at a gallop. Raoul liked her to be lean, athletic, highly-strung, and she wanted to please him, to fuel those fires of his that she couldn't live without, that were burning her life away on her own self-chosen funeral pyre.

Just before eight o'clock she went into the bathroom and took the Heinlich ring from its antiseptic fluid and rinsed it, inserting it deeply, shuddering at its chill, at its alien, mechanical shape inside her flesh. Then she opened the shutters and the french windows, even though it brought the cold night air into the room, and began listening for the engine-note of the Lamborghini and the rhythmic shrilling of its tyres on the mountain bends.

Her body was already responding to his approach through the night out there, her nipples hardening, tingling, the wetness coming between her legs. *But what if, for the first time in their life together, he were too tired?* Would it be a relief, not to be seized, bruised, plundered? Or would it leave her with a craving that would drive her mad within an hour?

17

AT THE HOTEL D'ANTOINE

BOARDING SWISSAIR FLIGHT 320 at Geneva, Raoul Cavaille hesitated as a stewardess took his fur-lined overcoat to stow for him, and thought of turning back, of seeing Szala again, *demanding* to see him.

'*Voilà votre place, M'sieur Cavaille.*'

He looked at the stewardess for an instant with his face blank. No, there was no point in going back. Szala wouldn't see him. *There is nothing to be done*, Szala had said.

'*Merci, Suzette.*' Most of them knew each other in the first class section of these flights; Genêve-Côte-d'Azur was almost a commuter line.

Nothing, Szala had told him, sitting there with his enormous bulk overflowing the arms of the chair, his thick, fleshy hands lying motionless on the desk, his colourless eyes glinting within their pouches, cold, reptilian. *There is nothing to be done. We can only wait. And you, my good friend, can only hope.*

George Szala was the only man whom Raoul feared. Turning the scales at more than twenty-nine stone, so obese at thirty-four years of age that it robbed him of breath merely to walk to the dinner-table, George Szala, part-Swiss, part-German, part-English and Oxford-educated, was the personification of one of man's most repulsive vices: greed. This was not why Cavaille feared him. He feared him because Szala, in his need to satisfy his greed, recognised no considerations of humanity, charity or even mercy. If anyone became a threat to him in his business life – he had no other – or even came close to jeopardising his position, Szala would cut them down – *had* cut them down, three of them in the last four years to Raoul's knowledge: Monteith, Kleinhoffer, Lucchese. Monteith had been sent down for twenty years at the Old Bailey in London for fraud and had hanged himself in his cell within a week of starting his sentence. Kleinhoffer had been found in his apartment in Bonn, slumped in the shower with the air still sharp from cyanide fumes. Lucchese had fallen from the platform of the metro in Rome, in his hand a note reading *Francesca, my heart of hearts, I shall wait for you.*

There was nothing ever criminal in Szala's treatment of those who became a threat to him. They had made mistakes; they had played with fire, perhaps; or they had failed to meet their obligations at one of the major stock exchanges. Sometimes they needed only a little time, a little patience; sometimes they would beg Szala for a second chance, offering exorbitant compensation once they were on their feet again, the kind of chance that was commonly granted a business associate in the world of international finance where if one fell, many might fall. But Szala cut them down, because his greed was based, as all greed is based, on fear, on insecurity – so that he *had* to do it, just as a snake strikes when it is threatened.

Raoul Cavaille, as he lowered himself into the chair that George Szala had courteously offered him, reflected the man's fear, because Raoul had come close to threatening his position.

'You were too ambitious, my good friend.' Szala spoke educated English, but fruitily, like a well-fed bishop, because of his huge chest and his plump, fleshy mouth. 'Ambition is laudable, in my opinion, but – '

'Tell me what happened.' Raoul, half this man's size and with energy vibrating in him like discordant music, looked small, tense, dangerous. He cut Szala short because otherwise he would pontificate, as always. To have arrived before even middle-age at the head of an organisation – International Commodities Trust – which owned banks, exchanges and financial research corporations was probably the cause of his pathological obesity, it was thought; self-induced stress had driven him to an insatiable appetite for food. It had also led him to lecture his business associates on their moral shortcomings. This might have been merely tiresome if it hadn't always preceded his decision to cut them down.

'The Merchant Guaranty Trust in Jersey has been ordered to cease operations pending official enquiries.' Szala waited, a strange light coming into his small unblinking eyes as he watched the blood leaving Raoul Cavaille's face. 'Henry Simpson has been arrested but within two days will be freed on bail, thanks to my intercession.' His bulk leaned forward an inch. 'Would you care for some coffee?'

Raoul didn't hear the question. He was already computing the situation, the damage done, the ways out, the legal considerations involved and above all the danger from Szala, the appalling danger from Szala.

'And Deutsche Eurotrust?' he asked, his throat tight.

Szala leaned back again, his immense arms lying across the desk like felled timber. 'Deutsche Eurotrust is of course implicated. Critically implicated. So is Lausanne Affiliates Insurance, and so is Taiwan Textile. And so are you, my good friend.'

Aware of the smell of shoe polish, Cavaille got up and paced restlessly; a cab had splashed him a little as he'd got out of his limousine and he'd asked for a shoe-shine at the hotel. The odd thought went through his mind that whenever he smelled shoe polish again he would remember this day, this hour.

'Taiwan will ask for time,' he said, and turning, found Szala's monstrous head tilted watchfully towards him like one rock balanced on another.

'People always ask for time. They let time run out and then they ask for more. But there is never any more.'

In a moment Cavaille asked in a strained voice, 'Will you close Taiwan Textile?'

'No. I will *fore*close *on* them.' He watched Cavaille flinch.

'Lausanne would be able to carry us through for a few months, until the enquiry – '

'Carry *you*, perhaps. Not me. I'm not personally implicated, after all. Nor is International Commodities Trust. At the moment I'm in the clear.' He waited until Cavaille stopped pacing and looked down. 'And of course I intend to remain in the clear. And to remain in the clear I shall need to initiate immediate action.'

'Taiwan.'

Szala appeared to consider, though Cavaille knew he was simply pausing for effect. Szala had considered everything before he'd called him in here. 'Taiwan, yes. And Zurich Bullion.'

Cavaille moved across to the enormous redwood desk and stood poised over it, staring into the little eyes buried deep in their pouches. At this moment Cavaille, his black pin-striped jacket open and thrown back, his hands on his hips and his head thrust forward like an eagle with its wings held open in the attack posture, might have seemed able to offer force against the man at the desk, to match threat for threat. But he was powerless and they both knew it; it was the primitive man reacting, not the sophisticated financier.

'Zurich Bullion would have to file for bankruptcy if you moved in on them,' he told Szala.

'Yes.'

'There'd be twenty thousand creditors. Twenty-five.'

'Twenty-two thousand, three hundred. Yes.'

'With claims in the region of a hundred and fifty million Swiss francs.'

'Two hundred and four million. Yes.'

Cavaille went on staring at him for a moment and then swung away from the desk, unwilling to face any longer the fat, monstrous shape of his own personal Nemesis. And what about Henkel, of Zurich Bullion?

Henkel would shoot himself. A year ago when he'd told Cavaille about the US-linked money-laundering operation he was setting up, Cavaille had warned him, but he'd brushed it off, pulling a drawer of his desk open and showing Cavaille the revolver. 'I have my insurance,' he'd said lightly. That wasn't insurance, Cavaille had told him. 'My escape route, then.' Henkel had worked in the French Resistance as a young man; for him a bullet through the brain was the answer to everything.

'I'm not implicated,' Cavaille said as he swung back to look at Szala, 'in terms of criminality.'

'No. But you are implicated.'

Cavaille drew a quick breath. 'How long will you give me?'

Szala looked pained. 'Always the same question. But surely you must have got wind of this before I telephoned you?'

'Yes. I flew straight to Paris, then London.'

'Ah.' A faint smile. 'Trying to put out the fire.' The smile grew larger, fleshier, and a sibilance began rising from the plump mouth, like wind escaping from a balloon, at first in little gusts and then bigger ones, until the body itself started shaking, its flesh heaving and wobbling inside the Savile Row suit as the small piggy eyes squeezed shut and the repulsive sound went on escaping as Cavaille watched, sickened. When he couldn't stand it any longer he turned away and stood facing the corner windows, where drizzle clouded the glass. When the loathsome sounds behind him died away he turned again and found Szala wiping his eyes with a white silk handkerchief. 'Rushing about,' he said in small piping tones, 'trying to put out the fire. You're the same as all the others, my good friend. You people always over-reach yourselves – and then when disaster appears on the horizon you're facing the other way.'

When Cavaille believed he could speak with a steady voice he said briefly, 'Offer me a deal, Szala. There are several possibilities, you know that.'

'A deal . . .' the huge man said softly, his hands shifting around on the desk with just the tips of his fingers touching the surface, as if in search of something, reminding Cavaille of two enormous crabs. 'A deal . . .'

Cavaille waited, sitting down again and crossing his legs, studying one black, brilliantly-polished crocodile shoe. Szala looked up.

'I'm sorry. I'm afraid I can't think of anything.'

'Give it a little thought. Give it a few days.'

'Why should I?'

'Because if you destroy me, you'll destroy others, who might be useful to you in the future.'

Szala said slowly, 'Anybody who puts himself in a position where he can be destroyed can hardly be of any use to me.' His hands began shuffling across the desk again, faster now, the crabs sensing prey. 'A few days . . .' Then they stopped, and Cavaille thought he could hear something squealing. 'Yes. There may be a possibility.' He looked up. 'I'll be in touch.'

'*Eh bien . . . Madame est servie.*'
  '*Merci, Gaston.*'
'*Voudrez-vous que je reste?*'
  '*Non.*'
'*Très bien, Madame. Bon appétit.*'

The waiter's attention did not include the visitor; Gaston had not even glanced at him since coming into the room. At the Hotel d'Antoine a visitor to one of the Imperial suites was never acknowledged, unless the host made it clear that no discretion was called for. It was probably the only hotel on the entire French Riviera where a king could entertain a chorus girl in *absolute* privacy.

Bowing to Madame de Valoise, Gaston led his matronly little assistant from the room, leaving the polished teak-wood serving-trolley by the table, heavy with covered silver dishes and damask napery. A display of fresias stood on a side table, flown from Paris this afternoon. In the chased silver bucket the champagne had been uncorked.

'It was wonderful of you,' Mario Romano said gently, 'to invite me here. I didn't dare hope. Some champagne?'

Thérèse watched him as he took her glass then his; watched his dark, still boyish face – a face from a portrait by Michelangelo, the face of an angel.

But Mario Romano was no angel, as she knew.

'It's been a long time,' she said. They were speaking in English, by instinctive agreement; the mood of the evening was not French and sophisticated, nor Italian and romantic, but businesslike, despite the setting and the exquisite Oscar de la Renta ivory tussore dress that clung to her waist and tilted her breasts and left her shoulders naked and glowing flawlessly in the candlelight. The dress too was businesslike, if that kind of business had to be done; she didn't yet know; she only knew that Mario could be dangerous.

She hadn't asked him to tell her more when he'd telephoned her at the Chateau, saying that he'd run into Jacques at the Club d'Hiver a few days ago, and found him still 'crushed' by his father's death. If Mario could be of any service in this hour of grief, Thérèse must let him know.

And that was enough. She had sensed danger.

'A long time,' he nodded, smiling his beautiful smile, 'yes, it's been a long time. But you've not changed.'

It must have been three or four years. They'd met by chance at a beach party in Cannes, with a hundred and fifty guests dispersed among the Roman-style marquees and along the sands, with the light of flambeaux casting shadows as far as the creaming surf. Everyone was in fancy dress, and Thérèse remembered how Mario's medieval armour had got in the way as they'd lain together out of sight behind one of the tents, and how he'd cursed it softly while she tried not to laugh.

He raised his glass. 'To your incomparable beauty.'

'Oh Mario, you're *so* Italian.' But she relaxed, just a little. Whatever threat this man might offer her, it would be offered with grace, artfully wrapped and courteously presented. To a woman like Thérèse, who had so much to hide and so much to fear, it made a difference. Even a battle to the death could be fought with chivalry; her greatest fear of all was that of naked cruelty.

Lifting the massive silver covers, Mario tempted her with a little *ballotine de lapereau au foie gras, pistaches et truffe*, and later some *aiguillettes rosées de canard au fondant de légumes*, pouring first a glass of Pouilly Fuissée and then some Pommard, swirling it for her in the glass to taste, in deference not to the celebrated creator of *Maquillage de Valoise* but to a woman whom he wished the wine to please. That was Mario: he was born to make any woman feel infinitely precious. What a waste the man was, flitting from bed to bed along the whole length of the Riviera . . . it was time he fell in *love!*

'You'd see what I mean,' he was saying now, 'if you met her.' He'd brought the conversation round to this girl he'd come to know, Celeste, someone he'd taken pity on and was trying to help.

But what did it have to do with Jacques?

Jacques was the centre of their attention tonight, though he hadn't been mentioned yet.

'She lives with her mother, an invalid, in one of those cramped little apartments in the rue Princesse Florestine, *three* floors up and with no lift. It occurred to me Thérèse' – and he touched her hand briefly – 'that you might feel disposed to let them have one of your apartments along La Condamine. They'd so love the view of the harbour. *Un peu de Grand Marnier?*'

'*Non. Du cognac.*'

He poured it for her, and a glass for himself.

'Thank you,' she said. 'An apartment?'

'It's not a great deal to ask.'

She said nothing. She owned dozens of apartments along the coast, some of them vacant at this time, one of them on the Condamine – Mario had done his research.

She savoured the fumes of the cognac for a moment, then said, 'Tell me a little more about this girl Celeste.'

'There's not much of interest. She's just one of those shy little spinsters one meets now and then – '

'Hardly your style, Mario.'

He laughed gently. 'I have a heart, you know. She's such a nice person, and she can't afford the kind of place I'd like to see her in – she's only an assistant to Maître Dorlhac, the attorney.'

Thérèse felt a tremor go through her.

So there it was.

Maître Dorlhac, the attorney to the de Montigny-Villiers, a man privy to the family's most intimate affairs. Maître Dorlhac, whose 'shy little' assistant was obviously under the spell of Mario, for whom she would probably do anything, even to the breaching of professional confidence.

And he'd done it so sensitively, as she knew he would when the time came – she'd had to *persuade* him to tell her more about this girl Celeste, and even then there wasn't 'much of interest', except that she worked for Maître Dorlhac . . .

'I really don't see,' she told him easily, 'why I should provide your little friend with a residence on La Condamine – or anywhere else.'

She wanted to be sure.

'Why don't I ring for them to take these things away, Thérèse? Then we can talk without interruption.'

'Very well.'

When the trolley had been taken out and the door was closed, Mario stood looking around the suite, admiring the shot-silk walls and the Florentine scrollwork. 'You live in beauty, wherever you go, don't you?'

'I've worked for it, Mario.'

'Oh – ' he raised his hands quickly, smiling ' – of course you have, you deserve everything you have in your life. And this is such a restful little retreat for you here; the atmosphere at the Chateau must be distressing at a time like this. I feel for Prince Jacques, you know. It's been hard for him.' He drew a chair close to hers, leaning towards her with his elbows on his knees and his hands clasped together, his posture intimate, confiding, his dark eyes troubled. 'I'm not of course very close to the family, but like most people I have the greatest admiration and respect for Princess Charlotte – and Jacques too. I believe he should inherit, you know. I believe he'd find the – ' he searched for a moment ' – the strength. The ability. Don't you, Thérèse?'

She was listening very carefully, and thought before she answered.

'I think so, yes.'

'But his mother doesn't agree, perhaps. She sees him as a playboy.'

'Yes.'

She watched him, aware of the sharp, devious mind behind the beautiful Michelangelo looks. What Mario was telling her now was the extent of his knowledge, the extent of his power over her and over those at the Chateau de Beausoleil. He wouldn't reveal more than was needed to convince her; then he would make his demands, whatever they were.

'Have you tried to persuade the Princess that her son can be the only possible choice?'

'I have.' There was no question of her refusing to answer, to discuss it with him. They both knew that.

'And does she listen?'

'I'm not sure. She knows I have Jacques' interests at heart.'

'But of course,' Mario said softly, and looked deeply into her eyes. 'But of course.' She looked down, her breath coming faster.

So he knew everything.

'It would be nice to think,' he said, 'that by some miracle Princess Charlotte could find her health again; then the question of the inheritance wouldn't concern us. I hear she's rallying a little, thanks to her new nurse, the American girl. Lynn, is it?'

'Linda.' As he knew perfectly well. He knew *everything*. He was simply playing with her.

'It's rather interesting,' he said, looking at his hands now, 'that the Princess decided to bring someone from so far away. Don't you think?' He glanced up quickly, to catch her expression.

'She's talented, obviously.'

'And devoted to her patient.'

'Yes.'

But why was he talking about the nurse? Was she important in some way?

'She's also charming, I understand. Prince Jacques spoke of her with – ' he opened his hands ' – with a certain affection.'

'He's under stress at the moment. It's natural for him to seek comfort where he can find it.'

'Ah.' He seemed to consider this. 'In any case the Princess wouldn't encourage a relationship between her son and a temporary nurse. Would she?'

'I imagine they wouldn't have much in common. I don't know anything about her, Mario. Should I?'

'Perhaps there's nothing to know.' He tilted his balloon glass until the last of the cognac touched the rim, watching it carefully. 'I saw her at the Hermitage a few nights ago, by the way, dining with the Compte de Beauvais. They made an attractive couple.'

'What are you trying to tell me?'

He tilted his glass back and drank, savouring the spirit. 'Nothing at all – I'm an insatiable gossip, that's all – it's part of my job, to know who's dining with whom. I'm delighted that tonight you chose to dine with me.'

He'd simply parried her question about the nurse, and she couldn't persist. Instead she changed the subject, because there was something far more important that she needed to know.

'This . . . protégée of yours, Mario. What would happen if she lost her job with Mâitre Dorlhac? I mean, supposing – ' she waved a vague hand, sending a sapphire flaring in the candlelight ' – supposing someone complained, for instance, of an indiscretion, perhaps, or a breach of professional confidence. You see what I mean?'

'Of course.' Mario looked into her green eyes for a moment, saw that they were serious and drained his cognac, putting the glass on the table beside the fresias and going behind the chair where Thérèse was sitting. He cupped her face, then touched the lobes of her ears, circling them with his fingertips. 'It's too late,' he said softly, 'much too late. Besides, if anyone were foolish enough to harass my little protégée it would have the gravest consequences, and for so many innocent people. I'm sure you don't wish for that.' He slid his hands down to her bare shoulders, stroking them with sensual fingers as his voice became infinitely gentle. 'What I hope with all my heart that you might wish for, my lady of the sea-green eyes, is the most *tempestuous* affair with your ardent and devoted slave, Mario Romano, whose blood is already afire at the very thought . . .'

18

THE GIRL FROM MEMPHIS

'HAVE YOU HEARD about the *monte-en-l'air?*'

Bibi was breathless with the news, limping as quickly as she could to grasp Linda's hands the moment she came into the music room. 'Last night?' Her blue grey eyes were wide with drama.

Linda stood just inside the room, aware of the sunlight coming through the tall windows and the smell of polish from the furniture and the beautiful shape of the piano with its sweeping rosewood curves – all familiar things now, because they'd chosen the music room for their daily French lesson, since no one else came here these days. All familiar things, in a world that had just ended for her.

'Have I heard about what?'

'The *monte-en-l'air*. The cat-burglar! He robbed the Villa de l'Aube last night, and took *all* the Baronne de Lépée's jewels!' She stared into Linda's face, waiting.

'That's too bad,' Linda said.

'What's the matter?' Bibi was suddenly concerned. 'Are you all right?'

'Yes.' Her voice sounded dead, and she heard it, and tried to force life into it. 'The Villa de l'Aube? Isn't that quite near here?'

Bibi tugged on her hands. 'Tell me. Tell me what's the matter.' Suddenly she was near tears.

'Nothing's the matter.' But the child's worry was getting through to her, and she put her arms around Bibi and spoke against the soft fair hair with its blue ribboned pigtail. 'It's just that things happen in life, Bibi, good things and bad things – you know that. I've had a bad day, that's all.'

'It's only nine in the morning, yet!'

'A bad yesterday, then.'

'What happened yesterday? *Please.*' She struggled free and

stared up at Linda again, her eyes wet. 'I'm your friend, aren't I?'

Even feeling as numbed as she did, Linda remembered how easily this child could be hurt. 'Of course, darling. You're my very best friend.'

'Then we've got to tell friends *everything.*'

'Some things aren't easy to tell, Bibi.'

'Is it because of the accident?'

'Yes'. That was a lie, but a get out. For the past three days everyone had been talking about 'the accident'.

Linda had been the first to hear of it. She'd been changing to go out for the evening, bothered because she'd only brought one formal dress to wear and Michel de Beauvais had already seen her in it; but she'd been too excited to worry about it for more than half a minute, because the last time she'd seen Michel at the Hermitage he'd promised to 'make a few enquiries', and see if he could find out why she was here, why she'd been chosen among all those other applicants by Princess Charlotte – and why she had the strange feeling that she'd been here before.

Then the little chambermaid, Marianne, had called her to the phone.

'Mademoiselle Terman?'

'This is she.'

There was a short silence; then the woman's voice came hesitantly. 'This is – this is the Compte de Beauvais' secretary, Mademoiselle. I see from his private appointment book that you were to have dinner as his guest this evening.'

'That's right. I was just – '

'Mademoiselle Terman, I very much regret – ' there was another silence, then '– I regret to inform you that there was an accident this afternoon on the RN 7. M'sieur le Compte will be unable to keep his appointment with you this evening.'

'You mean he was injured?' She'd already learned that Route Nationale 7 between Paris and the Riviera was the most dangerous motorway in the country.

'Yes, Mademoiselle. He was fatally injured. Please excuse me now.'

The line had gone dead.

'He was a brilliant young man,' Princess Charlotte had told Linda the next day. 'I had just offered him a major part in managing my estates.' She had slept most of that day and in the evening had asked for morphine, which was unusual.

'There's some kind of *mystery* about the accident,' Bibi told Linda now, and led her across to the brocade settee by the windows, which had become their favourite place to sit. 'Did you see this morning's papers?'

'No.'

'Poor Linda.' Bibi put her thin little arm around her shoulders. 'You were going to have dinner with him that night. What a *shock!*' Bibi never raised her voice, but always laid emphasis on the most important words, sometimes hissing them fiercely. 'You should have come to find me – I would have helped comfort you.'

'I know.' Linda gave her a little squeeze.

'In the paper it said there was another car involved – they found black paint on his dark blue Citroën, and some damage that must have happened before his car rolled over – shall I get *Nice-Matin* for you to see? It said – '

'No, Bibi. It won't change anything.' Since hearing that shocked, halting voice on the phone she'd been trying to shake off a feeling that she was somehow involved, that it was because Michel had been making enquiries about her that the accident had happened. But she was beginning to think in this kind of way after her first few weeks at the Chateau – everything here seemed larger than life, more dramatic, more menacing. Even Michel's inviting her to dine with him that night had been mysterious, as she'd felt at the time.

'You weren't like this yesterday.'

Bibi's voice was a whisper, breaking into her thoughts.

'What?'

'The day before yesterday,' Bibi said slowly, 'and yesterday, when we had our lesson, you were upset about the accident. But you weren't like this.'

'You're imagining things, Bibi. You always are.' She looked at her watch. 'We've got twenty minutes left. Now give me some more parts of speech, OK?'

But as she looked into those clear, watchful young eyes she knew she wasn't deceiving Bibi. Something else had happened, yes, apart from the shock of Michel's tragic death, but it was only to do with Linda herself, only to do with her own ego, her own small world. The one that had crashed around her.

Gee, but he's really something . . .

A voice in her mind, just a voice, saying it over and over, and strangely enough an American voice, Suzie's, Suzie Spinoza's.

Hi! I'm Suzie Spinoza.

A voice in her mind.

She'd been visiting the Princess when Linda had come back from the town, from her almost daily trip to the Pharmacie du Marché. The English girl, Lady Houghton-Downe, had been there too, and introduced herself.

'We're staying here for a while.' She'd taken Linda aside before they'd left. 'You're doing a simply *fabulous* job with Charlotte – I'd heard she was *so* much better!'

There were always people visiting the beautiful rose-filled room in the east wing, except when the Princess was tired and Linda kept them away. 'I'm delighted there's someone here from the States,' Princess Charlotte had said, 'for you to talk to. Although little Bibi tells me your French is coming along famously.'

'*Elle est très gentille, Madame.*'

'There you are, you see!'

Le petit Baron came to visit sometimes, approaching the huge bed slowly as if he weren't quite sure if he were welcome, then trotting to take Princess Charlotte's hand the moment he saw her smile. Madame de Valoise came every day, stepping straight off the cover of *Vogue* with her perfect skin and those incredible green eyes; Madame Cavaille was often there, beautiful too, like her sister Charlotte had been once, but usually tense and trying to conceal her nerves. *Her husband beats her*, Bibi had once said in a fierce whisper; and sometimes Linda had noticed bruises on her arms, and felt pretty angry about it, but of course couldn't say anything.

Dr Chirac came every day, still distant but often paying Linda a compliment; Madame Leclerc showed up to busy herself with the curtains or the bedside table or the roses, though she too had decided to make her peace. Others came, some of whom Linda didn't know, though her patient was pleased to see them for a few minutes.

And Jacques came.

Jacques. Smiling to her, his eyes full of warmth, even though they hadn't been together or even spoken for three days now. Three days, by the calendar.

Then four.

The last time Suzie, the American guest, had come to visit

Princess Charlotte was yesterday. 'I'm from Memphis, Tennessee. They say you're from New Jersey, right?'

'Right.'

'A long way from home.'

'It's kind of getting shorter,' Linda smiled, 'every day. At first I thought I was on a totally different planet, you know? Now I'm starting to get used to it.'

They talked for a while in Linda's room, because Suzie had asked for some aspirin. Also she didn't sleep too well. 'There's so much going *on* around here, isn't there!'

Linda took a liking to her straight away: Suzie was vital, friendly and easy going; she also had great looks, with a tawny skin and bronze eyes with flecks on them when she smiled. But she was a bit of a hypochondriac . . . first aspirin, then something to make her sleep. 'I guess it's my conscience or something.'

Linda said she'd have to take her blood pressure and pulse and ask a few questions: had she always had trouble sleeping, did she have any worries on her mind, was she on any kind of a diet, or medication?

'I can't make you out a prescription, Suzie, but there are a whole lot of things you can get over the counter: I'd suggest *Bonne Rêves* or *Somnivon* – made in li'l ole Noo Jersey.'

Suzie had talked for a while, bubbling over with the 'far out lifestyle' over here in Europe, her first visit and she'd already lost a fortune she didn't even possess in the first place – 'Daphne played it for me at the casino, in a *private room* – ' and she'd spent a whole evening with a real live sheik who wanted to *marry* her, and there was this whole incredible Chateau – 'Right out of Disneyland but for real – ' where she'd been invited to stay, kind of like as a guest of a guest, and the fantastic people here, actual Princes and Princesses and everything, and hey, what about Prince *Jacques* – 'Gee, but he's really *something* . . . He's taking me out to dinner tonight, just the two of us, and then we're going on to a night-club, can you imagine? With *him?*'

19

NIGHT DRIVE

'WHAT DID I DO?'

Here under the trees the air was very still, and Linda's voice sounded louder than she'd meant.

Jacques stood with the riding crop in his hand, holding it against his leg, tapping it gently; he looked uncertain, puzzled.

'I don't understand,' he said.

She'd seen him from the conservatory, where she'd been trying to find a gardenia for Princess Charlotte, because she loved their scent. Jacques had been walking back through the riding park from the stables, and for a moment she'd simply watched him, the straight back and the long legs and the angle of his head as he'd kept his eyes on the ground, sometimes slowing as a thought came to him. Then without really thinking about it she'd opened the door of the conservatory and gone to meet him under the trees, wanting to face it, to get it over with.

'I just mean,' she said, 'what did I do to make you start avoiding me, day after day?'

But already she was wishing she hadn't decided to confront him, expecially out here within sight of the Chateau and its many windows. She was in her white linen coat and pants; Jacques was in jodhpurs and a hacking jacket; they must have looked like a couple of people at a fancy dress party, and there was a bitter kind of truth in that, because they didn't really have anything in common.

'Have I been avoiding you?' he asked her, and came closer, throwing down the riding crop and holding out his hands. But she moved back quickly and dug her own hands into the pockets of her coat. 'We've seen each other every day,' he said, and he sounded genuinely puzzled.

'When you've come to visit with your mother, yes. But I was

just there, like a part of the furniture. You've never gone out of your way to see *me*.' She shrugged. 'That's all I meant.'

'I've been – ' he hesitated, and she knew what he'd been going to say.

'Busy?'

He tilted his head but didn't look away. 'I've been preoccupied. I'm sorry – I didn't realise you thought I was avoiding you.'

'Forget I said anything.' She turned to go, now wishing very hard indeed that she hadn't been seized by this stupid impulse to talk to him. They were having the kind of conversation where nothing meant anything, because they were speaking a different kind of language.

'Don't go,' he said quietly.

She swung back to look at him and felt tears coming, because that was how it had all begun, when he'd been standing up there on the verandah in the sundown and seen her standing in the doorway and said, *don't go.*

'Look,' she said tightly, willing the tears not to come, 'I think I'm talking about something that never really existed, Jacques. Let's call it love.'

In a moment he said, very gently, 'Love . . .' and stood turning it over in his mind. And that was when her heart really broke, right in that instant, because the word didn't have any meaning for him and she could see that and it hurt, it hurt like hell and the tears were coming now and she turned away and began running blindly under the trees, her white rubber-soled shoes slipping on the dead leaves and a bird darting out of cover, startled, and the tears drying on her face because she was running so fast – but he was faster.

'*Linda!*'

She tried to escape him, scared now, running scared again as she'd always done as a young kid because once some guy had run after her and tried to catch her along a footpath on her way home from school – it was something she'd never got over.

'*Linda!*'

She tried to go faster but the fallen pine needles were slippery and she tripped on a tree root and tried to save herself but couldn't, and pitched headlong until she felt his arms around her just in time. She began struggling free, angry now, and he didn't resist; he just let her go; and now she couldn't run any more because she hadn't faced this thing yet, she hadn't got it over with and until she'd done that she'd never be able to forget.

'What was all that, then?' She faced him, brushing the tears away. 'What did it mean, the things we did, the things we said? Was it all just nothing?' But even as she heard what she was saying she began questioning it herself, trying to remember the things they'd said, trying to remember the vows they'd made, the solemn declarations of undying love – *but had there really been any?*

Jacques stood watching her, his dark eyes pensive, his whole attitude puzzled. Then he said carefully, 'In America, don't you have affairs?'

She stared up at him, still out of breath from running, and wondered if she'd heard it right.

'Affairs?'

He nodded slowly. 'Love affairs.'

Somewhere the bird – the one they'd startled when they'd run through the trees just now – flew back to its branch, calling thinly on the still morning air, a plaintive note, despairing; and again Linda felt her heart break, just at that small sound, as she knew now it was going to go on breaking in the days ahead, whenever she caught the scent of a gardenia or heard the call of a bird.

Slowly she said to Jacques, 'That's all it was?'

He didn't answer, but just let the question go on repeating itself in her mind, until she understood. Yes. That was all it was. An affair. A love affair.

Her voice came sharply. 'We call it sex.' She stood closer to him, her eyes locked on his. 'In America, we, the American people, call that kind of thing sex. Maybe it isn't in the Constitution but that's the word we have for it, or one of the words, sex, a roll in the hay, a one-night stand, you name it, we do it – sex.' She watched him flinching, his eyes refusing to look away, to look ashamed, but flinching, maybe not at the heat of the anger in her voice but at the crude way she was putting it because these were the only words that sprang to her mind and she wanted to hurt, to be bitter, to let him know what she thought of him now that he'd made her understand what they'd really been giving each other, a roll in the hay.

'Please,' he said in a moment. 'Don't let yourself – '

'Sure I have affairs in America, you bet I do. I have them over there and I have them here and I'll probably go on having them all over the place, wherever I can find a man I can turn on – it's healthy, OK? It clears the sinuses and promotes cardio-vascular circulation and maintains the hormonal balance and – and – oh God . . . oh my God, I – I don't really mean to say things like – ' and she folded her arms, hugging herself as if she were freezing cold suddenly – even her teeth were chattering and she just closed her eyes and squeezed them tight and felt his arms go gently around her again and this time she didn't try and get free because they weren't a danger any more, his arms, they didn't mean anything and she didn't want to cry her heart out with him holding her and trying to comfort her because all that was over now and she was out on the other side of it.

On the other side of the affair.

'I had no idea,' he said after what seemed a long time. 'I had no idea.'

'That's OK.' She left herself as she was, leaning against him with her legs straight and her head resting on his chest and her hands just folded together somewhere, not around him, no, not around him, because that was over too. It was just that he was gentle and friendly and didn't mean her any harm so it was OK to stay like this for another minute or two while she got her breath and could finally stand away and let him go and get on with her life again in the new world that was waiting for her out there, a world without Jacques.

'It was just that I suddenly saw you standing there, Linda, that night, and you looked so very lovely, with your eyes – but never mind that now; you came there at a time when I needed someone very badly, you see, because the day was dying and I was thinking of my father and how I wished I could have talked to him before – but that doesn't matter either. It's difficult for you to understand, because you are a woman and most women take sex so much more seriously than men. That's why they – '

'Please spare me the homespun psychiatry.'

She felt him tighten. 'I'm sorry. I'm just making a pathetic attempt to excuse myself for not understanding – for hurting you. But Linda, when other men entertained you, in your own country, did you always believe they'd fallen in love with you?'

'No. But this time it was different, that's all.'

'How was it different?'

'Let's call it culture shock.'

'Please,' he asked her. 'I want to understand.'

She eased herself out of his arms and stood back a little, looking up at him. 'All right. It's really very simple. This time it was different because – because this time, it was I who fell in love with you.'

Then she walked away and didn't turn her head until she reached the conservatory – and then she had to, just for one last look, but he must have gone into the trees because she couldn't see him anywhere, and the world looked suddenly so terribly empty.

* * *

The noise in this place was deafening. They were playing hard rock, acid rock, heavy steel, you name it, they played it, and the noise came blasting out of those bright chrome amplifiers as big as the back of a school bus and it made Suzie feel that she ought to be leaning towards the noise like she was in a gale force wind, or it'd blow her over.

'*Comme vous êtes formidable!*' The guy with the headband and the Buffalo Bill moustache was yelling at her, dancing like crazy, right down on his haunches and laughing up at her.

'Me Jane, you Tarzan!' Suzie yelled back, and felt a shoe strap go.

'*Comment?*'

'I only speak American!'

'Ah! You – uh – very formidable!'

'That's the first time anybody's ever told me *that!*'

She waved him goodbye and hobbled across to the bar and took off her shoe. The strap had broken clean away so she took the other shoe off and yelled to the bartender for a juice. She couldn't see Daphne anywhere; she'd last seen her dancing with a very sexy looking guy in a tuxedo, and if she knew anything about Daphne by now she'd be out there somewhere in a car or the janitor's closet and she'd come back in ten minutes looking flushed and with one shoulder-strap hanging down and there'd be that weird haunted look on her face, and when Suzie asked her if she was OK she'd throw her blonde head back and flash that dazzling Marilyn Monroe smile.

Suzie had recently started to wonder whether she ought to light out of this rich man's paradise scene and hole up somewhere normal before Daphne blew her entire stack and took off her clothes and got arrested and tried cutting her wrists on her way to the hoosegow, and maybe that sounded funny but there was something about Daphne that warned her she was ready to blow, and Suzie didn't want to be there when it happened. Other times she had a strong feeling that if she lit out of here and left Daphne she'd blow anyway and it would be Suzie's fault.

'*Darling!* I wondered where you'd gone!'

'That's funny,' Suzie said, 'I was wondering just the same thing about you.'

And sure, there it was, that weird expression on Daphne's face, like a little kid would look when she'd done something she shouldn't have. *Had* to do – but shouldn't have.

'Why are you looking like that, darling?'

That's funny, Suzie thought of saying again, but I was just wondering . . . What she said was, 'This place is so noisy my head's splitting, how about you?'

'Then let's go.' Wanting to please Suzie, anything to please Suzie because she couldn't find her just now, thought she'd lost her. *If I thought I couldn't see you again, I think I'd die.*

Out in the Jaguar, accelerating along the Grande Corniche towards Monte Carlo, Suzie checked her seat belt for the third time, watching the trees and the apricot coloured rocks flash by in the headlights with a knot tying itself tighter and tighter in the pit of her stomach. She knew the bodyguard was somewhere behind them and that was why they had to lose him – Daphne had explained the game she always played – but was it worth getting themselves smashed up all over these apricot coloured rocks with a tree sticking through the windshield?

'I hate to sound chicken,' Suzie said at last, 'but could you slow down to maybe something like a hundred and ten?'

'Don't you like it, darling?'

'I'm about to throw up.'

Daphne flashed her that brilliant show-girl smile, her small hands caressing the thin rim of the wheel. 'I've never crashed a car yet.' She shot a glance at the mirror again.

'The thing is,' Suzie told her, 'I wanted to ask you about Sheik Ahmed. I've decided to marry him.'

Daphne's foot came off the throttle so fast that the motor's braking effect pushed them against their seat-belts. Daphne checked the mirror again and stood on the brakes and threw the Jaguar into a side road and pulled up with the tyres squealing and switched off the lights and cut the motor.

'What decided you?' she asked, her tone over-bright.

They watched the scenery flush with light and then go dark

again as the bodyguard's car went zooming past the side road flat out. Its sound died away and there was just the ticking of hot metal from under the hood. Daphne put the facia lights on and looked at Suzie in the glow. The clock said 2:46 a.m.

'Mr Ariche called me,' Suzie said, not actually answering the question. What had decided her was this whole situation with Daphne. Whatever Suzie wanted, she got; she even got a whole lot of things she didn't really want, like jewellery and perfume and fox furs that made her feel like she was a kept woman – and not kept by a man, even. She'd take all this from a man, sure, because men were for digging in, deeper and deeper through the bullshit till you got to the gold. That was legitimate. But this was different, and she liked this strange little head-case of an English girl enough to want to be liked back, and she couldn't do it if she was dependent on her. Sheik Ahmed of Abu Talha could be the answer.

'His Majesty has asked me,' Mr Ariche had said on the phone in that soft, courteous voice of his, 'whether I can have the very great pleasure of conveying to him your acceptance.'

So it was for real. Mr Ariche had said that if her decision was 'in the affirmative' he would send a limousine to the Chateau de Beausoleil for her and they could discuss immediate arrangements and meet with His Majesty for a celebration party before their departure together for Abu Talha. A month ago, gee, she would have said yes and hit that limo so hard it would have bust the doors open. *How rich is he?* she'd blurted out to Mr Ariche at that dinner party, *I mean it couldn't be less important, but* . . . And Mr Ariche had looked at her and said softly, *You don't think three billion dollars is important?* A month ago she would have done anything to get herself off the poverty line and out of those stinking broken spring beds at the truck stops, but now, today, tonight . . . OK, she'd gotten soft, living with Daphne, gotten choosy. Abu Talha was a hell of a long way from Memphis, Tennessee, if she ever wanted to run back home, and there'd been all those guys with robes and head-cloths and jewelled daggers and everything – they'd be her neighbours, OK?

And there was the thing Daphne had said about their liking for kinky sex and their dominant ways. Did that mean horse-whips? *Camel*-whips?

'He called you,' Daphne was saying, 'and you actually said "yes" over the telephone?'

'No. I told him I'd let him know in a couple of days. But now I've decided.'

Daphne's face was pale in the glow from the facia lights. 'I see. Oh well – goody!' But the first tear was creeping down her cheek and she couldn't look away from Suzie and Suzie knew it was because Daphne was going to lose her and wanted to remember her face, kind of etch it into her memory forever. 'Can I come and see you sometimes, in Abu Talha?'

'For Christ's sake!' Suzie said and put her arms around the poor kid and waited for her to get through the crying fit; but there wasn't one this time and Suzie knew why. This time it was too big for just crying, and if she let Daphne out of her sight for one little minute from here on she'd go and do something terrible. 'Look,' she told her, 'I guess you have the message by this time but I might as well spell it out for you. I came over here to Monte Carlo to find a rich man to marry, right? And I haven't found one yet – except for this sheik. And he's *asking* me to marry him – I'm not even having to seduce the hell out of him first. Makes sense?'

Another tear fell, this time on Suzie's bare shoulder as they sat like the babes in the wood, holding on to each other in the dark. It was warm inside the car and the air was filled with their mingled perfume – Daphne's *Arpège* and the *Mitsouko* she'd bought for Suzie – and it was time they went home to bed, Suzie was thinking, but they weren't going to get any sleep before they'd worked this thing out and they might as well do it right here. 'I know it sounds odd, Suzie, but I've got a sort of presentiment.' Daphne's voice was very quiet – quiet, not soft, quiet but with a kind of cutting edge to its tone; and she'd called her 'Suzie', not 'darling', and that always meant the bullshit was over for a minute and she was talking for real. 'I mean about dying. I've got a presentiment that I'm not going to last terribly long. And – '

'You're pooped right now, that's all. We both are. It's three in the morning, and people get depressed at this hour.' She watched the pale reflection of Daphne's face in the windshield and Daphne didn't know she was doing that, and the look in those smokey-blue eyes was creepy, a kind of staring into someplace else, like she was watching her own funeral.

'No, Suzie, I know what I'm talking about. And what I want to tell you is that I've already given instructions that everything I've got is to go to you.'

Suzie waited a couple of seconds to see if she could hold on to herself somehow and then she knew she couldn't because it was just coming right up out of her in a kind of hot wave and she was hitting the door of the car open and yelling at Daphne – 'For Christ's sake won't you understand I don't *want* anything more from you? Don't you see I can't go on taking and taking and *taking* till I haven't got any pride left?' She got out of the car in her stockinged feet, holding the door open. '*And do you think a million bucks or ten million bucks would mean a goddamned shit to me if I'd gotten it because you were dead?*'

She slammed the door shut and began running through the dark, and the crazy thing was that she found herself thinking she was going to rip the feet off her panty-hose this way.

20

IN THE RIDING PARK

THE SERVANTS HAD brought chairs to the little mezzanine floor in the east wing of the Chateau, and of course vases of roses. From her bedroom Princess Charlotte could walk as far as the mezzanine without tiring herself too much; she was no longer able to go downstairs and out of the building to the rose garden, and though Linda had said she would go there again as soon as she'd regained her strength, both of them knew it would never happen. Charlotte was often in pain these days, and had fallen twice, trying to cross the room from her bed without anyone's help. The tragic death of Michel de Beauvais had grieved her, and she'd sent Jacques to Paris to represent her at the funeral.

The mezzanine had therefore become an alternative to the rose garden, which its three windows overlooked; from it one could see right along the wide carpeted passage as far as the grand staircase. But nothing spoken of here could be overheard – even by little Bibi, who had an ear at every keyhole! – for people would be seen approaching along the passage, and the conversation could be broken off, or turned to small talk.

'Raoul has a very good mind,' Toinette was saying. 'A quite brilliant mind.' She was sitting with her back to the middle window, and her face was half in shadow. Charlotte thought how beautiful her sister was, with her pale ivory skin and her raven dark hair drawn back in a chignon, reminding Charlotte of the face she'd once seen in the mirror before the malignant cells had begun moving through her body and slowly destroying it.

'He has a brilliant mind for business,' she agreed in a moment, 'but you know what I think of him as a man.'

Toinette hugged her arms under the thin woollen sleeves; the bruises of last week had begun clearing, and three days ago when Raoul had come home early for the weekend she'd not been subjected to attack. He'd thrown her across the bed and begun ripping at her clothes, but then had stopped suddenly and become still for almost a minute while she'd lain there wondering what was happening to him. Then he'd started shaking with emotion of some kind, and his breath had rasped in the quiet room as if he'd been running. Finally he'd pulled away from her and left her lying there with her senses rioting because she'd been bracing herself for the onslaught and it hadn't come.

'I'm tired,' he'd said at last, and walked like a somnambulist into his dressing room. 'I'm tired, as I told you on the telephone.' And Toinette realised then what had happened: his erection had failed him, and for the first time since their marriage. And this had shattered him.

'If I wanted to leave him,' she told Charlotte, 'I could. I'm sure you know that.'

'I can't see why you – ' but her sister broke off. 'It's nothing to do with me, of course, except where it concerns the inheritance and the estates. If you were willing to take them over then they'd become yours, just with a signature; but not while you're married to Raoul.'

'Without him, I couldn't manage them.'

Charlotte was silent for a while, feeling the pain begin creeping into her legs as it always did at this hour in the afternoon; soon Linda would be along to take her back to bed and put pillows under her feet to drain the blood away. She'd begun to feel the onset of desperation in these last days; there'd been a part for Michel de Beauvais to play in the inheritance, but now he was dead, and there was no one else, unless she decided to listen more to Thérèse and consider handing over to Jacques. She was certain of one thing: Raoul Cavaille would never get his hands on the properties of the de Montigny-Villiers. Edouard had loathed his brother-in-law, knowing how brutish he was, and for the sake of Edouard's memory alone she could never allow such a thing to happen.

'Your husband is brilliant, as you say, Toinette, and I want you to make me a solemn promise.' Her pale, wasted hand rested for a moment on her sister's arm, then she drew it away, to hide it under her plaid blanket. 'You must promise that Raoul will never be allowed to gain the slightest degree of control over the properties of our family, because of his marriage to you. He'll try, I know that. And so do you. Promise me, then.'

Silence fell again, and through it the cry of the peacocks rose from the lawns beyond the rose garden. In a moment Toinette said helplessly, 'Very well, I promise. But I can't – ' she turned her head to look through one of the windows, wanting to avoid her sister's gaze – 'I can't exercise any control over him, if he decided to bid for some of your companies. I don't understand enough about high finance to stop him. He – '

'My own advisers and the heads of those companies will stop him, Toinette. What I'm asking of you is that you won't lend your name to any attempt by Raoul to touch the estates.'

Toinette turned her head back and looked steadily at her sister. 'I can promise that, yes – but what's it worth? It's only a formality. He's strong, Charlotte, and very determined.' Her voice became tense and she leaned closer. 'I can give you whatever promises I like – and I'll keep them as best I can; but I can't promise you what *he'll* do.'

'Would you divorce him, Toinette? If I asked?'

'No!' She said it at once and without thinking.

'Do you enjoy being . . . treated as you are by that man?'

Toinette moved away, hugging herself, crouching a little, staring through the windows at the lowering sun. 'No. Of course not. I hate it.'

'Then why – ?'

'Because there's more to Raoul than just that. A lot of women envy me, do you know?' She faced her sister again. 'And even if they knew how he – how he shows his passion for me, they'd still envy me, and take my place if they could. And some of them do know – and would still do it. He's got some kind of dark magic for me, Charlotte.'

'And you can't escape its power?'

'It's not like that. I don't want to, and never shall.' She looked down. 'Sometimes I've thought about leaving him, yes, but it's at those times when I know without any question that I'll never do it. Life without Raoul would be like life without the sun.'

Charlotte was watching her with something like shock in her eyes; Edouard had been so gentle with her. But Toinette had always been like this – restless, passionate, driven by needs and frustrations known only to herself. 'One day, perhaps,' she said quietly, 'Raoul will leave you.'

'For someone else?' Her eyes grew wide.

'Yes.'

'I'd kill her. Or him.'

Charlotte looked away. She didn't want to hear any more about this man with his 'dark magic'. She only wanted to keep faith with Edouard and see the small but precious world of the de Montigny-Villiers in safe and kindly hands.

'Of course Raoul has asked you to plead for him,' she said in a moment.

'Yes. He'd like the estates. Who wouldn't?'

'Then you may tell him, Toinette, that I shall spend the rest of my few days doing everything in my power to see that he'll never have them.'

On board the yacht there was no feeling of any movement; the sea was halcyon calm. From the stern one could see the lights strung out along the coast from Cap d'Antibes to Monaco. The laughter of the guests carried across the water to the fishermen putting out their lobster traps in the shallows.

The two-thousand-ton *Sahara*, the size of a destroyer, had left dry dock a week ago in Marseille after refitting, and Sheik Ahmed of Abu Talha had thought it a good occasion for a party. She was his favourite vessel, among nine others registered in his name in Panama.

'She has said no.'

Julius Ariche, toying only with a glass of passion fruit in deference to his host's religion, had spent the last hour trying to decide exactly how he should break the news; finally he'd made up his mind to be brief about it, and he was now watching the Sheik's reaction closely.

It was sharp and immediate, a sudden spark deep in the eyes, a compressing of the lips. For this man, with the power of life and death in his own country, it was the equivalent of an outburst of rage.

'Why?' His voice was silky, reminding Ariche of the sound of a sword being unsheathed.

'I believe the lady is overwhelmed, Your Majesty. I can understand that.' He noticed one of the male guests lurching a little as he made his way aft, a woman on his arm; Ariche half turned, hoping that Sheik Ahmed would turn with him and not see the guest. His host was very tough with drunks at his own parties; he detested them, and anyone Sheik Ahmed of Abu Talha detested was in big trouble.

So, thought Julius Ariche, was Miss Suzie Spinoza.

But then her life, as she knew it now, was already over, whether she became one of Ahmed's wives by consent or by force. It was simply a question of time, of how long it would take for this eagle of the desert to tear her to pieces and throw them to the sands. But the difference to Ariche was substantial; he would be asking half a million US dollars for this piece of merchandise, providing he could sell it; if his customer had to seize it by force and have it shipped out by night he wouldn't be paying anybody for anything. There'd be a risk, of course; in his own country Sheik Ahmed was the law, but here in Europe he had to behave himself. It was to avoid that risk that he'd engaged the services of Julius Ariche.

'You've talked with her?'

'At great length, Your Majesty.'

Actually the phone call had lasted precisely two minutes, which had been quite long enough for him to get the message. And the message was no. Ariche believed that it was something to do with the Lady Daphne Houghton-Downe. It looked like a close lesbian relationship, and the English woman's immense wealth would have influence over the American girl. It was well known at this level of international society that Lady Daphne was a nymphomaniac, but that didn't stop her from engaging in homosexual affairs; in much the same way, Ariche was certain that Miss Spinoza was a prostitute, but many of her kind were lesbian. It might be that Ahmed posed a threat to Lady Daphne, and that was an interesting situation, for an Arabian sheik to be in contest with an English noblewoman over an American prostitute, with the stakes in terms of money very high.

'You don't think you can persuade her?'

Ariche turned quickly to his host. 'I shall go on trying, of course. Your Majesty requires this woman, and I shall therefore use my utmost endeavours to procure her.'

Ahmed's hooded eyes had flicked to look at the drunken guest, who had now come within earshot, and in the next second one of the attendant aides was moving in. Ariche gave the guest five minutes more on board, and this would prove to have been his last invitation. Ariche could already hear one of the power boats starting up.

'In two weeks from today,' Sheik Ahmed told him, 'I shall be leaving with my retinue for Abu Talha. Please see that Miss Spinoza will be available to me at the palace on my arrival.'

Three hours later, just before midnight, the *Sahara* was dropping anchor in the Port de Monaco, and her guests were escorted to the quayside by robed aides of the Sheik. Among them were Raoul and Toinette Cavaille, and shortly afterwards the voluptuous throb of the super-sports Lamborghini was echoing along the winding streets to Beausoleil.

As they went into their suite at the Chateau they heard the telephone ringing, and Raoul answered it.

'Hello?'

'Szala.'

Toinette noticed Raoul's sudden attention – he crouched slightly, gripping the phone and turning away from her, as if he wished suddenly she weren't there, weren't listening. But she knew it wasn't a woman calling him, especially at this hour, and at the Chateau. It was something to do with business; since he'd come back from Geneva he'd been nervy and quick tempered, shut in with himself. And he'd aged, appallingly, in just these few days; he was grey-faced and stooping, as if someone had driven a fist into his stomach with terrible force. And he hadn't wanted her, and that was the worst, because his urge had always been fierce.

'How are you?' he said into the phone.

'Very well indeed.' The voice, like the man, was fat, and the words came rounded from the fleshy mouth. 'I must apologise for phoning so late.'

'Not at all; we've only just got in.' Even the man's apology was ominous; he was in a mood to play – and Szala's games were so dangerous.

'I won't keep you. You asked me to give your situation a little thought, and I have done that. So let me suggest one or two propositions that might appeal to you. I'm assuming of course that the possibility of saving yourself has its own appeal.'

'It does.' Raoul was aware of his wife's stillness in the room, and as he half turned with an impatient gesture she went to the brass trellised cabinet between the windows and poured some cognac, bringing it across to him. But he shook his head quickly, and she went to sit on the end of the Grecian couch, the glass still in her hand, determined to stay in the room.

'Would you for instance,' Raoul heard Szala's voice on the line, 'be prepared to sell me your drilling project in Canada? The Golden Rift territory?'

'I can't,' Raoul told him straight away. He'd been prepared for this proposal. 'The estimates for the mineralisation are ten million tons, grading 0.075 ounces of gold per ton. Lucas would never let me sell.'

'How could he stop you?'

'By bringing in the consortium. I don't have total control.'

'That's a pity.' Szala's mood had changed rather quickly. Already tired of playing, he was ready to sulk, and to hit out like a child in a tantrum. 'Then let me suggest you offer me your Mideast Property holdings.'

Without real hope, Raoul asked, 'For how much?'

'I was thinking in terms of five million pounds sterling.'

Raoul's mouth tightened. 'Their market value is nearer twenty million. If I sold out at your price I'd have to lose Marbridge International and Vivatex, just to pay for the loans outstanding. I'd be bankrupt.'

'I could force the sale.'

In a moment Raoul said wearily, 'Then you must force it. But I thought you'd phoned me with a viable proposition.'

'I have, but I thought we should just clear the decks a little, before I offer you a final chance.' Szala paused for a moment. 'In fairness, I should warn you that if you find this last suggestion unacceptable, nothing will save you. Now do you understand that, Cavaille?'

'Yes.' He waited, aware of his wife's presence again as she sat watching him.

'Very well. Now this sister-in-law of yours,' Szala's voice came smoothly, 'Madame de Montigny – er – I'm sorry, but her full name escapes me – '

'*La Princesse Charlotte de Montigny-Villiers.*'

'Ah, yes, thank you so much. I remember your telling me that sadly enough she hasn't much longer to live. Is that right?'

'Yes.'

'I thought so. And I've been doing a little research on your behalf, and my proposition – my *final* proposition – is this. If you were able to persuade that lady to leave her estates in your good hands, I would settle for the major vineyard, Chateau de Bourget-Delahousse. Its present value has been put conservatively at forty-five million French francs. I would be generous and allow you to keep the rest.'

'There's danger everywhere.'

Thérèse de Valoise shifted in the saddle, loosening the reins and letting her horse graze. In the distance she could see the east wing of the Chateau, with the morning sunshine winking on the glass roof of the conservatory. A small figure in a track suit was running between the trees, and in another minute disappeared. Linda, the nurse.

'All I can think of,' Jacques said, 'is that my mother is dying.' His Arab gelding took a side step, restless, and he stilled it. He and Thérèse had ridden hard for almost an hour, and their mounts were steaming in the sharp air. In a moment they moved off at a walk, to warm them down.

'I know how you feel, Jacques. In the last few months your whole world has started turning upside down.' She reached for his hand and he took it quickly, grateful for her understanding. 'But there are other things – important things – that we've got to think about.' As they walked their horses under the trees she felt an urge to confide in him completely, to go back into the past and bring everything into the light of the present day, astonishing him, seeing him rein-in suddenly and stare at her in disbelief. But he had enough to contend with, and it could even unhinge his mind at a time like this.

'You're talking about the estates,' he said. 'I know I ought to be responding to the crisis and making the effort to go into training and everything, but it wouldn't work, Thérèse – you know me inside out; I'm just not capable.'

'You're intelligent, Jacques, in a lot of other ways. You could learn. You see, the danger is that unless you give it at least a try, Raoul will do everything he can to take over, through Toinette. And you know what your mother thinks of Raoul.' As they rounded the park past the stables they slowed the horses a little. 'I love this place, Jacques. It's my only haven. I can't think of it in any way as partly my own, but it's the only real home I've got. But my situation's very difficult. Your mother and I have an understanding; there's friendship between us despite everything, and I desperately want to help her, to see her go peacefully, knowing the estates are in safe hands. I can call on half a dozen top management people in my own enterprise – *Maquillage de Valoise* – to give you their expertise and talent and support if you took over here, just as you'd have mine. But I can't go to your mother with an offer to do this.' Her green eyes looked down. 'I loved your father very much. We all did; but with me it was different. He loved me too, in his way – though not as he loved your mother. But it didn't leave me with any privilege here, or with any right to call this place my home. I'm still a stranger, to you and your mother and everyone else, someone who came in from the world outside, an intruder. In a way, I'm even an embarrassment – '

'I don't think of you like that – ' he swung in his saddle, taking her gloved hand – 'none of us do!' He could remember her when he was still a child, asking his governess who the beautiful lady was with the green eyes and the pretty dresses. 'She's a friend of the family,' Miss Wilson had told him in her brisk English way, 'a good friend of the family.'

'I know you don't think of me like that, Jacques, but we've got to be practical. I'm not of the blood and I don't bear the family name.' She reined-in her mare and faced him steadily. 'The only hope I've got of protecting the estates is through you. I've tried to persuade your mother that you'd acquit yourself well if you took over, that you'd accept the challenge if it were thrown to you. You're young, strong, courageous, and you're the rightful heir.' She gave a little pause. 'Don't you understand?'

He didn't look away. She'd been saying things that no one else had, putting into words a different vewpoint he'd never considered.

'I didn't think of it as a challenge.'

'I know. But that's what it is, and that's why I put it like that.' She turned in the saddle. 'Look.'

He followed her gaze, and saw the Chateau in the distance, framed by the trees beyond the green sward of the riding park, with the sunlight glinting across the windows and the turrets rising gracefully against the pale morning sky.

'You've seen it before, Jacques, as a child and then as a man; you've got used to it; but it's still one of the most beautiful buildings in France, and it's your home. But if you want to go on living here you might have to fight for it, and if once you start fighting then you'll have to win.'

Again the urge came to her to say more, to tell him *why* she wanted him to accept the challenge that he hadn't even seen was there. But it was more than she dared do. So she sat in silence, with the horse moving gently under her as it grazed, tearing softly at the short winter grass. Birds called from the pinewood, as they always did here where the trees were thickest, and from far away an airliner lifted from Nice-Côte-d'Azur and began turning across the sea, its faint sound rising. Still Jacques said nothing, and she waited, knowing that she'd said as much as she could and that another word might strike a wrong note and bring down all that she was trying to build.

He moved at last, turning back in the saddle and looking at her with his eyes clouded in thought. 'Next week,' he said slowly, 'I'm racing the boat.'

'I know.' So she'd lost. The speedboat trials across the waters outside the Port de Monaco was one of the first sporting events of the winter season, and posters had been displayed in the town for a week now. And it was all he could think about. 'Good luck,' she said bitterly.

'What?' He'd caught her tone.

'And please be careful.' She'd been obliged to see this event last year, as the guest of someone she didn't want to offend. The boats looked as dangerous as the cars in the Monaco Grand Prix – they went like bullets and it was difficult to believe there was a human being inside them. The year before that, a *pilote* had been killed.

Jacques looked down. 'Boys' games,' he said wrily. 'I know that's what you think. But after the trials – ' he brought his head up again – 'I'll talk to my mother, and tell her I want to inherit, when – when the time comes.'

Thérèse brought her horse closer. 'Do you mean that?'

'Of course.'

She took a deep breath. 'Then give up the trials, Jacques.'

'It's too late now. I'm the premier *pilote*, and everyone's looking for me to win.'

She reached for his hand. 'Then be careful,' she said again. 'There's so much at stake now.'

21

THE EAVESDROPPER

'I HAVE A LITTLE surprise for you.'

The crimson Alfa-Romeo purred softly through the lamplit streets of the Principality, its tyres squealing a little as it took the corners, because Mario always drove fast, and cleverly. Celeste had never told him, but to drive with him in this sleek, shining sports car brought her close to orgasm; it was the way he caressed the thin-rimmed wheel with his strong sunbrowned hands, the way he swung the car so rhythmically through the bends, as if he were dancing with a woman. Before she had met Mario Romano, she had needed to stroke and fondle and explore herself, alone in her cold bed, thinking of Michael Jackson or Robert Redford or Prince Albert of Monaco and 'what it would be like' with them, before she could bring on 'the feeling'. But after these few first weeks with Mario she had to be careful even in the shower, not to excite herself. She felt drawn taut, like a violin string, needing only the slightest touch to send her into a delirium of vibrations.

Before she had met Mario she hadn't been alive, or known what life meant. These days when she looked at herself in the mirror she saw someone almost beautiful, with glowing eyes and a mouth tender with secret smiles. Her few friends had noticed it too – the checkout girl at the supermarket and the janitor at the apartment house and the thin, bony woman with the hare lip who came to tune her mother's piano. And yesterday Maître Dorlhac himself had said with unaccustomed familiarity that 'while flowers usually bloomed in the spring, she seemed to be more responsive to the winter time . . .' He'd retreated into his inner office at once, closing the door and leaving her to blush unseen.

'I'll give you three guesses,' Mario told her, his white smile flashing and a lock of hair stirring in the breeze. The night was mild and he'd lowered the canvas top.

And there it was again, the magic of Mario. With Mario there were always surprises, and mysteries, and guessing games, as if he and she were living in a fairy story all the time, hand in hand on their way through an enchanted wood. Tonight they'd gone to Gianni's, to sit in the lantern light and talk softly at the small round table while Francisco had brought them pink, tender prawns still sizzling from the pan, and *Saltimbocca* with the juice poured over it the instant before the dish was set down on the checkered cloth, and then *Zabaione*, which Celeste adored, because she'd never tasted it until the first time she'd dined with Mario, at Chez Bacco.

And after Gianni's, tonight, they'd made love in the arabesque room in his apartment, with the scent of sandalwood rising from the brass bowl above the divan and the soft lilting of flutes drifting from the stereo and her soul flying around the room in the shadows, released for a while from her body, where the fires of lust were leaping. And now, with her blood still singing and the wind of their movement playing through her hair, they were racing through the streets in his scarlet car to some other part of the enchanted wood where he'd chosen to take her.

'Only *three* guesses!' he smiled to her again.

Sometimes, lately, she had caught herself thinking that it had only been by chance that she had come to meet Mario, and that it might never have happened. That would have been terrible, unthinkable; there would have been this shining world full of light and colour and excitement, shut off from her by a door that had never opened. It would have been as terrible as if he were to leave her now.

'We're going to the Casino!' she called to him above the sound of the car, though she secretly hoped they weren't; he'd only taken her there once and it had looked rather boring.

'Try again!' he told her.

'To a night-club!' But again, she hoped it wouldn't be that; she didn't want to sit with a lot of other people, drinking cold fizzy champagne.

'No! You've only one more chance – ' and he leaned his dark head closer – 'but I'll tell you we'll be there alone, just the two of us.'

And the astonishing thing was that so soon after she had been with him, naked and leaping and tossing in ecstasy, he only had to say that they'd be alone somewhere together to send an immediate sensation deep into her body. But perhaps it wasn't so astonishing, no . . . He was Mario.

'In a fishing boat!' she laughed in pleasure. They'd done that once, sailing along the silver pathway the moon had burnished for them on the water.

But he didn't take her in a fishing boat. A few minutes later they were climbing in an elevator with gold-framed mirrors and red carpeting, and when they stopped at the sixth floor Mario took her across a little hall and unlocked a door, throwing it open and stepping aside for her.

'Look around, my lovely Celeste. Tell me your thoughts.'

It was one of his favourite phrases, *tell me your thoughts*, asking her for the intimacy of her mind.

As she went forward into the apartment she saw the whole of the harbour spread before her through the window, for this was on La Condamine and from here you could see the yachts and the lighthouse and then the streets rising to the beautiful Centre de Congrès and above it the Casino and the lights of the streets going higher and higher until they reached Beausoleil, half-lost among the pine trees. Celeste went from room to room and window to window, now seeing the Palace, apricot-pink and floodlit high above the town, and now the twinkle of lights across the bay as far as the harbour of Larvotto and the softly-lit windows of the Sporting Club at the end of the peninsular. Wherever she went she saw fairyland.

When she turned at last she found Mario standing in the middle of the biggest room, watching her, his dark eyes mysterious.

'It's so beautiful,' she told him breathlessly.

'It's not furnished, of course.' The floors were of limed oak parquet and the woodwork everywhere was ivory, with small fluted columns and arches and deeply-panelled doors, the ceilings rising from the walls to form a half-dome of Venetian moulding. 'If you can imagine some nice carpeting,' Mario said, 'maybe royal blue or apple green or just champagne, or primrose, or turquoise . . .' he shrugged. 'And maybe silk curtains, or rich white damask, or satin, or tussore, or perhaps brocade . . .'

He wandered about, pleased with Celeste's reaction, going from window to window as she had, his eyes moving upwards across the view to the north, higher and higher until he was looking at the Chateau de Beausoleil, its lighted windows half hidden among the trees. He thought of Thérèse de Valoise, and for an instant held his breath.

'You sound like an interior decorator,' he heard Celeste saying from behind him.

He turned from the window. 'I advise people sometimes,' he smiled.

'It's going to look wonderful, however it's furnished.' She couldn't stop gazing around her. 'What are we doing here, Mario? Who does it belong to?'

Mario went over to her, and took her hands. 'We came here so that you could look the place over. And if you like it, then it belongs to you.'

She laughed again. 'You're always making jokes.' But this one she didn't understand.

'At the moment it belongs to a friend of mine,' he said seriously, 'someone who wants to thank me for a small service I did them.' He gave a shrug. 'I'm comfortable where I am, but you told me your own place was a bit too small, and there's no elevator. Do you think your mother would like it here?'

Her grey eyes were wide. 'But we couldn't possibly afford it, Mario!' She was beginning to feel worried. He obviously didn't understand how things were with her.

'I'm not explaining myself too well. If you like this apartment, you can have it. All you need to do is sign the deeds and all those boring papers, you know? And then you'd have to choose the furniture and get it delivered. The place is being offered to me furnished, so there'd be nothing for you to pay – all the bills would be taken care of.'

'But Mario . . .' She went on gazing into his face with her eyes still wide. 'If the apartment is being offered to you, I don't see what it's got to do with me.'

So he took her down into the street again and they drove to the little all night café on the corner and ordered bowls of hot *soupe à l'oignon*, and she remembered she had a cassette for him in her bag, and give it to him.

'Thank you,' he said, 'and this is what it all has to do with you, don't you see? You offered to help me when I didn't know where to turn, and now I'm in a position where that other client of Maître Dorlhac can no longer make a nuisance of himself. So I – '

'It was successful?' she asked eagerly. Mario had never

mentioned what was on the tapes, so she'd believed they weren't of any use to him.

'You have completed a perfectly successful mission,' he told her with mock solemnity, 'and now you can come in from the cold.' He slipped the cassette into his pocket. 'In fact tomorrow when you go to the office you can take the recorder out of its hiding-place.' It had begun to worry him too, because already she'd brought him enough secret information to enable him to run the good Maître Dorlhac straight out of town if he wanted to, let alone a startling insight into the secrets of the Chateau de Beausoleil. There was no further need for little Celeste to run the risk of discovery.

'Mario,' she whispered feelingly, 'I'm so glad you're out of danger at last.' She reached for his hands across the table. 'To be able to do something for you makes me feel . . .' her soft eyes dipped away, and she didn't finish.

'So the least I can do,' he said in a moment, his voice lowered dramatically, 'is to fix you up with a little place along La Condamine.' He made a show of glancing around him furtively. 'In Russia, you know, they award their top intelligence agents an entire hunting lodge on the banks of the Volga.'

For a while she entered into the game, as always, but then grew serious. She'd done so little for him, and couldn't possibly accept such a magnificent gesture of thanks. It took him quite some time to persuade her. She was now shivering with the onset of nerves, determined not to let him go on spreading the world at her feet like this, yet beginning to picture herself choosing and ordering all the things she'd need to furnish such a fabulous apartment, seeing them delivered and seeing herself telling the people how she wanted everything arranged . . . There was now a tug-of-war going on inside her, and Mario felt it was time to say the one thing that would make up her mind.

'Think how happy your mother would be, Celeste.'

So they ended their evening with a cup of *chocolat chaud* and Mario drove her home to her shabby little place along the rue Princesse Florestine with her bemused and sleepy head against his shoulder all the way, dreaming her dreams, and it wasn't until she was standing on the doorstep watching the scarlet sports-car growing smaller and smaller along the street that she stopped waving and realised that for the first time since they'd met he hadn't said when he would see her again.

'She was absolutely overwhelmed, of course.'

There was a clanking noise, and then the clicking and whining of the camera.

'I'm delighted.'

That was Thérèse. She sounded sarcastic.

'You can move around for a minute. Asking you to keep still is like holding a tiger on a leash.'

Now *that* was a funny thing to say.

There was a draught coming from under the door, sending dust up her nose. She felt a sneeze coming on, and stifled it, because it would mean she'd have to get up and run down the corridor to do it and then come back, and that would be a nuisance because she didn't want to miss anything. The draught smelled of carpeting and wood-smoke and the perfume Thérèse was wearing – this was the one that had been created especially for her, that no other woman in the world was allowed to buy; they'd called it, of course, *Thérèse*, with her permission, and then they'd asked her if they could put it on the market and she'd said no, even though they offered her five million francs. She'd told them they were impudent. That was Thérèse for you!

'I'm not sure I like that.'

Like what? Oh yes, Mario had called her a tiger on a leash.

'I'm speaking of your magnificent animal vitality.'

Mario said something more but the sneeze was coming and she cursed under her breath and got off the floor and went scampering along the corridor. She always had noisy sneezes, and Madame Leclerc said it was because she felt guilty, listening at keyholes. Old bitch. *Vieille saloparde!*

Inside the huge salon that was part of her suite in the Chateau, Thérèse adjusted a shoulder strap and checked it in the long gilded mirror. The camera clicked again and she turned quickly.

'Don't you *dare* print that one, Mario!'

'But it was so natural . . . so *insouciante!*'

'The contract specifies posed portraits.'

Mario left the array of matt-black lamps and moved close to her, his eyes soft in his beautiful Michelangelo face. 'What pictures I could take of my lady of the sea green eyes, if she would only tear up the contract . . . I would let the light play softly across her exquisite breasts, first caressing the nipples to bring them erect, and then touching them with my tongue to leave highlights on them . . .' He sighed wistfully, and she stepped back before he could use his hands, because the instant he touched her she'd be lost.

'For God's sake . . .' she whispered, 'it was only last night!' But his ardour made her feel so young again.

That night when they'd dined together in her private suite at the Hotel d'Antoine, and he'd leaned over her chair from behind and told her he wanted a *'tempestuous'* affair, she'd believed it was simple flattery, to soften the knowledge he'd just given her – that thanks to his connection with Maître Dorlhac she was in his power. Since then, her private and rather austere lifestyle had exploded into a blazing infatuation with this young Italian photographer, this cunning, dangerous intriguer who for years had been infiltrating the private lives and public scandals of the Côte d'Azur. Almost in her fiftieth year, Thérèse de Valoise, creator, founder and supreme matriarch of a company that had replaced Arden itself in the front rank of the international cosmetics industry, had in the past few days become the slave of this street-wise con man from the Neapolitan slums, drawing him against her quivering body and clinging to him until he'd conjured little flames with his devilish fingertips and then fanned them with kisses until her libido was on fire and she raged with its heat, pulling him into her and crying his name, locking her legs around his own as if to capture him, to enslave him as he'd enslaved her, not letting him go because if she didn't reach the climax that had become the one paramount need in her life she'd suffer the torments of the damned.

It was the same for him, she knew. 'That night,' he'd said a little time ago, 'I just thought it might be amusing for us, a little *divertissement*. I didn't know it would be like this.'

Now he stepped back and tilted his head, appraising her pose again. 'A little to the left, please, to *your* left, and could you lift that classic head just a centimetre?'

She moved as he asked, unused to being photographed. It was something she'd never allowed to happen – the gradual erosion of her world-class image by public exposure, even though her looks could have claimed the front cover of the classic glossies. But after that first evening with Mario she had totally surrendered, and for the first time granted the exclusive interview that *Paris Match* had been clamouring for since she'd first walked onto centre stage.

'That's perfect,' Mario told her, 'now please don't move . . .' He took six shots with the repeater and gestured for her to relax.

'You didn't mention my name,' she said in a moment, 'did you?'

He looked up from the camera, a new lens in his hand. 'Your name?'

'To Celeste.'

'To *Celeste* . . .' he said slowly, as if having to search his memory. 'But of course not. You said you didn't want me to. But it was frustrating, because I'd have liked her to know it was you she should thank, not me.'

'She didn't question it?' Thérèse hadn't the slightest interest in the girl – except that she was Mario's source of information, and therefore dangerous.

'Of course she questioned it.' He changed the lens and dropped the old one into its black velvet-lined box. 'I told her the truth – that I'd done someone a slight service and they wished to acknowledge it.'

'I see.'

A slight service . . . the promise of silence. It was the blackmailer's tool of trade. Yet Thérèse had done nothing wrong; she wanted Jacques de Montigny-Villiers to claim his rightful inheritance, that was all, and Mario could destroy her hopes with a single word in the right quarters. But no, that wasn't all, really. Charlotte was dying, and she must be allowed to die without ever knowing the secret that Mario knew, and could tell if he wanted to.

Thérèse would do anything to stop him. She could be dangerous, too.

'I don't want to tire you,' he said, and took six more shots on the repeater and switched off the lamps. 'Tell me more about your childhood, if you feel like it. So far it's been fascinating.'

His contract with *Paris Match* had still to be signed, but the fee for the interview with photographs had been settled at two and a half millon French francs. He realised now that Thérèse would have granted it simply because he'd changed her into a young girl again, at least for a while. His inside information about Prince Jacques had ceased to be necessary – yet it was always there if he ever wanted to use it. In the past he'd hit certain unsympathetic celebrities along the Riviera for a million or two, yes, but they'd never been women, and he'd usually given most of it away to some private charity of his own; the luxurious apartment on La Condamine had been a farewell gift to Celeste. He would probably never ask Thérèse de Valoise for anything again; his affair with her was all that obsessed him now. Of all the women he'd known so intimately this one was supreme, not because of the rioting carnality he'd discovered in her – though that was exciting enough – but because of all she represented: great wealth, and great power, together with a beauty and a presence and a reputation that made every photographer in the world reach instantly for his camera the moment he saw her – usually too late.

Born in the slums of Naples, Mario had always been drawn to people like this; they dazzled him, fascinated him. To capture this one for himself, to touch her firm, sinuous body wherever he pleased, to plunge himself into her and hear her begging for more, always for more, was so heady for him that for the first time in his life he'd started an affair that had begun to dominate him. Already he'd begun wondering what his life would mean without Thérèse de Valoise . . . not forever, but for a single day . . .

'And then my benefactor came along,' she was telling him now, 'and everything changed.'

She was sitting at one end of the Louis XV love seat, and Mario was on the floor, one of her stockinged feet between his hands. The tape recorder was nearby, its cassette turning.

'And who was he?'

She looked away, her green eyes catching the light from the windows. 'He's been dead for a long time.'

'So it wasn't Prince Edouard.'

'No.'

Mario waited. She could give him her benefactor's name or they could invent one, as she chose; it had been agreed.

'He was very rich, and – '

'If he's been dead for some time,' Mario interrupted, 'I imagine we can use a pseudonym?'

She turned back to him. 'I think so.'

'All right.' She would check the finished interview when he'd written it, and change anything she liked; that too had been agreed. 'All right – he was rich. And?'

'He was very fond of me, and set me up in a little beauty salon of my own, in a back street on the Rive Gauche. That's how I began.' She went on to tell him more, leaving out names and certain events that she didn't ever want published; yet she realised that Mario might already know them, though he never gave any indication. 'By the time I was twenty-three,' she told him, 'I already had a staff of four sales girls, and people were asking where else they could by my products.'

'Success,' Mario smiled, 'and so soon. Your benefactor must have been delighted.'

She looked down. 'He travelled a great deal, and I wasn't to see him again.'

The winter sunlight, slanting through the south windows and flooding the room, was also in the corridor outside, lighting Bibi's blonde pigtail as she lay full-length on the carpet with her ear to the gap below the door. She couldn't hear *every* word they were saying in there, but she'd already heard quite enough! Every time she felt she'd got abreast of what people were up to, something new came along, and the *last* person she'd expected to see at the Chateau was Mario Romano, the celebrity photographer. Bibi had only –

A sound was coming from somewhere and she pressed herself off the floor to listen better, ready to run. People *always* interrupted her whenever she found something really *juicy* to listen to. It wasn't as if –

Someone was coming up the stairs!

She gathered her thin black-stockinged legs together and went hobbling along the corridor just in time, ducking around the corner and peeking back between the wall and the big potted fern, her heart thudding. It was Madame Leclerc, as *usual*. Things would be a lot better around here if that old bitch got the sack – she was *always* trying to interfere with people.

A minute later Bibi was sitting with her knees clasped on the windowsill of the little dormer room upstairs, on the top floor of the Chateau – her favourite thinking place – getting her breath back and going over what she'd heard in Thérèse's room. She'd only met Mario Romano twice, once at the Palace when there'd been a charity reception for the Red Cross, and the second time at the Hotel de Paris, where her governess had taken her to watch the famous people being interviewed by Radio Monte Carlo on the occasion of a film gala. The first time, Bibi had been rather young, but the second time she was *quite* old enough – at twelve and a half – to fall instantly in love with the dark-eyed, Italian looking photographer and miss her next three days of lessons because of what they'd decided was a bilious attack, since she couldn't eat. Actually it was a severe case of *chagrin*, because of what had happened outside the Hotel de Paris: she'd managed to leave there just in front of Mario so that she could drop her lace handkerchief for him to pick up. But he hadn't even noticed, and when she went back for it she found some awful black and white dog actually *peeing* on it because it had fallen at the bottom of a stone pillar.

So now her beloved Mario was having an absolutely red hot affair with Thérèse de Valoise . . . Well, it couldn't be helped. She knew from the exhaustive enquiries she'd made that he was always having an affair with *someone*, so it might as well be the beautiful Thérèse. Bibi didn't resent it, because Mario was *hers alone*, locked in her heart, and nothing could ever change *that*.

She slid off the windowsill and went to listen at the open doorway, but couldn't hear anything; this old place was always creaking and bumping because of the timbers shrinking, as Henri the chauffeur had said. (Henri was having his own bilious attack these days – he'd been so sure of getting Linda to fall for him.)

She went back to the windowsill, where the sun was, and where she could keep her eye on the stone-paved porch that made the entrance to the Chateau. To be able to see people coming and going told her a *great* deal about what was happening in the world. And these days there was so much to keep track of! Raoul and Toinette were going through some sort of trouble – he'd come back from Geneva the last time looking like a ghost and Toinette would hardly answer if you spoke to her. Charlotte was worried stiff about Jacques taking part in the motor boat trials, but he said he couldn't get out of it now; and poor Linda was still breaking her heart over him – but then they *all* did that for a while when he'd thrown them over for someone lese, and this time it looked like being the American girl, Suzie. That wouldn't be so bad, because Bibi rather liked her and the way she said things – 'You're a real live countess and everything? Well, gee, I guess that's something I'll be writing home about' – but Jacques shouldn't have treated *Linda* like that, because she was the most wonderful and generous person Bibi had ever met, and she was *fun* and terribly good looking – which should have appealed to a man like Jacques – and so gentle and patient with Charlotte that even that old bitch Mme Leclerc gave her a thin kind of smile now and then, which was enough to crack her face open.

Poor Linda! Sometimes during their French lessons Bibi had come close to blurting out how sorry she was, but she knew Linda well enough to realise it wouldn't be any use; she was a very private person and not the kind to cry on anyone's shoulder. She wouldn't even want to *talk* about Jacques now – she'd have too much pride. And in any case –

Bibi heard something again, and went to the doorway. This time it hadn't been a creak in the timbers, she was certain of that. A door had opened somewhere, and she could hear voices – and one of them was Mario's. He was leaving!

She whirled out of the little dormer room and took the back staircase, going down two floors and flitting along the gloomy passage that led past the kitchens and the cook's quarters and the boiler room, tugging open the narrow door that led straight into the main hall. Then she stood still for a moment and listened, getting her breath and darting a glance around her. Mario couldn't have come down the stairs yet, or he'd be crossing the hall by now and going out through the main door.

She began climbing the stairs, listening. There were footsteps some way off and higher up, but no voices. Mario must have said goodbye to Thérèse at the door of her suite, so he'd be alone now – *hooray!* She climbed higher, and had reached about halfway up the enormous staircase when she saw Mario just starting down from the top. And then a funny thing happened. The moment he saw her, he lost his footing somehow and fell down, grabbing at the banister-rail in an effort to save himself. And it flashed through Bibi's mind that he'd done it on purpose, though she couldn't possibly imagine why.

She hurried up the stairs to help him.

22

AN UNKNOWN HAND

THEY CAME ON each other, Linda and Suzie, halfway along the corridor between the mezzanine and the grand staircase, and when Suzie saw the athletic figure in the nurse's white pants and jacket she thought of ducking into the nearest room, but there might be someone inside.

'Hi,' she said, and flashed a token smile that didn't reach her eyes. She had to pass the other girl and she couldn't just stare straight ahead.

'Hello,' Linda said. She didn't smile. 'Do you still want to see me?'

Suzie looked back, half-stopping. 'I – uh – no. No thanks.' She made a throw-away gesture with one hand. 'It wasn't anything important.' She turned to walk on, but Linda stopped her again.

'I'm sorry. There were things on my mind, that's all. Why don't we go in here?' She opened a door nearby and stood waiting.

Suzie hesitated, wishing she could duck out of this. A couple of days ago the cramps had started again, and the nurse had been in the dining-room at breakfast time, so Suzie had asked her if she could see her for a minute. Linda hadn't even smiled, and for Suzie that was pretty devasting; if there was somebody she knew even slightly and they didn't smile when they ran across each other she always felt she must have offended them. But Linda had been so friendly before that, when Suzie had been to visit with the Princess – she'd asked about something to make her sleep and Linda had been very helpful. But in the dining-room two days ago she'd just said coldly, 'I'm sorry, I'm here to care for only one patient.'

Suzie thought it was maybe something she'd said, but she couldn't think of anything. Linda was still waiting for her by the doorway, so she thought she'd better just go on in. It was a little room like a study, maybe, with just a table and a few upright chairs and some paintings on the wall that must be real old because she could hardly tell what they were meant to show.

'How can I help you?' Still no smile.

'It's just these cramps.' She leaned her butt against the mahogany table, folding her arms.

'Why don't you sit down,' Linda said, 'and relax. What cramps?' She took a chair opposite, drawing her feet up on the rung.

'Around here. It happens – '

'Are you going into your period?'

'Yes.'

'When is it?'

'The fifteenth. In three days.'

'Do you always get these cramps?'

'I guess not. It only started in the last couple of months.' She was still trying to think what it was she'd said wrong.

'When did you come to France?'

'Around a month back.'

'On a vacation?'

'Kind of.'

'You're not sure?'

Linda's tone was indifferent, and she looked away most of the time, like she was thinking about something else. Suzie began looking for a chance to cut this short and get out of here, because she couldn't stand not being friendly with people, unless of course they got her fighting mad about something first.

'Yes. I'm on vacation. But it doesn't really bother me too – '

'I remember you telling me this was your first trip to Europe,' Linda cut in. 'And even though you're having a lot of fun it's a stressful situation – getting packed and making plans and then the voyage and everything. You're probably producing too many prostaglandins, like a lot of us do around this time.'

She waited for Suzie to say something, but nothing came for a moment because Suzie *remembered* now – sure, she'd told this gal how fired-up she was about coming out here – *This place is right out of Disneyland but for real*, she remembered saying, or something like that, *with all these fantastic people, princes and princesses and everything, and hey, what about Prince Jacques – gee, but he's really something. He's taking me out to dinner tonight, just the two of us, and then we're going on to a night-club, can you imagine? With him?* And she remembered the way Linda had stared at her and then turned away suddenly. Suzie hadn't got the message right then, but now . . .

O-o-*kay*.

'Sure, I guess it's the prosta – how's that again?'

'They're like hormones. Don't worry about it. Are your breasts tender?'

'Now you mention it, yes.' Suzie got out of the chair, pulling the hem of her Pierre Cardin cashmere sweater straight. (Right – *Daphne's* Pierre Cardin sweater.)

'That's pretty common too.'

'So I just forget about it.'

'Unless there's real pain, then I'd suggest a couple of aspirins three or four times a day for the two days before the date and during the flow.' She got up too, and led the way to the door. 'I don't know if we can find Motrin or Anaprox here, over the counter but Ibuprofen would do the job just as well and that's not on prescription, at least in the States. They're effective prostoglandin blockers. Or if you don't go for drugs, try a vitamin B complex every day, with 100mg of B–1 and 500mg of B–6 – you want me to write that down?'

Suzie asked her to repeat it. Then she said, 'And maybe I'll cut down on the night-clubs, right?'

Linda looked down, opening the door. 'Late hours don't do any of us a lot of good, whatever kind of fun we're having.'

'You know something? I don't find it that much fun, unless you're with some guy who's really interesting.' She lowered her voice and went straight into a sisters-under-the-skin routine. 'Prince Jacques, for instance – you remember I told you he was dating me? Now *he's* interesting, my God, but he never even tried to lay me – which I'd been kind of expecting. I got the distinct impression he was being faithful to somebody else – you know how we get these vibes? A *real* nice guy. OK, so no late nights and I guess no coffee and cigarettes and sugar and all that jazz – have you ever wondered why it's mostly the bad things that turn us on?'

'It's the standard complaint.' Linda closed the door after them, and caught sight of Bibi limping along the corridor towards them from the grand staircase.

'Look,' Suzie said, 'I really appreciate your advice, OK?'

Linda gave her a quick smile for the first time before she turned away; then she hesitated and turned back, and the smile wasn't there any more. 'Any time,' she said quietly. 'And I appreciate your kindness, Suzie. But for your information I have absolutely no interest in Jacques de Montigny-Villiers, nor will I have in the future. So if he dates you again, feel free.'

She turned away again and saw Bibi waving to her as she hurried along the passage. 'I've been looking for you!' she called.

'What's up?' Linda thought at once of her patient.

'Someone wants your help,' Bibi said, breathless. 'He's got a broken ankle.'

'Who has?'

'Mario,' Bibi said, and flashed her a look of bottled-up excitement. 'Have you ever met him?'

'I don't think so.' They reached the staircase, and found the man sitting a little way down, hugging one ankle.

'Get some ice, Bibi, and hurry up.' Linda bent over the man on the stairs and gave him a brief smile. 'I'm a nurse.'

'It's nothing serious,' he said, but his face was tight with pain.

'Let me get there.' He took his hands away and she felt the ankle gently. It wasn't broken and there was no swelling yet. 'Does it hurt to move it?'

'I'd rather not try. I'm a bit of a coward.'

'Heroes are the worst.' She palpated the ligaments, and found no laxness or swelling. A glance at his face discovered no loss of colour, which was surprising if he were in so much pain that he didn't want to move his foot. 'I don't think there's anything broken,' she told him. 'It's probably just a sprain; but you'd better get an X-ray taken as soon as you can. Right now I'd like to get you somewhere more comfortable where we can apply the ice. Can you put your arm around my shoulder?'

He was sitting propped against the wall in the corridor when Bibi came puffing up the staircase with two ice-trays and a plastic bag.

'You do pretty well,' Linda smiled. 'I think I'll make you my new assistant.'

'Is it broken?' Bibi asked, though she had her doubts. She didn't see how anyone could deliberately *break* something, whatever the reason.

'It's fine, Bibi.' Linda hit the ice cubes into the bag and made a pack. 'How did it happen, did you slip on something?'

'It was pure clumsiness,' Mario smiled ruefully. 'I'm not used to marble steps.' He held his hand out. 'Mario Romano, at your service.'

'My name's Linda. I'm pleased to meet you.'

'Linda Terman, of course. I've heard so much about you.'

Bibi sat on her haunches, watching Mario's face all the time because she couldn't look anywhere else. He was *beautiful!* No wonder Thérèse had decided to have a red-hot sizzling affair with him, even at her age!

'You've heard about me?' Linda asked him. She felt somehow alerted.

'Of course. People tell me how very professional you are, and what a wonderful job you're doing for Princesse Charlotte.' He tilted his head, and when Bibi saw the lock of dark hair fall decoratively across his brow she nearly swooned. 'I saw you at the Belle Epoque a little while ago, didn't I? Dining with the Count de Beauvais?'

Linda watched him steadily now. 'Yes.'

'That was tragic,' Mario said, 'I mean the accident – you heard about it, of course?'

'Yes.' Linda had a strange impression of things coming together. That was the only way she could have described it, if she'd been asked. The late sunlight was streaming through the windows of the mezzanine, right at the end of the long corridor, and slanting across the red carpet as far as here, where these three people had met together in an impromptu tableau – Mario Romano, a stranger to her, little Bibi – in love for the first time, by the way she was staring at him – and herself, crouched in the sunlight and holding the ice compress around Mario's ankle while he talked of Michel de Beauvais, who was here too, in a strange way. The air was so still, and the corridor was so quiet that they were speaking in hushed voices, as if they were afraid of disturbing ghosts.

'They thought there was something funny about that car crash,' Bibi said. 'The police.' She watched Mario as steadily as Linda. 'Do you think there was?'

'Nobody knows.' He looked back at the child gravely. 'But I wouldn't be surprised.'

'Why not?' Linda asked him.

He looked from Bibi to her. 'Because nothing surprises me any more. Not on the Riviera.'

Their eyes held. Linda believed he'd just turned her question aside, giving a glib answer; but she couldn't force him to tell the truth.

'They're still making enquiries, aren't they?' Bibi said. She didn't really know much about the Count de Beauvais except that he'd been something to do with Charlotte's business affairs; she just wanted to keep Mario's attention, because tonight when she went to bed she was going to go over and over this little scene and listen again to everything Mario was saying now, with his *delicious* Italian accent, and watch again his strong, poetic face, which the sun had tanned to the colour of the sandalwood pencil-shavings that got all over her desk when she was taking her lessons. (She was late – *horribly* late – for her algebra lesson from Mlle Pinal, but it couldn't be helped, because *nothing* was going to get her away from where she was now, in seventh heaven, and anyway Mlle Pinal could keep herself busy with her hand up her skirt for a while.)

'They're still making enquiries, yes,' Mario answered, though Bibi didn't even remember what the question was. 'But – ' he gave a *wonderfully* expressive shrug – 'you know what it is. Sometimes it's difficult to get at the truth.' His eyes moved to Linda's again, and for the first time she realised how handsome he was – a bit too handsome, really; she could believe he was the local Don Juan around here. But he hadn't made macho inuendoes about her own looks, and that was a change; instead, he'd called her professional, which was a genuine compliment.

'Did you know Michel?' she asked him. The ice in the bag was melting a little and leaking out, forming a puddle on the carpet, but she didn't do anything about it.

'Michel?'

'De Beauvais.'

'Yes. But then I know everyone here along the coast. Or I know something about them. It's my job.'

'That's how you know about me?' Linda asked quietly, and sensed Bibi looking at her.

'Perhaps.' His dark eyes were cloudy as he watched her. He seemed to have entirely forgotten the pain of his ankle; the ice must be doing the trick. 'It must be quite a change of scene for you,' he said thoughtfully.

'A change of scene?'

'From New Jersey.'

Icy water began trickling over Linda's hand, and she moved the plastic bag, folding the end over more securely. 'Are you getting wet?' she asked Mario.

Her smile was put on, as Bibi could see. Bibi was picking up a lot of atmosphere in the air here, and found it very intriguing. She was more certain than ever that Mario had faked that fall on the stairs. At first she'd just caught the idea in her mind, which often happened to her – she'd see things going on that other people missed, except for *le petit Baron*, who knew a lot more than anyone would believe. She hadn't bothered to ask herself why Mario had deliberately fallen on the stairs like that; she knew that sooner or later she'd find the answer.

And now she had. It came to her as clear as if it were written on the wall behind him. He'd wanted to meet Linda, and needed an excuse. There wouldn't have been much point in falling down the stairs unless someone were watching: he would have had to yell out and cause a fuss, which wasn't his way – he was a very deep one, Mario Romano, and he liked to do things quietly. But when he'd seen her there, coming up the stairs, he knew she'd go and fetch Linda; and if she hadn't, he'd have asked her if there were a nurse in the building. *Because he knew there was one.*

So why did he want to meet Linda, right in the middle of an affair with Thérèse? Even Mario wouldn't take on two at once (three, really, but Bibi hadn't told him yet that he was hers alone).

'How did you know I was in New Jersey?' Linda was asking. She'd tried to sound casual but Bibi wasn't fooled.

'I forget who told me,' Mario said. 'Isn't it true?'

'Yes. It's true.'

'There must have been a lot of competition,' he said, 'for a position with a princess on the French Riviera.'

'Yes.' She watched him all the time now, wanting to catch his every expression.

'It's simply a compliment to your reputation, as a top professional.'

'Not really. There are rather a lot of nurses with my qualifications.' Even as she heard herself saying it, she caught echoes from the past.

This was the same conversation she'd had with Michel de Beauvais at dinner that night, not long before he died.

'Then we're lucky to have you here,' Mario said softly.

'Thank you.' She took the ice-bag away from his ankle and gave it to Bibi. 'But it wasn't luck, M'sieur Romano. And you know it.'

'Do I?'

'Yes.' The late afternoon sunlight had crept away from the corridor now, and shadows were moving in. She felt their chill. 'You know more about me than you'll say. So does Princess Charlotte, and so did Michel de Beauvais.' She turned to the child beside her. 'And so do you.' She shivered suddenly and her voice echoed along the empty corridor with almost a cry of despair. *'Why won't you tell me? Why can't anyone tell me what I'm doing here?'*

* * *

Later she was ashamed.

Alone in her room at ten o'clock that night, she was leaning at the open window to watch the moonlight across the bay. It was almost ten o'clock, and in a few minutes she would go into the room next door for a last look at her patient before turning in. The reason why she was feeling ashamed was that she'd been letting things get to her lately, where she should have taken them in her stride; and she realised how much she'd changed in the little time she'd been out here. Sure, things had gotten to her plenty of times in New Jersey – problems with her patients and one or two of her supervisors and her ex-husband and her landlord – but it had seemed a natural part of life: in life you had problems like everyone else and you had to cope with them the best you could. The difference was that back home in New Jersey she'd coped pretty well, taking each day as it came and dealing with it. Also, she'd had friends over there, and people she could go to even if they weren't actually her friends. She'd been sheltered and surrounded by a whole major hospital, and it had given her a degree of authority and security.

She'd known where she was.

Out here it was so different. The things she had to cope with were totally strange to her: the deepening mystery of what she was doing here at all, and the wild, heart-wrenching affair she'd let herself get into with Jacques, which had reached right down into the depths of her spirit and brought out emotions and passions she'd never have discovered in New Jersey, where life was practical and more or less predictable and down-to-earth. (It was the first time she'd caught herself thinking of it as an affair, and for a moment she felt a lurch. Sure, that's what he'd said it was, at least for him, and that was what she must try and see it as. OK.)

Out here she didn't have any friends, except for Princess Charlotte and Bibi, but one was dying and the other was a child; she couldn't burden either of them with her problems. And there weren't any problems, as a matter of fact, or she'd go do something about them. Give her a train crash or a subway accident or a five-car pileup and she'd cope with whoever it was that came in, that was *brought* in, bloodied or screaming or with a leg hanging off or covered in vomit or all of them at the same time, sure, she'd know what to do. Life had been simple back there. Out here there was no crisis; it was just that she was lonely, and scared, because there were people here who knew things about her that she didn't know herself, and that was an assault on her own conception of her identity, of reality – and it was frightening. As the sun went down over the hills west of the Chateau and the shadows came creeping along the ornate and silent corridors, they came creeping from some other time in some other world, touching her and chilling her like they had this afternoon, when she'd made a fool of herself in front of Mario and Bibi.

A thought came to her now, as she watched the lights of the town and the molten silver of the moon across the bay, that she'd never considered before. There'd been times when she'd believed in Jacques, and times when she'd felt a kind of pace and rhythm coming back into her life – shopping for things down at the pharmacy and seeing Dr Chirac for consultations and taking lessons with Bibi and jogging in the park – times that had made her feel that she wouldn't mind staying on here for a while – maybe a year or two, getting to understand French medicine and custom and language, to extend her knowledge of the world and what made it tick. But tonight she knew that as soon as her patient in the next room had died, she would leave France and go back home. There was nothing to –

Her thoughts were interrupted by a slight sound outside the room, and she opened the communicating door quietly, crossing to the big four-poster bed. Her patient was sleeping, but fitfully. There was nothing within her reach that she could have touched, to make the kind of sound that Linda had heard. She went to the door and looked into the passage outside, and thought she caught movement near the grand staircase, but couldn't be sure, because there was no more than a glow from the shaded lamps along the walls.

Bibi?

There'd be no reason for Bibi to come along the passage secretly, no reason for her to eavesdrop at Princess Charlotte's door – though according to various people it was the child's favourite source of information . . . The sound she'd heard was just the creaking of the building: this place was more than two hundred years old.

She went back into the room, where the Dresden clock on the night-table showed a minute before ten. She poured a glass of distilled water from the pitcher and dropped two Sonoril tablets into the palm of her hand, in case the Princess needed them during the night: she often woke naturally and lay for hours, turning restlessly rather than ask for anything. There was something trying to get Linda's attention, and she became aware of it, and clearing her mind for a moment and concentrating on the two pills that lay in the palm of her hand, consciously noting their size. They were slightly smaller than Sonoril, but she'd just shaken them from the Sonoril bottle, so she poured a half-dozen into her hand and took them over to the single lamp that was burning and looked at them carefully. They were all the same size, but slightly smaller than normal.

She checked the label of the bottle, and recognized the spidery handwriting of the dispensing pharmacist, and remembered the way he'd written over the figure '4' of the prescription-number more heavily to cover a mistake – he'd originally written '2'. So – it was the same bottle as usual, but since she'd administered the last two tablets the contents had been changed.

She looked across at the sleeping face of her patient. Princess Charlotte wouldn't have done such a thing; she'd told Linda so many times that she had infinite trust in her care, and had never questioned Dr Chirac's prescriptions. But the contents of this bottle had been changed. These weren't Sonoril, so what were they?

Linda sat down slowly on the little embroidered chair, and stared at the cluster of matt-white tablets in the cupped palm of her hand, while the shadows in the room began crowding in on her and the hairs at the nape of her neck began rising.

23

PRINCE JACQUES

THE SEA WAS still choppy after the three-day mistral and there was a reported cross-wind from the south at seven knots, but nineteen of the competitors in this year's Marine Cup de Monaco speed-boat trials had qualified for tomorrow's finals and Prince Jacques de Montigny-Villiers had gone out to break three records, the last two his own, piloting his fourteen-foot 90 h.p. cathedral-hull *Flying Fish* around the course in a final seven minutes, five and one-fifth seconds that had brought a spontaneous cheer from the group of competitors and officials on the quay.

His tinted visor salt-filmed and his muscles sore from the pounding of the fifty-knot run, Jacques brought his boat in slowly, respecting regulations and giving way to a little blue sail-boat that was tacking across the water from the port.

Most of the men gathered on the quay felt inspired by Montigny-Villiers' performance, but one or two had said earlier that he had the devil in him today and was out to commit suicide: to qualify for the finals in a sea this choppy was to do quite enough; to go out and break three records was to take the kind of risk that none of the others had any stomach for. A degree too much rudder on the turns at the buoys or a slight increase in the planing-angle when the hull was already slanting upwards at twenty degrees across the short, sharp waves, and the boat would flip over like a fish and send its pilot into the sea with the speed of a stone from a catapult.

But for Jacques there was a positive factor that he balanced against the risks: he felt released. Crouched at the wheel and sending the small, powerful projectile across the surface of the sea with the spindrift flying against his life-jacket and the engine's roar reverberating in his rib-cage and the pounding of the hull sending its shockwaves through his body, he entered that strange altered mode of consciousness that the Japanese called *satori*, the state of grace that all world-class athletes come to know, the zone of consciousness into which they move when they work at the limits of their skills and power – and a little beyond.

'It's a good way of forgetting,' Jacques had told another competitor this morning. 'Risky, expensive and rather noisy, but the best way I know.' Last year his father had been here, a man loved and respected throughout the Principality and the Côtes-d'Azur, as was Prince Rainier himself. On the occasion of the Marine Cup trials, Edouard de Montigny-Villiers had come down to the harbour to encourage Jacques and mingle with the other *pilotes* and ply them with questions about their boats and their seamanship and their ambitions, standing on the quay with his feet spread apart and his hands thrust into the side-pockets of his duffle-jacket and his easy laughter bringing an ambience of carnival to the event, taking the strain off their nerves and helping them to the state of relaxation that would ready them for competition.

This year they missed their friend Prince Edouard, his son most grievously of all; and for Jacques there was the certain knowledge that next year his mother would be gone too, taking her beauty and her gentleness and a few of her beloved roses into the cold stone vault where his father was already lying. This too Jacques could forget for a while every day, spurring his black stallion through the park at a breakneck gallop and sending the small boat roaring across the sea. And the other worries: his promise to Thérèse that he'd talk to his mother after the trials were over, and offer to take on the huge responsibility of the estates, to train himself rigorously for a task he'd no desire to do. And the worry of what he'd heard this morning – from Linda, the nurse.

She'd been icily circumspect, requesting a few minutes of his time and addressing him formally, her eyes indifferent and her tone distant.

'I felt that you were the first person to inform, *Monsieur le Prince*.' She'd looked crisp and professional in her white uniform, standing out against the dark oak panelling of the library, where he'd asked her to meet him.

'Naturally, my first thought is that you must have been mistaken, *Mademoiselle*.'

'Of course. But I wasn't. The fact that I thought I heard someone moving around in my patient's room isn't important. Whoever changed the tablets might have done it earlier, when I was downstairs at supper. But they were changed. You or any other lay person wouldn't notice the difference – it was very slight. But I've administered thousands of that particular tablet and I know its character. The new ones weren't only smaller; their texture was different, too – almost imperceptibly smoother to the touch.'

'Very well – the tablets were changed. But why is it so important?' He sounded impatient, because he still felt guilty about having given her the impression that he was in love with her. But didn't she realise that he couldn't take any woman seriously at this point in his life, when his heart was too numbed by death and approaching death to concern itself with love?

'It's important,' Linda told him coolly, 'because I didn't imagine anyone would have made the change just for something to do. So I took the new tablets down to the pharmacy and had them analysed. The people at the pharmacy aren't officially allowed to carry out analysis and they don't have all the necessary equipment, but I know the man there quite well since I've made purchases almost every day since I arrived here, and he obliged me. From his own experience in handling drugs – greater even than mine, since dispensing is his specialised field – he's assured me that the new tablets are prescribed under the commercial name of Coumadin.'

'I'm sorry, Mademoiselle, but that doesn't mean anything to me.'

'It will. Coumadin is an anti-coagulant, a valuable and useful agent for preventing blood-clotting and therefore used a great deal in the treatment of cardio-vascular disease. It's saved countless lives, but it would end your mother's.'

Jacques took a step closer to her. 'It's some kind of poison?'

'Toxicology isn't involved. But your mother's ability to clot blood and temporarily repair broken blood vessels is already undermined by her disease. I'll put it simply for you, *Monsieur le Prince*. If I'd started her on those tablets in the belief that they were the usual sedatives she would have suffered gross internal haemorrhage inside of a few days, and there would have been nothing we could do to save her.'

'*Mon Dieu!*' Jacques said very softly, and went on staring at her in lingering disbelief. But she'd given her report in the same clear, decisive terms she might have used in a court of law, and they'd carried absolute conviction. 'Have you told Dr Chirac yet?'

'He's the next person I've got to inform. I told you first because you're the closest relative to my patient, and it'll be for you to decide what has to be done.'

He nodded, turning away and going to a window, fists bunched on his hips and his leather riding-jacket pulled open. He'd ridden to the Chateau straight from the stables, where Linda had telephoned.

'This couldn't have happened by accident, Mademoiselle? A mistake on the part of the dispenser? Of anyone?'

'No. It wasn't a new bottle; I'd already used around a dozen tablets – the normal ones – before someone unscrewed the cap and changed the contents.'

'My mother doesn't have long, in any case – ' Jacques turned from the window – 'but this would have ended her life much sooner. Is that right?'

'Weeks sooner. Maybe months.'

'Are we talking about an attempted murder?'

'Yes. I don't see what else we could be talking about.'

He was silent for a time, his thoughts touching on a host of ideas and glancing off again as he tried to bring this horrible situation into perspective and look at it logically, unemotionally. *But someone had tried to kill his mother*. How could he think of that without emotion? Without anger? Rage? Watching Linda, he could see that beneath her cold, formal attitude she also was shocked and angered; her life was the giving of care, and someone had tried to harm one of her patients.

'Is my mother alone at this moment?'

'No indeed, M'sieur.'

'Who is with her?'

'The Countess Bibi.' Seeing his frown, she added, 'She's extremely bright, and absolutely devoted to *Madame la Princesse*, as I'm sure you know.'

'Yes. Yes, she – ' he broke off and pulled a chair nearer the one where Linda was standing. 'You must please sit down, Mademoiselle.' His voice had gone very quiet, and more than once he'd glanced towards the door. 'I have to ask you something. Do you have any idea who might have done this thing?'

'No. I'm simply an employee here; I don't know anything about your family's private affairs.'

He lowered himself into the chair opposite and leaned his elbows on his knees, his hands clasped and his eyes on Linda's. 'You realise that the law might require you to report this matter to the police?'

'I'd certainly have to in the United States, either personally or through one of my supervisors.'

'I am going to ask you not to inform the police. At least until I can find out a little more.'

'I'll have to leave it to Dr Chirac.'

'You are obliged to tell him?'

'Absolutely. It concerns his patient's welfare.'

'Yes, of course. Then I'll also talk to him myself. You see, I want to keep this from my mother. It would upset her – frighten her.' His thoughts were still disjointed, even as he tried to speak logically. His mother would be upset, and frightened – but would she be surprised? She might guess at her enemy's identity, and at once. And their motive. Was it to do with the estates? With some knowledge that she possessed, that could compromise somebody?

'I certainly won't tell your mother, M'sieur. I agree – it would increase her suffering. I shall also make sure she's never left alone, even for a minute. At night I'm going to lock both doors and sleep on a couch in her room – I'll make some excuse.'

'Thank you.' Some of the worry left his face for a moment and his eyes softened.

'I'll be keeping all her drugs under lock and key – there's a cabinet in the room. I also suggest you carry a beeper on you, all the time you're within range.'

'Very well. Where do I find one?'

'I'll ask Henri to see to it.'

'Thank you.' He hesitated, then went on. 'As you say, the private affairs of my family are deeply involved in this appalling act. And I realise that – ' he didn't know how to put it, and again hesitated – 'that no member of my family has the slightest interest for you, except for my mother. But since you meet some of them every day, and talk to them, I would be grateful if you'd tell me of any suspicions that might occur to you. You may have complete trust in my confidence.'

Linda looked down for a moment, then met his eyes again. 'My sole concern is for my patient. If there's anything I happen to learn that might affect her welfare, I'll be sure to report it. Not otherwise.'

'I understand.' Jacques again tried to compose what he wanted to say next, so that she too would be able to understand. He got to his feet, moving the little upright chair to its place in the corner of the bookshelves and turning to face her again. 'So I have to thank you, Linda, for saving my mother's life, if only for a little time. I also want you to know that your devotion to her is the one thing that gives me comfort in my rather bleak and distressing existence. It makes me regret all the more deeply that without meaning to, I caused you pain. Please try to – '

'If you'll excuse me, *Monsieur le Prince*, I must get back to my patient.' She turned and went to the door, and in a moment was gone.

Eh bien . . . At least he had tried.

His first thought was to cancel his engagement in the Marine Cup trials; then he reconsidered. It was best to give the appearance that life was going on as usual, so today he was here with the other competitors in the Port de Monaco, making what attempt he could to join in with their high spirits. Standing on the quay with the waves slapping at the great stone slabs and the wind fretting in the lanyards of the yachts at their moorings, he gazed across the water at the marker buoys riding the chop with their penants fluttering in the spindrift and their bright checkered paintwork shining in the late afternoon sun. Tormented by the news that Linda had brought him, he found his mind churning with suspicions, conjectures and wild, unreasonable assumptions, to the point where he must seek relief again in physical action, if only for a few minutes.

It was a little after four o'clock when he moved across to the commandant of the Yacht Club, under whose direction the trials were being held, and requested a final timed run over the course. One or two of his friends tried to dissuade him; he was in a strange mood today, and it had already tempted him to send his boat over the course with an almost suicidal recklessness around the turns.

'Three records, Jacques,' said Willi von Klee, 'and you're still not satisfied?'

Jacques gave him a short answer that he didn't catch, as he left the group and shrugged into his orange life-jacket and put on his visor, going down the three stone steps and dropping into his boat. Within a minute the powerful engine was throbbing into life, and the crimson-painted *Flying Fish* was nosing from the harbour into open water, leaving a curving wake.

Later it would be said that the trials should never have been run this year, with a seven-knot wind blowing and the sea so dangerous.

24

DREAD TIDINGS

THE LETTER WAS delivered by hand to Monsieur Julius Ariche at the Hotel de Paris two days later. The envelope bore the waxed seal of the Sheikdom of Abu Talha, which also appeared at the top left-hand corner of the missive itself. On opening it, Julius Ariche noticed the faint scent of sandalwood, due to the incense that was always burning in Sheik Ahmed's apartment.

> *Dear Ariche,*
> *In three days' time I shall leave with my retinue for Abu Talha, and will, as I informed you, expect to find the party of interest awaiting me there at the Palace.*
>   *Upon the satisfactory discharge of your services in this respect, you will receive the remuneration agreed upon.*
>
> *With my good wishes,*
> *Ahmed of Abu Talha*

Julius Ariche glanced across at the calendar on the gold-tooled leather desk-top and noted the date. Very well, then. It shall be done, Your Majesty.

At this stage of the operation Ariche was often presented with a choice. Either he could contact the 'party of interest' – in this case Miss Suzie Spinoza – one more time and try to persuade her into marriage with his client, or he could simply conclude the business by having her seized and shipped to Abu Talha, insensible and incognito, without ticket, passport or identity.

From his knowledge of the lady, having spoken with her and also observed her from a distance in the hotels and the Casino, he had come to the conclusion that she was a small-time prostitute who had come to the Riviera either to extend her activities or to capture a rich husband, and who had chanced to strike up an acquaintance with the blonde English heiress, who was taking her around as an amusing companion. On the one hand Ariche didn't feel that this scenario was promising: Spinoza wanted a man, and a rich man, but all the time she was being housed and fed and given clothes to wear, she wasn't going to grab at *any* rich man, especially one whose exotic background might frighten a conservative American girl away. On the other hand, if she had to be seized and shipped out as a white slave, she was the perfect candidate, without background, substance or authority. It would cause as little disturbance as catching a chicken by the neck and tossing it into a sack.

During his career in import-export, Ariche could recall three such incidents. Four years ago a young woman had agreed to marriage with an African diamond-broker and had changed her mind at the last minute. Ariche was there when she was dragged from her small blue Citroën near the Champs Elysées and bundled into a waiting limousine with tinted windows and *Corps Diplomatique* number-plates at three o'clock in the morning, her scream cut off abruptly as the door had slammed shut on her. It was more than an hour later when a *flic* had noticed the small blue car, its engine still running and the driver's door hanging open. Last year Ariche had been there when a very pretty schoolgirl, chosen by an agent of an eros centre in West Berlin, was rendered unconscious by the application of an ether-pad and taken from her bed, through a window and into a private taxicab on the outskirts of London. Her price at that time, when the German mark had been worth more against the pound sterling than now, had been seventeen thousand pounds, a small enough sum that Julius Ariche would not have worked for except that the eros centre in question was a customer of long standing. And only three months ago in Rome, he had been there – of course he was *always* there – when a young singer from the junior opera company had boarded a train for Florence and was never seen to alight from it at her intended destination. She had been selected by a Pakistani horse-breeder who liked his mistresses to sing grand opera for him before he brought out the whip. There was, as Julius Ariche knew so well, no accounting for tastes.

Although the necessity of seizing the merchandise by force was always a little risky, it gave him a certain pleasure – a pleasure that would have been erotic in a normal man. As a young boy he had enjoyed catching flies and dropping them onto a spider's web, to watch the ensuing struggle. Today, the women he dealt in offered much the same spectacle in the moment of their capture.

So it would be with Miss Suzie Spinoza.

* * *

'How high is it?' Bibi asked.

'I'm not actually sure about that.'

'You mean you don't know?' Bibi turned her head to look at Suzie in the back seat.

'I guess that's what I meant.' Suzie was always phased by the way kids could put you in your place if you didn't say exactly what you meant.

'It's a hundred and fifty-one feet high,' Bibi announced. 'The index finger is eight feet long.'

They were talking about the Statue of Liberty. Bibi was sitting in the front of the Lancia next to Henri, as she always did on these shopping excursions, because if you let people like Linda or Suzie or *anyone* good-looking sit in the front, Henri wouldn't keep his eyes on the road, and that was very important when they went round the hairpin bends into Beausoleil.

'Have you seen the Grand Canyon?'

'I guess I never did.'

'It's two hundred miles long.'

'Well isn't that something?' Suzie was trying to fix this kid's age, and thought it was maybe twelve or thirteen. You could ask an American kid that age the name of a brand of tampon, but would it be OK in France? She couldn't ask Henri. The best thing would be to look along the shelves until she saw the right kind of picture on a box.

'And it's five thousand feet *deep*,' Bibi said.

'I've heard it's kind of impressive.'

Henri swung the wheel and turned into the Avenue de Verdun. A dark grey taxi turned off the Boulevard de la Turbie and followed the Lancia, keeping pace.

'I'm mad about America,' Bibi said. 'I read a lot about it, because I'm going to go there one day.'

'Maybe I can take you home with me,' Suzie said lightly. 'Put you in my pocket.'

Bibi turned her head again, this time slowly, and gave Suzie a look with her clear grey eyes that told her a whole lot of things, chiefly that this kid might look twelve or thirteen but was nudging thirty, and didn't care for being talked down to. It was going to be perfectly OK, Suzie knew now, to ask Bibi where to find the tampons.

'That's partly why I like Linda so much,' Bibi said, 'because she's American.'

As Henri turned into the Boulevard de la République a Mercedes limousine pulled up in the Rue du Marché. Both the limousine and the dark grey taxi carried radio antennae.

'Do you like Linda?'

'I guess she's pretty nice.' But hard to get to know. Oh boy, the way she'd frozen Suzie dead in her tracks like that, saying she couldn't care less about Prince Jacques . . . He'd obviously stood her up, which was a shame.

'We go first to the pharmacy?' Henri asked them.

'If that's OK with you,' Suzie said with a glance at Bibi.

'Yes. It's a good place to park, and we can go to one or two other shops from there.'

Henri pulled up and got out and went round to open the doors for his passengers, but Bibi was already on the pavement and Suzie was climbing out. It was nearly four in the afternoon, and the warm sunshine was filtering through a slight sea-haze to the south. The air was still, and the sound of a speedboat in the harbour came clearly into the streets. Henri would have liked to be down there, watching the preliminary runs, but he wouldn't be free until the evening. At least there was the compensation of escorting the young American into the town.

'If there's any help I can offer you with the shopping, Mademoiselle, you have only to tell me.' Henri's smouldering black eyes lingered on the American girl's face, noting its every feature. 'It would give me the greatest possible pleasure.'

'Thanks.' Suzie finally had to glance away. Jesus, these Frenchmen could get you right into bed just by looking at you . . .

'Come on!' Bibi said, and took her hand. They'd be all day if she let Henri start his manoeuvres.

The Mercedes limousine had not moved. It was parked some hundred yards away, and one of the tinted rear windows had been lowered a few inches.

The grey taxi had stopped at about the same distance, higher up the street, but now it began moving towards the stationary Lancia where Henri was standing.

Suzie and Bibi were now walking along the pavement, hand-in-hand, between the Lancia and the pharmacy.

At this moment the distant roaring of the speedboat near the harbour cut out suddenly, and Henri glanced up, but could see nothing because the buildings hid the sea. He frowned, thinking the engine of the boat had seemed to cut out rather abruptly.

'Look,' Suzie told the little countess, 'I need a few things I'm not sure how to ask for in French. Will you help me?'

'Of course I will.'

As they neared the pharmacy the grey taxi gathered speed suddenly, passing the Lancia and then braking as it swerved in towards the kerb. There was very little traffic at this hour, and only a few people on the pavement, none of them anywhere near Suzie and Bibi. Henri was still standing by the Lancia some distance away, intent on the sounds coming from the harbour; he noticed the taxi swerving towards the kerb but assumed the driver had seen a fare signalling.

'Can I find Max Factor here, Bibi?'

'They've got almost everything.'

As the taxi reached the kerb the rear door came open and for an instant a hand was visible on the door lever; then it was slammed shut and the vehicle pulled away again, the sunlight sending a reflection from its windscreen across the police car cruising past from the opposite direction.

'What about candies?'

'They keep those too. As a matter of fact I was going to suggest we bought some.'

Suzie gave a little laugh as they went into the pharmacy.

'*Framboises?*'

'It just means raspberries.' Bibi gave her the small round tin, and Linda looked at the picture on the lid. '*La Vosgienne*,' Bibi said, 'means the "Girl from the Vosges," which is a district in France. It's just the trade mark. Some things don't translate very well.' She wondered why Linda didn't look pleased with the tin of *bonbons*. 'Is Charlotte all right?'

Linda hesitated. 'She's fine. Shall I open these right now?'

'We'd better not. Suzie's just treated me to a huge praline sundae down in the town. This is the stuff you asked for.' She gave Linda a brown-paper package.

'Thank you, Bibi.' Linda put it onto the little marquetry table inside the door and turned back to look at her, trying to reach a decision. And then she did. 'Come on in, won't you? I'd like to talk to you.'

'What about?' Bibi wouldn't normally have asked, because talking to Linda was the best thing in her life; but Linda had sounded serious, though she was pretending not to be.

Linda quietly closed the communicating door between her room and Princess Charlotte's after looking in for a moment, then came back as Bibi limped across to the deep Louis chair which was her favourite place in here. 'It's about my patient,' Linda said quietly. She'd decided to talk to Bibi as a nurse, to get the message across that this was going to be official, and not some kind of game they were going to play. Sitting in the big chair with her legs dangling, Bibi found herself looking up into Linda's lovely but unsmiling eyes. 'And what I'm going to tell you has to be in absolute confidence, OK? The only other people who know about this are Prince Jacques and Dr Chirac, and they're not going to be telling anybody.' She pulled up a brocaded stool and sat facing the child. Child? In a lot of ways Countess Bibi was very grown up; otherwise they wouldn't be having this conversation. 'So is it a deal? You'll keep this a secret?'

Surprisingly, Bibi hesitated, gazing back into Linda's eyes, her own solemn and steady. Then she said slowly, 'I never give away secrets that people *tell* me. I only tittle-tattle sometimes, about Mademoiselle Pinalle and Madame Leclerc and people like that, because – ' she looked away, her wide grey eyes on something that Linda couldn't see; then she looked back again – 'because I can't help it, I suppose. But I never give away secrets that people have *told* me, and asked me to keep.' She put her fair head on one side, and the pony-tail hung down against the dark brocade. 'Do you see the difference?'

'I think so.'

'All right, then. But apart from *that*, I would *never*, *ever*, in the whole of my *life*, give away anything *you* told me, or anything *about* you, whatever it was. And I don't need to cross my heart, do I? Because you know it's true.'

'OK, Bibi. I'll go with that.' Linda looked down for a moment, touched, and then said, 'OK, this is the secret. Somebody around here is up to mischief, and we have to put a stop to it because it could get serious.' She went on to tell Bibi about the switching of the tablets and what it could have brought about, glossing over the medical details but making sure that Bibi realised the situation already *was* serious.

Even as Linda told her story she felt doubts that she should be burdening these very young shoulders with something that amounted to attempted murder, assuming that the 'mischief-maker' knew the consequences of her giving her patient those anti-coagulants. But there was nobody she knew here whom she felt she could trust – except the little countess. When she'd told Dr Chirac, he'd told her flatly that she must have made the mistake herself, confusing the two bottles. She'd said that if he really believed that, he must immediately inform the authorities and have her charged with gross and culpable negligence, but he'd astonished her by saying it had been the kind of mistake anyone could make and they must both forget it. *Was that the standard of medical practice in France?* She didn't believe it – the French had a fine reputation in this field. Then why was he taking it so lightly? If her patient weren't already in danger she would have insisted on Dr Chirac's going to the authorities, so that she could at least clear her name; but it was only this one man who thought she'd made a mistake, and he didn't have her respect in any case; and an enquiry would mean her immediate suspension – which would leave Princess Charlotte unprotected. That was unthinkable, and she'd decided to sink her pride.

She made her report to Prince Jacques and Dr Chirac – her patient's closest relative and her physician. But now she needed help, and from others.

'It's like this, Bibi. We have to make sure that Princess Charlotte is never left alone, even for one minute, day or night. I can't be here all the time, though I certainly won't be jogging any more in the morning, or going into the town with Henri. I'll have food sent up on a tray – it won't be difficult to make a few changes. If – '

'But you can't imprison yourself?'

Bibi was perched forward now on the edge of the huge chair, and began making it clear that she understood the situation perfectly well – and knew what to do about it. Linda needed exercise, and Bibi would 'sit in' for her every day. She'd recruit one of the servants to keep watch on the corridor outside from the mezzanine, taking it in shifts with someone else. They –

'It has to be someone we can trust absolutely, Bibi.' Linda didn't know any of these people here at the Chateau; all she knew was that when a family fortune was to change hands twice within less than a year, there was usually a struggle for position and heritage, and what she had to tell this thirteen-year-old girl was difficult. 'Even when someone very familiar to you comes to visit with the Princess, they mustn't be left alone with her. Even people close to her.'

'Except Jacques.' Bibi was watching her steadily.

'Prince Jacques?' Linda looked away. 'I don't know. But if you say he's OK . . .'

'I do. You can trust him with *anything*.'

Except my heart. The thought flew through Linda's mind, catching her unawares. She let it go. It was just a tattered shred of the past still on the wind.

'OK,' she said, looking up at Bibi. 'But nobody else. Right?'

'Right.'

As they went on making their plans, Linda opened the package Bibi had brought from the shopping expedition, and found the two electronic beepers she'd asked for. She gave one to Bibi. The other she'd give to Prince Jacques.

'The transmitter's on the night table by Princess Charlotte's bed, where she can reach it. If you're in there and she's sleeping, you can press the button and I'll get the signal, and so will Prince Jacques – he'll have one as well. OK?'

Bibi inspected the beeper with interest. 'American know-how,' she said. 'Fantastic. Do I just put it in my pocket?'

Linda showed her how to carry it. Then she said quietly, 'I guess you're not very old Bibi, and I'm sorry to have to bring you into things like this. But I want you to know that without you, I'm not really sure how I could keep Princess Charlotte safe.'

Bibi slipped off the chair and stood close, looking up at her with her grey eyes wide. 'That's the most important thing we've got to do,' she said gravely. 'But whatever it was you told me we had to do, that would be the most important thing for me.' Then her eyes narrowed and she spoke in a half-whisper. 'Besides . . . I'm the best one to help, because I know a lot about the people in this Chateau . . . an awful lot . . . And what I don't know, I can find out.'

She only stayed a few minutes longer, and was on her way to the door when someone began knocking on it, lightly but very fast, and when Linda opened it they saw Madmoiselle Pinalle standing there in the corridor, her face ashen.

'There's been an accident, down in the harbour. It's Prince Jacques . . . it's Prince Jacques . . .'

25

CRISIS

TOINETTE WHIRLED TO face Raoul.
'*What made him crash?*'
He stared at her.
'How would I know?'

She turned away, fixing the diamond earring Raoul had just given her. He'd found it somewhere on the floor – she was always losing them.

'I don't know,' she said, and tried to calm herself. In a few minutes they would be downstairs in the hushed, shadowed dining-room with whatever guests happened to be there. She would have to seem natural. That was part of her life, always having to seem natural, smiling to order during polite conversation, her long sleeves hiding the bruises. 'But I remember your saying that Jacques mightn't have long to live, the way he takes so many risks. It seems . . . such a coincidence.'

Raoul came close to her, holding out one sleeve for her to fasten the cufflink; he could never manage them when he was nervous. It was one of those mundane little rituals between a husband and wife that belied, tonight, the enormous tension between them.

'You're so melodramatic, Toinette. Do you imagine I'd tamper with his boat? I don't know the slightest thing about engineering.'

Her eyes flashed. 'Is that all that would have stopped you?'

'Of course not.' He held out the other sleeve.

'Anyway you've got plenty of people who'll do things for you – whatever you tell them to do.'

She thought of Michel de Beauvais, pulled from the wreckage of his Citroën on the RN7 only weeks ago. The police were still investigating the cause of the accident. Only a few days before it had happened, Charlotte had told Toinette in confidence that the Count de Beauvais might be offered a major interest in the estates.

Had Raoul known? He could have found out; he could find out anything he wished, with that man Dorlhac's help.

'You need to throw away this shirt,' she told her husband. 'The cuff's begun fraying.'

He thanked her and moved away, with more things on his mind than a frayed cuff. 'It was a rough sea, that's all,' he told Toinette. 'They're already saying the trials should have been cancelled, or postponed. If Jacques had been killed, someone would have been blamed.' There'd be an enquiry in any case; Jacques was going to live, but it had been a close thing; they'd said the speedboat had flipped over without warning and then reared up, to crash down across the floundering *pilote*.

'He was very experienced,' Toinette told him.

'He was taking *risks*, as he's been doing since the day his father died.' Raoul moved close to her again, lowering his voice. 'I told you before: Jacques offers us no impediment.'

Toinette kept her distance, a chill running through her as she went to the mirror and checked the line of her dress, turning her dark head to inspect the chignon. And what if Jacques *had* 'offered an impediment?'

It had begun with the telephone call from Geneva, from Szala. She hadn't known what he'd told Raoul, but that was the night when he'd failed to make love to her, the second time; and in the long dark hours he'd told her, very simply, what would have to be done if he weren't to face ruin and public shame. At first he'd told her only that his one chance lay in his acquiring the estates; later he'd made it clear that he expected her to help him – and at whatever cost to her conscience.

To Raoul's knowledge – through Dorlhac, the lawyer – Charlotte had still not made a will, for reasons of her own. If she died intestate, the estates would pass automatically to her son, Jacques. If that happened, the way would be clear. Jacques was incapable of running the estates and in any case had no stomach for it; Raoul and Toinette – who was, after all, Jacques' aunt – could easily move in and take over, leaving him as the mere titular head of affairs with a small fortune of his own to squander. And if anything happened to him the estates would automatically pass to Toinette, the next in line.

'So it all depends,' Raoul had told her with his black eyes holding hers, 'on *when* your sister dies. If for any reason it happened before she made a will, my worries would be over. And you, Toinette, would find yourself the mistress of the de Montigny-Villiers fortune.'

She'd told him it didn't interest her: she'd never want for security. He'd said then at least she should imagine how she'd feel as the wife of a ruined and disgraced financier, her name linked with his in the international headlines. She'd said she could face that; she'd never cared what people thought about her. But then she'd realised that she didn't have any choice. Whatever her own feelings, she was going to do exactly what Raoul wanted her to do. *He had a kind of dark magic for me*, she'd told Charlotte a little time ago. Charlotte had asked, *You mean you're in his power?*

Yes. When this man's eyes looked deep into her own she was lost, and she knew that if ever she attempted to challenge him, to defend herself against him, he would break her will. This was as clear to her as if she'd seen it somewhere carved in stone.

So she had agreed to do what he'd asked her, and taken the phial of tablets from him – *where had he obtained them?* – and gone into her sister's room; and as she had quietly approached the bed, listening to Charlotte's feeble and arrhythmic breathing, she'd had to go through all the excuses in her mind, the logical, intelligent reasoning that had allowed her to come into this room in the first place, stealing upon a living human being, *her own sister*, with intent to bring an end to her life.

Charlotte was already dying, with only a little time left, perhaps only a few days, perhaps no more than one. She was ready to go, 'to join my darling Edouard,' as she'd told Toinette more than once. All she was hanging on to her life for was to see the estates in safe hands. For this she suffered increasing pain, day after day. Toinette could end her suffering so easily, and ensure the safekeeping of the estates – in the capable hands of Raoul. There was no one more experienced in the management of substantial enterprises than he, and the only reason for his present difficulties was that a business associate – a man called Henry Simpson of the Jersey Guaranty Trust – had failed to fulfill his obligations and left Raoul critically exposed. The de Montigny-Villiers assets would be secure in his care, and would even prosper – a fact that Charlotte would be ready to concede if she didn't feel such a personal dislike for him.

Toinette understood this; Charlotte was afraid for her, thinking that Raoul's treatment of her was gross and unthinking cruelty.

But that wasn't true. His dark, compelling need to ravish her to the point of injury had sensed a response from her own deep cravings, the instant they'd met. She couldn't hope to explain this to Charlotte, whose life knew only gentleness, and she hadn't tried. There was only one solution, and Raoul, with his practical and ruthless attitude to all human affairs, had shown it to her. And she'd been powerless to refuse.

His voice broke into her thoughts as he shrugged into his dinner-jacket and pulled down his cuffs. 'Jacques is your nephew, Toinette, and you feel a natural regard for him. So let me tell you this – and you know I never lie. Whatever happened to his speedboat, I had no hand in it. From all reports the sea was dangerous, and he was driving himself to break record after record, taking the most appalling risks. So you can put it out of your mind.' He brought his feet together and bowed slightly, darkly handsome, a smile glittering in his eyes. 'Let me tell you also that you've never looked so captivating as you do at this moment. Shall we go down?'

'Yes.'

She would go down to dine with him tonight. She would go anywhere with him, tomorrow, the next day, and all the days of her life. She would do whatever he asked her to do, even the most heinous deeds, because she had no choice. The only thing that could ever save her from his dark power would be darker still – death itself, hers or his own.

* * *

'*Oui. C'est l'infirmière privée de la Princesse Charlotte de Montigny-Villiers, Docteur.*'

A telephone rang and the nun answered it.

'*Mademoiselle, voulez-vous –* '

'*Qui est là?*'

'Do you speak – er – *parlez-vous Anglais?*'

Another telephone began ringing and the orderly picked it up. The nun nodded to Linda. 'Yes. One moment, please.'

The doors of the operating theatre opened again and two surgeons came along the narrow, bright-lit passage, their heads together in conversation, blood staining their gowns.

'*Mademoiselle?*'

'Yes?'

'In here, please.' The nun was beckoning. Two more orderlies hurried past, one of them dropping a clipboard and stopping to pick it up.

Linda followed the nun. The smell of ether was drifting along from the operating theatre. Everyone seemed to be talking at once.

'Docteur, il'ya quelqu'un qui vous demande . . . '

'Non – c'est un journaliste – '

'Où est Docteur Chirac?'

The doors opened again and a nurse wheeled a metal trolley into the passage, bright instruments tinkling, bload-soaked swabs crimson under the light.

'This is Dr Barnes, Mademoiselle.'

'Good-evening.' He smiled to Linda as the nun left them. 'You're his mother's private nurse, I understand.' He spoke with a British accent.

'Yes, Doctor.'

'All right, I'll give you the score, as best I can.' He was a short man, his hair tufting below the green linen cap, the mask hanging loose around his neck. His eyes were red-rimmed and his face drawn: the team of surgeons had been operating for seven hours non-stop. Linda had reached the Centre Hospitalier Princesse Grace three hours ago and had been trying all the time to get news, even a scrap of news. They'd just kept on telling her they didn't know anything definite yet. 'Dr Chirac's on another emergency,' the Englishman said, 'but he's asked me to talk to you. I wangled a stint here for the winter – too jolly cold in London.' He gave a weary smile, then turned to the X-ray pictures that covered the whole of one wall. 'I suppose Prince de What's-his-name was lucky, considering. Smashed the right femur to bits – look at this – sub-trochanteric, transverse, cominuted – ' he prodded the plate – 'but we've got most of it together again and I dare say he'll be able to walk all right, with a bit of a limp.' He glanced at Linda, his eyes crinkling as he attempted another weary smile. 'He's young, of course, and very fit, quite an athlete from all reports.' He looked at the plates again. 'Let's see – fractured pelvis – bi-lateral through the acetabulum – this is a better shot – nothing too difficult. A lot of laceration over most of his body, because the boat came down almost on top of him – we've sewn him up all right but there'll be a few scars. The worst damage is to the face – ' he broke off as a nurse looked in.

'Excusez-moi, Docteur – téléphone.'

'Who is it?'

'*Le Docteur Maillard. Il est –* '

'Tell him I'll ring him back, would you? And look, Marie, do you think some kind soul would bring us a nice pot of tea?' He turned back to the X-rays. 'Yes, his face came in for rather a lot of punishment – look at these. Malar and zygomatic arch fractures, displacement of the floor of the orbit – Doctor Fresnay went through the mouth and did some rather nice elevation under the arch – this is the clearer shot – and this one – he's extremely good at this kind of thing. What these pictures don't show, of course, is the tissue damage. He's already under plastic surgery and he won't be out of there before midnight. God knows what he's going to look like when they've finished with him, but they're first class chaps; I've worked with them before, in Nice.'

Linda thought of that lean, aristocratic face with its handsome profile, and felt an instant of compassion. 'Is there any internal damage, Doctor?'

'Nothing nasty, no. It was kind of – ' he clenched one fist and brought his open hand across it – 'a kind of skimming process, and of course the water saved him quite a bit. Six inches to one side – the *wrong* side – and he would have had his skull smashed in.' He turned away and gave a noisy sneeze. 'Allergies, allergies . . . they say it's the olive trees down here. Are you from America?'

'Yes.'

'Jolly good show. I've done a bit of work in your Bellevue Hospital. So there we are. Optimistic prognostications and all that.' He offered a charming smile that this time reached his eyes. 'If you're going to take over nursing him when he gets home, I dare say he'll recover pretty rapidly.'

'Thank you, Doctor.' Linda picked up her sling-bag from the metal stool. 'Look, I want to reassure his mother as much as I can, but she'd want to hear the truth. Have the plastic surgeons expressed any hope of real success?'

Dr Barnes looked down for a moment. 'I'm told this patient was a rather good-looking chap.'

'Yes.'

'Well now, since you want the truth – ' he gave a little shrug – 'I believe what they're going to try for, as hard as they can, is to make him . . . what we might call socially acceptable.' His tired eyes met Linda's again. 'You know, so that he can go around without people thinking he's some sort of a freak.'

'They're going to do the very best they can, Madame.'

In the quiet of the room, Princess Charlotte watched her, the rose-shaded lamp casting soft shadows. It was gone midnight.

'But it won't be easy for them. That's what you mean?'

'It'll be a challenge.' Linda put her hand on her patient's. 'You know the kind of success they can have these days with plastic surgery. Dr Barnes told me these two specialists are first class. But in any case I think we should all be thankful that he's alive and already recovering. He's very strong, and very fit, and whatever we try to prognosticate at this moment in time, I believe the actual results will prove better.' She kept her eyes on Princess Charlotte's as she spoke; she'd learned early in her training that to look away when she was giving a critical opinion was to make the patient feel she was hiding the truth.

After a time the Princess said quietly, 'Very well, then. We must thank God for His mercy.'

'Yes. It could have been so much worse. And now you must sleep, with nothing on your mind. He's through the crisis, and from here on he can only gain strength.'

But as she quietly locked the door of each room and got ready for bed, the doctor's words kept coming back, disturbingly. *So that he can go around without people thinking he's some sort of a freak . . .*

Other thoughts haunted her as she smoothed the night-cream into her skin, with the lights turned low. The tragic accident to the Count de Beauvais was never far from her mind, and now it was overlaid by the shocking and deliberate attempt on Princess Charlotte's life and the accident to her son, only hours ago. Linda remembered the feeling, soon after she'd arrived here at the Chateau, that there were dark undercurrents at work, strong and malevolent forces that she couldn't hope to understand. For a while, when her belief in Jacques had rescued her from her fears, she'd gotten these ideas out of her mind, putting them down to culture shock. But now they were back, and more insistent, crowding her from the shadow. Everything had started going faster, whirling deeper like a dark maelstrom as one crisis followed another, as if Prince Edouard's suicide had set off a train of events where death and the closeness to death were beginning to weave a sinister design.

As sleep came fitfully, more than an hour later, the last thought in Linda's mind was that whatever had brought the onset of headlong violence into the life of this ancient family, it must run its course, for no power on earth could stop it.

26

THE NEW PATIENT

'I WOULDN'T IF I were you, darling.'
'Why not?'
'He's not for little you.' Daphne watched the waiter pour some more champagne. 'You see, I *know* a lot of these people, so I can save you some trouble.'

Suzie covered her glass as the waiter tilted the magnum again. 'I'm fine.' She looked back to Daphne, who seemed a little depressed tonight. She'd only danced a couple of times since they'd come into the night-club and she hadn't gone off anywhere with a man and come back looking strange, and it was already three o'clock in the morning. Another thing that Suzie had noticed was that Daphne had started looking across at the door, like she was expecting someone. The place wasn't crowded, maybe fifteen or twenty people in here; the trio was playing mostly blues. 'I thought he looked quite interesting,' she told Daphne.

'He did, Suzie, and he is. And he'd marry you like a shot because he's just got his fifth divorce and is obviously keen on you, but if you like the idea of living in wedded bliss with a man who spends most of his time selling armaments to all those little countries so that they can kill each other off, and the rest of his time with little boys in Berlin and Tangier and Marakesh, I'm sorry for you.'

'Oh Jesus. I didn't think he looked that way.'

'Darling, he'd fuck a donkey if that was all he could get.' That was another thing Suzie found different tonight. Daphne didn't normally say things like that. 'He's terribly rich and he's got a title but that doesn't mean a bloody thing.' She glanced towards the two gilded doors again, then drank some more champagne, the diamond bracelet on her wrist flaring in the light. 'All he needs a wife for is to make him look respectable, but of course they can't stand him after a while. There are all kinds of rich, you see, and

222

they have their own kinds of sex. There are the tycoons who've started from nothing and built an empire, but that's all that turns them on, and anyway they get so bloody tired from wheeling and dealing that they haven't got any strength left for romping in bed. Then there are the ones who were born with so much energy that they can buy and sell a goldmine and a couple of African republics and half the stock in Harrods and then take on a dozen call-girls and even their wife if she's around, all in one day, before they can get to sleep.'

Suzie noticed a man come in and stand looking around for a minute. A waiter went up to him but he just motioned him away and sat down alone at one of the tiny tables where the lighting was so dim that he pretty well disappeared. Daphne had seen him, and was taking her elbows off the table and sitting back, pulling her silver-lamé stole around her shoulders.

'Then there are the rather dreary aristocrats who were born with lots of money but don't know what to do with it, so they spend most of their time in places like this and drink themselves under the table and wake up in the arms of a totally unfamiliar lady who's just emptied their wallets and given them AIDS.' She'd begun speaking faster now, and was trying so hard not to look across again at the man who'd come in that it showed. 'Then there's the old-money type, usually *very* rich and mostly Jewish – they tend to be small, quiet, self-effacing family men who wouldn't be seen dead with a floozie and wouldn't know what to do with her anyway – they look on women younger than themselves rather paternally. Now if you could find one of *those*, darling, providing you didn't mind officially changing your religion, you'd be all right. Now I've simply *got* to go and tinkle.' She flashed what Suzie thought was a kind of scared smile and left the table, going through the archway opposite the doors and not looking at the man who'd just come in.

Suzie hesitated, got a hold of the huge champagne bottle by the neck and was trying to tilt it over her glass without dropping it when the waiter arrived from nowhere.

'*Permettez-moi, Mademoiselle.*'

'Thank you.'

She hadn't meant to drink any more than three glasses tonight (if she didn't count them, the whole thing got out of hand), but she was bothered about Daphne. She'd been getting more and more bothered about her since the night when they'd been racing along the road up there and Daphne had screamed to a halt in a side lane and told her that when she died she was going to leave everything to her. Maybe it had been OK to get things straightened out but it had taken a bit of doing and Suzie had made her run a good half-mile before she'd tripped and sprained her ankle and ended up sitting on her fanny on the ice-cold hardtop letting rip with the really classic winners out of the truck-driver's vocabulary while Daphne had held her tight and begun sobbing her heart out and then started laughing and wanting to know what on earth a shit-kicker was.

By the time she'd half-carried Suzie back to the Jaguar and they'd driven home along the Grande Corniche the whole thing had gotten more or less worked out. They'd curled up on the rug in front of the fire and held their frozen hands around mugs of rum toddy and decided that Suzie would have to change her mind about marrying Sheik Ahmed of Abu Talha because if she were only going to do it just to show she could be independent of Daphne, it wasn't worth it.

'Look, darling, I won't give you another *thing* if you don't want me to, but *don't* go and fling yourself at the nearest Arab before you've found out a bit more about him. I'd never forgive myself if you came to any harm.'

Suzie hadn't argued very much. She'd been doing a lot of thinking the past few nights because she didn't sleep too well, and the more she'd thought of those guys with their flashing eyes and their curved daggers the more she'd realised she'd feel more at home with just a regular millionaire from Texas or Florida with a couple of oil-rigs or an orange grove who didn't have any funny ideas about taming a gal with a camel-whip.

In fact she was pretty sure, as she sat here starting in on her fourth glass of Dom Perignon, that she'd maybe just missed doing the craziest thing she'd ever done in the whole of her life so far, and if that guy Ariche called her again tomorrow she'd drop the phone like it was a live rattlesnake.

The man at the little table over there wasn't there any more. She'd only just noticed. He hadn't gone out again because the doors were right opposite and she'd have seen him, and he wasn't sitting at the bar. Well Jesus, even Daphne wouldn't lay a guy in the ladies' room. Would she?

Suzie was restless and uneasy. She had the strongest feeling that it wouldn't be very long now before all that neurosis stacked up inside of her was going to blow. It didn't make Suzie feel any better when Daphne came back from the john in a totally different mood. Most of tonight she'd been depressed, and now she was starry-eyed and flashing her showgirl smile and talking nineteen to the dozen about how good the life was down here on the coast and how they ought to come here more often, things like that, not waiting for any answers, just letting it all come out in a whole torrent of joie de vivre.

'But you're tired, darling.'

The flow stopped suddenly and she was looking at Suzie with concern.

'I'm OK,' Suzie said.

'No, it's bed-time. Here am I bubbling away and it's almost tomorrow.' She beckoned the waiter and signed the bill and got up, and that was when Suzie saw she'd dropped something and picked it up and gave it to her. It was a 100-franc note.

'Is that mine, darling?'

'It sure isn't mine.'

'Oh goody, pennies from heaven!' She held it out to Suzie, laughing gaily. 'Why don't you – ' then she stopped, and put the bill in her purse. 'Sorry, Suzie, I'll never learn, will I?'

Once in the crimson Jaguar, Suzie dozed off, hit by the fourth glass of champagne and a wave of sleep. Daphne looked down at her once or twice but didn't disturb her. It was difficult not to talk any more because she felt so happy, but poor little Suzie had *so* much to put up with – this wasn't really and truly her kind of life and all she wanted was a nice rich man who'd be kind to her and then she'd probably settle down in a cottage in the country and raise a lot of perfectly *marvellous* children, and Daphne would visit them with lots and lots of presents and they'd – well no, not lots and lots because Suzie would have all she wanted at last, just a few toys and a pot of caviar, just as a gesture. Everything would be wonderful!

She span the wheel and sent the car through the bends with the tyres shrilling a little, glancing down and making sure that Suzie's seat-belt was buckled and then gazing ahead again through the windscreen to watch the sweep of the lights bringing the rocks and the trees out of the darkness, coloured and beautiful and making a magic picture-show, faster and faster until it all began blurring a little and she felt an instant of warning and shook her head to clear it, yes, the speedometer needle was on the high side of 130 kph and she'd left that silly bastard a long way behind this time without having to swerve into a side-road, serve him right, bodyguards were such a *frightful* bore.

But she didn't take her stockinged foot off the accelerator because there wasn't anything else on the road at this time of night and it was perfectly all right to throw this lovely lovely motor-car through the bends and go faster and faster and listen to the roaring of the slipstream and watch the dark green of the pines and the apricot-coloured boulders go swinging by with only a foot to spare on the hairpin bends as she changed down and sent the Jaguar up the hillside towards La Turbie and the Chateau with the engine howling as she – watch it, darling, *watch* it, yes, that rock was *very* close . . .

The tyres gave a sudden scream as the car heeled over with the headlights going dizzy across the trees and the little stone walls that stopped people from going right over into the void and she hit the brake and brought the wheel over and heard gravel from the roadside shooting out from the wheels and rattling against the rocks with a sound like a machine-gun, what marvellous fun but she mustn't overdo things, they had to get home safe and sound.

Then she didn't remember anything for a while. The really horrid part began when they were in their room at the Chateau and she was dancing, faster and faster in the middle of the room with the flames in the fireplace strung out in a circle all round her and Suzie calling something to her, something she didn't really understand because she had to concentrate on keeping her balance or she'd go flying right through a window by centrifugal force *it was fun it was fun but she wanted to stop now and she couldn't, she just couldn't –*

Flames in a ring around her –

'Daphne, for Christ's sake – '

Poor little Suzie with her white face and her small hands reaching out and trying to stop her but all she could do was go faster and faster – *faster and faster and laughing a lot, screaming with laughter –*

'Daphne are you OK, are you high on something – ?'

Whirling and whirling with the flames in a ring all around and I'm frightened now, terribly frightened –

'Suzie I'm frightened darling for God's sake help me – '

Hands reaching out and then Suzie's arms – 'It's OK, honey,

I'm with you – ' her arms trying to get hold of her – 'but listen, what are you on, I need to know what you're on – '

'*It's cocaine – it's bloody cocaine and it won't let me go and I'm so terribly frightened!*'

Arms holding her tight now and Suzie's voice coming through the flames as they began slowing down – '*Take it easy now, OK? I'll go get Linda.*'

'I want you to keep this safe for me.'

Linda took the envelope; it was thick, and bore a wax seal and the words, *To be opened only in the event of my death*.

'Should I put it in a bank, Madame?'

'No. But hide it somewhere. No one is to open it but you, do you understand?' Her eyes were fixed on Linda's, waiting intent.

'Yes.' She went into her room and put the envelope under her things in the bottom drawer of the dressing-table. Later she'd think of somewhere safer. When she came back, Princess Charlotte was taking a few steps across the room to one of the windows that overlooked the rose garden. Surprisingly, she'd rallied soon after the news of her son's accident, and for the last two weeks had even spoken to him on the telephone. She was the kind of person who, already suffering, would react to a crisis by reaching for hidden strength and somehow finding it.

'What time is it, Linda?'

'Almost ten o'clock. He shouldn't be long now.' She took a deep breath, and tried to forget she hadn't slept more than a couple of hours during the night. She'd lain awake until past three o'clock trying to reach a decision; then Suzie Spinoza had come to her room and she'd had to go and bring the English girl down from her high.

The decision she'd had to reach was to do with Prince Jacques, and it wasn't easy. Two weeks ago Princess Charlotte had told her that she wanted Linda to nurse him from the moment he came home from the hospital. She would ask Dr Chirac for a new nurse for herself. *I know your skills*, she'd told Linda, *and I know your depth of devotion to a patient. Jacques is more important than I am now, and I want you to give him everything you've been giving me.*

Linda had refused. She'd been engaged specifically to nurse Princess Charlotte, and there were RN's right here on the coast with her qualifications who could care for Jacques. It was then that Princess Charlotte had let her know that few things escaped her, despite her being for the most part confined to her bed. *He didn't mean to hurt you, ma chère, and I think you know that by now. Put it out of your mind. He needs you.*

Linda had said she wanted a few days to think about it. Maybe she could forget the closeness she'd once believed there'd been between Jacques and herself; she had to take things like that in her stride. But there were other problems that seemed insurmountable – and she'd have to handle them alone. Before the boat crash, Jacques had been able to take full responsibility for dealing with the situation concerning the switched tablets. Now he wouldn't be able to have anything on his mind but his recovery from massive injuries and their attendant shock.

But someone had tried to bring an end to Princess Charlotte's life, and nothing could alter that. They might even try again.

Linda couldn't tell her patient why she mustn't ever be left alone again. If Linda were going to look after Jacques, she'd have to change her room, and the new nurse would take over the one she had now, where Bibi was doing her lessons all day so that when Linda had to leave for a while, Princess Charlotte would have someone near. But how would she explain the situation to her replacement? If she told her there'd been an attempt on this patient's life, she'd quit the job right away – or ask for Dr Chirac's instructions, only to be told that no such attempt had been made, and that Linda had simply got the tablets mixed up. There'd seemed to be no way out, until Linda had offered a compromise.

'I'll nurse Prince Jacques,' she told his mother, 'but only if you agree to remain under my care as well.'

'It would be too much for you.'

'No. There are only the two of you. In my hospital I nursed ten.'

'But with others helping you.'

'I'm sorry Madame. If you insist in bringing in a replacement to care for you, I'll have to leave here altogether.'

In a moment the Princess had said searchingly, 'You must have your reasons, Linda. Strong reasons.'

'Yes.'

'And you can't tell me what they are?'

'Madame, I can only ask you to trust me. I know what's best for both you and your son, and I'm capable of nursing you both, day and night.'

Again a question had come into Princess Charlotte's eyes; but she'd decided to dismiss it. 'There would be a great deal for you to do, *ma chère.*'

'It wouldn't tax me to the point where I couldn't do it well.'

So it had been agreed, and now Princess Charlotte moved across the room to another window, where she could see part of the gravel driveway where it curved through the pines.

'How long will it be, Linda, before my son will walk again, with the sunshine on his face?'

'Pretty soon, if there aren't any complications.'

Princess Charlotte's withered hand rested on the window-sill, her fingers picking at a blister of paint. 'How soon? Do you mean weeks, or months?'

'Weeks.' It was only an educated guess; she just wanted to tell her patient what she needed to hear.

'Then I might see him walking again, before I leave you all?'

'Why certainly.'

'I would like to think so.'

The doors of the ambulance came open, and he could smell the scent of the pines.

Hands reached for the metal stretcher, moving it, shaking him and sending pain through him like forked lightning.

'Easy, now . . .' a voice said; he heard it faintly through the bandages.

'Welcome home, *Monsieur le Prince.*'

He didn't answer. They'd only hear a feeble croaking.

Their feet sounded, crossing the flagstones. The big double doors were opened, and there were more voices. The stretcher heaved and swayed, suffusing his body with pain. Light crept at the edges of his smoked glasses, between their rims and the bandages; the light went piercing through his brain.

They'd told him he must stay another two weeks at least in the hospital, but he'd insisted otherwise. He would need a full-time nurse at the Chateau, they'd told him, and would have to learn physical-therapy exercises at the hospital. He'd agreed, though someone had said his mother had demanded different arrangements. He didn't care. He wanted only to be home again, where he could begin to think things out; there was no peace at the hospital, and he felt disoriented there.

The things that he'd have to think out were going to be

unpleasant, and there'd be a point reached where he'd need to decide whether to go on living, because of that quiet voice he'd overheard, soon after the final operation.

It's too early to tell, but one thing's certain. He won't be recognisable as the man he was. The most we can hope to do is to make him recognisable as a human-being.

They'd thought he was still under the anaesthetic.

'Be careful,' someone said now. 'Georges, get behind me, in case we trip.'

The stretcher began tilting end-to-end as they started up the grand staircase; there was the scuffling of careful feet, and heavy breathing.

'We shan't be long now, *mon Prince*.' It sounded like Henri, the chauffeur.

Someone missed his footing on the stair-carpet and the stretcher lurched, then steadied. Pain flared through him like sudden fire, searing his bones.

Recognisable as a human being.

Like *le petit Baron*, then, a creature that had to slip into the shadows at the slightest sound and lurk there unseen, unknown. Ice, this time, froze his nerves, where before there had been fire.

Then they were in a room, with the sound of shutters being closed, and muted voices. He was lifted onto a bed, and had to clench his hands into fists until they were senseless, so as not to cry out.

'Poor Jacques,' a voice said, and a small hand touched him. He shrank away. *He was untouchable now. Didn't they know?*

'Bibi,' a woman's voice came softly, muffled by his bandages, and then, 'I'd like you all to go now, please. Thanks for your help.'

After a little time the door was closed, and it was quiet, but he sensed he wasn't alone. He would have spoken, but the slightest effort, even moving his tongue, brought pain.

'How do you feel?'

From the darkness behind the smoked glasses, behind the bandages, he said: 'Who is that?'

'I'm Linda Terman, your nurse.'

It was a minute before he could find the strength to speak. '*I don't want you. Get someone else.*'

'I can't do that. I'm following your mother's instructions.'

'Tell her I want someone else.'

Time went by; he couldn't tell how long; the pain was flowing through him like slow fire in the dark. Then her voice came again.

'I am to be your nurse. Those are your mother's wishes. You'll have to forget yourself now, and start thinking of others, for the first time in your life. It's the only way you'll ever pull through.'

27

THE SNATCH

THE HOTEL NOVA-PARK ELYSÉES in Paris is tucked between the Champs-Elysées and the Plaza Athénée. There are only seventy-three rooms but some of them are quite spacious. The Royal Suite, comprising twelve rooms alone, covers almost five thousand square feet of richly-carpeted floor-space. It is not considered very expensive at an approximate rate of US$5,000 per night because it offers a private roof-top garden, private telex machines, Agence France-Presse and Reuters news bulletins, conference-chambers and dining-rooms and a bar for each living-room. There are five bedrooms and seven bathrooms with gold-plated fittings. The windows are bullet-proof and a Rolls-Royce is at the permanent disposal of guests. By way of a bonus, Mlle Margaret, on the ground floor, is considered the most attractive hotel receptionist in the whole of Paris.

The décor is sumptuous, with mauve and marble predominating. Its glib description as 'sheik chic' derives from the fact that many of the hotel's guests are Arabs.

It was from the Royal Suite on this cool December morning that Sheik Ahmed of Abu Talha telephoned an unlisted number in Monte-Carlo, to inform Monsieur Julius Ariche that he would be in Paris for two days on his way home, and that he would arrive at the Royal Palace in Abu Talha two days afterwards, and would of course expect to find the 'party of interest' – Miss Suzie Spinoza – awaiting him there as agreed.

A photograph of the young American girl was propped against the telephone as Sheik Ahmed was speaking. It had been taken by a hired cameramen with a telescopic lens the day after Ahmed had fallen violently in love with its subject. Even from a distance, the camera had faithfully registered the lady's startling good looks: the deep amber eyes shining from a mass of raven-dark hair and the long, expressive mouth breaking into that generous, almost erotic smile. The slight graininess on the photograph enhanced it, lending it a hint of mystery. It was this exquisite face that Sheik Ahmed had seen in his imagination whenever he had lain with one of his wives, since the day when he'd first glimpsed it.

A man of lively imagination, he was able already to picture the moment when Suzie Spinoza would be brought before him for the first time, on the night of his arrival at the palace, with two of his favourite eunuchs dragging her forward by the thongs around her wrists, and her naked body scented for him by her women attendants. The first time, he would use the whip lightly; he'd only be playing. Later it would be different; there'd always been that strange tendency in his behaviour to these women that led him to inflict more and more pain on them the less they aroused him; or perhaps it wasn't so strange; surely they deserved it. Even this American girl would lose her ability to arouse him after a while. It was simply a sad fact of life.

'It has to be done tomorrow, at the latest. Your deadline is noon, the day after. Friday.'

The voice of Julius Ariche was scarcely raised above its habitual softness, but he knew that the man on the other end of the line would be listening carefully. Ariche would be giving his action team fifteen per cent of the half-million US dollars he'd receive for this item of merchandise. Under his calm exterior and the softness of his tone he was seething with anger – at himself, for not having succeeded in enticing Spinoza into an act of marriage with the Sheik, with his action team for their lack of success in securing the merchandise before now, and with Sheik Ahmed himself, for taking his private Boeing 727 to Paris with his entire retinue without first warning Ariche that the deadline was so close.

'Tomorrow,' he repeated into the telephone, 'at the latest. I shall expect you to make absolutely certain next time.'

A private executive jet was already waiting for him on the tarmac at Nice Airport, with the crew standing by. The papers were prepared and the procedure rehearsed. He would board the plane together with Miss Spinoza and a registered nurse. The scenario was that the American lady was a wealthy socialite on her way to a private detoxification clinic in Switzerland, which would explain her slurred speech and her inability to walk unaided. In point of fact she would be under a heavy dose of Dopla–23, a drug that Ariche had used successfully before, since it comprised a sedative together with a temporarily mood-altering constituent which put the subject into a state of mild euphoria, inducing the unquestioning acceptance of whatever was going on.

'Next time, M'sieur,' the voice came on the line, 'we shall make absolutely certain, yes.'

It wasn't until almost twenty-four hours later, soon after seven o'clock in the evening, that the crimson Jaguar belonging to Lady Daphne Houghton-Downe was seen to leave the Chateau de Beausoleil. As it purred down the hillside road towards Monte-Carlo the dark-grey privately-owned taxi took up station not far behind. A radio-telephone call was already going out, informing Monsieur Ariche that contact had been made with the target vehicle.

Fifteen minutes later Suzie Spinoza and the English milady were greeted by the maître-d'hotel in La Salle d'Empire, at the Hotel de Paris, and escorted to their table. Outside in the Place du Casino, the grey taxi was now parked within sight of the Jaguar. The black Mercedes limousine belonging to Julius Ariche was on the far side of the square with its chauffeur standing correctly near the driving-door, hands behind his back and his eyes in the shadow of his peaked cap. A rear window of the car was open a few inches, though nothing inside could be seen through the tinted glass.

Suzie Spinoza, as Daphne would later remember, was in a subdued mood this evening. That silly business of the cocaine trip a few days ago had unnerved the poor darling. (Actually it *hadn't* been so silly, it had been absolutely *bloody*, but with any luck it wouldn't happen again because she wouldn't smoke such a big rock.)

'It's not nearly so bad as you think, darling,' she said brightly. 'It happens to *lots* of people.'

Suzie watched her in the light of the shaded lamp, her tawny eyes thoughtful. 'Sure. And *lots* of people keep on with that junk and finish up – ' she stopped herself from saying 'dead' because Daphne was always talking about being 'doomed' – 'finish up on the funny farm. The thing is, I'm going to take care of you from here on out. OK?'

'But what a *bore* for you, darling.' She reached her hand across the table and pressed Suzie's. 'Now please don't worry any more about it. You're looking so absolutely *stunning* tonight that I'm probably going to lose you.' She meant of course that she'd lose

Suzie for a while to some dashing young stud – who might be with someone Daphne could do it with in the Jag, of course, though she didn't actually feel like it just now. That was the trouble with the bloody stuff – smoke a little bit and your libido hit the ceiling, but take too much and it put you off. It wasn't so easy to measure things when you base-lined because the rocks weren't always the same size; but she didn't like using a needle because it made the whole thing seem so *medical*, and people would notice the marks.

'Is that all you're having?' Suzie asked her. She'd ordered smoked salmon.

'I'm going to save room for some Crêpes Suzette, darling.' That was another thing: coke took your appetite away.

She watched Suzie covertly during their meal, realising that this American girl was turning her on more and more every day, with that slow, sexy smile and that husky voice and the way she walked, her slim hips swinging like a model's on a catwalk. But it just wouldn't do, would it? She was getting such a lovely lot of Suzie's company at the moment but of course it couldn't last. Sooner or later she was going to lose her to whatever rich and handsome man she finally decided to marry. They'd see each other *sometimes*, but it wouldn't be the same.

Somewhere deep in Daphne's confused and haunted mind there was the certain knowledge that on the day she didn't have Suzie any more, she'd want to die. And she knew the way.

It was an hour and fifteen minutes before the maître d'hotel settled the blond mink stole around Daphne's shoulders and escorted her and the American lady to the doors.

'It's only half-past eight, darling. What would you like to do?'

'Whatever you say.'

'I'd love to play a little roulette, but I know it worries you.'

They stood by the Jaguar, their furs keeping the cold from their bare shoulders. Across the flowerbeds, on the far side of the square, the window of the Mercedes limousine was lowered another inch. Higher, near the Avenue des Beaux Arts, the engine of the taxi started up.

'Watching you lose a fortune at roulette won't worry me any more,' Suzie smiled ruefully. 'Whatever gives you the kicks you need, OK?'

Daphne stepped close to her, a shadow crossing her face. 'You really are such an absolute darling. God knows what I'd do without you.'

'You won't have to.' Suzie had been riddled with guilt ever since that cocaine trip: recently she'd been throwing Daphne's kindness back in her face and all the time the poor kid was mainlining and not saying a thing about it.

The walked across the corner to the Casino, leaving the Jaguar outside the hotel. As they went up the steps a flash-light glared for a second and Daphne recognised Mario Romano taking a picture of someone getting out of a limousine, all smiles and sequins and long legs, a junior film actress of some sort.

'A hundred thousand francs,' Daphne was laughing to Suzie as they went across to the *salons privés*, 'that's my limit for tonight. Then we'll go and dance at the Club, shall we?'

'Whatever turns you on.'

Outside the Casino the dark grey taxi turned the corner and cruised to the top end of the square, the radio-telephone giving its electronic ring. The man sitting next to the driver picked it up.

'*You missed your chance*,' the voice of Ariche came, so softly that the man's scalp crept. He'd seen what happened to people when they did something that Julius Ariche didn't like.

'M'sieur, she wasn't alone. Until we can get her alone it's too risky, believe me.'

As the taxi crawled past the Mercedes the man turned his head, but could see nothing through the tinted glass of the limousine; he just felt a chill in the air.

'*Listen to me*. When they leave the Casino, follow their car and crowd it against the kerbside. Then make the snatch. *Do you understand me?*'

'But M'sieur, I – '

'*Do you understand me? I want you to make the snatch.*'

'As you say, M'sieur.'

The woman sitting in the rear of the taxi had heard the voice of Ariche over the telephone, and leaned forward. '*Merde*, has he gone crazy?'

'But of course. He – '

'Listen,' the driver cut in, 'what are we talking about? How many times have we done it before? We have to do it fast, that's all. We need fifteen seconds, twenty at the most. You know that.'

'And make sure she doesn't yell the place down . . .'

'*Alors*, you don't know how to stop a woman screaming?'

The taxi turned at the top of the square and started down again, double-parking alongside a small red Alfa-Romeo. The engine was switched off. As the driver sat looking through the windscreen he was aware of his heart-rate quickening. Ariche was right. If they didn't make the snatch tonight they'd overrun the deadline and lose Spinoza and twenty-five thousand US dollars each, *merde*, it didn't bear thinking about. They'd done it before and they could do it again; the moment the Jaguar started up and left the square he'd crowd it and they'd make the snatch.

But it never became necessary to do that. The events of the night, like the events of every other night and every day in the course of human affairs, were taking their place in the orderly sequence arranged by destiny; and sheer luck came down on the side of Julius Ariche.

As Daphne threw her first chips down on the roulette table, Suzie missed something.

'Oh, Jesus – I left my bag in the restaurant. Can you believe that?'

'We'll go and fetch it darling.'

'*Mesdames, Messieurs . . . Faîtes vos jeux, s'il vous plaît!*'

The wheel began spinning, and the ball was dropped in.

'You don't need to come with me,' Suzie said, 'it'd break your luck. I'll be right back.'

'Are you sure?'

'You bet.' She turned her head with a laugh as she moved away – 'No pun intended!'

A minute later she was walking down the steps of the Casino. Alone.

At the top end of the square an engine started up, and the dark grey taxi began moving off. On the far side the chauffeur was climbing behind the wheel of the Mercedes limousine.

On the ornamental clock over the Casino, between the two sculpted goddesses, the hands showed 8:44. At this hour the restaurants were crowded, and few people were about: one or two bored chauffeurs talking by their cars, some visitors walking down past the flower gardens, pointing to them in pleasure. The air was still, and the square quiet.

Then several things happened at once.

In the *salon privé* the roulette wheel slowed and the little ivory ball came to rest in No. 7. Daphne had laid her bet on four numbers at the other end of the baize but was no more than momentarily disappointed: she never gambled to win, but only to have fun. But she felt Suzie's absence, as she always did these days when they were separated for only a few minutes; and she picked up her fur from the back of the chair and left the *salon*, hurrying a little to catch up with Suzie.

In the square, Mario Romano, who had reserved a table for himself and Thérèse de Valoise for 9 p.m. at the Astoria, in the Avenue Saint-Michel, was slinging his camera-gear from his shoulder and walking across to his Alfa-Rome, which was parked outside the Hotel de Paris. He noticed the Mercedes limousine and recognised it as belonging to Julius Ariche. He also noticed Suzie Spinoza, whom he'd not seen since the dinner party thrown by Sheik Ahmed of Abu Talha, but decided not to stop and say hello to her because he didn't want to keep Thérèse, his dinner-guest, waiting.

Inside the taxi, as it slowed towards the pavement near the Casino, the driver was preparing himself for the task ahead, though there would be little for him to do except concentrate on a fast getaway without attracting attention. The other man was reaching for the door-handle, ready for action. He was strong, athletic and very determined, the kind of man who would not let anything get in his way – which was why Julius Ariche had selected him. His was the major role in the operation, and he was perfectly capable of performing it. He had, in any case, no intention of throwing his share of $25,000 onto the pavement by making a mistake. His name was Claude. In the rear of the taxi, the woman was also ready with the door-handle. Her task was crucial, but she would have no difficulty; she was young, charming and had a disarming smile, which were all that was necessary. Her name was Héloise.

High above them all, the hands of the clock reached 8:46, and at the same time Mario Romano broke his stride on a thought. His subconscious had been putting a few things together, concerning the presence of Julius Ariche and Suzie Spinoza in the same place and at the same time. He knew how Ariche made his living. Mario himself lived by his wits, and was always alert. Instinctively, he stopped and turned.

At the same instant Daphne Houghton-Downe appeared on the top step of the Casino, looking for Suzie.

The taxi swerved in to the kerbside and the rear door came open.

'Excuse me!'

Suzie, ten or twelve feet away, turned at the sound of the

woman's voice and saw her framed in the open doorway of the taxi. Suzie went over to it.

'Do you speak any English?'

'Sure.'

'Thank God!' The young woman looked helpless but relieved. 'I'm trying to tell this driver to take me to the Candlelight Club, but he says he's never heard of it.'

Suzie was now standing right beside the taxi and its front passenger-door came open suddenly and a man came diving onto the pavement and in the next instant Suzie felt her arms pinned as the woman drew back quickly into the taxi to make room. Suzie was overwhelmed by a whole kaleidoscope of impressions as they flooded her senses – the strong square face of the man right up close to her and his hard cruel eyes and the pain in her arms as he flung her towards the open door of the taxi and the smell of exhaust gas and Daphne coming down the steps in the distance with her mouth open and her hands waving frantically and then a rush of terror and the sound of her own scream rising before a thick hand was clamped across her mouth and she was pitched headlong into the taxi.

The driver was gunning up and calling to the man on the pavement, but as he hurled himself back through the doorway Mario Romano reached the spot and slung his heavy camera-gear at the man's head, half-missing him but bringing him to a stop for an instant, and in that instant Mario brought one foot against the back of the man's left knee and it jack-knifed.

Someone was screaming again. Daphne.

'*Suzie! Oh my God – Suzie!*'

The man spun round and smashed a fist into Mario's face and he staggered and went down but rolled to break his fall and sprang up again, diving for the man's legs but too late: the man lurched into the taxi and slammed the door and the engine gunned up and that was when Daphne's bodyguard came across the pavement at a fast run and dropped into a trained bent-legged stance in front of the taxi with both hands on his gun.

'*Ev-rybody fer-eeeze!*'

The satin-nickel steel-framed .38 calibre Colt Super-Auto Combat Commander was aimed through the windscreen at the point between the driver's eyes.

Mario Romano had been around celebrities long enough to recognize a fully-trained bodyguard who knew what to do with a weapon that size and he lunged for the rear door of the taxi and dragged it open and chopped the edge of his hand down on the woman's wrist as she clung onto the handle and then he went inside and got Suzie. The woman obviously hadn't seen the bodyguard and his gun because she was in the back, and she tried to break Mario's hold on Suzie so he flattened one fist and drove it with medium force into her throat and heard her choking for breath as he pulled Suzie onto the pavement.

The driver had a decision to make and he made it. He could tell a private bodyguard from a plain-clothes cop and he realised that all this guy wanted was to rescue the girl in the back, and once she was safe on the pavement he'd probably lose interest, so he gunned the engine again and threw the taxi around in a tight curve with its tyres shrilling and the rear door slamming shut; but there was something he didn't know about this particular bodyguard, which was that in the six months he'd been assigned to protecting Lady Daphne Houghton-Downe there hadn't been a single minute's action and tonight he was bored out of his mind and that was why he loosed off nine rounds in beautifully-controlled succession into the rear tyres and blew them off the wheels of the taxi and sent it careening across the road into a tree as the door burst open and the people inside poured out and began running for their lives while Mario Romano kept his fist on the automatic-shot trigger of his camera and took enough pictures to paper the walls of Monaco police-station, including the Mercedes limousine in the background.

28

LA CONDAMINE

'I WOULD LIKE them closed.'

Linda came away from the shutters. 'I'll close them in a little while,' she said patiently.

'I want them closed *now*. Don't you understand?'

'Of course.' Linda stood by the bedside for a moment. 'I also want you to understand, *M'sieur le Prince*, that as your nurse I'm responsible for your welfare.' She bent to straighten the edge of a blanket. 'Your eyes need light. So does your pituitary gland and so does your mind. If you brood in the dark all day you'll get more depressed than ever – and you wouldn't believe the effect the spirits have on every single cell in our bodies.'

It had been a week now since he'd left the hospital, and a dozen times Linda had believed she'd have to call in someone to help her. Jacques had been sinking deeper every day into a state of mind bordering on the suicidal. The day after he'd come home she'd found broken glass all over the floor of the bathroom: he'd smashed the mirror with a bare fist after seeing his unbandaged face for the first time. The following day he'd locked Linda out of his room and it had taken Madame de Valoise nearly half an hour, calling to him through the door, to persuade him to open it. Yesterday when Linda had finished walking him across the room a few times she'd gone across the corridor to turn Princess Charlotte's bed, and when she came back she'd found Jacques packing his toilet things into a valise. He said he was going back to the hospital, 'where the nurses would listen to him.' This time it had needed Charlotte to come to his room and persuade him to stay.

During this long week, Linda's feelings had swung between elation at the challenge to her skills and endurance, and near-despair as Jacques had become increasingly depressed. She understood the reasons, of course. For years she'd nursed male patients who'd lost their looks or their manhood or both, because of accident or disease; and men, whose vanity was greater than women's, suffered more. Jacques, too, had once been handsome; now he couldn't even face a mirror, even though she told him over and over that it was early days, that he should get his mind off what he looked like until three or four months had passed. Many times she'd sat on the edge of his bed and spoken to him quietly, while he'd lain helpless and anonymous behind the sunglasses he refused to take off when she was in the room.

'I told you in the beginning, *mon Prince*, that this has come as the first real challenge of your life. It may have occurred to you that we're all interested in seeing how you deal with it. Personally, I think you have enough pride to show us who you really are.'

'You don't understand.'

'I understand much more than you think.'

Sometimes he listened to her. Sometimes he asked her to leave him in peace. She wasn't sure how she could have handled things if it hadn't been for the people who'd rallied around her – Bibi, Madame de Valoise and even Suzie Spinoza.

'You know something?' Suzie had told her yesterday. 'You make me feel so goddamned *useless*.'

'I do?'

'The way you brought Daphne down from that high. The way you're caring for everyone. Jesus, you make me feel like a parasite.'

'Sorry about that.' Linda was bent over the washbasin in her room, soaking bandages in antiseptic; the pharmacy had been out of the impregnated kind. 'How can I help you, Suzie?'

'I guess I came here to ask what I can do about the way I am – I've gotten the running – uh – you know, kind of loose colon.' She leaned in the doorway, her arms folded, watching Linda.

'How long have you had it?'

'Since a few days ago, you know, when they tried – '

'That's just after-shock, Suzie. Don't think about it any more.' When Daphne and her bodyguard had brought Suzie home she'd been almost catatonic – it had been a pretty frightening experience for her.

'OK, I'll try. I also need to know if there's anything I can do to help you.'

'Like what?'

'Scrub floors. Empty bedpans. Hold people's hands.' She gave a hopeless little shrug. 'Jesus, I don't even know what a nurse does. Isn't that terrible?'

'You pretty well summed it up, except that we don't do floors – or windows.'

But Suzie had meant what she said, and by the end of the day she'd started working shifts with Bibi to see that Princess Charlotte wasn't ever left alone, and some of the time she'd spent sitting on the edge of the huge four-poster bed, telling stories about her life in Memphis, Tennessee, having of course to leave out most of it and make a lot of it up, while Princess Charlotte listened and slept and wakened again to ask how Jacques was now, always the same question, how was he now?

Thérèse de Valoise hadn't left the Chateau since Jacques had been brought home. Some of her day she spent talking quietly with Charlotte, and Linda had the feeling the two women were drawing closer to each other, maybe because Charlotte didn't have long now: she was becoming more and more dependent on drugs to keep down the pain; or maybe they were each seeking the other's comfort at a time when Jacques' life was suddenly going through tremendous and traumatic change. Most of the day Thérèse spent in the room across the corridor, talking to Jacques and helping Linda with his dressings and the exercise programme the kinetherapist had ordered for him, and helping him especially with his state of mind, his desperate need for reassurance.

Again, Linda had the feeling that Thérèse and Jacques had become closer during these last distressing days. Lying awake one night as the half-moon had covered her bed with a milky light, Linda had the impression that the Chateau had become like a ship at sea where storm waters were rising, so that those on board were moving together to share their courage.

'I hope you realise,' Madame de Valoise had told Linda one morning, 'that you're an inspiration to all of us here.' She was leaning at one of the windows to feel the sun on her shoulders, and spoke softly because Jacques was sleeping. The extraordinary beauty of this woman, Linda thought, had in some way deepened since she'd first met her; the lustrous, rather mysterious eyes had taken on a warmth that hadn't been in them before; she listened with quiet attention, and so often sensed people's meaning before it was put into words. 'After all,' she went on, 'you came here as a complete stranger, knowing nothing about us; yet you've done more for us than it seems we've ever been able to do for each other. Do you know what I mean?'

'Not really.'

Linda was holding one of the aluminium crutches that Jacques had to use when he walked, and Thérèse came from the window and took it from her, leaning it against the wall and coming back to stand close to Linda, her voice hardly above a whisper, her eyes intent. 'You're tired, my dear. Tonight I'll look after him, and get him what he wants.' She took Linda's hands. 'What I mean is, all of us here have been isolated from each other, pursuing our own selfish lives, shut in with our fears and our ambitions – you know what I'm talking about; you're very sensitive. And then – ' she hesitated, glancing down for an instant – 'then Prince Edouard died, tragically and unexpectedly, and we were all left hurt and bewildered and stricken. And just when we needed someone who could – ' she shrugged – 'I don't know, someone who could show us how to care, to be selfless, how to find courage – you were suddenly in our midst, a stranger.' And Linda was astonished to see the green eyes filling. 'A stranger with a heart bigger than all of ours put together.' In a moment she let go of Linda's hands and stood away. 'I just wanted you to know.'

In a moment Linda said quietly, 'Thank you. But I – I guess it's just the kind of job I do.'

'No. It's the kind of person you are.' She turned away, her shadow slanting on the sunlit floor, a jewel on her hand glowing like a prism; then she seemed to make up her mind to say something she might have left unsaid. 'I'm a celebrity, Linda, and considered very chic, very sophisticated. But I came from modest beginnings, and underneath all the glitter there's a deep simplicity. I believe in things like fate, and the influence of the stars – I'm very superstitious. But I don't think I'm being naive when I say that you're not here among us by chance. You're here to do great good, and save us from ourselves.'

And in the instant Linda's mind was flooded again with questions. 'Do you *know* this, Madame de Valoise?'

'No.' She made to turn away, and stopped. 'Let me put it differently. Yes, I know it. But I don't know how.'

That night, she made up a couch in Jacques' room, and Linda slept almost the whole night through.

Visitors were a problem. So many people wanted to speak to Jacques, to cheer him up and reassure him, but he wouldn't see most of them. They were always in the corridor – Mme Leclerc, Mlle Pinalle, Daphne Houghton-Downe and Suzie and Bibi, even Henri the chauffeur and Claudette the cook. Linda had to explain that her patient was slowly improving, but that it would tire him to talk to people at this stage. But two of them he allowed in, just for a moment, perhaps because they were children, and wouldn't judge him on his drastically-changed appearance.

Bibi had held his hand for a moment, smiling her most beautiful smile. 'Just think of it, Jacques. If that damned boat had come down a bit harder you wouldn't even be here now, and I'd be crying my heart out night and day. Nothing's *all* bad, ever, is it?'

The other visitor he allowed to see him was Guillaume, *le petit Baron*, who crept softly into the room and stood hesitantly beside the bed, his misshapen features barred by the light coming through the slats of the shutters, his small hand warm in Jacques'.

'I've found a bird's nest,' he said, his tongue slurring. 'As soon as you can walk in the garden again, I'll show it to you.'

Linda had been in the room at the time, but neither she nor Guillaume could see the eyes of the man in the bed, because of his dark glasses. But his head had been turned to watch his young visitor, Linda remembered later. It was during the night when she was awakened by something like a low cry, and hurried across the corridor, to find Jacques lying on the bathroom floor with both his wrists cut and spurting blood.

* * *

'It's exquisite, Celeste!'
'I'm so glad you like it, Maman.'

The two women, one younger and more slim than the other, stood in the middle of the spacious salon and looked around them at the archways and fluted columns and panelled doors. The curtains had been delivered and hung only this afternoon, and their gossamer tussore fabric framed the lights of the Royal Palace in the distance. The carpets, of a deep champagne hue throughout the principal rooms, still smelt of newly-woven jute, and stray threads lay here and there, unnoticed by the installers.

Celeste had worried the question: should she ask her mother to help her choose the furnishings, or should she simply invite her along here to their sumptuous new apartment, already decked out? The idea of surprising her had been irresistible. Mario had always been full of surprises . . .

'But Celeste, how is it that he – ' The frail, bewildered Mme Duvivier stopped herself in time. It wasn't her business.

The relationship between mother and daughter had settled itself over the past four years since the one man in their lives – M'sieur Duvivier – had been taken in an ambulance to the Centre Hospitalier Princesse Grace at three o'clock one morning, to be pronounced dead on arrival, of a massive cardiac arrest. After their shared grief had cried itself out they had moved to the shabby little apartment in the rue Princesse Florestine. M'sieur Duvivier, a bank clerk with *Crédit Lyonnais*, had left only a few investments that were not worth selling at the time of his death, and Celeste's salary from Maître Dorlhac was modest.

Mme Duvivier knew of course that her daughter enjoyed male company from time to time, though she never came home late, nor did she have anything to say about her few 'friends.' Secretly, her mother hoped with all her heart that Celeste would find a husband; but it didn't come to pass. Celeste was not pretty, though certainly not plain; those soft, contemplative eyes and her air of secret interests should alone attract any man with the sense to notice them. At the age of twenty-nine, Celeste should be thinking seriously about taking a mate, if she were to have children.

Then at last this young photographer, Mario, had appeared on the scene, and Mme Duvivier's prayers seemed to be answered – and, perhaps, Celeste's, for she spoke of him sometimes, and enjoyed his company more and more often.

This evening, Celeste had caught the unfinished question, and as she and her mother sat in the kitchen eating sardines on toast – there'd been no time to prepare anything more fitting to the occasion – Celeste explained that she'd been able to give Mario her professional advice over some legal matters, enabling him to benefit handsomely. It wasn't, after all, far from the truth.

'Such generosity, Celeste!' Mme Duvivier was delighted with this sumptuous expression of Mario's regard for her daughter. Celeste's company in their cramped apartment had never been exhilarating, but their evenings had been passed pleasantly enough with their embroidery and the television and occasionally a game of cards. Once her daughter was settled with a husband, her mother looked forward to a life of her own, with her piano – she was making progress – and the undemanding company of a little dog; Celeste had never wanted one: she said they were smelly and noisy.

'I tried to refuse, Maman, as you can imagine; but he wouldn't have it.'

'Such a wonderful man!'

'Yes,' Celeste said quietly.

For the last two weeks – two weeks and a day – since she had watched the crimson Alfa-Romeo growing smaller along the rue Princesse Florestine, she had thought of Mario constantly; and then the copy of *Nice-Matin* had been lying on the kitchen table one evening, where her mother had left it for her to see. On the front page, Mario's picture had leapt before her eyes!

KIDNAP ATTEMPT FOILED

Dramatic Scene Outside Monte-Carlo Casino

Late last evening, M. Mario Romano, the Paris Match photographer, hurled himself to the aid of a potential kidnap victim – whose name is for the moment being withheld at the request of the Monégasque Police Department – and dragged her bodily from a taxi in which her assailants were attempting to abduct her by force.

Details had followed, and that night Celeste had not slept before midnight, her mind and heart filled with the image of Mario, who had proved himself not only gallant, charming and generous, but a hero . . .

It had been a reminder of him that had gladdened her heart; yet she had finally found sleep with tears drying on her cheeks. Since she'd watched the little sports car disappearing along the street that night, Mario had twice sent flowers – but to both of them. The only time he'd telephoned, his voice had not lost its warmth, but he'd said he was in a noisy bar and couldn't talk for long – he was so very busy now, with the winter season on the Riviera at its height and so many celebrities arriving. Again, there'd been no mention of when they would meet again.

'I should have brought something to cook, Celeste!' Her mother poured a little more wine. 'We should have had a chicken, at least!' She dabbed delicately at her mouth with a paper napkin.

'It was because I wanted to surprise you, Maman.'

I've got a little surprise for you . . . His head close to hers in the Alfa-Romeo.

'I still can't believe it. You must tell Mario I'm overwhelmed. You'll be sure to do that, won't you?'

'Yes.'

After the first few days she'd wondered if she'd done something wrong, something to offend him. But she couldn't think of anything – he was so confident, so carefree, that it would be almost impossible to hurt his feelings. But if that was what she'd done, she'd want to die.

'And wait till he sees the furnishings you chose!'

'Yes.'

Then she had wondered whether it was because her 'secret mission' was over, and successful, so that he had no more need of her. Perhaps this beautiful apartment had not been by way of thanks, but a parting gift . . .

It couldn't be that.

That would be too cruel, and Mario wasn't cruel.

'The first time he has a chance of seeing the place,' her mother said, 'I shall make myself scarce, don't you fear.'

'There's no need, Maman.'

Her mother cleared away the dishes, and found some Crême Caramel from her shopping-basket and put it hesitantly onto the table. 'The dessert, *ma chère*, though it should be at least Crêpes Suzette on this occasion!' She looked suddenly at Celeste. 'Why don't we run down to the shops and bring back a bottle of champagne?'

Her daughter's eyes were cast down. 'Perhaps tomorrow, Maman. Or the next day.' Though tomorrow she should spend the evening out again, alone, as she'd done last week, pretending to meet Mario. She knew how much her mother was hoping for her to find a husband, but what she could do?

'Tomorrow I'll do some extra shopping, Celeste, and we'll celebrate.'

'That would be lovely.'

Later, when her mother had gone to bed, Celeste went quietly from window to window again to look at the shimmering lights of the town. This apartment was on the sixth floor, but if she pressed her nose to the glass she could just see the street immediately below. But it was empty, and she turned away.

29

A Terrible Party

'I WANT YOU TO give me your word that you'll never do that again. Or anything like it.'

Her voice came quietly in the moonlit room. He could barely see her face through his dark glasses; there was just the sheen of her cheek, silvered by the moon, and the glistening of her eye.

'Leave me alone,' he said.

His wrists were throbbing. Dr Chirac, called from his bed, had come here and put sutures in. Perhaps the throbbing meant infection; he didn't know about these things. But the doctor and the nurse were both capable, and they'd see to whatever had to be done, if infection were setting in. And if there were nothing they could do, then no matter, it wasn't important. Nothing was important any more.

'I'll leave you,' Linda said, 'once you've given me your word. I'll take it. I'll trust you.'

Some kind of feeling in him stirred. Perhaps that was important, yes: somebody's trust.

'It's not important,' he said, 'don't you see?'

'Your life?'

'Yes.'

'It may not mean much to you right now, but that's just because you're still in a lot of pain.' She leaned closer. 'Dr Chirac is the only person I told, because I had to. We're telling no one else – least of all your mother. Can you imagine what it would do to her?'

Jacques went on listening to the soft, urgent voice coming through the moonlight. No, he hadn't imagined what it would do to his mother; he hadn't thought about anything except that he wanted oblivion. It would have been terrible for his mother, yes, if he'd succeeded: first her husband, and then her son . . . And at this of all times, when all she wanted was peace of mind.

'You should know,' he told her bitterly, 'that suicides never think about others.'

'That's right. If they did, they wouldn't want out.'

'Want out?'

'They wouldn't give up. When other people mean anything to you, you want to go on living.'

He felt an urge to take off his dark glasses and look at her, and read her eyes; but he hadn't the courage. 'That's all that matters to you, isn't it?'

'What?'

'Other people.'

With a soft laugh of disbelief she said, 'What else is there?'

He pushed himself higher on the pillows. 'Do you know what made me do it?'

'Of course.'

'How can you know things like that?'

'It's not difficult. You just have to listen. But in this case I wasn't listening hard enough. I shouldn't have let him come to see you; but he's such a wonderful little person, and he's been worrying about you all the time, asking about you.' She paused a moment, seeing tears shining suddenly on his face; she reached automatically for the tissues on the bedside table, then changed her mind, deciding to let him think she hadn't noticed. 'I would have blamed myself, if you'd succeeded.'

That too should have occurred to him, he realised; he would have left a lot of pain behind him. But all there'd been in his mind was the scene Guillaume had conjured up: the two of them, hand in hand, crossing the open expanse of the lawns where people could watch them, and pity them, while they looked for birds' nests . . . two freaks, finding shelter in each other's company.

In a moment he shifted again on the pillows, feeling pain shoot through his hip, waiting until he could speak normally. 'I think I should apologise.'

A sigh came out of her, and for a moment she closed her eyes and let the relief go floating her along. So this man wasn't a typical suicide; it had just been the impact of sudden horror. She could understand that.

'There you go,' she said, and found herself smiling, because of the relief and because there was something so strange in hearing an apology from someone who'd just cut his wrists – and gone at them really hard. The true suicide never apologised: the very act was an attempt to make the whole world apologise to him. 'But there's something you need to understand,' she said. '*Le petit Baron* was born that way, and there's nothing we can ever do for them – I mean physically. They can't get any better. But you can. You're healing well and you'll go on healing. There were no burns, you see – they're the worst, believe me. All that's going to happen to you is that you'll look a little different, maybe even a lot different. But you'll still be the same person, and feel the same. We'll know who you are.' She got up from the edge of the bed, checking the night-table with a glance.

'No,' he said quietly, 'you won't. There'll be other changes, too, when I've found out how to make them.'

Linda looked down at him. 'The healing process is like that. It kind of brings us out of ourselves.' She checked the water-jug and straightened the pillows.

'Brings us out – ?'

'Gives us a new perspective on everything.'

'I see. You're leaving now?'

'It's almost morning, and I'd like to get a little sleep. It's been a busy night.'

She'd meant it to sound wry, amusing, but his voice was broken when he spoke again, with an attempt at formality. 'I – I'm extremely sorry for the trouble I've caused. And of course you have my word that – that I shan't worry you like that again.'

'Of course you won't, *mon Prince*. You've made the turn.'

Raoul Cavaille pulled the sleek black Lamborghini off the road with the tyres churning up gravel and the headlights sweeping across the pine trees. He doused them and cut the engine.

'*I don't believe you.*' He was furious, frightened.

'Why not?'

'Nothing's happened. She's still the same.'

'Then they were no good, that's all.' Toinette leaned her head back against the seat squab and shut her eyes. 'The tablets were no good.'

'He – I was assured they'd be effective.'

'Then the nurse must have noticed the difference.' She climbed out of the car to follow him; he was standing on the edge of the drop, where a low wall had once been built to stop vehicles going over, though the stones had been broken away over the years. She always followed him. *When would she stop? How could she break the spell?* He stood like a dark predator, staring down at the chateau among the trees, the moonlight reflected from some of its windows. He was frightened, she knew, because of the telephone-call he'd made from the auberge where they'd had dinner, higher in the foothills at La Turbie. He'd received a message to call Geneva but the line had been engaged when he'd tried to telephone from the Chateau – three or four times, his hand shaking as he'd spun the dial. Then at the auberge he'd tried again and got through, and come back to their table with the blood gone from his face. Frightened because of that monstrous toad Szala.

And furious perhaps because the German at a table near them had made eyes at her the whole of the evening. Raoul's jealousy was as fierce as all his other emotions. *I would kill any man who tried to take you away from me, Toinette*. He'd said that on their third evening together.

'I've ordered something else.' He spoke without turning his head, his eyes fixed on the turrets and the cypresses below.

'What do you mean?' She'd drunk almost a whole bottle of wine tonight without intending to, and to a certain extent her fears were anaesthetised. Since Raoul had been stricken by his obsession with the fortunes of the de Montigny-Villiers her life seemed to have plunged over a brink, like the one where they were standing now, and she was falling all the time, crying out in vain for help. In vain because only Raoul could help her.

'Something else for her.' His voice carried on the quiet air like a death sentence.

She swayed suddenly, and had to steady herself by reaching for him. It wasn't because of the wine. It was the feeling of terror, like a blow from the dark. He was going to make her try again. It had been days after the last time before she could look at herself in the mirror, face her own reflection without seeing herself as a monster, vicious and depraved.

'Raoul, I – '

He steadied her, looking deeply into her eyes, already sensing what she was going to say. 'Listen to me, Toinette.' His hand was on her arm like a steel hook, hurting; but she was used to that. His voice came sibilantly on the pine-scented air. 'Your sister is suffering. She doesn't have more than a few days now, at most a few weeks. She's longing for release. You know that. We all know it. Meanwhile we're going to go on living, and we have to think about ourselves, too.' He tightened his grip and she caught her breath; he didn't release her. 'What you have to do will take only a minute. Then you can forget all about it, forget that it ever happened.' He turned his head. 'Look down there, Toinette. Isn't it beautiful? In the moonlight, in the sunshine, it's always so beautiful. The Chateau de Beausoleil, the seat of great fortunes, of great power. Within a very little time it's going to be yours. Ours – since nothing will ever separate us. There is the Chateau, and you are to be the chatelaine, gracious, imperious, and with everything in life that any woman could possibly ask.' He lifted his other hand and brought the tip of his forefinger to the tip of his thumb, leaving only a tiny space between. 'And you're worried about something this size, Toinette, one little capsule.'

She stood shivering.

'You're asking so much, Raoul.'

'To gain so much, for both of us.' He held her more gently now. 'But it must be done soon. Tomorrow, before midnight, at the latest. I have to telephone Szala the next day, and tell him that everything has . . . been attended to.' He touched her brow with his lips, and she noticed how cold they were. 'You'll do it for me, Toinette?'

She closed her eyes, to escape his relentless gaze. In the darkness she felt herself scurrying like a small animal seeking escape, scratching at the bars of a cage, round and round and round, finding no way out – because this man would never leave her, and she couldn't leave him. She'd known it since the day they'd met.

'Yes,' she said. 'I'll do it for you.'

'You promise?'

'Yes.'

Forty-three kilometres from the coast, north of Sospel in the Alpes Maritimes, the black armour-plated Mercedes belonging to Julius Ariche was sweeping through the curves of the D2204, heading for the Col de Brouis, where the staff of an ancient farmhouse – rebuilt and modernised but preserving its original appearance – had been alerted by radio-telephone an hour before.

In the rear of the limousine Ariche sat alone, his hands lying perfectly still on the padded leather arm-rests and his short body leaning forward slightly, unconsciously assuming the tensed, alert attitude of a creature suddenly made aware that it has become the attention of a beast of prey.

Héloise has talked. They were the only words spoken over the telephone directly to Ariche an hour ago; the caller had then rung off. But Ariche hadn't questioned the warning; only a well-wisher could have sent it – perhaps the driver of the grey taxi, or Claude, the snatchman. Under the white glare of the light in the police station in Monte-Carlo, someone had at last broken, worn down by the merciless interrogation. It had been Héloise, the young and charming lure who had coaxed Suzie Spinoza across the pavement that night, within reach of the taxi and Claude's powerful arms.

Very well. Monsieur Ariche had options. It wasn't the first time that someone had squealed, and the ancient farmhouse, with its apple orchard and its rose-red walls and its steel-lined sliding panels deep in the cellars, was not the only refuge available to the Levantine. This one had been set up within a strategic distance of the Riviera, since much of his business was conducted there. He could stay at the farmhouse for weeks, months if necessary.

'M'sieur, s'il vous plaît.'

The voice had sounded discreetly over the intercom. Ariche moved a switch.

'Well?'

'There is a police-car behind us, with its codes flashing.'

The driver had seen it in his mirrors.

'Then slow down and let it go past.'

'Very good.'

But the police-car was not overtaking them; it was now following closely behind the Mercedes, its coloured lights flickering across the chromium.

'M'sieur?'

The driver was waiting for new orders. Ariche gave the situation a moment's thought. If Héloise had talked at all, she would have held nothing back; it would be very much in her interests to assist the Monégasque police as best she could, now that she'd started. The number-plate of the black Mercedes would have been flashed to the French gendarmeries throughout the country, the instant it was known.

Ariche brooded, ensconsed within the smoked-glass windows of the limousine. They had not been exceeding the speed limit: the driver knew Monsieur Ariche's standing instructions on such matters. The only reason for the police car to have come up on them was because the *agents* wanted to talk to him. Again, Julius Ariche had options. The last time a car had closed up on the

Mercedes was a year ago, when a certain Sicilian, who had believed Ariche to be poaching on his preserves, had attempted to object. Ariche had given a brief order to his bodyguards, and when the armoured limousine had driven away from the scene thirty seconds later, three men – among them of course the Sicilian – had lain by the roadside with their arms flung out and the reek of cordite heavy on the air.

But the people in *this* car were the police. They could be similarly dealt with, of course; Ariche required his personal escort to maintain a programme of rigorous training: they were virtually Commandos out of uniform, and a couple of policemen would present no problem. But later . . . later there would be many problems; one could not leave *policemen* lying by the roadside with their arms flung out, and hope to remain in business. The description and number of the black limousine would automatically have been reported on the radio the moment the police had sighted it.

'Pull in to the side of the road,' Ariche said briefly over the intercom.

A moment later the two gendarmes came up to the Mercedes on foot, both hands near their guns and one of them carrying a mobile cellular telephone.

'I want everyone out of the car,' the lieutenant ordered, '*one at a time.*'

Julius Ariche was the last to leave.

'Your *carte d'identité, M'sieur*, if you please.'

They stood in the moonlight, five men, two in uniform. When Ariche had left Monte-Carlo an hour ago, within five minutes of receiving the message over the telephone, he had decided not to bring the escort car with him. It might have attracted attention and in any case the extra man- and fire-power would have been unnecessary, whatever the situation.

The eyes of the police lieutenant looked up from the identity-card and into its owner's face. 'M'sieur Ariche, you will accompany us to the border of the *Principauté*, where you will be handed over to agents of the *Gendarmerie Monégasque*, who wish to question you. Would you like to make a brief statement?'

'No, thank you.'

But Ariche's eyes flicked suddenly to look at the nearest bodyguard and there was immediate movement. The two gendarmes reacted quickly enough and one of them had his gun halfway out of its holster before the order came to freeze, but that was much too late. The bodyguards had practised this kind of exercise a thousand times since they had entered the employ of Monsieur Ariche, and they went through it with perfect precision. Within two minutes the gendarmes were handcuffed to each other, one of them with his arms round the steering column and through the wheel of the Citroën DS. The ignition key, together with the keys of the handcuffs and the gendarmes' revolvers, lay somewhere in the undergrowth a dozen yards away, and the electric cable to the radio antenna was draped across the driving seat, torn from its connection.

It was seven mintes from the moment when Ariche had told his driver to pull in to the side of the road, at the same time ordering 'exit procedures'. There would be another ten or fifteen minutes to wait.

'Offer them cigarettes,' he told his guards, and moved away into the bushes, taking the opportunity to relieve himself. The necessary decision-making had already been done, and Ariche was left at leisure to reflect bitterly that it had been a woman – a *woman* – who had disrupted his life in this way. The next time he ordered a snatch, it would not be made gently.

The emergency lights of the police car were still flashing; they had been left on deliberately, and the two bodyguards stood with their hands behind their backs, watching the moonlit sky. The helicopter came directly in from the south, following the *Chemin Départemental* 2204 and sighting the lights of the police car without difficulty.

It landed in a clearing not far from the road, and Monsieur Ariche was taken aboard. Within twenty minutes it would land in the close vicinity of a farmhouse near Castel-Vittoria, across the Italian border, where Ariche would arrange his onward journey to Tripoli, via Tangier. There was at this time no extradition treaty extant between Libya and the French Republic.

As the helicopter prepared for take-off, the co-pilot leaned towards his passenger, a small box in his hand. 'Some Turkish Delight, M'sieur Ariche?'

'How kind of you.' He took one. They thought of everything, these people, and knew his fondness for this particular confection, especially in time of stress.

There was only one problem. The pilot's night vision was excellent, but nevertheless it was still night, and when the rotor-blades of the helicopter touched the top of a pine tree on take-off they shattered on impact, and when the fuel-tanks burst as the machine hit the ground, the glow could be seen from as far as the Col de Brouis.

The Levantine died with his bladder empty but his Turkish Delight still undigested.

Suzie had thought it was going to work out OK, but now she knew it wasn't.

'Are you all right, darling?'

'I'm fine.'

'I've been dancing with such a *marvellous* man – he says he's a sailor on leave from the French fleet. Can you imagine anything more *convenient?*'

Suzie gave a quick false laugh. So it wasn't going to work our after all. Linda, the nurse, had said she'd have to get her friend along to a detoxification centre – there were several in Switzerland, not too far away. Or she should try getting her to talk, because there seemed to be something on her mind, it wasn't just too much money and too much time on her hands, Linda had said. How could she tell? But if she'd said it, it had to be true. Linda was so *aware* of people. Suzie had watched her yesterday, nursing the Princess. Jesus, the *patience* of that gal, the understanding . . . Suzie could have gone on watching her forever, while the eyes of the poor woman in the bed followed her everywhere, adoringly.

And the job she'd done with Daphne, that time when she was on the high, talking her down, talking her down all the time while Daphne went on yelling until Linda's quiet voice and some of what she was saying began getting through – it was a matter of setting up a trusting relationship, she'd told Suzie later, you just had to listen and let them know someone cared, till they were quiet enough to let you shoot the Haldol in, or whatever kind of psychotropic agent you decided was best, if that was the word she'd said.

So Suzie had talked about a detoxification centre and Daphne had said she didn't need one, it was perfectly all right really, but she just felt a teeny bit miserable sometimes and the last time she'd overdone things. She wouldn't do it again.

'He told me that the way I danced, the whole of the fleet would mutiny just to watch me!'

'Terrific.'

'Oh darling, I'm talking too much – what a *bore* for you.' She pushed her glass of champagne away, and suddenly the fun was over; her face had kind of crumpled, and Suzie felt terrible – she didn't ever want to put Daphne down. 'Doesn't life strike you as a sort of frightening merry-go-round, Suzie? And we can't get off? Because we all want something, and it's here, even though we don't know what it is. We've got money, we've got men, we've got enough champagne to drown in, so perhaps that's what we end up doing, drowning in too much champagne.' She watched Suzie with her bright, feverish eyes. 'Don't you think?'

'No.'

Daphne looked as if she'd hit her. 'Listen,' Suzie said and took a small cold hand in hers across the table – 'that's not really you. It's just your act, to cover up something you can't tell people about. Right?' She was relying a lot on what Linda had said.

But it shut Daphne up in a second – you could hear the door slam.

'Oh, we've all got something we'd like to tell people about, darling, it's not just little me.'

Suzie wasn't quite getting the drift, and it worried her. Daphne was high again, OK, but it wasn't on champagne, it was on coke, and she was close to the edge. Something had just changed in her, gone snap, and it was to do with telling Daphne she was covering something up that she ought to tell people about. Suzie felt the blood leaving her face. Jesus Christ, you had to be so goddamned careful with people, or you'd send them right over the edge. She wished Linda was here – she'd know what to do.

'All I mean is,' she said, 'I'm ready to listen to anything you want to say, I mean it'd be absolutely OK with me.' Daphne was watching Suzie with her eyes trying to laugh, or cry, and not managing to do either.

'That would be marvellous darling.' She went on gazing at Suzie without saying anything, or even trying to say anything – Suzie was getting a whole lot of vibes now but she wasn't sure what they meant. At last Daphne smiled, a perfectly normal-looking smile, a real one, from a real person. 'What a wonderful friend you are to me, Suzie.' The smile grew warmer, shimmering on the small pale face. 'Look, I've just seen someone I know, and I'm going to leave a message for them at the desk, and when I come back we'll talk about it, shall we?'

'Sure. Fine. We'll talk.'

Daphne's smoke-blue eyes lingered on hers for another few seconds and then she turned away and walked between the tables until Suzie couldn't see her any more because of all the waiters and the dim light in here.

Maybe a breakthrough. Right? Maybe it was really going to work out OK after all, if she could get Daphne to talk to her and get whatever it was off her mind, like Linda said. That would be fantastic. No more coke and no more –

Then Suzie got up and knocked over her glass of champagne as she grabbed for her bag and jostled her way between the tables and saw the waiter and caught his arm and said – 'my friend left a message for someone – '

'The lady who – '

'Right – she left a message for – '

'But yes, *Mademoiselle* – this way, please.' At the desk he spoke to the receptionist and took the slip of paper, handing it to Suzie. 'She told me to give it to you when you left, but – '

'I'm leaving right now – ' She unfolded the piece of paper and read the few words and took off through the archway and across the lobby with a woman in red giving a little yelp of surprise as she bumped into her and went on and hit the doors before the guy could pull one of them open for her and suddenly there was the night and the cool air and the white reversing-light of the Jaguar as it backed out of the line of other cars – '*Daphne! Daphne!* – ' tugging and pressing the door-handle but it wouldn't – '*Daphne, for Christ's sake!*' – tugging again and the door came open and she ducked inside and switched off the motor and jerked the key out and clenched it in her fist and said – '*No, sweetheart, it's not going to be that way, OK? I'm not letting you out of my sight again till we've talked, you know what I'm saying?*'

Then she just went on sitting there while some guy came and hovered around outside, probably the bodyguard, and Daphne sat with her small white hands on the steering-wheel and stared straight in front of her through the windshield, breathing very fast and then slowing down while Suzie talked to her the way Linda had done, but this wasn't the same kind of high, because of the message she'd left – *Sorry, darling, but it was such a terrible party*.

'Take it easy, sweetheart, that's all we have to do.'

Rubbing her hands, trying to get the circulation back, her favourite emerald ring on tonight, worth a million goddamned bucks or something but what did that add up to when the hand was so cold, so deathly cold, but it could have been worse, it had *meant* to be worse, with this car hitting up the kind of speed she always drove at with the headlights streaking through the dark and the tyres squealing and tonight something else, sure, the smashing of glass and metal against the tree, the one she'd chosen, and then nothing, the party over, that was all, *the terrible party*.

'Take it easy, sweetheart, you're home now, you're safe with me.'

'Yes.' Such a small voice as she turned her head to look at Suzie, understanding at last what she was saying.

Breathing slower now, pretty well normal, and her eyes looked OK, kind of quiet, coming out of shock, maybe, wondering why she was still alive.

'We're going to talk a little,' Suzie said, 'and you're going to tell me just what's on your mind, this thing that's been bugging you, right? Because it's time now. I want you to tell me all about it, sweetheart.' Rubbing her hands, so small, so cold, rubbing the life back in.

Daphne's eyes on her, very calm now, and not even any tears coming.

'All right, darling. I will.'

30

THE VISITOR

'I'M SHATTERED.'

Thérèse smiled, picking out another album. 'Then I'm flattered.'

Mario came into the room from the balcony, looking more romantic than she'd ever seen him before, more Italian, his monogrammed beach-robe exposing his chest – ornamented with just the right profusion of hair, not too pink, not too macho – and his strong legs and slender, graceful feet. A lock of his dark hair hung carelessly over one eyebrow; the morning sunlight turned his olive-brown eyes to gold.

'I can't believe you're serious,' he said, bewildered.

'You mean you don't want to believe it.'

Thérèse was determined to make light of it for both their sakes, but it was proving less easy than she'd imagined. That was because she'd never realised she'd like him more at the end of their affair than at the beginning. It was usually the other way round: most affairs just burnt themselves out, to leave only a wisp of smoke, a little ash.

'Is that why you cried last night?' Mario asked her.

'Probably.' She turned the huge pages of the album slowly, taking care not to finger the photographs. 'I didn't realise you were so talented, Mario.'

He came and stood over her, looking down absently at the photographs as if he'd never seen them before, as if they didn't represent most of his life's work.

'What did I do wrong?'

Thérèse looked up at him against the light from the open french windows. 'You blew your cover.'

'What precisely does that mean?'

She'd never seen him so upset. 'When we began this affair, it was because you forced me into it. I could use the word blackmail if I wanted to be dramatic. You made me think that if I didn't offer you my body and soul on a plate, you'd do me great harm. True?'

Mario turned away impatiently, turned back, his face dark with worry. 'Look, I wasn't going to – '

'But that was the deal, wasn't it? A "tempestuous" affair, with a rather nice apartment on La Condamine for your little spy.'

He flinched at that, and she felt a pang of remorse.

'That's the impression I meant to give,' he admitted quietly. 'But in fact – '

'But in fact you would never have done me great harm, Mario, would you? Or even a very little harm. That's what I began to find out, as we got to know each other. And I finally realised you weren't a Machiavellian arch-fiend after all, but a very gentle young man with romantic ideas.'

'Is that all?' He sounded angry, and she tried hard not to smile.

'These days, darling, it's a lot. Despite all the roses and anniversaries and Valentine cards, very few men actually like women. You're one of them.'

For a moment he looked at her with his eyes clouded; then he pattered barefoot to the balcony and came back with the tray of coffee, pouring a cup for Thérèse. 'But you're not ending our relationship because you've found out it's not being forced on you.'

'No. It's because of a lot of things, really.' She bent to the tray to take more cream. 'A very dear friend of mine is dying. Charlotte has only a few days now, and I can't offer you the passion and the excitement that I'd like to.' With a note of bitterness she said, 'There's nothing quite so crippling to the libido than the certainty of approaching grief. And I'm worried about Jacques, too. We don't know yet what that crash is going to do to him – what it's going to leave him like. And above all, I don't want the rather lovely relationship we've developed to burn itself out in the usual way. Please try to understand.'

'Quit while we're winning?' he said sourly.

Thérèse let silence come in, wanting him to go on listening to what he'd just said. It took a moment or two before he sank onto his haunches and laid his hands on her knees, looking up at her. 'Yes, I understand what you're saying. It's just that I'm going to miss you, terribly.'

'Thank you, Mario. And I'd like to say this. It was terrific.'

He smiled at last. '*Vraiment*, my beautiful Thérèse, it was terrific. Tempestuous.' For a moment he lay his brow against her knees while she touched his head; then he moved away from her and poured himself some coffee. 'So I'm talented, you believe? It's taken you long enough to discover that.'

It broke the tension, and she laughed easily. 'I said I didn't realise you were *so* talented, Mario. These pictures are stunning.'

'*Paris Match* thought so. They've just approved my interview, by the way, and they'll use *all* the pictures I took of you.'

'Congratulations!'

'Thank you. It will make a nice . . . memento.'

'Among so many others.'

Thérèse found herself admiring the way he was taking his disappointment. Well yes, to be fair to herself it was more than just disappointment. He'd miss her, certainly, but for him there was the shock of rejection. That was never easy for anyone. How many times had this happened to him? Perhaps she'd ask him, before she left his apartment.

'I've noticed a trend,' she told him, 'in your work. You took so many children, this year. Look at these – pages of them.'

'A trend is a trend. They come and go.'

'But there's always a good reason for them. I know – I'm in cosmetics. This one's exquisite, this little girl.' She looked up from the album. 'You've never had any children?'

'No. I've never been married.' He was sitting on the floor, his legs angled behind him, his eyes on the square of sunlight made by the french windows; he was only half-listening to her.

'You've never committed yourself,' she said.

He shrugged. 'Perhaps it's that.'

'It takes courage, Mario.'

'Then I don't have it.'

'You were quick enough to rescue Suzie Spinoza from that gang of thugs. But it's not the same kind of courage, I know.'

'Suzie?' He turned his head. 'Oh, yes.' He looked back through the french windows at the cumulus piling in the south. They said there was a mistral rising again. Suzie, yes, with those fantastic looks. American. American girls were fun.

Thérèse closed the heavy album and went to sit on the floor beside him. He wasn't listening to her, but for reasons of her own she wanted his attention. 'You've had a lot of affairs, Mario. How many times has this happened?'

'This?'

'How many times have they ended it, not you?'

He gazed at her for a moment in surprise. 'This is the first time.'

'The *first* – ' Thérèse looked at him in astonishment. 'Oh my God . . . You must be feeling suicidal!' She wanted to laugh outright, but it would hurt him even more.

'Suicide never crosses my mind,' he said with dark solemnity. 'Most of them attempt to kill me when I leave them.'

'I can believe it.'

'I'm not fishing for compliments.'

'I know.' She threw an arm around his shoulders suddenly, the laughter going on inside her where he couldn't hear it. 'My poor Mario . . . What a terrible thing I've done to you.'

'Perhaps it's a good lesson, no?' Her face was so close to his that he could have kissed her by barely moving; but he resisted the temptation. Even if she brushed her mouth against his cheek, he wouldn't kiss her. *He would refuse!* Or try.

'Perhaps,' Thérèse said, 'yes. The best lessons in life are the hardest. This could be a breakthrough for you, Mario. Choose carefully, in your next affair, and – '

'There'll never be another one!'

Thérèse said nothing. Either he was being gallant, or deciding he couldn't face another lover walking out on him. It had come as a tremendous shock to his masculine ego.

'You must be going, Thérèse. I don't want to keep you.'

She kissed him lightly on the cheek, and got to her feet. 'You're right, I'm flying to London at noon.'

He stood up quickly, knocking a coffee-cup over. '*Merde! Oh – pardon!*'

Her laughter held a note of tenderness.

Before she left him, she said, 'Mario, I'm a little older than you, and perhaps even a little wiser. Let me say this.' She picked up her green silk bag. 'You said that some of the women you've left have tried to kill you. It's time you found one who would die for you. Then you could take the most stunning pictures of her for the rest of your life – and of your lovely daughters.'

He watched her, brooding, and again there came into his mind the captivating face of Suzie Spinoza.

'I don't know,' he said absently. 'I can't say what will happen.'

Thérèse kissed him gently on the mouth, lingering there for a long moment, the last. 'Nobody ever knows what will happen. That's why life is so interesting.' As he opened the door for her, she turned once more. 'But if this proves to have been your last affair, Mario, I hope it was at least one of the best.'

His dark eyes glistened suddenly as he took her hands in his. 'It would be so easy to lie, Thérèse, simply to be courteous. But I don't have to, and I'm sure you know. It wasn't the best, because there were no others . . . no others that I could ever remember now.'

'How did it get broken.'
'I was walking.'
'On your own?'
'Yes.'
'You shouldn't do that.' She snipped some more of the bandage away; the blood had dried, making it difficult.

'I was not asking for a lecture,' he said stiffly.

Linda soaked a swab, dabbing at the edges of the bandage. 'When you feel like walking, I want you to call me on the beeper. That's what it's for. I couldn't care less about the smashed vase, but I do *not* want you walking on your own, do you understand?'

He didn't answer. Behind the dark glasses, behind the swathes of bandages, he felt a burning resentment. He'd been trying to deal with it, to understand it, but so far he hadn't succeeded.

'If you fall over because no one's with you, you risk breaking your hip again. It just makes sense, that's all.' She dropped the bloodied swab into the dish. 'Look, I need to get the rest of this bandage off as soon as I can. If I rip it away it won't open the wound or do any harm, but it'll be rather painful. How do you feel about that?'

'Do what you have to do.'

She did it quickly but the pain flashed right through his body, reaching areas he'd thought were still numb.

'OK?'

'Yes.' Saliva gathered in his mouth.

It could only be guilt – the resentment. By French standards this young woman had behaved absurdly – it had been her fault. Culture-shock, yes. For a few days he'd been able to see it like that, as a minor accident of the heart that he'd unwittingly caused. Then the guilt had started, and in his mind he'd had to bring up arguments in his own defence; but the guilt had got worse, because he'd started seeing the matter from Linda's point of view instead of his own. And finally he'd found it was possible to feel just as guilty as if it had been his fault alone. His remorse hadn't given him any peace; he'd begun sleeping fitfully, waking to see her face, her tears fresh on it, waking to hear her voice . . . *What did it mean, then, the things we did, the things we said? Was it all just nothing?*

The day had come when he couldn't get her out of his mind. But he couldn't go to her, talk to her: he'd already made his apology, or tried to. And she'd been so formal with him since that day in the riding park, so icy.

But Linda, when other men entertained you, in your own country, did you always believe they'd fallen in love with you?

No. But this time it was different, that's all. Her head high as she'd face him, her shoulders back, the tears running but her voice perfectly under control. *Because this time it was I who fell in love with you.*

But there'd been nothing to be done, and so the guilt had grown worse, and the remorse, until he'd accused himself in his mind without mercy, unable to talk to Linda or to anyone else about it, though sometimes he'd been on the point of letting his mother know how he was feeling. It had made things no more bearable when she'd told him quietly, 'Linda is so wonderful to me, Jacques; I'm grateful to God that she's with me through these last days of my life.'

So wonderful . . . and that was the woman he'd unthinkingly hurt so deeply . . .

Nothing to be done. Nothing, except revile himself, day after day, brooding, hating himself, until the day came when the sea was choppy with white-caps and the salt was flying and they'd said, *Three new records, Jacques, and you're still not satisfied?*

The records had meant nothing to him: the risk in breaking them was what he needed, had to have, so that if the gods wanted to put a price on his guilt then he'd pay it.

She'd been there in his thoughts as the boat had reared and crashed down, blotting everything out.

'How do you feel?'

He opened his eyes. 'What? I feel – ' but it couldn't be said. It was too late now; it would always be too late.

'Are you OK?'

'Yes.'

'You can rest now, if you'd like. Do you need anything before I go?'

A long time seemed to go by. 'Nothing that – '
'Yes?'
'Nothing.'
Linda waited, trying to divine what was on his mind, but he'd shut himself in again, as he did so often. She checked the patient environment for the last time and left the room, quietly closing the door.

'Hi,' Suzie Spinoza said as Linda came into her room. 'How is *M'sieur le Prince* making out?' She was picking up a little French here and there when she talked with Linda.

'He's fine.' She checked the little clock at her bedside, surprised to see it was gone eleven. 'He's started to move around on his own, which is a good sign, though the ornaments come in for a beating. Listen, I didn't know it was so late, Suzie – bless you for taking over.'

'Any time. You know something? I'm learning a whole lot of new things, being around someone like you.' She got out of the brocade chair, dropping her copy of *Paris Match* onto the stool and slipping on her snakeskin shoes.

Linda moved to the doorway, listening for a moment. Princess Charlotte's breathing was steady, rhythmic. In the soft lamplight her brow had no shine on it; earlier there'd been a little fever.

'I'll say goodnight,' Suzie told her.

'Sure. Sleep well, Suzie, and thanks again. Oh – nobody came along here, right?'

Suzie turned at the door. 'Only her sister – Toinette.'

Linda was taking off her white coat, and stopped with one arm still in its sleeve. 'You told her the Princess wasn't to be disturbed?'

'Sure. But she got pretty insistent, said she had something important to tell her. So I let her go on in.' She wondered why Linda was looking so uptight suddenly, not moving, her coat only halfway off. 'I mean, her own sister, wasn't that OK?'

31

GHOST FROM THE PAST

'WHERE HAVE YOU been?'

'Just helping Linda. Did I wake you?'

'It doesn't matter. I'm glad. Now I know you're back.'

Suzie slipped between the sheets, taking Daphne's hand. 'Are you cold?'

'Not really.' Her voice was sleepy. 'Sweet dreams, darling.'

Suzie moved close to her and slid an arm around her shoulders. 'Everything's OK, sweetheart.' It was Daphne's nerves making her so cold; that's what Linda had said. In a way, Suzie had kind of taken on a patient of her own in this poor little rich kid, someone she could look after instead of herself. And Jesus, it was about time.

Watching the glow of the firelight on the ceiling, she started worrying again about the way Linda had taken it when she'd told her Charlotte's sister had paid a visit tonight. It was OK, Linda had told her, she didn't have to worry over it; but she'd gone in there to look at Charlotte real fast. Why?

There was so much going on around here. It was like there was a curse on the place – was that kind of thing actually possible? Since Prince Edouard had killed himself – she'd heard all about it from that weird kid Bibi – it seemed things had started to go wrong for everyone. OK, for everyone except Linda. She was the person who was holding the entire place together.

Daphne stirred, and Suzie listened for the beginning of another nightmare, so she could wake her before it got bad. Daphne was going through a whole new phase since she'd made what she called her confession. She wasn't on the coke any more, and that was fantastic: Linda said nobody could just knock it off cold-turkey without the most awesome withdrawal symptoms, so it had to be because Daphne hadn't been in too deep, or it was such a relief to have got that stuff off her mind that she didn't need to freak out any more.

But it had been scary. The confession bit.

Suzie had got into the Jaguar that night and made sure her seatbelt was real tight, but Daphne drove quite slowly down the mountain road, not talking much, very quiet, so quiet that Suzie sat there waiting for something to blow, but it didn't. They went right past the Chateau and down to Monte-Carlo, along La Condamine and onto the quayside. The night was very calm, with the moon in its third quarter just touching the sea.

Suzie remembered every minute, every sight and sound; they'd driven slowly along the quayside, and there was a thin, lonesome-looking girl sitting on one of the capstans, huddled in a windcheater and watching the boats; she turned her pale face as they went past, then looked at the harbour again.

'I want it to be here,' Daphne said when she pulled up and cut the motor. 'By the boats.'

'OK.'

There was the *Mariana* sitting there, the longest yacht in the port, and the *Princess Charlotte* right alongside, all white and gold, then a whole bunch of small boats with thin masts and furled sails rocking together and pulling at the ropes. Stars were reflected in the still water, sprinkled across it. Daphne got out of the car and went to stand near the edge of the quayside, and Suzie caught her up right away in case she was going to do anything stupid. Another car had followed them here, the bodyguard's; it was parked not far away, giving Suzie a good feeling; since that time outside the Casino she'd had a lot of respect for those guys, Jesus, this one had saved her life, him and Mario the photographer.

'Remember I told you a little about my sister,' Daphne was saying, 'my step-sister?'

'Sure.'

'She was a bit older than I was, and got everything first, remember? And I hated it. And of course I hated *her*.' She stood holding herself, kind of hunched against everything, and when Suzie put an arm around her she could feel she was shivering, in spite of the mink she was wearing. Shivering so badly that Suzie couldn't hold her tight enough to keep her still. 'It's all right, darling. I'll be all right . . . I think.' She stood staring at the boats, the little ones. 'Look, I – I don't want to be a bore, Suzie, so I'll cut it short if I can.'

'Sure. OK. Whatever makes you feel comfortable.'

Then before she knew it Daphne was shaking so badly her teeth were chattering and she turned suddenly and held onto Suzie with her eyes squeezed shut – '*Oh Christ, oh Jesus Christ*' . . . Saying it over and over, like praying, and that was maybe what she was doing, her small body shaking all the time, worse in a way than the coke trip had been, there was no screaming and yelling this time, it was just quiet, and scary, and Suzie began praying too, inside.

It took a long time, and when it was over, Daphne pulled herself free and stood with her head down for a minute and then turned slowly to look at the boats again.

'I hated her, was that what I was saying?' Her voice sounded almost normal now, just very quiet.

'That's right,' Suzie said.

'So I began doing naughty things. I was four, then, about four years old, and Sandra was six. Edouard and Charlotte were staying with my people – they were old friends, you see, actually Edouard was my godfather. Anyway – ' she stopped and let out a breath and then brought her head up and went on in that quiet, toneless kind of voice like she was reciting something that didn't really interest her. 'Naughty things, yes, like pushing her when we were coming down the stairs, just in fun, and putting mustard in her corn-flakes to make her sick. Then the fun got serious, you see, and I took the wedge from under a ladder she was climbing on and it tipped over and she broke her arm.' She stopped right there, and just stood looking at the little boats, shivering, and when Suzie was getting ready to say something to reassure her, Daphne started talking again, this time going faster and faster, like she was being drawn towards the edge of a waterfall and couldn't stop.

'Then – then soon afterwards we sneaked off together without Nanny seeing us, and went onto the lake in a boat – one of those tiny things with a sail, not much more than a toy, and a puff of wind came and turned it over and we fell out, and I started swimming for the edge of the lake. I was a good swimmer – we both were – but Sandra's arm was still in a sling and I heard her screaming for help but I just went on swimming and the noise she was making got fainter and fainter and there you are you see, I told them I tried to save her but couldn't because I wasn't strong enough, they'd call it manslaughter wouldn't they, or homicide by negligence, or was it murder do you think, *was it murder, Suzie –* '

'No, of course it wasn't, you don't have to – '

'*But Christ Almighty she died don't you see, she died and it was my fault –* '

'Look you were four years old – '

'*But I knew what I was doing and I knew it was wrong!*'

'You were just a little kid, honey, you didn't really mean – '

'*I killed my sister.*' She whirled and clung to Suzie and Suzie hung on while the terrible shaking started again and went on for minutes while Suzie didn't see there was anything else for her to do except ride it out till it was over, though she stared past Daphne to where the bodyguard was standing, his arms folded and his head tilted back a little as he looked in their direction, watching them steadily, wondering what the hell was going on, or had he seen Daphne this way before?

No. Suzie didn't think so. This hadn't happened before and she didn't think it was going to happen again. Just to make sure, she asked Daphne: 'Have you told this to anyone else?'

'No. No.' The shivering had stopped at last, but her hands were icy.

'Let's get in the car, sweetheart, and we'll go home.'

Suzie drove, while Daphne lay back with her head against the squab and her eyes closed and her face white, a sheen of sweat on it. A case for Linda again, Suzie thought. Jesus, what would they do without Linda?

After a minute she said slowly, 'You were around four years old when – when the accident happened, right? And she was maybe six? But didn't you tell me earlier that what you couldn't stand was her getting sex first, before you could, and a car first, things like that?'

'Yes, but don't you see, that was the whole trouble.' Her voice was calm, a little slurred, like she was coming out of shock. 'That was the trouble – *she was always there . . . she was always with me, even after she was dead . . .*'

'Kind of haunting you?'

'Yes. That's it exactly. But I – ' she broke off, and a deep sigh came out of her. 'OK, we don't have to talk about it any more, sweetheart. We'll just go home and get some sleep now.'

Suzie felt there was no point asking any more questions, making Daphne go on talking about this thing. She'd brought it all to the surface now and got it over with after – how long? – more than twenty years, maybe twenty-five. Her mind would need to settle now, let it all die down. The questions in Suzie's head wouldn't make any difference; they were just something to think about while she put the Jaguar through the mountain curves higher and higher towards the Chateau with the headlights of the bodyguard's car in the mirror. OK – could Daphne have saved her sister, helped her to reach the overturned boat where she could cling on till help came? Maybe. But that was just an assumption. Had Daphne gone on swimming away deliberately, hoping her sister would drown? Not necessarily; it could have been in her mind that she was certain she couldn't help Sandra, didn't have the strength at that age, so she thought the only thing to do was get to the shore and bring help. And then afterwards, with the shock of seeing her fished out of there, limp and cold and streaming with water, she'd gone into a guilt reaction that had grown worse and worse, out of all proportion, and finished up convincing herself she'd killed her sister.

That could happen, sure, in a sensitive kid. *Four years old* – the age when everything was larger than life, ten times larger, and more frightening, more terrible. Suzie shivered suddenly. What a thing to have to live with! Ever since that day, Daphne had tried to live a normal life, not saying anything to anybody, not letting anything show, while all the time she'd been growing up there'd been her dead sister growing up beside her, still getting everything first, never leaving her in peace . . . Until she'd met Suzie, who looked so like Sandra, and begun giving and giving – clothes, kindness, security, anything she needed, hoping desperately to make it up to her, to Sandra, and earn forgiveness.

As the sleek sports sedan cruised between the pines along the driveway to the Chateau, Suzie looked down at the girl beside her. Daphne's face was still bloodless, and her body was so limp that only the seat-belt could be keeping it upright. Her eyes were closed, but Suzie couldn't tell if she were sleeping or quietly tormenting herself, watching them bringing her sister home for the last time, her hair still streaming from the lake, a little six-year-old ghost who would haunt Daphne through all those years, until now.

'We're here,' Suzie told her gently.

Daphne's eyes came open, and for an instant there was fear in them. 'Where?'

'Home. The Chateau.'

'Oh.'

'And tomorrow you'll be OK, sweetheart. Starting a whole new life. Because she won't be here any more.'

'Are you all right?'

Linda turned, starting a little. 'Yes.'

Bibi watched her from the open doorway, her clear grey eyes unblinking. 'I came to take over for a bit, if you want me to.'

Linda stood away from the dressing-table, where she'd been leaning, totally lost in thought, when Bibi had crept quietly up to the doorway. 'Just for ten minutes, honey, sure, while I go and check Prince Jacques. But don't let *anyone* into Princess Charlotte's room.'

'I never do.' Watching Linda, Bibi realised that Suzie must have let someone in, otherwise Linda wouldn't have said that. Suzie was the only other person Linda trusted to keep watch. *Who was it she'd let in, and why was Linda so worried?*

'How was the math lesson this morning?'

'I threw my calculator at Mademoiselle Pinalle. Since she'd caught me with it I thought she might just as well have it.'

Linda forced a smile. The reason why she'd been so deep in thought was that she didn't know whether to confide in Mme de Valoise or go on taking total responsibility for Princess Charlotte. The moment Suzie Spinoza had told her last night that she'd let Toinette Cavaille in here, Linda had gone straight to the drawer in the writing-desk where she kept her patient's medication secured. The drawer had still been locked – but it was possible that Mme Cavaille had a key. The medication itself didn't look as if it had been tampered with – but if tablets or capsules *the same size and colour* had been switched, she wouldn't be able to tell. She'd not the slightest reason to suspect that it had been Charlotte's sister who had made the switch before; it was simply that *everyone* had to be suspect, except Bibi and Suzie, the only two people Linda believed she knew well enough to trust.

This morning she'd asked Bibi to go into the town with Henri first thing, and bring back duplicate medication; then she'd thrown the old bottles and phials into a trash-can. She'd hidden the new batch behind a loose panel in her bathroom, where the cold-water pipes ran, almost doubting her own sanity as she did so. Was she becoming paranoid? Hiding things behind secret panels was a lot more typical of one of these people here in the Chateau than of a healthy-minded all-American girl out of Trenton, New Jersey.

OK, so the place had got to her. There wasn't anything she could do about that; all she cared about was seeing that no harm came to her patients, and if that meant behaving like a thief in the night, very well.

She'd checked Princess Charlotte thoroughly and regularly for any unusual change in her condition since she'd learned that Mme Cavaille had been in here, explaining to the Princess that the medication had been changed slightly and that Dr Chirac would need a report on its effects. She'd hated lying, but the alternative would have been to tell her that there'd been an attempt on her life and that Linda feared another one . . .

'Can I look at the Handbook while I'm here?'

Bibi's quiet voice aroused her from her thoughts. 'Sure. If that's how you get your jollies.'

'My *what?*'

'Get your fun.' Some of the photographs in the surgical section of her *Registered Nurses' Handbook* were enough to give any kid nightmares.

' "Get your jollies . . . " ' Bibi said with a soft laugh, 'I'll have to remember *that* one!'

Linda gave her the book and checked her watch. 'I'll be across there with Prince Jacques for maybe twenty minutes, OK?'

'OK.' She looked up at Linda with her eyes wide and steady. 'And *nobody* is coming in here, don't worry.'

Linda shot her a grateful glance from the doorway, then crossed the passage and went into the third room along, opening the door quietly in case Jacques were sleeping. But the bed was empty, and the door to the bathroom was open. Hurrying, she looked in there, remembering how she'd found him the last time; but the place was empty. Worried now, she went quickly to the big walk-in dressing-room, but he wasn't there either. And then she saw his crutches leaning against the wall in the corner of the room, in their usual place.

But he'd never leave this room on his own because he was still traumatised by the change in his appearance, and anyway he couldn't walk out of here without the help of his crutches.

Linda caught her breath, glancing quickly around the room. The shutters were as she'd left them, a little way open; the bedclothes were thrown back, but not disordered; Jacques' medication was on the night-table where it should be; and his dark glasses were – *his dark glasses were there on the table too*, even though he'd refused ever to take them off except when she was changing the dressings. He'd never allow anyone but herself to see his face without them.

She broke for the door.

32

THE STAINED-GLASS WINDOW

THIS TIME THE pain was unbearable and Toinette had to cry out before Raoul would stop.

Tonight he'd regained his virility – she didn't know how or why; perhaps because she'd told him that she'd been in to see Charlotte and had done as he'd instructed her; perhaps because he believed now that the estates were almost in his hands. All she knew was that the moment she'd slipped out of her afternoon dress to change for dinner he had attacked her without warning, and within minutes she was spreadeagled on the Chinese rug in front of the hearth, his hands tearing at her clothes and his great phallus ravaging her, the heat of his strong hard body like a fire against her own until at last the cry was forced out of her and he brought a hand against her mouth.

It was over now, and the room was quiet. Anyone coming here would find two seemingly civilised people, a devoted husband and wife changing for dinner, she in her oyster-satin dress by Calvin Klein, a rope of pearls at her throat, he looking elegant, distinguished in his London-tailored dinner-jacket and scarlet cummerbund. The black lace briefs Toinette had been wearing were out of sight in the bathroom, torn and flecked with blood; the bruise on her neck would colour beneath heavy makeup.

'Are you ready?'

Her voice was toneless. This was the time when she always had to drag herself painfully back to the semblance of normality, because he expected it of her. With Raoul, the other side of his nature was able to regain its ascendancy almost at once; for Toinette it required longer to change from a nymph plundered in the forest by a brutish satyr to a woman restored for a while to civilisation; but to please him she resumed the role of a loving wife as soon as she could.

'Give me three minutes,' Raoul told her. 'I must change these cuff-links – diamonds are so vulgar.'

Toinette was on the balcony finishing her glass of Punt e Mes when he came looking for her. The evening air was calm and no more than cool, carrying a hint of woodsmoke from the village. She had been trying to still her mind, so as to go down the grand staircase and into the dining-salon looking soignée and serene on her husband's arm; but her thoughts were still whirling, coloured and strident and terrified, like the raging of a nightmare. This too was familiar; it was always at this time that she was driven to face the truth and the future. How much longer would she let herself be torn and bruised by this man's sadistic lust? When would she come to realise that unless something happened to help her, she would remain a slave to this Svengali for the rest of her life?

Each time it happened, she thought of leaving him, of running so far and so fast that he could never catch her up, never find her. But deep inside her was the knowledge that she must do more than run, however far and however fast, if she were to be free of him.

When Raoul came onto the balcony she was leaning at the low stone balustrade, one slender hand to her ear-lobe.

'I've done it again, Raoul . . .' Her smile was nervous. 'Please don't be cross.'

'You've lost another earring?' His tone was no more than chiding. He could never be cross with her at a time like this, when his body was still suffused with the afterglow of the ravishing.

'It's not really lost this time. I was trying to tighten it, but it went down just here.'

Raoul moved to her side, and looked down at the massed leaves of the creeper that clung to the wall.

'Can you see it?'

'Yes. Just below that thick branch. But if I take my eyes off it I'll never find it again.' In vexation she said, 'It's one of the lovely sapphires you gave me for my birthday.'

Raoul leaned over the balustrade. 'I can't see it. Is it within reach?'

'You'd have to climb over and hang on, darling, then you'd find it easily. But I don't want you to take the risk.'

His smile was quick and charming, the male in him responding to challenge. 'Didn't I tell you? I used to be a cat-burglar!' He swung a leg over the balustrade and found purchase on the thick branches of the creeper, then swung his other leg across and hung on with one hand. 'Am I close?'

'Yes. A little bit this way. Can you see it?'

'No.'

For Toinette there was a last moment of hesitation that she would always remember, and then she slipped off one of her pretty champagne-coloured shoes and brought the stiletto heel down hard on the back of Raoul's hand, the one that was clinging to the balustrade. Then she turned away and leaned with her back to the stonework and closed her eyes, with one thought quite clear in her mind among all the others that were crowding in – that if he hadn't asked her a second time to kill her sister she would never have been able to do this. But that had been too much, and when he realised she'd disobeyed him he would have been furious, and more brutal than ever before. She wanted an end to pain.

Behind her there was the hectic rustling of leaves and a brief cry, then silence for a moment, then a thud coming faintly from below; and in the soft evening light Toinette Cavaille stood there frozen in this moment of time, a young and beautiful woman leaning on a chateau balcony, her eyes closed and one shoe dangling by its strap from her hand.

'D'you imagine there's a kind of jinx on this place?' Suzie asked.

'Could be.' Linda flopped into the big cane chair, drawing her feet up in the yoga position; she couldn't remember when she'd last sat down anywhere. The little ormolu clock on the dressing-table stood at five after midnight; Bibi was asleep on a camp bed in Princess Charlotte's room, on what she called 'night guard.' Suzie had been here only a few minutes, and Linda just didn't know whether she should accept her offer to stay for a while, in case anyone came in here and Bibi didn't wake. Locking the doors didn't amount to much – there'd be spare keys in a place like this. And anyway she had a feeling that the Princess wasn't in danger any more; it was one of those vibes that had been coming to her from nowhere since she'd become part of the life at the Chateau, where there were so many tensions, so many undercurrents of intrigue.

'You want me to go look at her?' Suzie asked.

'Who?'

'Toinette.'

'No. I'll take a peek in a while.' Linda had left Mme Cavaille sleeping, lightly sedated; she'd been in shock for more than an hour, relapsing after the police had questioned her. They'd taken the body away soon after they'd got here, and Mme de Valoise had given them the necessary identification. Princess Charlotte hadn't yet been told; Linda didn't know what the news would do to her, of a death so close.

Suzie sat on her haunches on the floor, watching Linda from beneath her dark silky lashes. 'Gee, you're really something else, you know that?'

'Pardon me?' Linda turned her head, aroused this time from thoughts of Jacques . . . of Jacques as she'd last seen him . . . of Jacques and the things he'd said . . .

'Did they train you to cope with life this way,' Suzie asked her, 'or did it come with the genes?'

'It's the job.'

Quietly and with a gentle smile, Suzie said, 'Bullshit.'

Linda shrugged. 'You learn how to cope, under training, sure. And when you hit your first hospital job. Life's pretty real in those places.'

'But you have to have something in you, first. Right?'

'I guess it helps.'

'D'you think *I* might have what it takes?'

Linda waited a moment, surprised, then said, 'I don't know enough about you, Suzie, or your past. As a guest of the French nobility and the close friend of a British heiress, it could be your life has been too sheltered up to now, for this kind of work.' Linda shrugged. 'I imagine you want me to be frank.'

'Oh, sure. And you're right – I've been spoiled rotten for the past couple of months, since I came to Europe. But – '

'What did you do before then?'

'I was a whore working the truck-routes out of Memphis, Tennessee.' She laughed softly at Linda's expression. 'But I guess that doesn't qualify me for the nursing life either . . .'

Linda said slowly, 'And you tell me *I'm* really something else?'

'The thing is,' Suzie said, her amber eyes serious, 'I got myself a patient, in a way, all on my own. And I think I cured her.'

'You mean Lady Houghton-Downe?'

'Right. She's doing OK now – she's off the dope. I'll tell you about it later, maybe, if you're interested, though I'm not actually sure whether I played the role of a nurse or a priest. It's given me the idea, though, of going into the same kind of thing you're doing. See, this is the first time in my life I haven't felt I'm just a two-bit tramp. And watching you, seeing how you go about things, has been one hell of an experience.' She got off the floor, tugging her gold lamé jacket down. 'Meantime your day isn't finished, so if you need me along here – *any* time, day or night – you know where to find me, just down the passage.'

After she'd gone, Linda remained in the big peacock chair for a while with her feet tucked under her, thinking about Suzie, and about the man on the flower-bed with his arms flung out and his head pillowed on the geraniums, and about Toinette Cavaille with her shocked white face, and the police detectives who'd come to investigate the accident, and Mme de Valoise with her green eyes flickering over Toinette for an instant with that strange expression that had come and gone almost before Linda had caught it. And when the events of the day came crowding in too fast she got out of the chair and went to the mirror above the dressing-table and drew her hair back and stared at herself for a minute as if she needed to remember who she was, and that she had a life to live too, if only she could remember where she'd put it.

Then she began thinking again about Jacques . . .

Of all the events of the day, that had been the most astonishing, the most electrifying.

When she'd found his room empty and run into the corridor, she'd seen him in the distance, right at the end, standing perfectly still and looking in her direction.

At first she hadn't believed her eyes – it wasn't Jacques; it had been someone else. He couldn't have walked that distance without his crutches, and he would never have left his room without his dark glasses, which gave him a feeling of security. Linda had walked slowly along the corridor, seeing, as she got closer, that yes, it was Jacques, Prince Jacques, standing tall again with the help of the stick at his side, his head framed by the stained-glass windows of the mezzanine, their colours thrown by the afternoon sunlight to fall across his shoulders from behind, like a mantle. As Linda drew near, with the colours playing across her eyes, he said very quietly:

'I'm sorry if you were worried.'

His voice was perfectly calm, perfectly steady, with that low resonance in it that she'd forgotten, or had stopped noticing. His dark eyes rested on her own, as if they'd softly alighted there. It seemed a long time before she answered him.

'I couldn't find you.'

It wasn't what she'd meant to say; but then, what had she meant to say? Her mind was struggling to understand what he was doing here, how he'd managed to come this far.

'I know,' he said.

She threw out a hand, confused. 'Did someone – did someone help you?'

'No.'

'I see.'

But she didn't see. She knew what his injuries were, and what they allowed him to do, and not do; she knew how much movement and how much pressure it would take to build up the degree of pain where he'd have to stop, to freeze, his eyes squeezed shut and his teeth clenched; she knew what his threshold of pain was; and she knew the terror he'd felt, and expressed, when someone – Thérèse de Valoise – had once come into his room and found him without his dark glasses hiding half his face. So, putting it all together, she knew it was impossible for him to have got here by himself, and with his face exposed to anyone who might come along.

'I don't understand,' she heard herself saying. Surprisingly, she felt tears on her face.

'Understand?'

'Yes.' She didn't brush the tears away; they were still coming, and she might as well let them; they weren't to do with the usual things, pain, or grief, things like that. It was just that she hadn't ever seen a miracle; they'd never been part of the job. 'I don't understand how you got here. Or what made you do it.'

After a moment he said, 'I didn't have any choice.'

'Any *choice?*'

He could have stayed where he was, couldn't he, in the comfort of his bed, hiding behind his dark glasses? It would have been easier for him to –

Then suddenly she understood.

'The only alternative – ' he began saying, but she cut in without being able to stop herself.

'I know. I know, yes, of course – yes, yes – '

'Then I'm glad.' He sounded surprised.

'I – it's just that I didn't know what kind of man you were. I didn't imagine you could ever do a thing like this.'

'I didn't,' he said, 'either.'

She looked at him in surprise. 'Then what happened?'

'I changed, I suppose. Or I found something I didn't know was there.'

She thought about this, but it was too much to handle, and she began coming back to her senses. 'Look,' she said, 'you've absolutely *got* to rest now. I'm going to fetch your crutches, so stay exactly – '

'Then you *don't understand.*' His voice was louder, and a note of anger came into it. 'But I want you to. I want you to know that I had time for a lot of thinking, just lying there day after day, and after a while I found I didn't want to go on lying there and sulking and brooding about my face and trying ineffectually to cut my wrists, because the one person in the world who meant anything to me, the one person I'd come to admire above all the rest was having to watch me go through my adolescent antics. And you'll never know how ashamed I was, this morning, just this morning, and how furious I was, when I suddenly came to see myself as you were seeing me. And that's why I had no choice. And if you go and fetch those crutches I shall throw them straight through the window. *Now* do you understand?'

She watched him with the tears drying on her face; they were beginning to itch now, so she wiped them away, quickly, wanting to pretend they'd never been there, because she'd seen a lot of people in relentless pain and a lot of people die agonizing deaths while others wept for them in uncontainable grief; and sometimes she'd seen things, yes, that had come close to a miracle, and she ought to have been ready for this one. It shimmered in her, like the coloured light that came from the windows.

'Yes,' she said, 'now I understand. But – ' a sigh came suddenly, drawing the tension out of her – 'but I've got to be practical. You've overtaxed your strength, and – '

'There's something else I want you to know.'

Linda watched him steadily, defeated. There was nothing she could do with this man. His eyes glinted, catching the light and reflecting it; his face, with the long scars running from the brow to the chin, and with the rows of sutures puckering the skin, was a total stranger's – she'd never been able to remember, after the accident, what he'd looked like before. But now, as his voice vibrated on the quiet air of the mezzanine, the memory came back to her, little by little, and the scars gradually began losing their raw lividity, and she saw him as she would later, when the healing had done its work.

'We were both lucky,' Jacques told her evenly, without emotion. 'I didn't know that our love affair was the last I would ever have. Looking as I do – as I will, even when the healing's finished – I won't ever ask a woman to feel any kind of love for me again. *Nothing is going to change my mind about that.* So I was lucky that the last woman I knew was you, Linda, and I want you to know that I'l cherish the love you gave me for as long as I live.'

She looked down, felt restless; she didn't want to hear this; whatever they'd had was over, had been over long before he'd crashed his boat. All she could feel for him now was admiration, the admiration of a nurse for a patient who'd made it through a nightmare and come out with his pride intact.

'And you were lucky too,' he went on, 'because our affair didn't become more than it was – at least for me. If that had happened, you would have been saddled with this – this freak of nature for years to come. That was an escape for you, and I thank God for it.' From the grounds below the windows there came the cry of a peacock, sharp and disturbing, in contrast with the quiet warmth of his voice. 'We've both suffered, in different ways. What I did to you, quite without intention, preyed on my mind until I longed for some kind of release from my self-anger – and I found it. Some of them said the sea was dangerous, that day, but only those close to me could know that I was driving myself to virtual destruction.' His mouth moved painfully in a wry grimace. 'And I came close. Very close. They thought I'd gone mad. Maybe. But only you will ever know the truth.'

As the silence drew out, Linda felt the need to say something, something to let him know at least that she understood. But what could she say? She believed everything he'd told her, but it was outlandish, crazy – mad, yes, as he'd said himself. He'd felt that much remorse that he'd crashed his boat as a desperate, unconscious gesture of atonement?

'Jacques, I – don't really know – '

'Please, Linda. Please don't say anything. I only wanted you to know these things, and there is nothing you need say. It's over now, and we can start forgetting. What happened out there on the sea didn't change anything; it didn't make up in any way for the harm I did to you. But my mind still won't know any peace unless you will offer me something I hardly dare ask of you. Your forgiveness.' His hand reached out, hesitantly, and as she looked into his eyes she saw an infinite longing, and her own hand reached out for his, quickly, in the pool of coloured light.

33

A Hundred Red Roses

'WHAT TIME ARE you meeting him, *chérie?*'
'At seven, Maman.'
'Then you'd better make haste!'
'Yes.'
Celeste went to the mirror, shaking out her soft blonde hair and turning her head, tilting it, making all the gestures that were necessary, in case her mother could see her through the doorway, going through all the questions that every woman asked herself when she was about to meet a man – hair too wild, eye-shadow too deep, skin-tone right for candlelight?

Then, hearing her mother at the piano, Celeste went slack suddenly, turning away from the mirror, the pretence no longer necessary. Her heart, which had once leapt and danced at this hour of the day, was quiet, as if sleeping, ready to forget. But she would wait a few more days, always a few more days . . . before she began the painful process of letting her mother realise that – that things had changed, that the little red sports-car wouldn't be –

Quickly she picked up her book from the bedside table and slipped it into her bag, her movement surreptitious, so that anyone watching might have believed that it was something that her mother wouldn't have liked to imagine her reading; but it wasn't that; *A Brief Reassessment of Napoleonic Law* was surely above reproach – it was simply that *maman* wouldn't expect her to be reading a book – *any* book – during an evening with her beloved Mario.

'Where is he taking you tonight, *chérie?*'
'*Le Sorrento!*'
From the piano her mother watched her hurrying through the beautifully-furnished salon, slinging her blue suede bag from her shoulder. 'But *Le Sorrento* is closed on Tuesdays!'

Celeste faltered. 'It is? Then I must have got it wrong. It'll be *La Chaumière* – he loves taking me there.' She blew a kiss and hurried out – 'I won't be late, Maman!'

Along the corridor she slowed her steps; there was no need to hurry now. In the richly-pannelled elevator she opened her bag and took the book out; its sharp corners would damage the suede. Then she got out her purse to make sure there was enough money in it to buy herself a pizza at the little place around the corner, where the tubular lighting was bright enough to read by, without straining her eyes.

Across the hallway, her footsteps echoed on the green marble floor, sounding of loneliness.

He stared at the ceiling.

He'd been staring at the ceiling, he realised with uneasiness, for three days now, shaking with an unaccountable fever. Its cause was obvious, of course, but for the first twenty-four hours, since Thérèse had walked through the door – *that* door over there – he'd told himself it was the 'flu, or fatigue from overwork, with the rush of winter visitors coming through. Then, after he'd crawled from his bed and boiled himself some spaghetti and tried in vain to eat a little of it, he'd trudged back to bed and faced himself and his predicament, and had decided that it had simply been the assault on his ego that had laid him low and raised his temperature to the hundreds. An assault which had left him taken by surprise – not to say astonishment! – and outflanked, undermined and overwhelmed.

He, Mario Vittorio Emanuel Romano, the most priceless treasure the gods had ever offered womankind, the most experienced and practised virtuoso in the art of courtly love, the one man above all other men along the French Riviera with whom, in fair and unbiassed comparison, Don Juan would seem a male chauvinist pig, had been rejected, for the first time in his life and right in the middle of an affair. *Rejected*. Worse, without even a scene, without even a modest show of tears, screams or curses. Worse yet, without even the titillating risk of being mown down by a battered Citroën 2–CV the next time he crossed the street!

Then on the third day – *this* was the third day – Mario had found himself remembering one or two things that Thérèse, in her gentle wisdom, had said to him. His memory of her had been refreshed by the sudden apparition of a delivery-boy at his door, half-buried beneath a vast bouquet of roses. Mario had stood them in a bucket in the very middle of the room, where he could see them the whole time. The slightly vulgar slogan on the gold florist's label – which he was sure Thérèse had never seen – had prompted him to tear it up and throw it away, on top of the cold spaghetti. *If You Can't Say It With A Hundred Roses, It Can't Be Worth Saying!* But the personal message from Thérèse, which she must have sent by hand to the florist, had stirred his memory of her.

A souvenir, dearest Mario, of our passing joy. But since no woman can send a man flowers, these are not for you to keep. Give them to someone you love – but choose carefully! Thérèse.

Her gesture had touched him, and he now decided to sit up in bed and stare at the roses instead of the ceiling, while those things she'd said before she left him went echoing through his mind, with his own voice answering.

I've noticed a trend in your work . . . You took so many children, this year. Look at these – pages of them.

A trend is a trend. They come and go.

You've never had any children?

No. I've never married.

You've never committed yourself.

Perhaps it's that.

It takes courage, Mario.

And then, on her way to the door, she'd become quiet, and solemn.

Mario, I'm a little older than you, and perhaps even a little wiser. Let me say this. You said that some of the women you've left tried to kill you. It's time you found one who would die for you. Then you could take the most stunning pictures of her for the rest of your life – and of your lovely daughters.

It was this thought that began running through his mind again and again, until at last he got up and washed and showered and put on one of his midnight-blue silk suits, with the gentle words of Thérèse de Valoise still coaxing him; and that was why, some ten minutes later, when the slender and wistful Celeste came down the steps of her apartment building in La Condamine, she saw the little red Alfa-Romeo standing there with Mario staggering under the biggest bouquet of roses she had ever seen.

34

Morning

It was 3 a.m. and pitch dark when Linda was awakened by what had sounded like a low cry, and slipped into her bathrobe, hurrying on bare feet through the doorway to Princess Charlotte's room.

Bibi, on the camp-bed in the corner, hadn't stirred.

'*Ma chère* . . .'

Linda moved quickly to the huge four-poster bed. 'I'm here, Madame.'

'*Ma très chère* . . .' The thin, bloodless hand reached from the bedclothes, and Linda held it gently, her other hand on Princess Charlotte's brow. It was dry and cold – too cold.

'I'm going to get you a – '

'No, Linda, I need nothing now . . . nothing more now. But listen to me.' A surprising strength came into her hand as it gripped Linda's. The moon, in its first quarter, sent bars of light and shadow from the half-closed shutters, touching the gaunt face of the Princess. Linda felt the tension going out of her as the nerves settled; it was a feeling she'd known so many times, and she knew without any question that her patient was right – she didn't need anything more, now; there was nothing to do, nothing to fetch for her. 'Listen to me, my child . . . When – when this is over, I want you to open the envelope I gave you. You kept it safe?'

'Of course, Madame.'

'Then soon you will know everything . . . You remember I promised that one day you would understand?'

'I remember. But please – '

'Let me say this . . . I would like to say more, much more, but there's so little time.' She fought for breath, but her hand still held Linda's tightly, though it trembled now. 'I could never have believed how much love you showed me, *ma chère*, in the last days of my life, coming here as you did, a stranger. You were so wonderful to me, so wonderful . . .'

Linda held the thin, cold hand in both her own, giving it her warmth, listening to what her patient was saying but at the same time letting her mind run ahead – would Dr Chirac be at the hospital now, or at home? If the Princess asked to see her son, should Linda wake him right away? He needed –

'What time is it, Linda?'

'Three in the morning, Madame. If – '

'A bad time . . . a good time for me, but a bad time for other people . . . So inconvenient . . . Would it harm my son, to be disturbed?'

'No. But it's going to take a few minutes to bring him here.'

'I will wait. It's important, you see.'

'Of course. I'll fetch him. And who else?'

'No one. Only Jacques.' Linda was relieved; Princess Charlotte's sister, Toinette, was still under light sedation; her husband's accident had left her traumatised. 'There are only two people I wanted to talk to, before – before I leave, *ma chère*, and one of them is Jacques. The other, of course, was you.'

'Then I – I'm privileged, Madame.' There was more Linda wanted to say, but now wasn't the time; there'd never be a time. In her mind were some of the things she'd said to all those other patients; they'd been so varied, of course – some had died badly, with no thought for the living, while others – most of them – had died well, considerately, courageously, leaving her with feelings that had taken on a deeper meaning at the borders of life and death. Finally, as she held this cold, fine-boned hand in both her own, she said what she'd said to so many of them; but she wasn't just repeating a formula – it had been true then and it was true now. 'I'm losing a friend, *Madame la Princesse*, but you're leaving me with so many things I'm going to remember, for such a long time.' Then she heard herself adding something that was for Princess Charlotte alone. 'Knowing you has been a kind of blessing.'

She was surprised, as she rested her cheek for a moment against the dying woman's, to feel a tear pass between them, because at a time like this there were so many practical things to deal with, and there was no place for emotion.

'Such an exquisite gift, my child . . . and I wasn't expecting it . . .'

'Poor Jacques. It hasn't been your year, this one, has it?'

He turned his head a little, watching the shuttered window in the east wall, where light was creeping; it had been the thin notes of a bird that had caught his attention. It was almost morning.

Like others, Thérèse de Valoise had quickly learned to engage only his eyes during conversation, but now, sitting opposite him in the velvet Louis XV chair, she was able to study his face, and for the first time felt hope that it would heal successfully, and leave him with a passable appearance – even intriguing, with those fine eyes of his. The thought of it eased her heart.

'It hasn't been a very good year,' Jacques said quietly, 'for any of us.' He turned back to face her. 'You've lost a very dear friend.'

She looked away. 'Yes.' Was 'friend' the right word? She'd been the mistress of Charlotte's husband, as everyone had known; yet Charlotte had not only tolerated her countless visits to the Chateau over the years, but had personally invited her. Perhaps it was their shared love for Edouard, their respect for him and for each other, that had allowed friendship and understanding to grow between them; it was often the way, in a wife-mistress relationship. 'Yes, she was my friend, dearest Charlotte. Everyone's friend.'

She leaned down to the small table, where little Marianne, the maid, tears wet on her pale face, had put a tray of hot milk for them, and some biscuits; she'd made to stir the embers in the hearth, but Thérèse had gently stopped her; it was a time for embers, not for the leaping of new flames. But the room was chill, and they sat hunched in their padded dressing-gowns.

'A little more, Jacques?'

'No. No thank you.' He still found it difficult to drink anything. 'You've been a great strength to me, Aunt Thérèse, all through this year.'

'Then I'm glad, *mon cher*.' He hadn't called her 'Aunt' for a long time, not since he was a child, a dark, leggy boy with grazed knees and dizzying energy. *Are you really my aunt? Because if you are, it means I can't marry you when I grow up, and that would be terrible!*

In the dim light of the room, Thérèse watched him obliquely. *No, Jacques, I'm not really your aunt. What I am to you, though, you would never believe. But then, you will never know.*

'And you've found a new strength of your own,' she told him, spooning the skin off the hot milk and putting it into the saucer. 'Linda told me what you did.'

'What I did?'

'She called it the "miracle." '

'Oh.'

She meant the way he'd left this room by himself and walked all the way to the mezzanine. Miracle? No. But it had taken some doing, yes; halfway there he'd had to stop, propping himself against the wall with the pain trying to consume him like a fire. That had been his point of no-return; he'd known quite clearly that he couldn't go back, because it would mean he'd been defeated, and that would have sapped the strength he'd need, which would have brought him down and left him spreadeagled on the floor, unconscious and humiliated. On the other hand he'd known just as clearly that he couldn't go on, either; the mezzanine had looked infinitely far away, a pool of coloured light as insubstantial as a chimera, unattainable. He'd stayed like that for a long time, with the pain trying to burn him down; he'd been lucky, because later he'd realised he must have lost consciousness for a while: the beams of coloured light had lengthened along the corridor when he'd next opened his eyes. Propped like a burning stake against the wall, he might easily have toppled and crashed down.

But it hadn't been the beams of light that had reached out to him, giving him courage; it had been the thought of Linda, with so much courage of her own, that had led him to the mezzanine; at one point, when he'd begun losing consciousness again, he'd believed he could see her standing there, waiting for him.

Linda . . .

'She told me it shouldn't have been possible,' he heard Thérèse saying quietly, 'to get there by yourself. I suppose you realise how much admiration she has for you?'

He looked away. 'No. She – she was my inspiration, that was all.'

'And still is, I'm sure.'

Jacques looked at her quickly, and his tone was cold. 'I'm her patient, Thérèse, and she is my nurse. There's mutual respect, of course.'

Thérèse let the silence go on for a little, sipping at her milk, watching the light of the new day reach the brass knob of a fire-iron in the hearth, and set it shining.

'It's over, then, is it? The affair?' She added quickly – 'She didn't say a word to me about it, Jacques, not a single word. But of course I knew.'

He glanced around him, restless. 'A chateau's a small place, I suppose. But for your information, yes, it's over. It was over weeks ago, and there's nothing left. Nothing.'

'She . . . speaks of you kindly, Jacques.'

His hand moved in a gesture of dismissal. 'That's her nature; she'd speak kindly of the Devil himself.' He hesitated, fretting at the tassel of his dressing-gown, and when he spoke again his voice was firm. 'You're the only one I have left now, Thérèse – the only person I can talk to, and be frank with. And I know that you won't let this go any farther. But there's a risk of boring you.' He waited.

'I've always been fond of you, Jacques; and from this day forward I want to fill the gap that's been left in your life, however poorly but as best I can. So don't speak of boring me; your happiness is close to my heart.'

His eyes were wet suddenly and he had to glance down. 'Thank you. Then I just want you to know this. I thought that was all it was, at first – an affair. And when Linda found out, it – it was very painful for her. But now she's through it, and for her it's really over. For me, oddly enough, the worst has still to be dealt with, because I hadn't been able to keep her out of my mind since I realised how much I'd hurt her; and then when I came to know her, day after day when she was nursing me, I was faced with something I hadn't realised before, because I'd changed, quite a lot – matured, if you like, since the crash and the way it left me.' He moved his elbows back, so that he could grip the arms of the chair, needing some kind of token support. 'Linda won't be here much longer, and when – when she leaves us, I'm going to have to deal with the fact that I shan't ever see her again.' His dark eyes lifted slowly, and Thérèse saw naked anguish in them. 'And I would rather go through again . . . what I've been through since the crash, than the first weeks of my life, after she's gone.'

In a moment Thérèse asked him quietly, 'Does she have any idea that you feel like this?'

He said sharply – '*No*. But that doesn't make any difference. Even if I hadn't destroyed the love she felt for me once, I wouldn't have her saddled with a freak. Do you understand?'

'But my dear, you – '

'You *must* understand. It's over now. And it's going to stay like that.' He looked away, his fingers fretting on the arms of the chair. 'That's all I wanted you to know, Thérèse. Now please let's talk about something else.'

She said in a moment, 'Very well. I'll respect that.' She asked him if there'd been time to talk with his mother, before the end came.

'Yes. A little.' He moved suddenly, easing himself out of the chair with the help of his cane and taking a few steps towards the nearest window, while she tensed, ready to help him if he stumbled. 'A little, but enough. I said I'd take over the estates. I knew she wanted me to. We – '

'Jacques!' Thérèse said quickly. 'I can't believe it!'

'You don't think I can do it?'

'I didn't think you'd *want* to.'

'I want to do what has to be done – the way she'd want it done. She and my father. I owe them that.'

'I'll help you,' she said, 'if you like, just in the beginning. *Maquillage de Valoise* is almost running itself by now. I'll have the time, and I can reach the most qualified advisers in Europe.'

He half-turned, and the rubber tip of the cane squeaked on the parquet floor. 'I know. And bless you, Thérèse – I'll need some help, yes, in the beginning.'

He moved again, painfully, and she knew that he'd set himself the goal of reaching the window. The man who would soon assume the captaincy of the de Montigny-Villiers estates was taking the first few steps, and they were likely to be more difficult than all the rest. Watching him, the woman in the chair, herself the head of a vast international enterprise, was sharply aware that a milestone had been reached and passed, in her own life and in the fortunes of this beleaguered family. She herself was intimately involved, far more than Jacques would ever know.

After so many years.

Since she was seventeen, an impoverished *midinette* slaving with chilblained fingers at a sewing-machine under the roof-tops of Paris. Since Prince Edouard – among several other adventurous aristocrats – had been . . . how old? Not much older than Thérèse, though he was already married then and going through the bittersweet agonies of trying to remain faithful to his new bride and at the same time savour his last fling behind the scenes of Parisian society.

Then suddenly things turned more serious. Almost inevitably

the young Thérèse became pregnant – and with a child she had no hope of providing for. She didn't even know who the father was, though at that time he could only be Prince Edouard or one other paramour's – the generous, ardent Compte de Lucinge. It was then that Thérèse, an orphan with no resources, was made aware that destiny was not always to be against her, for the child was only a month old when Prince Edouard came to her and offered to adopt it. He confided in her that a bitter disappointment had come into his married life: it was destined to be childless. His affection for Thérèse led him to propose that her child, a son, should be raised as his own, and made his legal heir. At that time Princess Charlotte had no knowledge of the liaison, and would assume the child to be the issue of total strangers.

Thérèse was willing enough; unable to afford even modest comfort for her infant son, she was delighted to see him welcomed into a family where he would lack for nothing. In compensation for the loss of her child – though she needed none – Prince Edouard set her up in a small business of her own as a beautician, since she had a flair for the use of cosmetics.

That period of her life had proved to be momentous and far-reaching. Within the year she was obliged to take on two young assistants and move to larger premises. In Paris, the flower of the European capitals, her natural ability to make other – especially older – women feel pampered and indulged, together with her instinctive knowledge of décor and presentation, brought clients flocking to the small golden door tucked discreetly among so many others along the fabulous Champs Elysées.

Freed from economic anxiety, Thérèse began to regret having given away the child she could now have afforded to raise. There was nothing, of course, to be done; but she was still seeing Prince Edouard from time to time, and in fact could now be considered his mistress; she deliberately, therefore, eschewed any form of contraception, eager to bear another child – which this time would certainly be Edouard's, since she had renounced all other lovers. It was not long before she discovered a vital truth of which Edouard himself was probably ignorant. Whatever Princess Charlotte's condition, *he* was sterile.

The true father of her child, then, was her earlier lover, the adventurous Compte de Lucinge, who later was to meet his death in a riding accident in the Bois de Boulogne.

The child had been christened Jacques.

He stood before Thérèse now, the personification of one of the two secrets with which Thérèse de Valoise intended to die. She was not so sentimental as to yearn for her son to acknowledge her after all these years. The childhood title of 'aunt' was perfectly acceptable, and their affectionate relationship could scarcely be made closer simply by Jacques' knowledge of what she was to him. It would even be embarrassing for this young man suddenly to be faced with the truth.

Let it rest as it was. She would now, in any case, be filling the gap that Charlotte had left, with the happy prospect before her of helping and encouraging him in his new role as the head of the estates, and whether she did it as a close friend or his mother wouldn't make the slightest difference. Legally and in his own mind he was Prince Jacques Edouard René de Montigny-Villiers, but he was not of the blood, and to be told the truth would only confuse and hurt him. Let it rest.

The other secret which Thérèse would forever keep sacrosanct was the reason for Edouard's suicide.

You'll never tell anyone, Thérèse. Especially Charlotte.
Very well.
Do I have your solemn promise?
You have, Edouard. I promise.

At that moment she hadn't known what he was to do; it would be an hour or so before she slipped quietly out of the Hotel de Paris on that fateful morning and climbed into her Ferrari, just before dawn. To many people the situation wouldn't have seemed crucially important. Cancer of the prostate was operable, and with a good chance of success. But despite Edouard's having taken a mistress, his adoration of Charlotte had been profound, and her respect for him was a major need in his life. To his mind the site of the growth and the ensuing impotence of which his doctors had warned him were shaming to a man of his pride, and would diminish him in Charlotte's eyes. In addition, his own brother Philippe had died under the knife, and Edouard had afterwards felt an obsessive fear of surgery. These two factors together he had found insupportable.

But Edouard, nothing could ever diminish her love for you.
This is an appalling thing, Thérèse. Shameful. Ignoble.

Once she'd realised what he was leading up to, she had argued with him all that tragic evening.

For a man of your age and with your constitution, Edouard, the chances of complete success are far above average. Surely you know that.

Please don't talk about it any more. I implore you.

His fear was chilling, paralysing. Thérèse realised that even if he would let them put him on an operating-table his fear alone would work against him, perhaps fatally.

But she'd gone on pleading with him, for his sake, her own and most of all for Charlotte's, knowing how the news would devastate her. He had been adamant. And before she took her leave of him, he'd asked that they should make love for the last time, such was his need of faith in his own virility, even in the eleventh hour of his life. And so the matter had been done, though God knew how she'd found the heart for it. As they'd moved together in the sacramental rite of Eros, she realised she was offering him the simplest gift of womanhood, the assurance that when he died it would be as a man.

Afterwards there had been a last glass of champagne, and only when he opened the door of his room for her had he come close to putting into words what he meant to do.

Tell her I'll be waiting for her.

She had conveyed his message, and now they were joined again, Edouard and Charlotte, and as she watched the silhouette of the young man with the cane taking his painful steps towards the window, Thérèse had the presentiment that for Jacques the long night was over. A shiver of awe passed through her, for the thought seemed to fly from her mind into his, as he managed the last step and gently opened the shutters.

'Look,' he said, 'it's morning.'

35

THE LETTER

LINDA'S HANDS WERE shaking as she unlocked the little drawer in her dressing-table and took out the envelope that Princess Charlotte had given her a week ago. It bore Linda's name, and below it the words, *To be opened after my death.* On the back it was sealed with the crest of the de Montigny-Villiers.

If it hadn't been for Bibi, and the few words she'd spoken that had left Linda dumbfounded, she would have held this oblong cream-coloured envelope in perfectly steady hands, as the morning sunshine crept across the room. But because of what Bibi had said, she wondered how she dared break the seal and open it.

She'd been in the portrait gallery half an hour ago, the small salon that opened from the hall at the bottom of the grand staircase, the room where *le petit Baron* had startled her the first night she'd spent here in the Chateau de Beausoleil. That was nothing compared to what Bibi had done this morning.

Linda had gone there on an impulse. Up to that time there'd been a lot to do; Dr Chirac had been here to meet with the attorney, Maître Dorlhac, and supervise the removal of Princess Charlotte's remains by the undertakers. People had needed comfort, and as usual came to Linda for it – little Guillaume and Mlle Pinalle and Henri and Marianne and others; then Princess Charlotte's room had to be tidied and the huge four-poster remade. Linda had been glad of the need for activity; she knew that later it would come home to her that the woman she'd nursed for so long, and grown to admire and finally to love, was no longer here, no longer anyplace where she could reach her again.

And then, when the people had gone and the carved oak doors of the entrance hall were closed against the sunshine, quiet had come to the Chateau, with hushed voices sounding from closed doors. It was then that Linda felt the urge to go to the portrait gallery and see Princess Charlotte again as she'd never seen her except here – young and in health and beautiful, so very beautiful, with that expression, warm and faintly smiling, that had reminded Linda of someone when she'd first seen it, someone she knew, but couldn't quite place.

Bibi caught sight of her through the open doorway to the hall, and came quietly in, slipping a small cold hand into hers and pressing it gently, her grey eyes wistful.

'She was so beautiful,' Linda said in a moment.

'Of course,' Bibi answered softly, 'just as you are. She was your mother, didn't you know?'

She tucked the envelope into the pocket of her white linen coat and went out of the Chateau by way of the winter-garden and across the lawns, reaching the rose-garden where she'd sat so often with the Princess. The sunshine was warming towards noon, and the only sound except for the occasional call of a bird was the muffled beat of hooves on turf, where horses were being exercised in the riding-park.

There was a moment, as Linda sat down on the cane chaise-longue, when she told herself that she would never break this seal, open this envelope, never in her life. She would find somewhere to burn it, just as it was, perhaps in the smouldering bonfire across there near the kitchen-gardens; then she would go into the Chateau and call Dr Chirac and ask him to engage a replacement nurse for the Prince de Montigny-Villiers; and then she would pack, and leave. Henri would take her to the airport.

Because this was not her place, here in this ancient Chateau among these timeless trees. She'd come here from right across the Atlantic, and back there were people she could understand, living a life she herself had been used to since she was – since she was *born*.

It was then that the envelope in her pocket drew her hand there despite her thoughts of destroying it unopened. Because, if what the strange little countess had said was true, where *had* she been born?

When she'd asked Bibi what in heaven's name she was talking about, she'd said, 'It was just something I happened to overhear, that's all.' She'd stood there staring up at the portrait. 'But look, you can see the likeness, surely?'

The waxen seal crackled as Linda ripped open the envelope and began reading.

My dear child,

You are watching me write these words, as you move about the room, taking such wonderful care of me. Where will you be sitting to read them, when the time comes, as soon it must? In the mezzanine, with the sunlight coming through the coloured panes, or in the rose-garden where I used to sit with you? I shall know soon; I shall be there. You will be very close to me.

But I don't believe I have much time left, now, and I must be as brief as I can. I shall simply give you the facts of the matter, and let you read between the lines and share the feelings we had during these strange times – I, and my beloved husband, and others. Try your best to understand our agonies of mind, our hasty resolves, our seeming foolishness. And if you find things difficult to grasp, remember that I write this on my death-bed, from which the view is a little different.

To my task, and with haste.

My marriage with Edouard knew great joy, but also a keen disappointment. It was childless. A year after we had been together, I went for an examination, to learn from my doctors that I was – in their idiom – fertile. (It makes me sound like a cabbage-patch, don't you think?) This could mean only that my dear husband was lacking in this regard. I knew his pain that our marraige was without issue; we both yearned for a child.

So I gave him one. (You will already see, my dear Linda, that the letter you are reading is the most private and secret document imaginable, yet I have no slightest fear that you will ever divulge one word of it.) The child I produced was from the loins of Prince Philippe, Edouard's brother, who at my urgent entreaty agreed to the brief union that was necessary. He loved Edouard, as I did, and we entered into this stratagem for his sake – to furnish him with an heir and a child whom he could love; it would not be his, yet would be of the blood of the de Montigny-Villiers.

When I became pregnant, my husband was overjoyed. (I learned later that he too had submitted to an examination and had been pronounced sterile. He now ridiculed his doctor, certain that the tests had been faulty. His doctor, kind soul, pretended to agree.) Eventually the child was born, to our delight. But fate was again most cruel. By chance, when

Edouard was at his doctor's clinic, he learned that the tests he'd undertaken earlier were not, in fact, inaccurate. It was impossible for him to sire a child.

In the face of his pain, his humiliation, his accusations against me, I stoically denied my infidelity. Yet it was in vain. The child was now six months old, and my husband, distraught and embittered, made secret arrangements for its adoption and deportation overseas – he would not bear its presence in the country, let alone his house! Poor Edouard . . . With difficulty I forgave him, just as later he would forgive me.

The child was a girl, and in America, where she was given into adoption through the services of Maître Dorlhac, she was rechristened. By now, you know her name. It is Linda.

The stiff, cream-coloured paper was trembling in Linda's hand, and as she raised her eyes to the ancient stones of the Chateau, her mind was whirling with the onrush of thoughts the letter had released.

So this was where she'd been born! No wonder she'd had those strange, bewildering sensations of *déjà vu* . . . those flashes of intuition that she hadn't come *here* from across the ocean, but had come *back!* She'd been too young to remember this fairy-tale castle, these sunlit lawns and trees, yet the memory of them must still be in her subconscious, and the memory of that lovely woman who had come into her life too late for them to know each other. Her natural father she'd never seen; Bibi had said, yes, he'd died in a mountaineering accident; but she knew his face; it had looked down on her whenever she'd passed through the portrait gallery.

The cry of a peacock came from beyond the topiaries, raucous in the noon stillness, and for a moment her mind went spinning into a vortex again as the past caught up with the present. Had there always been peacocks here, and had she heard them, when she was too young to know what they were?

She was drawn back to the letter in her hand, and felt a sense of wonder as she realised how close the Princess was to her still.

And by now, your thoughts must be in a whirl, I know. It's such a lot for you to deal with. But the facts of the matter are easy enough to put to paper. With the help of good friends in the United States, I was kept acquainted with your journey through life, from the kindergarten in White Plains and then to the high school and finally to the nursing college and the three hospitals where you devoted yourself to the needs of others, as you did to me. I never believed I would see you again; while my husband was alive it was impossible; yet in this life events can swing us without warning into new directions. From the anguish of Edouard's passing I was granted a little joy, however brief – the chance to see you, and to know you for what you are . . . a beautiful young woman with a heart big enough to share with so many people like me, who have need of you.

You mustn't think that my husband was cruel to me, Linda, in taking you away from me. Men, as you know, are vain creatures, and the ego of the male is sensitive. Within a few short months of sending you out of France, Edouard was plagued with guilt and remorse; yet he couldn't countenance bringing back another man's child to live under his roof. He proposed adopting another, a boy, who could one day inherit the estates and take charge of them. Again, we agreed upon a secret stratagem. For the protection of my husband's pride and the family name, I pretended pregnancy, and was taken to a private clinic to 'bear' another child. I don't know to this day who his natural parents are; under French law the anonymity of adopted children is protected; but he was of good stock, and healthy. We came to love him as our own. He was given the name of Jacques.

Only Maître Dorlhac and a selected few among the staff of the private clinic know the truth; it was not necessary to swear them to secrecy; their vocation, which is also yours, imposes strict discretion, as you know.

Then came the two tragic twists of fate that led you to be here today at the Chateau de Beausoleil, reading these words. I was told that I had leukaemia; a year later, Edouard reached his decision to leave this life, perhaps unable any longer to watch my suffering, though I shall never be certain of his reasons. After his death, I made up my mind to bring you here if I could – but this presented a problem. I didn't know you then as I do now, and it was essential that you understood the paramount need for secrecy. Were it ever to be known that you were my child, and the child of Prince Philippe, it would also be seen that my beloved husband was deceived by me, and even though my reasons were honourable, I couldn't allow *this, since I hold his memory sacrosanct. For Jacques it would mean confusion and humiliation, as you can well imagine; although by adoption he is legally entitled to the appellation of prince, and is heir to the estates by natural succession, he is not of the blood: he entered the house of de Montigny-Villiers a stranger. Linda, my dear, I know you will see that he is spared this knowledge for as long as he lives.*

Linda looked up from the letter, once more obliged to wrench the familiar world around and somehow see it in its new perspective.

Jacques, a stranger here.

The implications were bizarre. She herself, a US citizen on the staff of a hospital in New Jersey, had been born here in France, the daughter of a prince and princess and with the blood of this noble house in her veins – yet the memory was only in her subconscious. Jacques had come here as a stranger, yet had grown to know this place as his home, and today as his possession. As she thought of his life up to now, she had to close her eyes against the sunshine, avoiding tears but feeling her heart go out to him. He'd loved the man he'd believed was his father, only to lose him, and tragically. Loving the only mother he'd ever known, he'd lost her too, soon afterwards; and at her death-bed, as if some malevolent witch had chosen to fulfill an ancient curse, he'd become a stranger again, this time to himself, his face unrecognizable and his body crippled.

That extraordinary thing he'd said, in the little mezzanine that day when he'd walked there on his own, came back to her. *What I did to you, quite without intention, preyed on my mind until I longed for some kind of release from my self-anger – and I found it. Some of them said the sea was dangerous, but only those close to me could know that I was driving myself to virtual destruction.*

She didn't want to think about that. It'd be easy to say that these Europeans, with their dark passions and their sense of drama, preferred living their lives theatrically; but things like this went on in the New World too, where life was supposed to be so enlightened and sophisticated, with men on the moon and everything. Sure thing, there were crimes of passion, suicides and suicide pacts, lovers' quarrels ending with a gunshot; it was just that for most people the pace of life was so high that they didn't have time to take much notice.

A jingle of harness came from the distance as a rider passed close to the edge of the park and she looked around quickly, thinking of Jacques. But it wouldn't be him; it'd be a few weeks, even a few months, before he could sit on a horse again. She looked down at the last page of the letter. The writing was feeble now, and she found it hard to make out some of the words – they must have been written only days ago, and just in time.

So you see why it was a problem, to bring you here. If I had even hinted at the truth in a letter, 'out of the blue,' you would have thought I was deranged; after all, you'd never even heard of me! This explains why I chose a more plausible way of catching your interest . . . it's now a little joke we can share. Shall I tell you how many applications I received before yours arrived? A hundred and thirty-two! Thank goodness you suspected nothing – or did you? Perhaps you did . . . but you came to me, and that's all that matters now. At last you know how your life began; by your blood and birthright you are of the house of de Montigny-Villiers and the title of princess is yours, and always has been, though I know this will mean very little to you – the democratic Americans are no more than mildly amused by our archaic usages.

You should know that I have bequeathed the estates to Jacques, as the legal heir. You would not, in any case, wish to be saddled with the complciated task of managing them. It had been in my mind to 'make a match' between you and the Count de Beauvais, if he were able to catch your interest. That is why I suggested he should offer you his attentions. He, as a shrewd businessman, and you, a Montigny-Villiers, would have made ideal partners. But alas . . . his life was cut short so tragically. As things are, to make an important bequest to you would be to invite curiosity, and risk exposure of the truth. I am therefore bequeathing you a substantial annuity, to be drawn from the estates for as long as you may live, in recognition of your devoted services. This is acceptable practice, and will raise no questions in people's minds. I know you will understand my reasoning. To thank you adequately for the joy you have brought me would be impossible.

The handwriting was thin and sloping now, and Linda had to guess at some of the words; they'd been written only two days ago, when she'd asked Princess Charlotte . . . when she'd asked her mother . . . if she ought to be making the effort, when she badly needed rest. Linda had thought she'd merely been writing to friends.

Finally, I hope you will find it in your heart to think kindly of Jacques, despite the past; he would never give hurt to anyone in the world intentionally, least of all you, whom he so much admires.
And so, Princess Linda de Montigny-Villiers, my lovely child, I must leave you now. It is growing late, and I am to meet my beloved again, my dearest Edouard. He –

There was a break, and a mark where the pen had slipped across the paper; then a few more words, now in her native tongue – *vraiment, la vie est très étrange – et triste, parfois – mais maintenant – Edouard je viens – je viens à toi –*
Another mark and then nothing.
Nothing more.
That had been when Linda had found her asleep against the half-raised pillows, the pen still in her hand, the last page of the letter on the floor. That evening, the Princess had given her the sealed envelope.
As Linda picked it up now and slipped the folded pages of the letter inside, the soft breeze stirred the scent of the roses, reminding her instantly of the woman who'd loved them so much, the woman who'd told her so often, when Linda had questioned her, that she had only to be patient for a little longer.
Soon you will understand, ma chère . . . Soon you will understand.

36

HOME

ONCE AGAIN THE gates of the horse-paddock had been thrown open, and two of the grooms from the stables were directing the visitors' cars. Once again the catafalque, smothered this time in roses, was borne from the chapel to the family vault, while women, veiled in black, wept softly.

The morning was fine but cool, and the air sweet with the scent of pines. Of those gathered here, many were thinking of Princess Charlotte de Montigny-Villiers, whose death they were here to mourn; others, closer to her, felt release from the daily anticipation of her dying, eased by the thought that her suffering was over. For a few, the world had been changed, a little or in great measure, by her death.

Linda stood a short way from the circle of relatives, and was able now and then to watch them as the priest intoned his prayers. She looked most often at Jacques, secretly astonished at the strength of will he'd found from somewhere since he'd made that miraculous journey as far as the mezzanine, alone. Yesterday she and Suzie had helped him negotiate the grand staircase for the first time, using only the silver-knobbed malacca cane; today he stood without it, his back straight but his shoulders twisted a little because of his damaged hip; he'd left the dark glasses in his room, along with the crutches.

Once, while her eyes were on him, he looked up suddenly, and it was a moment before she could glance away. She'd been finding it difficult in the last few days to visit him and see to his dressings and medication without remembering some of the things he'd said to her a long time ago, in the small dormer room under the roof. But that was typical of the nurse-patient relationship; people started to get too close, emotionally. In a week now, maybe even less, she could hand him over to a nurse from the village.

Near Jacques stood Maître Dorlhac, his eyes cast down and his pale hands clasped together in front of him. A short time ago, when he'd greeted Linda at the edge of the crowd, he'd given a discreet little bow. '*Mes homages, Madame la Princesse.*'

'You mustn't ever call me that,' she'd told him quickly. He was one of the few people who knew the truth.

There was a certain warmth in his eyes. 'I know. But just this once, I wanted to greet you as I should. This family is close to my heart, and I knew you a long time ago, before you can even remember.' A smile touched his eyes. 'Welcome home, *ma Princesse.*'

The priest was nodding now to the pall-bearers, and they moved towards the coffin.

Suzie Spinoza stepped back to make room. Daphne had lent her a black silk dress to wear today, and they stood side by side in the pale sunshine. Yesterday, Daphne hadn't believed it when Suzie had told her.

'A *nurse?* But darling, I thought you wanted to find a rich husband!'

'That was before. I guess it's Linda – she's really something, isn't she? I think what I'm looking for now is myself, and when I've found it, I'm going to do something useful with it. Does that sound crazy?'

'Of course, darling. But if – ' and Daphne had stopped right there, looking at her with her blue eyes particularly smokey as she considered; then she said, 'No, it doesn't sound a bit crazy, when you think what you did for me. You'll make an absolutely marvellous nurse.' Then the dazzling smile came back. 'And anyway you'll have all those simply smashing doctors around you, and can just pick the one you want for a husband. There's nobody richer than *they* are!'

Behind Suzie and nearer the coffin, Toinette Cavaille, sister of the deceased, walked slowly among the others towards the vault, with Mme Leclerc supporting her. Under the black lace veil her face was still drawn, and her eyes flickered with nerves. But she was getting better, much better now. Linda, the nurse, had kept her under sedatives long enough for her to miss the funeral for Raoul in Geneva two days ago, on the excuse of prostration. She'd been frightened of being there at the cremation; with her mind still numbed with the shock of what she'd done, she could have believed that Raoul might have risen in some way from the ashes, to avenge himself. But now she could think more rationally, she realised that it had only been in the presence of that man that she'd believed she could never be free of his tyranny, even in death. She felt no remorse, no guilt. Murder was the taking of a human life, but this had been different: she'd exorcised the Devil incarnate, before he could hasten Charlotte to her death.

There'd come a time, perhaps, when she'd feel the need for confession, and then she'd go to the priest, and if her urged her to take the veil for a time as a way of repentence, she might do that; it would help to heal the bruises on her body and her soul.

The sharp smell of incense was in the air as the two boys in their robes walked beside Father Paul. Henri, the chauffeur, and Maurice, the head gardener, awkward in their stiff black suits, moved to the door of the vault, one of them inserting the huge key and turning it. The door swung open, and a shaft of sunlight pierced the darkness inside.

Half-lost among the legs of the crowd, *le petit Baron* watched the coffin, wondering how long the roses would live in there, and how long it would be before Aunt Charlotte got to Heaven. Very soon, surely, because she was so beautiful and God must love her, as everyone else had done. Guillaume would miss her, and would have sobbed at this minute, creeping away somewhere to hide his face; but a little time ago, Jacques had said that tomorrow they'd go bird's-nesting together in the trees by the riding-park, and Guillaume would show him some eggs; and this was a comfort to him.

Beside him, Bibi took his hand, watching Aunt Charlotte being carried into the dark. She wanted to cry out, to scream; it was as if something were being wrenched out of her heart; but she just went on standing there with nobody knowing, her grey eyes looking far beyond anything here.

She wished Linda were standing closer, but she couldn't, because nobody was meant to know she was one of the family. It was a secret that Bibi would have to keep forever, but that was all right; she kept a lot of them. The thing that troubled her the most was that she didn't know when Linda was going to leave, or whether there were any way of stopping her. Because when Linda left, Bibi didn't know what she was going to do. For the past two or three nights she'd been living in a kind of frozen nowhere-land, frightened of letting herself go to sleep at night in case Linda left before she woke, and when she slept at last, tired out, frightened of getting out of bed at daybreak, in case she found Linda gone.

She gripped Guillaume's hand very hard, and he looked up, surprised.

A little way from the throng around the vault, a woman stood watching as the two men swung the heavy iron door, an ember of lipstick showing behind her black lace veil, and the glint of green eyes. When the door was closed, she turned her head slightly and looked towards the tall young man who remained standing motionless for a moment with his dark head bowed, his shoulders twisted a little – her son the Prince de Montigny-Villiers, whom she could never acknowledge but would always love. He had suffered more than any of them, in a way, and a brief and silent prayer came into her mind. May the dark days be over for him now, and his house henceforth be blessed.

That was a week ago, and this morning Linda was standing in the gallery again, to look at the portraits for the last time so that she could carry the memory of these faces in her mind for as long as she could. She was looking particularly at the portrait of Prince Jacques, handsome, a little arrogant, quite unsmiling, a mask for the man she now knew him to be, sensitive, brave, troubled, and today faced with the challenge of finding himself again, and his place in life.

A shadow fell across the floor from the sunlit doorway, and Linda looked around. It was Bibi, standing perfectly still in that way she had, her grey eyes wide and unblinking, her blonde pigtail catching the light.

'Did you follow me here?'

Linda wished she could have taken it back, the instant she'd said it; but she'd wanted to be alone here, absolutely alone, because she felt the weight of something on her, something trying to change her, to move her in new directions. She didn't want to be disturbed, in case it upset some kind of balance.

'Yes, I followed you here.'

Bibi's voice was so quiet that it hardly carried, but Linda heard the hush of deep fright in it. She held out her hand, and in a moment the child came towards her, limping across the parquet until her hand was in Linda's, frozen cold. Looking down at the pale, pinched face and the hollow eyes, Linda saw she was beyond tears, far, far beyond.

'What is it, Bibi?'

'I don't want you to go.'

'How do you know I'm going?'

'You've been packing.'

'Sweetheart, you've just got to stop peeping through keyholes.'

'All right. Then I will. I'll do anything. Anything you ask. As long as you don't go.'

Linda took a slow breath, and got down onto her haunches so that Bibi was a little taller. 'It isn't as simple as that.'

'It is really. I know it is. I know *everything*. And I know that you mustn't go.'

'I have a job over there, Bibi, work to do, and friends to go back to, don't you – '

'There's work for you to do here, a lot of people to help. And we're your friends now, all of us here. You've come back to us, remember?'

Linda felt the weight shifting, and for a moment she wondered if she could duck out from under and go free; but she knew she couldn't do that; there was a decision she had to make, a big one, and she couldn't duck out of it. Something had changed, though; she'd been impatient when Bibi had come in here to disturb her, but now she had the feeling that only Bibi could help her. It wasn't just that the child knew everything about everyone because she listened at keyholes; she was also possessed of a weird kind of understanding, at a level where grown-ups had shut their minds down. Linda would have to listen to her, and very carefully.

'Sure, Bibi, I came back. It's what I've been told, and I believe it. But you already *knew* it, didn't you?'

'Yes.'

Linda held the wide grey eyes. 'What else do you know?'

'More than you. More even than you.'

In a moment Linda said, 'Then tell me about Jacques.'

'He loves you.'

It was said quietly, but Linda's heart lurched and her whole body tensed against the shock as the wave of feeling crashed through her and left her breathless. She hadn't been ready for it; she'd thought all that was over, that he didn't mean anything to her now. She heard Bibi's small voice coming through to her.

'Didn't you know?'

Linda opened her eyes and took a breath and said slowly, 'Bibi, tell me where he was born.'

The child put her head on one side. 'Would you keep it a secret?'

'Yes.'

'Cross your heart?'

'Cross my heart.'

'All right. It's important that we don't tell anyone, you see, because even he doesn't know. He was born in Paris. He wasn't born here, like you. He was adopted. He doesn't belong to the family. You're not related to him. Is that what you wanted to know?'

'I already knew. I just wanted you to understand that if I stayed here – ' she left it, because the wave was going through her again, more softly now, taking her a little way with it and then bringing her back, as if she were standing in strong surf. She didn't know whether to resist it or go with it.

'Don't worry,' the voice of Bibi broke through, 'I understand quite a lot of things.' Her small hands, still in Linda's, weren't cold any more, and her eyes had lost their look of desolation. The strange feeling came to Linda that she'd reached a decision and didn't realise it, but Bibi did.

'I want you to do something for me, Linda. It's nothing hard.'

In a moment Linda said, 'All right.'

'I want you to go across to the rose-garden, and wait.'

'What for?'

'Take a book or something to read. You're not in a hurry to catch your plane, are you?'

Linda looked at her watch. 'I need to leave here in half an hour.'

'That's long enough.'

'I wanted to thank you,' he said.

She stood facing him with her hands behind her back; she wasn't in her uniform, of course; she'd put on some slacks and a light blue sweater, things that wouldn't crease on the plane.

'How did you know where to find me?' Though she wasn't sure why she'd asked him that; she already knew.

'Bibi told me.'

'I see.'

She'd come to the rose-garden and sat on the chaise-longue, not bringing anything to read because it was so lovely here; she just let her eyes wander, half-closed, across the ancient stones of the Chateau, with the shadow of the pines softening the walls and lying like clouds across the glass roof of the winter-garden. *Which room had it been, the one she was born in? Which window was it?*

The cry of a bird came from the trees at the edge of the riding-park, where she'd been jogging that day when –

The sound of a door came, distantly, closing beind someone; then he was there suddenly, coming this way across the lawn, walking without the cane, his eyes on the ground so as to keep his balance, like she'd told him to do. He wasn't making very good progress, and she couldn't watch any longer, but got up and went quickly across to meet him.

'To thank you for all you did for my mother,' he said. 'And for me.'

'It was a privilege, *mon Prince*.' He moved slightly, putting his weight onto the other leg, and she said quickly – 'Look, you shouldn't be standing like this.'

'I didn't expect to be, so soon.' He was trying to smile, but the facial nerves were still numbed from the last operation. Nothing reached his eyes; she couldn't see what was in them, what kind of expression, but if she'd had to guess, she would have said he was looking at her like this, so intently, because he wanted to remember her for as long as he could.

She felt the wave coming again, and knew how uncertain she was, with nothing she could hold on to, and no strength to resist it now.

'I – I didn't expect to see you standing so soon either,' she said, 'least of all walking, and without even a stick. You've made the most miraculous progress.'

'Thanks to you.' The movement came to his mouth again, another attempt at a smile. 'I've also stopped avoiding mirrors.'

'And what do you see in them?'

'A kind of – a kind of amiable gargoyle.' The smile still didn't reach his eyes; there wasn't any room for it, they were so intense; she could see pain there, but it wasn't because he was punishing his body, standing here like this; it wasn't anything physical; it was like the look she'd seen in Bibi's eyes, a kind of desolation.

The wave came closer, rising.

'You look better than that,' she said. 'The healing's going on incredibly well. It's partly because you're – so determined.' The wave rose high, and she sensed its approaching force. "It won't be long," she heard herself saying, 'before you're quite handsome again, and then your admirers are going to start standing in line to kiss you. But I want to be there first, before anyone else. I want to do it right now.'

He tried to move away, his eyes confused. 'Linda, I told you I could never – '

'Don't say anything.' She took his face gently in her hands. 'Just let me kiss you, *mon Prince* . . . Let me be the first.'

The wave reached her and leapt and she went with it, letting it carry her along, carry her home.